Bar Flaubert

Alexis Stamatis was born in Athens in 1960. He has published six novels and six volumes of poetry, two of which have been published in the UK (*The Architect of Interior Spaces* was awarded the Nikiforos Vrettakos Prize). Arcadia published his first novel *The Seventh Elephant* to wide acclaim in 2000, while his second novel, *Bar Flaubert*, a best-seller in Greece, has been published in France, Italy, Spain, Russia, Serbia and Bangladesh. He currently works as a columnist for the *Ethnos* daily newspaper in Athens.

David Connolly has lived and worked in Greece for over twenty-five years. He is currently Associate Professor of Translation Studies at the Aristotle University of Thessaloniki. He has written extensively on the theory and practice of literary translation and has translated some twenty-five books by leading Greek authors for which he has received awards in the UK, the US and Greece.

Alexis Stamatis

Bar Flaubert

Translated from the Greek by
David Connolly

ARCADIA BOOKS

Arcadia Books Ltd
15-16 Nassau Street
London W1W 7AB

www.arcadiabooks.co.uk

First published in Greece by Kedros, 2000
First published in the United Kingdom by Arcadia Books, 2007
Copyright © Alexis Stamatis, 2000
English Translation Copyright © David Connolly, 2007

A catalogue record for this book is available from the British Library

ISBN 1-900850-57-5

Typeset in Bembo by Basement Press
Printed in Finland by WS Bookwell

Acknowledgements

`Death Fugue' is taken from "Poems of Paul Celan" translated by Michael Hamburger.
Published by Anvil Press Poetry in 1988

Arcadia Books Ltd gratefully acknowledges the financial support of The Arts Council of
England, the Hellenic Foundation for Culture, Athens, the Hellenic Foundation, London
and the Greek Ministry for Culture, Athens.

Arcadia Books supports English PEN, the fellowship of writers who work together to promote
literature and its understanding. English PEN upholds writers' freedoms in Britain and around
the world, challenging political and cultural limits on free expression. To find out more, visit
www.englishpen.org or contact
English PEN, 6-8 Amwell Street, London EC1R 1UQ

Arcadia Books distributors are as follows:

in the UK and elsewhere in Europe:
Turnaround Publishers Services
Unit 3, Olympia Trading Estate
Coburg Road
London N22 6TZ

in the US and Canada:
Independent Publishers Group
814 N. Franklin Street Chicago, IL 60610

in Australia:
Tower Books
PO Box 213 Brookvale, NSW 2100

in New Zealand:
Addenda
PO Box 78224 Grey Lynn Auckland

in South Africa:
Quartet Sales and Marketing
PO Box 1218 Northcliffe Johannesburg 2115

Arcadia Books is the *Sunday Times* Small Publisher of the Year

Dedicated to Nicole
and to the memory of Giorgos Heimonas

'We dance around in a ring and suppose,
But the secret sits in the middle and knows'
Robert Frost

Kill Dead Time

Kill dead time

I was down below, exploring her. My tongue teased the opposing skin, twisted it, smeared it with its warm lubrication. My mind wasn't in it though. My thoughts raced off, elsewhere. At one moment, my gaze fixed on the facing wall. It was my wall, marking the confines of my room. Three candles were burning in the silver candelabra. Their candescent light flooded the room. I drifted in their warm glow. I gazed again before me; only darkness now and a dim light in the distance. I proceeded. A stone door barred the entrance. I uttered the password. A crack opened in the middle of the stone. Light rain. I proceeded further still. Vegetation, mountain peaks, a stream babbling. Yet it was as if nature had faded away. Everything was black, draped in darkness, with only a dim light in the distance, a silver glimmer in the pitch-black forest.

'That's it...there...,' I heard her saying. As if I were being given orders through a loudspeaker, my mind was completely detached from what was happening, my body acted of its own accord, mechanically. I recall how, in the past, in similar circumstances, I would think of situations involving some rhythm, some mathematical sequence, in order to keep myself in that erotic flow. It was a good way of being there and not there without neglecting my partner. For, no matter how strange it may seem, that distance appeared to have worked beneficially.

'Yes, yes, Yannis, yes...' I heard her shout again, louder and louder, till her limbs gave way and she burst, uncontrollably surrendering her love. I took a deep breath. The room had a musty smell about it. As if an enervating gas were escaping through the cracks in the plaster and enveloping me. When I was sure that the modest ritual was over - from her point of view at least - I rolled over on one side. I was about to sit up in bed but she, thinking that I was getting up, rushed to put her arms around me.

'Yannis...it was so good. So different! Today, it was how I always wanted it to be. It was... it was just right.'

Just right and just rot, I thought. What's 'right' supposed to mean? How, when I'm not even really there, can she find it 'right'? If that was right, then what about the other times, the few times, that is, when I was there in body and soul? How right was it then? When I was *there*, when the veil enfolding us made me feel our bodies as one, why didn't she tell me just how right it was then? Just right and just rot. It was a mistake, a big mistake. Like all else, a big, fat mistake.

'Do you want to sleep here tonight?' she asked, lighting a cigarette.

'Manya love, I'm not ready to go to sleep yet,' - a trick that usually worked - 'why don't we go out for a drink?'

'Okay, I'll go and wash,' Manya replied somewhat irritated, and she got up.

Manya was an actress. Thirty-two years old, long, straight, red hair. Black, expressive eyes, with a blue circle around the iris. Her lips were fleshy, slightly protruding. Slender, with slightly accentuated hips. At that time, she was playing a supporting role in a TV comedy. She wasn't bad. She wasn't good either.

She entered the bathroom. I went into the living room and turned on the CD player. When Manya was in the bathroom, I never went in. Not that she'd forbidden me, but after love-making, there was something that made me want to leave her alone, to leave her to wash. The wind instruments began weaving above my head. Portishead. Lyricism with sharp stabs. I lit a cigarette, switched on the TV. Trash and more trash. I switched it off. Manya emerged from the bathroom wearing a bathrobe. She put on her make-up, a thick line of eyeshadow, she dressed and we left.

We walked along Mavromichali Street, then turned into Asklepiou Street. The first bar we went into was the Bright Lights, a popular haunt that recalled a French bistro. The moment I opened the door, I spotted Kostas Anagnostou, a friend and journalist, sitting at the bar. We'd known each other for a good few years. He was salaried, at the heart of the Fourth Estate. As a freelancer, I had a somewhat looser relationship with it. We didn't sit with him as I knew he wasn't too keen on Manya – a stuck-up starlet was what he called her. We stayed about an hour and then we went to the bar across the road, the 'Big City', a rock bar that hadn't progressed beyond The Clash and The Stranglers. Fortunately, there wasn't a soul there, and so at around three in the morning, I got rid of her quite legitimately, putting her into a taxi and waiting till it had turned the corner, supposedly noting the number.

I parked the old black Mini in my usual place in the cul-de-sac. Instead of going straight home, I decided to take a walk. Though it was April, Athens was deserted. The night warm. The Parliament building, beautifully lit, looked magnificent. In Harilaou Trikoupi Street, the Vovou office block seemed to be feeling the cold. Two or three transvestites on the street, they too now part of the setting. In Ippokratous Street, on a yard wall, red-painted graffiti: 'Kill dead time.'

I went to bed and fell asleep straightaway, without the previous hours dripping even one wet image. It had been some time since I'd had any dreams. Quite some time.

Hot chocolate or madeleine?

It was eleven-thirty on a Tuesday morning at the end of April when I sat down in my favourite armchair in front of the balcony door. I was drinking a coffee and gazing outside. On the streets of Exarchia, the cars and motorbikes had been performing their routines since early on.

Through the open balcony door, I could see the supermarket across the street. Above the main sign, I noticed a new one in red neon: 'Jacobs Suchard-Pavlides Chocolates.' I smiled. Uncle Demis's factory; the last Pavlides was a distant relative of my father. I recalled how, when I was small – six or seven years old – I'd go down to the factory in Piraeus Street and dip my hands into the vat of warm chocolate; I'd completely coat myself in it and the mixture would run from the palms of my hands. Even now, in my nose and mouth, that peculiar taste of hazelnut as it blended with the dark mixture, with the bitter taste of almond and, of course, that divine invention, Merenda! For years and years, I fed myself almost exclusively on Merenda. I used to get through a jar a day. After turning eighteen, though, I cut out sweets, just like that. The reason for my adult abstention from that chocolate paradise is most likely to be found in my excessively sweet apprenticeship in childhood. An age when everything comes in excess. And when you get older, you still have the recollection of that hot chocolate from your childhood that slowly melts in the mouth, a feeling that's now foreign to you, a sweet recollection, fused in the memory. A lost paradise; the only true one.

For sometimes, the recollection of a taste, even when it's not a small shell-shaped madeleine, is enough to bring back *temps perdu*.

I come from an old Athenian family. Markos Loukas, my father, is one of the most well-known writers in the country. My mother owns a small art gallery.

I lived with them until I was twenty-three, until, that is, I graduated from university. Afterwards, I went to the U.S.A. for postgraduate studies in Comparative Literature, began a doctorate which I never finished and returned to Greece to do my military service. After a round of two or three years working in private schools and colleges, I gave all this up just before turning thirty, took on some private lessons and began writing for various publications. In order to supplement my income, I worked for some magazines as a freelance writer; from interviews and features to cultural news and travel articles. In addition to all this – given that I had a good relationship with foreign languages, fluent English, Italian and German, and a little Spanish – I also undertook translation work for a small publishing company.

Writing is my great passion. Living in a house where the wall was synonymous with the bookcase – even the bathroom was full of books – it was only natural that my immune system wouldn't be able to resist the writing virus. I can't say my father exerted any pressure on me. On the contrary, he was quite against my decision to concern myself with literature. Eventually, as might be expected, I couldn't resist the temptation to publish my creative endeavours. Four years ago, I published, at my own expense, a collection of short stories, which, despite getting a couple of favourable reviews – reads smoothly, original themes – didn't sell more than three hundred copies.

What I always wanted, though, was to write a novel.

In appearance, I'm reasonably good-looking. Tallish, six feet two, brown hair, a thin face, green eyes, narrow arched eyebrows, a slightly crooked nose and, when I laugh, some funny lines that form around my mouth, rather like parentheses, making my delight appear forced – which it isn't.

As with most people, there's something about me that I don't like. I don't like it at all, I hate it, I'd like to be born again just so it wouldn't exist. And worst of all it's an imperfection that can't be put right: an unequal distribution. A genetic quirk led to my being born with my right arm roughly eight centimetres shorter than the left. No one in my family could ever give me a satisfactory explanation for this. Eventually, I set about investigating it on my own. There was no sign of this anomaly in either of the two families, at least for four generations back. The problem began to appear at around twelve, when my right arm suddenly stopped growing. The left continued to develop till I was seventeen, when the present difference of around eight centimetres became fixed. The first shock came with basketball, at which I was an especially good player. The ball no longer obeyed my commands, I could no longer perform my famous reverse dribbles, while my baseball passes, which used to reach their target with goniometer precision, now urgently required projectile correction. My skill had been forever amputated by eight lousy centimetres. During the same period, when the difference was now visible to the naked eye, my schoolmates began to make fun of me -'Hey, Loukas...you weirdo...'– but, fortunately, it didn't last long. The years at high school passed uneventfully, except for the second field of embarrassment: girls.

7

When the flirting began in the first class of high school, I'd always offer my left hand whenever I was introduced to a girl. Of course, that resulted in the girl being puzzled at first and ended by working against me, since it invariably provoked the question: 'So you shake hands with your left hand?' After not a few tragicomical episodes, I decided I'd offer my right hand, cleverly making sure to 'withdraw' the left so the difference wouldn't be so obvious, at least at first sight. The techniques I developed were numerous, based for the main part on some form of *trompe l'oeil*. I acted somewhat like a Renaissance painter; crooked stances, imperceptible raising of the left shoulder, bending of the spine to the right, a whole pile of tricks so that the girl would see the two limbs as equal in length as possible.

After some time, after Nana, that is, my first girlfriend, who never attached any importance to the matter, I began to reconcile myself with the problem. Naturally, I was always obliged to take my pullovers, jackets and shirts to the dressmaker's to have the right sleeve shortened. There were many people – and I'd checked this closely – who didn't notice it at all, but just as every complex is its owner's sole companion, so I too can't recall a single day in over twenty-five years when I haven't been concerned, albeit in passing, with this slight imbalance, this weirdo gene inserted in a generally sound, well-shaped body.

I have often reflected that whatever you are, it's always too little; however, it's this too little that from an early age encloses you inside a social shell: alienation.

I came to know love as a factory that was more fascinating than its products. Only on two occasions did I follow the process to the end. The first time, which lasted for four years, from twenty to twenty-four, was with Elda, a fellow student at university. We didn't put in very many appearances at the lectures; we were always going on trips and going through various emotional dramas that would end in exhilarating sex.

The second long-term relationship began when I was thirty-three and is still in progress, six years to the good. Her name's Anna, she's an art historian, ten years younger than me. We met one

Friday afternoon at the opening of an exhibition at the National Art Gallery. I'd gone alone, I was in no mood for company and all I wanted was to see for the first time from close up the works of my favourite painter, a French impressionist who used hardly anything but pastel.

Each painting was better than the next. The subjects were much the same: scenes from ballets, moments from the opera, horse races and, above all, young women. Women holding chrysanthemums, others holding anemones, women in the bath, women in the countryside. Despite his being a French painter working in Paris, the oriental influences were more than evident.

At one point I found myself looking at a painting that left me ecstatic. It was a woman sitting naked in an armchair, with her back turned. Her torso was leaning forward, her right arm was resting on the back of the armchair, while in her left hand she was holding a towel with which she was drying her hair. The painting was in pastel, with firm, sweeping strokes. My interest focused on the bones of the spine, which were sticking out of her back like an animal poised to attack. Yet, although the dominating feature was the twisted skeleton, it was something else that stole the show. A delicate hand, almost separate from the rest of the body, was gracefully holding the cotton cloth, reminding us that this delicate creature had just finished one of the most noble acts of the race: her personal hygiene.

At that moment, I felt a warm breath directly behind me. I turned round; a tall, slender girl with a pretty, intelligent face and black hair cut like a boy's. She was standing so close to me that it would have been rather silly not to have spoken. Before I could think of anything, the girl charged straight in:

'A women drying herself. Quite daring for the time, isn't it?'

'Yes,' I replied, putting the catalogue into my bag, stalling for time. 'I like the way the artist has captured her. An uncommon perspective. I like that element of the unusual.'

'Do you like unusual women?' she asked.

'I like what isn't easily comprehended,' I answered with a smile.

'Why do you think she sat up?' she went on, unrestrainedly.

'Perhaps he didn't understand...' I stammered.

'What didn't he understand?'

'What she wanted...herself.'

'Why don't men ever understand?'

Suddenly, there was an embarrassed silence.

'Well?' she said.

'Hang on a moment, we still haven't been introduced,' in order to gain a little time. 'My name's Yannis, Yannis Loukas.'

'Mine's Anna, Anna Rigopoulou.' A smile like a pink brushstroke lit her face.

Pretty girl, I thought.

The rest was what you'd expect. A year of ardent passion that I drained to the very last drop. A passion that I experienced in all its aspects. I lived through its transformations, its cataclysmic intensity, its tiny liquid drops as they evaporated. Her body was a landscape without end, a Russian doll that continually donned new garments, each more beautiful than the last. Though all this lasted just twelve months. When it eventually came to an end.

It came to an end and the passion faded. Just as with a bang it had been born, so with a salvo it expired, and I resolved myself to the fact that it was over, that it was destined to go on for just as long as it had lasted. What remained was a pleasant feeling that, for my part, turned into a kind of erotic resignation. A resignation that spread to other areas of my life and became second nature, a way of life. *I went through the motions out of habit.*

I didn't break off the relationship. Anna and I remained rather like friends and lovers at the same time. She was my worldly companion, an unofficial fiancée. She'd realized the change in my feelings, though she seemed to have accepted the new situation. I was sure that Anna suspected that there were other women in my life, but she never let it show. An undefined sense of duty kept her with me, a sense of devotion that patiently awaited its reward. But I was already gone, elsewhere. And this city was full of the opportunities that, albeit occasionally, give flesh and bone to that indefinite elsewhere.

I sipped the last drop of coffee and went into the living room. I switched on the computer and went straight to the previous day's file.

Whatever is decoded dies

After an hour and a quarter, I looked up from the screen. The text was before me; it covered three pages, nine hundred and twenty-five words. I'd send it to *Law 2000*, a lifestyle magazine. I printed it and began reading:

> *...He opened his eyes. For a while he didn't know who he was, where he was, what he was. A 180-degree panning round the room brought him to his senses. The objects were known to him, the air familiar, the smell recognizable. Yes, he was Nikos Marinos, thirty-four years old, single, a journalist. It was one-thirty in the afternoon and he had just woken up on his living-room couch in a two-roomed apartment in Metz, on that day, 4th July, his birthday, with a head heavy from his intemperate beer-drinking of the previous night.*

I went on reading the next pages that described his chance meeting with an old girlfriend, the recollections from their summer holidays of two years before, his invitation to her to have dinner together.

I read it again. It's not bad, I thought and I saved it onto a floppy disk. *Law 2000* had asked for a two-thousand-word article on bachelor life.

I picked up the phone and dialled the number of the chief editor: 'Hi Dimitris, it's Yannis. I've finished the piece, I'll send it to you.'

'Okay, Yannis. Daniel will have to have a look at it too.'

'If it's accepted, the fee's the same, right?'

'Yes, sure, a hundred thousand gross, bye then.'

In recent years, this had been one of my two main sources of income. Regular contributions to two magazines, less regular work for two more. The two standard magazines were *Law 2000* and *Individual*. I'd been at high school with Daniel Triandafyllides, the publisher of *Law*. He was a tough kid who went around on a motorbike. As a student, he'd got onto coke and all the rest, eventually going clean after a period of post-graduate detoxification in France. Being smart as he was, he soon grasped the spirit of the times – you enjoyed yourself, the enjoyment level was always one inch higher, you leapt but never quite reached it –

and he published three highly successful magazines that sold like mad.

As for my literary concerns, they were at that time confined to editing my father's autobiography. The ultimate goal, my novel, was a work constantly in progress. Or, to be honest, constantly in a state of postponement. For a good few years, I'd simply abandoned whatever I'd begun.

In the evening, I was awakened by the sharp sound of the phone ringing. At the other end of the line was Dimitris Papadopoulos, the chief editor at *Law 2000*. Daniel had rejected the piece.

'I'll send you some paid ads that need editing,' said Dimitris, trying to sugar the pill.

It was the third time in succession that the same thing had happened. I wondered why. I admit that it wasn't one of my best, it wasn't like the ones I used to write three or four years earlier, but with that kind of writing, you're walking a tightrope. Nevertheless, the fact was that I desperately needed the hundred thousand drachmas. I also wasn't very happy about the rejections. I decided to go and speak directly to Daniel.

Just a month previously, *Law 2000* had moved to a postmodern four-storey building in Kifissias Avenue, one of those that for some incomprehensible reason incorporates fragments of ancient Greek art in their facade. I went up to the second floor and gave my name to the secretary; a man strangely enough. After about ten minutes, the fellow announced that Mr Triandafyllides was waiting for me.

Daniel was standing in front of his desk.

'How are things, Yannis?' he said, welcoming me cordially.

'I've been better,' I murmured, and planted myself in an armchair.

Daniel sat down on his designer leather throne. The entire wall behind him was covered with a smoked-glass mirror, thus putting his interlocutor in the unenviable position of having to speak while gazing at his own reflection.

'What's that then, Daniel, some kind of postmodern interrogation?'

'A little test for my colleagues. The insecure ones keep checking their appearance, the self-confident don't care.'

'Then I've most likely failed, because I've already noticed that I'm getting fatter,' I retorted ironically.

'That's the trick. It's a special mirror that enlarges the reflection by twenty per cent.'

'You're a satanic one all right, a real Manson of the press,' I said, pretending to be serious.

Daniel laughed out loud.

'You've a way with words, Yannis, pity you're not able to write so well of late.'

'That's just what I've come to see you about. Is there some problem, Daniel, you've rejected my last three pieces.'

'Look, you're not new at this game. When you began, you remember what I told you. That your writing is at the forefront, your angle's new, exactly what every editor dreams of. You have to admit though that lately you've come to a standstill. Or rather...you've taken a step backwards. In this business, you have to be always moving forwards. You have to be on top of what's happening out there, and I mean globally, and choose whatever's hot, whatever's up front. Then you have to dissect it, fragment it, extract the essence. Today, Yannis, whatever is decoded dies. Instantly. Look how the young kids are writing. You have to break up the text, experiment with the syntax. We have to dismantle words in the same way we dismantle images. Whereas you've begun to paste them together.'

'It's true that I've come to the end of my limits. It's not in me to dissect either time or words. Okay, I've got stuck. Perhaps... It's my father's autobiography too. I'm tired of rummaging through his archives. But why am I telling you all this...' I said, seeing him adopt an expression that showed I'd got off the topic. 'What do you care,' I went on, 'you've got plenty to be pleased about. Apart from your Orwellian practices' – I glanced in the mirror and Daniel laughed – 'you're just fine. That's just how you were in school, a finger in everything...'

'All right, Yannis, I understand. We're friends. You're going through a rough patch. But here we're talking as colleagues. Everybody has a block at some point. Just don't let it get you down. Get on top of it so it won't get on top of you.'

'Don't worry, no one's going to get on top of me. Message received and understood. So long, Daniel, take care,' I said and got up out of the armchair, casting a last glance at my inflated reflection.

That evening, Anna had a family engagement. I phoned Kostas, my journalist friend who hung out at the Bright Lights. We arranged to meet there at around eleven-thirty.

'Hi there. What's that smile for? You're pleased because you trounced us again?'

'Can't say I didn't tell you. You lost it on the right wing. Yannakopoulos, Mavroyennidis.'

'Our turn'll come. We'll see who's laughing come the end of the season.'

'At least the team's doing well, because everything else is...'

'Oh, so we're feeling down in the dumps and remembered our old friend. Is that it?' said Kostas sarcastically.

'I'm not joking, lately everything seems to be going wrong.'

'You know what you need, Yannis? A bit of excitement. You're forty this year aren't you? Born in 1958, no?'

'Yes, 4th July, Cancer with Leo for horoscope.'

'Come off it, that's for old ladies. What matters is that you've got yourself into a rut, old friend. Same old tune year after year. Articles for magazines, wracking your brain to come up with topics, trying to adapt to every bloody style. That's not for your age, old boy. Either find a steady job and get it into your head that that's what you'll be doing for the next twenty years, or make a new start. Begin something new. And bear in mind that what I'm saying doesn't only apply to your work. I've seen you out at night with that bit of skirt. Why are you wasting your energy, Yannis? What's that little slut got to give you that Anna can't give you?'

'She gives me what Anna can't. And I get from Anna what I can't get from her.'

'Sounds to me like you've been taken in by all that stuff you write in your magazines. I thought you kept a distance...' said Kostas.

'Listen who's talking! With a new bird every other week...' I retorted, moving into the attack.

'Yannis, you keep making the most screwed-up mistake. You project yourself onto others. Me, old friend, I'm not you. I believe in what some wise bloke once said: love is the overestimation of its object. I don't want love, I want to screw, I'm not searching for anything through writing, I make money, I'm not imaginative, I'm realistic, I flutter around truth and I don't get burned, you dive straight in and become kindling. So let me get on with it in my own way and you see to it that you make some changes in your life. Anyway, let's have another drink. I've had enough of all this soul-searching bullshit.'

Kostas and I stayed until late, downing the drink. At around one, I bundled him into the car, drunk as he was, and took him home. Then I went back to my place and flopped onto the bed. I couldn't sleep. Between two and four, I watched *The Old Man and the Sea* on cable TV. Then I spent most of the night awake, thinking about Kostas's eyes, the fleshless backbone of the swordfish caught by the Old Man, and my own eight missing centimetres.

The autobiography

When, on approaching the milestone of his seventieth year, my father decided that he should reveal the course of his life to his readership, he realized that it would be an extremely tiring task, considering that this was a man with a compulsive obsession for hoarding whatever data might one day be useful to him. His mania for collecting naturally extended to the object of his work, with the result that the basement of the family home had been turned into a library-cum-storeroom.

Apart from being scholastic, however, my father was also intelligent, and so he sensed quite early on that he would need an assistant, an editor to sort through this pile of material. And because he was by nature suspicious, he knew he wouldn't find anyone better than me, someone who knew the subject and, in addition, someone who as a close relative would be under his total control. For my father, I was the personification of the ideal research assistant, who would delve into his huge archives and, always under his supervision, would classify, evaluate, and present him with the fruit of his creation, the flower of his fifty-year struggle with the written word. Reviews, unpublished stories, correspondence with other writers, interviews, notes, conference papers, drafts for novels never written and hundreds of other papers, files and envelopes had to be assiduously examined by me. It wasn't easy, but we finally managed to agree that the sort-out should be kept to a minimum and that the potentially mammoth autobiography should not exceed six hundred pages.

The book had progressed. I'd already been working on it for eight months and I reckoned that in another four months or so, my role in it would be finished. At the same time, my father was writing the text, which he showed to no one.

'It'll be a surprise for everyone,' he said, 'including the family.'

The time had come for the additional task that my father had insisted on: the sorting out of the blue bookcase. In the same basement where that enormous amount of material was stored, in the second room on the right, there was a blue bookcase with manuscripts and typed texts – novels and novellas – sent to him by aspiring authors, something that went on throughout the course of his career.

It was Wednesday, the day of the week that I devoted exclusively to the autobiography. My father and I had a meeting about what to do with his correspondence with Nikos Gavriel Pentzikis. This consisted of ten letters, from both sides, in which a heated argument unfolded concerning whether or not the stream-of-consciousness technique had been successfully assimilated into Greek literature. In his letters, my father, a fanatical opponent of the inner monologue, both reviles and is reviled by the author of *Mrs Ersi*. The expressions used by both of them would make the monks on Mount Athos want to hide their fondness for this pharmacist from Thessaloniki and make our academicians think again before confirming the rumour that had been circulating widely in the previous year, namely that my father was soon to join the ranks of the 'immortals' in the Academy of Athens.

Before meeting with him, though, I had to stop by and see my father's publisher, to give him some photos that were to accompany the text.

Panos Viliotis was relatively young, considering the twenty-odd years that he'd been at the peak of the publishing world. He couldn't have been more than around fifty. Well-preserved, with long grey hair tied back in a ponytail and an impeccable blue suit, he welcomed me from behind his high-tech desk. 'How are you doing, Yannis? It's been some time since I last saw you. When will you be through with it all?'

'I wish I knew,' I replied, at a loss. 'At present, I'm sorting through some letters, there's so much material, and he wants it all...'

'Yes, your father's more than a little scholastic. When do you think you'll both be finished?'

'I need another four months or so. Now, I'm about to start with all the manuscripts sent to him by young writers just after the dictatorship. There might be something interesting, though I doubt it. Most likely, he told them all where to go with their manuscripts. I think we ought to leave out the chapter on my father as an encourager of new writers!'

'What about you, Yannis, what are you up to? Are you still writing? I remember those short stories you published in *Patrol*. People said good things about them.'

'I keep trying to begin something, but it never comes out as I want it.'

'The dough's in the magazines, eh?'

'Yes, something like that,' I replied, making it clear that I didn't want to go on with the subject.

'Anyhow, if you do get anything finished, bring it to me to have a look at. After all, a little bit of post-war literary history must have been recorded on your genes.'

'The DNA alphabet is more complicated than the Greek one. When our chromosomes can be decoded into bytes, then we'll be able to speak with certainty about what's recorded and where,' I answered with the air of an expert.

'Then, dear boy, nothing will be written. Novels won't be written at all or they'll be written by computer programmes. It's just another product, don't you agree? Did you see Kokkiades on TV? Twenty-five years old, first appearance, best-seller, and just listen to him on literature in the next century. You'll load your computer with the characteristics of the hero, of the object of desire, of the bad guy, of the timescale, the type of conflict, you'll click on the narrative style of your choice and you'll choose between the thirty-three possible texts that exist. All the rest will be taken care of by the bytes. Just as we'll have "smart" drugs and "smart" homes, so we'll also have "smart" novels.'

'Except that the reader won't be especially "smart".'

Panos laughed and looked at his watch:

'You get your humour from your father. Come on, then, show me the photos.'

My father

'You mentioned on the phone about some phrase...'

My father puffed at his pipe.

'*Difficult to fight with your soul. It's an unequal contest. Like all wars...*'

'Like all...?' I asked.

'Wars.'

'Wars?'

'Yes, civil ones. Like all civil wars.'

'When did you write that?'

'I didn't write it. I felt it.'

'You felt it?'

'Yes. As soon as I woke up. It wasn't a dream though. It was that tender hour just before waking. When everything is in a state of semi-inertness...'

'It must have been the after-effects of some dream. That intermediate stage between sleeping and waking.'

'No doubt that plays some role. The closer a thought is at the time you wake up, the greater the effect of the dream's warmth on it. The person's at an intermediate stage, his mind is wandering in a fantasy.'

I smiled:

'Just imagine if you heard another father and son talking about such things. It still seems strange to me that I've a father who's a writer...'

18

'It struck you as strange even when you were small. I remember you secretly watching me through the door of my study.'

'Yes. I used to think that you lived somewhere else, in a strange land. Do you remember how I liked to listen to stories when I was a boy? At first, I thought that they came from beyond the world, from where music comes and numbers... When I first realized that my dad's work was to make up stories in our own home, where we ate and slept, I got quite a fright! Don't laugh! It was dangerous for a boy to live in a house with a father who made up stories and heroes.'

'Heroes? There are no heroes, only people. People, characters that visit me. It's a kind of co-existence,' said my father, who appeared to be enjoying the conversation. 'When I'm writing, I can feel them moving inside me, experiencing what I experience during the course of the day.'

'And when you finish the text, they go away. They go to sleep...'

'When the text is finished, it's they who belong to the readers. I'm the one who goes to sleep!' said my father, laughing. 'No, that's a lie, there's no sleep for me.' He went on, 'After I've put the final full stop, I go through a period of inner reflection, almost meditation, on the text.' I didn't ask him what he meant. It wasn't necessary. 'I sit and observe it,' he added, 'like looking at a painting. I note the balance, the volume, the correspondences. I want the finished text to breathe with sharp gasps, to crack open without revealing its openings. And it's there, in the cracks, that I try to entice the reader, to camouflage the hole so that the unsuspecting reader will fall in. But take note! I'm referring to a reversal that has to be justified by two things: by the particular weight of the characters and by the conflicts between them. Everything, but everything, has to be justified in a novel, Yannis! It has to be a perfect, flawless construction – like a building – with the supporting structure, the elements it supports, openings, even an expansion joint! The reader may see it all as being smooth and plastered, but inside there's a whole cosmogony: mortar, stones, bricks, cement, beams... The text's intestines have to work to perfection. Otherwise, dear boy, it collapses. It collapses and dissolves into its constituent parts.'

'Reversal... Though in your last book, not every page goes hand in hand with the previous one. Everything is linear. Everywhere detailed images, historical references completely documented, you've left nothing to chance. I remember somewhere how you even describe the cut of the lawyer's clothes. The narrative is chronologically constructed. Twenty-four hours in each chapter. The entire novel covers a week. The book's like one long sequence.'

'I'm glad you see it that way. Except that, to get to the end of that sequence, you have to read through some five hundred pages,' my father said with a wily grin.

'Come on, I didn't mean it negatively. You know how much I like it,' I said, apologetically.

There was a sudden silence. That often happened in conversations with my father. It was an unequal silence. For him, it was 'functional', part of the flow of the conversation. For me it was embarrassment, since, while it lasted, my father never stopped looking at me, and intently too, as if he were trying to gauge the impact that his words had had on me. Even as a young boy, I remember him with his beady eyes fixed on me from behind his glasses as if I'd done something bad. Now, of course, it was no longer Markos Loukas in his prime that I had before me. I had a seventy-year-old man, opinionated and capricious.

Outwardly, he was in pretty good shape. Tall, round-faced, stocky build, with a good crop of white hair for his age, a delicate well-formed mouth; he vaguely recalled his implacable friend, Pentzikis. His health in recent years hadn't been the best, a balloon to unblock his arteries, a prostate operation, yet these hadn't seemed to get him down.

My father continued to stare at me with an Apollonian calm. Markos Loukas was not the sort a boy would want for a teacher. A cool breeze that came unexpectedly through the half-open balcony door made him shudder. I got up and shut it and, returning to my armchair, I lit a cigarette and broke the deadlock:

'When's Mum coming?'

'I'm expecting her any time now.'

'I haven't seen her for a long while. It must be at least a month. How time goes...'

'A month. What's a month? You young people have a strange relationship with time. At my age, time flows by somewhat differently. Mine is coming to a standstill. When the biological hand reaches fate's slot, then time will point to my allotted hour.'

'Dad, I don't want you thinking like that...'

'Look, Yannis, I've always been a realist. Even in my collection of short stories, back in '65, when all the critics had a go at me – what's up with Loukas, the characters aren't convincing, the structure's unsound – even then I knew that my writing was realistic. I knew that everything that happened in the book was what the characters had either felt or were in a position to have felt. I told you, everything has to be justified. In any case, I never set much store by what the critics said...'

'That didn't stop you writing critical reviews yourself. All those years you wrote for *Narration*...'

'Don't forget that, first of all, I wrote under a pseudonym and, secondly, I chose books that I liked. I've also written libels, of course. Like in the case of that fraud, Matthaiou, in the period following the dictatorship,' said Father. Immediately, I sensed him wincing, as if he'd uttered something that was forbidden.

'What fraud? Who's Matthaiou?' I asked, astonished.

'Water under the bridge...'

'Come on, tell me. Besides it has to do with our work,' I argued.

'Nothing to tell, he was a strange fellow who'd sent me a text.'

'What text? Was it ever published?'

'No, thanks to me. He'd sent me a novel, God forbid... I went to a lot of trouble to make sure Hestia didn't publish it. He had people behind him in America. People with influence. Ginsberg, Burroughs and such like. Didn't you find anything in the archives?'

'Not yet.'

'Yes, that's one thing I most likely threw away. Anyhow. It was at around that time that we almost ruined our literature.'

My father had begun to raise his tone:

'Greece wasn't America! We didn't have a Dos Passos in prose; we didn't have a Cummings in poetry. We had Karagatsis and Seferis. That's why I fell out with Pentzikis. I'd no objections at all to stream of consciousness, even Faulkner used it. But that total disintegration, no respect for anything…Where's the structure, the characters, the sequence of events? Prose is not just jumping from one thing to another. Prose is footslogging, you need a steady step and keen eyes.'

I understood that my father didn't want to go on discussing this particular subject.

'I suppose you're talking about the trend in new novels after the dictatorship.'

'New novel? That wasn't a novel. Not even a story.'

'But there were some writers…' I began.

'Writers?' said my father, abruptly. 'Only in name. I'm a writer too. But something more.'

'Something more?'

'Writer is a noun and nouns get tired of standing alone. They look for an adjective to lend them support. I'm more than a writer.'

'Won't you ever stop talking in codes, Father?'

'I like codes, Yannis, I wouldn't have got where I am without them.'

'That cynicism,' I started to comment.

'Cynicism, Yannis, is adrenaline to an old man.'

'You've certainly got a way with words, Dad…'

'I've a way with them because I used to listen to them.'

I knew what was going to follow.

'From the age of fifteen, I accompanied your grandfather round the salons,' my father went on unstoppably. 'Always just behind him. And they were all there: Myrivilis, Karagatsis, Seferis, Terzakis, Prevelakis…'

'You don't have to tell me the story again. I've heard it countless times…' I said, almost pleading.

'You need to hear it again and again. I didn't spend all my days and nights with journals and glossy magazines. For the whole time that I was a student, for five years, I'd go twice a week to the houses of writers – your grandfather hung out with all the most interesting people – and I'd listen. I didn't speak, I listened. I made coffee, helped the women serve, emptied the ashtrays… Only if they spoke to me did I mumble something back to them. And like that, my mind eventually opened up. Through listening. That's how it is, literature calls for hard work. We don't just churn out a couple of incomprehensible phrases like Matthaiou and think we're through. That's where the adjective comes in that I was telling you about – and don't think I'm arrogant, but I'm more than just a writer. I'm a true writer.'

At that moment, we heard the sharp sound of the front door opening and, a couple of seconds later, my mother appeared in the living room with two large plastic bags full of shopping. A faint smell of perfume spread through the air, lightening the atmosphere. She stood at the entrance to the living room and stared at us, smiling. My mother is a tall woman, almost the same height as my father, very thin, her hair dyed a brown tint and, in recent years, quite short. Her face is slender, aristocratic, an accentuated nose, bright, green eyes, a slanting scar on her forehead, the result of a car accident when she was a child. Her movements are delicate, like those of a dancer. Her gait has something rhythmic about it, something imperceptibly affected, as if her every movement is obeying some personal choreography.

I got up and kissed her. She gently touched her lips against my cheek. My mother, like my father, was not particularly demonstrative. Effusiveness was not something held in esteem in the Loukas household. Our relationship was characterized by an emotional reservation, each member kept a safe distance from the other. It was by no means a coincidence that I'd never seen my parents kissing on the lips, nor ever holding each other's hand.

My mother is best described as 'indefinable'. Her motherliness is faint, like a wet windowpane, I never knew where I was with her, at times I felt her clinging to me like an oyster, without leaving me any space to breathe, at others like a limpet prised free and sinking to the bottom of the sea. I loved my mother, I loved that transient emotion she conveyed to me, I loved her in the way she fluttered around me like a butterfly. Her tenderness was so special that for many years I couldn't deal with it, until I accepted it as it was, I accepted that goodwill, that discreet tool that in our relationship drew the fine line separating parent and child.

My mother didn't stay long. She was tired, all day at the art gallery and then shopping, and she wanted to go and lie down. I proposed that we all eat together, but she didn't want to. She didn't eat much, two mouthfuls and that was it. I sat with my father a bit longer, we discussed one or two things about the book and then, since it was already late, we postponed the Pentzikis correspondence for the next day. I said goodnight and went down to the basement.

The blue bookcase

On opening the door, a strong musty smell took my breath away. I opened the small window of the *cour anglaise*, cursing the criminal architects of the '50s and the reinforced concrete visions of the Minister of Public Works of the time. The basement had three rooms, a very basic kitchen and a small bathroom. The one room was filled with the dozens of items collected by my father. Some were packed into large cases and others were piled in two oak chests. The other two rooms were filled with bookcases running from wall to wall, with two in the centre of each room, thus creating three inner aisles. The blue bookcase stood out like a sore thumb. It wasn't just the colour and the material – the only one made of iron among all the wooden ones – but also the height. It was noticeably higher than the others and reached all the way up to the plaster cove around the ceiling.

It was in the blue bookcase, then, that my father had stacked all the texts that various aspiring writers had sent him over the years. I suspected that he'd never even glanced at some of them, at least those inside the old-style files, where the knot appeared untouched, as if it had never been untied. Most of them, though, appeared to have been subjected to the test according to Loukas and, of course, had been rejected to great acclaim. The few that he had approved, some nine in total, had more or less all found their way into the hands of the reading public, given that Mr Markos Loukas was one of the major despots of Greek literature, at least for five or six years following the fall of the dictatorship. These occupied half the bottom shelf and had a sticker on their spine on which was written 'Prose/OK'.

My struggle with the pile of rejects was obviously going to be an unequal one. Naturally, I couldn't read them all, not even a representative section of each. Besides, the only reason that I'd go to the trouble was on the off-chance that among the defeated armada there was some frigate that had later become famous, having survived the first unfortunate battle at sea. I decided to begin by drawing up a list of names and titles.

After two and a half hours, I'd been through all the shelves except the last one. Two hundred and forty-four names filled seven pages of my notepad.

It was with some relief that I picked up the last manuscript. It was a mauve file tied with a blue ribbon. There was nothing written on the outside, neither the title nor the author. I opened it up. Inside was a note in pencil: 'Matthaiou/Novel. Reject'. I recognized my father's writing. Underneath was a large envelope, again without any writing on it. It contained some two hundred and fifty closely-written sheets tied with a thin string. The handwriting, though clearly legible, was very strange. The letters appeared as if carved; they stood out in relief from the tattered paper. The title, author and date were written on the first page in thick black felt-tip:

BAR FLAUBERT
BY LOUKAS MATTHAIOU
ATHENS, 1975

The name seemed familiar. Matthaiou... Matthaiou. Of course, it was the same man my father had been telling me about that afternoon. The 'fraud', the one who churned out 'incomprehensible phrases', that my father had gone to a lot of trouble to keep from being published by Hestia. I was seized by curiosity. I took the file and climbed down from the stepladder. I sat down on the only chair that there was in the basement and began to read:

CHAPTER ONE

oral mare
even neat

Suddenly.
Suddenly is the word. The dream comes like an oyster and attaches itself to sleep's tail. I blink my eyelids at the first ray of light: the image comes unstuck, falls and shatters. Suddenly.

25

In this night of the male, when the woman's inauguration is splendidly celebrated.
I arrived at the bar around twelve. 48th Avenue. The sign is in Greek: 'Bar Flober'. I hesitated before climbing the steps. A familiar smell. Like a warning. The steps winding. A spiral. Wooden stars, blue and white, like hooks from the curved ceiling. And a half-moon. Menacing. A flow of water. Muddy water. Mirrors, dust, heavy fabrics. And plants, dark plants, black stems and leaves, a pitch-black forest. Climbing up; discomfort. On the door upstairs, again the sign, this time in English: 'Bar Flaubert'. The association was lost. Bar Flober is one thing, Bar Flaubert another. Curiosity concerning the name. A dead white European author in the heart of New York.

Straight up to the counter. Lots of people and I didn't feel comfortable with so many people. Before, because now they tell me I'm okay. The atmosphere grey, smoke; like a battlefield. The battle I'd been waging of late. My gaze straight on Andreas, the Greek owner. Standing among the guests, talking to a girl, Andreas with a light-blue shirt, a dark-blue gaze. Hardly a girl, thirty-seven years old, almost twice my age, who worked in TV. She was wearing a huge earring. I went over to Andreas, who was standing with glass in hand. I was about to say something when a thin shadow passed fleetingly before me. Whether an angel or a demon, all I grasped was the moment, just a wisp of hair that like a diaphanous kerchief traversed the air - pitch-black as it was. I breathed her outline in its luminous aura. I stole a glance – her hair half-covered her eyes, three centimetres, oh those three centimetres! Just what was required. Andreas introduced us with some embarrassment. Her name was Leto. She was beautiful and slender and stooped as though shy. Something blind for a long time suddenly sparked. From the first movement of her head, I recognized the anger. At first I thought it was weakness, but it was anger, a dark anger, a black mound of anger, together with another emotion that I hardly knew. Only once previously had I felt it. Being a child, I didn't understand, I thought that I was responsible when the mouth twists, when the eyes glare. It's the eye, the whites of the eyes. That's where it shows. Anger. In women. For them, I'm no longer responsible. I'd replace the women in my life and christen them. With new names. She, no. We talked, I saw that she didn't look me in the eye. I saw *her as we talked and her features surged everywhere, broke like the sea against rocks. And it was this night of the male, when the woman's inauguration is splendidly celebrated…*

I read the first chapter in one go. I took a deep breath and went on with the second.

CHAPTER TWO

> *Nel mezzo del camino di nostra vita*
> *mi ritrovai per una selva oscura,*
> *che la diritta via era smarrita*
> Dante, *Divine Comedy*
>
> *[In the midst of life's path*
> *I found myself in a black forest,*
> *and my life as I knew it was lost]*

Ten months passed. Months of stone, cylindrical ones with openings as in an aqueduct where our love surged like a wave. I felt a dizziness planted in my insides by weakness. Because it was weakness that this love brought with it, and I had to protect myself. And my protection was for me to paste together the pieces and for her to see someone devoted. Leto became frightened. She saw happiness coming and she couldn't deal with it, couldn't comprehend people and happiness together. She was shaken. And she began the dismantling, with excuses, how she was supposedly offended by that insecurity in the corner of the eye. And even fewer touches. In the past, I'd been unable to bear it. Overly sensitive, I fell apart. Now, I was able to keep a hold. Even during sex, I was less and less tender. And she told me that one day she'd make me say 'I love you' for real, maybe in a year's time, she said something about a lifetime, and became upset, and her truth came out, and she looked it in the eye for the first time, though she was afraid lest it consume her, lest it consume the relationship, and she couldn't deal with it; she came out in spots, on the bottom right side of her cheek. There.

She accused me of being arrogant, ironic. You're losing me, she said. You're losing me. I'm leaving. And during the day she usually left. Only at night, each one's soul visited the other in sleep. When she woke up, always before me, she calmly got out of bed and made the coffee. In the afternoon, when she came home, she got the meal ready and cleaned the house. And that's how we went on. Full of anger, we continually spouted and fell, each of us like clay into the other's cracks. And a breeze, sweet and perspiring, burdened our hearts. Just kids, not yet nineteen, we didn't wish for tomorrow, because tomorrow was a lost cause.

Nevertheless, I wasn't the one to leave. One evening when I was lying on her belly and listening. I was trying to hear something, but nothing, darkness and silence. She told me she was leaving. And just like that, she took her beauty and disappeared. Since then, I've felt as if she swallowed me up. That her tongue performed its double duty. With one word she discarded me and with one movement she swallowed me. Since then I've lived there, in the body of the beloved, with her words saliva spread over my body. For ten months I'd removed the beauty from the black forest. And beauty is always greater than humans. When it's removed, you remain less than you are yourself. I'd search for her. Everywhere…

I went on reading. When I'd finished, the first rays of the sun furtively passed through the chinks in the curtains. I left the file on the floor and remained motionless for a while. Then I noticed that at the end of the two-hundred-and-fifty-page manuscript was a typed letter. It was from Matthaiou to my father:

Athens, 15 March 1975

Dear Mr Loukas,
I'm making so bold as to send you my novel Bar Flaubert. *It was written in Greece last year and has to do with my own personal experiences. I lived for many years in America, where I studied biology. It was there that I met with the leading representatives of the Beat Generation: William Burroughs, Allen Ginsberg, Jack Kerouac. I was a close friend for some time of the first two, though we've now lost touch. My return to Greece coincided with the 1967 coup d'état and for obvious reasons I was obliged to leave for*

Europe. I have published numerous studies in academic journals in Italy and France, together with short stories in English literary magazines. A text of mine was also published in the Greek magazine, Pali, in the sixties.

I would regard it as a great honour, Mr Loukas, if you were to take the trouble to read my manuscript, and even more so if you were to give me your opinion. I would like to express my deep respect for you and my confidence in the reliability of your judgement. I have already submitted the manuscript to Hestia.

With my most sincere wishes,
Loukas Matthaiou

PS. If you wish to contact me, you can write to me at the following address: 6 Sekeri Street, Kolonaki, Athens. My telephone number is: 722.435.

I gave little thought to the letter, as what I'd read before had left me stunned. It was only the first reading. I'd read it again and again, because what I had before me wasn't a story, it was as if someone had stuck a needle into my blood and had extracted the constituents of my most personal universe, things that even I hadn't suspected or, better, that I'd buried in the most secret crypts of my existence. It was as if I'd looked my soul in the eye.

Yes, in the eye, in the same way that I felt that this writer was looking at me. A man about whom I knew nothing, other than that twenty years before, my father had gone to great lengths to prevent his novel from being published. Being well aware, of course, of my father's views on literature and with our exchange in the living room still fresh in my mind, I wasn't at all surprised at his reaction. Nevertheless, he surely must have recognized the man's talent. What was it that had scared him? In 1975, Markos Loukas was all-powerful. Forty-seven years old, six novels to his credit, an associate professor at the university and a consultant editor at Hestia, he was the leading member of the select club of seven that held sway in the Greek literary scene. What was it that had scared him in the case of Loukas Matthaiou, with whom he shared the same name, one having it as a surname, and the other as a first name. I recalled his words from that afternoon: 'I've also written libels, of course. Like in the case of that fraud, Matthaiou, in the period following the dictatorship...'

Those words of his concealed anger. Anger and fear. And there were very few times that I'd seen my father afraid.

My father's ex libris

By the time I got home, it was already daybreak. The impression left on me by the manuscript was of a fluid text that resembled a sculpture in the making; a male figure that was indeterminable yet familiar.

I woke up at around twelve. I'd slept just six hours. I was uptight, something was needling me. I had work to do on the autobiography, on the Pentzikis correspondence. My mind, however, was on Matthaiou's hero, and on the author too. I searched through my archives in case I came up with some information. Nothing. Greek prose-writing, since the fall of the dictatorship at least, didn't include as much as a word from the pen of Loukas Matthaiou. It was as if the man had never existed, at least as a prose-writer.

I'd begun to despair, to the point that I started to wonder whether I should consider the matter closed, when I suddenly thought of Telemachus. Telemachus Anghelis was, among other things, a very well-known literary historian. A friend of mine for over ten years, he was what you'd call a walking encyclopaedia of Greek literature. He was the one who could tell you what pseudonym Taktsis used when out cruising, in which U.S. State Seferis's American publisher was born, what brand of cigarettes Skarimbas used to smoke... I called him straightaway on my mobile phone and we arranged to meet that evening in Kolonaki.

Before that, however, I had to see my father - not only about the autobiography.

I found my mother at home alone. My father had gone to the local café.

'I don't see much of him,' she said in a melancholic tone, 'he prefers the café with his friends...'

30

'A little men's talk is good for him,' I said, reassuringly.

'Your father's changed, Yannis, he's become grumpy. He's growing old and becoming difficult.'

'Just between us, he always was a bit eccentric.'

'There's his work as well.... But now it's getting too much. He's opinionated and capricious, he wants everything to be just as he wants it. It's so tiring. It's lucky I have my own outlets. What about you? How are you getting on? Is it progressing? Is that folder for him?'

'To tell you the truth, it's actually about that folder that I've come. It's a novel that someone had sent to father in '75 and he rejected it. One of the few things that have spoken straight to my heart. And I don't consider myself easy to please as a reader.'

'Who's the author?'

'You can't possibly know him. Even I don't know very much about him. Just his name and some information contained in a letter to father.'

'What's his name?'

'Matthaiou. Loukas Matthaiou.'

My mother, who all that time had been holding a cup of coffee, put it down on the table. She turned her gaze to the front door as if waiting for something.

'What...do you know him?' I asked.

'The name sounds familiar. I can't recall...'

'Mum, if you know something, you'd be helping me a great deal.'

Her intuition proved right as, before I was able to continue, there was the sound of the keys in the door and in walked my father, carrying the newspapers and two magazines.

'You'll have to excuse me. I'm going to change, I have to go to an auction,' my mother said, leaving the room.

'What's wrong with your mother, Yannis?' my father asked when she'd gone. 'Don't tell me you had a fight?'

'No. Sit down. I want to talk to you.'

My father sat down on the couch. I made myself comfortable in the armchair facing him. The afternoon light fell slantwise across his face and boldly outlined his features. I didn't look very much like my father. I noticed the two slanting lines that, starting from the base of his nose, reached down to his chin, as if wanting to delineate the area of his mouth, to accentuate the two lips that were as fine as a woman's. A charming dissonance in an otherwise manly face that beneath thick, grey eyebrows concealed two restless eyeballs, glinting from behind myopic lenses. Above, in the centre of his forehead was a birthmark, the family seal, proud and perfectly round. A circular concession on the part of the skin, roughly a centimetre in diameter, as if positioned precisely on the central vertical of the notional axis joining his two irises. A biological *ex libris*, a third eye, an additional controlling mechanism, superior even to that of the family gaze.

'Dad, I came across Matthaiou's novel in the blue bookcase,' I said, showing him the file.

My father seemed momentarily taken aback; he instantly recovered his composure, however.

'Matthaiou? Oh, you mean that hack writer we were talking about yesterday...'

'Well, I find his work extremely interesting and I'd like you to explain that hatred that I sense you have for him.'

'Hatred? What hatred? The man was useless, I'm telling you. You may like those ravings, but you'll do me the honour of allowing me to disagree. A hotchpotch of materials all thrown together.'

'Come on, I know you, you're as stubborn as a mule. Though Mum didn't seem to be too keen on him either.'

My father's third eye flickered.

'What, was it him you were talking about?'

'We weren't talking about him. We were cut short. Anyway, what could Mum tell me about Matthaiou?'

'Absolutely nothing. Your mother, dear boy, has not the slightest interest in literature. The only things she's bothered about are exhibitions and auctions. The people she associates with are all from the art world. She only has anything to do with writers when they invite us round for dinner. I have to admit though that it worked out well for us like that; it means we're not treading on each other's feet. At least, not often.'

'Dad, you're avoiding the issue. There's more to it than that,' I said, applying a little pressure.

'Listen,' he retorted, 'I've had enough of the matter. If that kind of pulp fiction is your cup of tea, then good luck to you. *De gustibus non disputandum...* I've said all I have to say about the man.'

'You haven't told me anything. I want to know where he is now. To talk to him.'

'Right, let's put an end to this once and for all, Yannis. After I'd read his monstrosity that you find so marvellous, I replied to his letter, giving my frank opinion; that it would be better for him to put down his pen and go back to the laboratory; he was a biologist or some such thing. His case even prompted me to write an article in *Narration* on the new trends in prose-writing following the dictatorship. Since that day, I've never heard of the man again, nor want to.'

'But what happened? He can't just have disappeared from the face of the earth.'

'I don't know. I told you, I wasn't in the slightest bit interested. Now, let's drop it shall we... Are you ready to start on the correspondence? Not that I'm particularly fond of Pentzikis, but at least the man knew about literature.'

I didn't pursue the topic. My father was annoyed, angry almost. Something had happened concerning that man, Loukas Matthaiou. I had to find out more.

I decided not to mention the irritating name again. The day went by calmly, without further excitement. We decided on which letters to include in the book and did whatever censoring was necessary, my father even wrote a short prologue. I left him in the afternoon as he was getting ready for his two-hour siesta.

At home, I read the manuscript once again. The fluid material began to take on a clearer shape. It was a man's head. His features were confused. From one angle, they reminded me of my father and from another of myself, but when I tried to picture him as a whole, it was someone else, someone strange and yet familiar. I was struggling with something that I was unable to put my finger on.

Telemachus

At around ten in the evening, I was at Leo's café-bar in Kolonaki Square. The bar was designer chic, completely transparent with the floor continuing out onto the street. I sat down at a table behind the glass facade, ordered a vodka and lemon and waited for Telemachus, who turned up a quarter of an hour late as usual.

A brilliant mind and loyal friend, Telemachus, apart from being a literary historian, was also an exceptional poet. His most recent collection, *Dust*, had been hailed as one of the best of the year.

'Hi, Yannis,' said Telemachus, 'good to see you, old friend.'

'How long has it been? All I seem to recall are answering machines and messages.'

'Yeah, Yannis... Never any time, for Christ's sake... How's the autobiography going? Is it coming on?'

'There's still a fair bit of work. What with my father's demands... Just sorting through the material in the basement is going to break my back.'

'He's kept everything, eh?'

'His favourite song is *Thanks for the Memories*,' I said, laughing. 'But you come up with some pretty interesting things. And this is where I need your brains. Does the name Loukas Matthaiou mean anything to you?'

'Loukas Matthaiou... That's a tough one.'

'You must know something. I can tell you that he once published a short story in *Pali*,' I continued.

Telemachus pulled a face, as if he'd been offended.

'I said tough, not impossible. So let's see what we have: Loukas Matthaiou. He must have been born around '38 or '39. As a young lad, he went to America to study, biology I think it was, and then he got involved with the Beat group, straight into the heart of the beast: Kerouac, Burroughs, Ginsberg, Corso. The whole damn gang of them. I've heard that there was a time when the Jew made a play for him, then Burroughs did the same. He came back to Greece for a short while at the beginning of the sixties, and Taktsis helped him to get a story published in *Pali*, under another name I think. Patras...something like that. He was back here again in '67, seems he'd decided to settle here, but it was the time of the coup and he left. Then I heard that he'd unsuccessfully tried to get a novel published under the name of Matthaiou. After that, he disappeared from the face of the earth. I once saw him in the flesh, in a club in

Kypseli in 1967, a few days before the coup of the 21st of April. He was a real good-looker. I've never seen a more handsome man. It's said though that he was a bit strange. Aren't you going to tell me where you got hold of his novel?'

'Sure, I found it in my father's basement and I read it in one go. It's amazing.'

'I tried to find it myself years ago. A friend in America had told me about it. There's a bit of a myth surrounding that work in certain circles abroad. And about Matthaiou too. The title has some reference to Flaubert, doesn't it?'

'Yes, the title is *Bar Flaubert*, though it doesn't have anything to do with the writer. Did I tell you my father had rejected it?'

'I don't think they had much in common.'

'Maybe, but so much so that even today he still doesn't want to hear that name. Something's not right, Telemachus.'

'It's very strange...'

'Listen, I've decided to dig up everything I can. Besides, not a lot's happening and my personal life's pretty much of a muchness. The whole business intrigues me more than you can imagine. I'm sure you know what I mean. A text opening up and spreading out inside you... The sad thing is that I can't find any clue, any lead on Matthaiou.'

'It seems that Uncle Telemachus is going to have to come to the rescue once again,' said my old friend, laughing. 'I can help you. I'll send you somewhere. To someone who must know much more than me. At least, he must have known then.'

'Who? What's his name?'

'Hansen. Arnold Hansen.'

Telemachus stopped for a long pause. He'd uttered the name as though part of a rite and now he was waiting. That was Telemachus Anghelis all over. He liked tossing out utterances like oracles and then waiting for them to drop. In this case, however, he was waiting in vain. Mr Arnold Hansen was completely unknown to me.

'So, who is he?' I asked.

'You must read books from the back cover! Arnold Hansen, dear boy, is a well-known American poet and much more; he was one of the first members of the Beat group, the man who typed out

Burroughs's *Naked Lunch*, who organized the poetry evening at City Lights when Ginsberg first read *Howl*, who arranged Gregory Corso's painting exhibitions. And, in addition, he also acted as Samuel Beckett's secretary.'

'Beckett... I can't imagine Beckett with a secretary. Anyhow, that's all very impressive, but what's the connection with Matthaiou?'

'Like I told you, when Matthaiou was studying in America, he went about with the Beat group. He was a very good-looking lad and all the gays in the group buttered up to him for his favours. Of course, Hansen knew all this first hand. And this, Yannis, is where we get back to the matter in question. For the last fifteen years, Arnold Hansen has been living in Greece, somewhere on the Lycabettus ring road. He lives alone in a house full of books and paintings, he's ill – some problem with his legs – and he has no one to take care of him. That man, who's a part of the history of post-war American literature, is growing old alone and destitute. Of course, up to a point, it's his own choice, he's rather unsociable and he hates interviews and the limelight. A few of my friends and I, mainly poets and critics, visit him every so often. We stay a couple of hours, have an ouzo, and when he's had one or two, he tells us stories from the past. You've no idea what my ears have heard about the various giants of literature. All of it off the record, of course. What the man wants is a bit of friendly company, something to ease his loneliness, so none of us has ever thought to take advantage of him. Back to our topic, then. I remember that, one evening, when he was talking about the Beat crowd, Arnold mentioned your friend Matthaiou. It seems he knew him quite well. I think he's the only person in Greece who may be able to help you, though I don't really understand your obsession with it all.'

'Let's not go into that. It's personal. Go on with what you were saying.'

'As you wish. I can send you to Arnold, though it has to remain between us. Or, even better, I can arrange for us to visit him together. He knows your father and I know he respects him. But we have to agree on something beforehand. You won't mention to anyone whatever he tells you. I want you to understand that. Not to anyone.'

'You have my word, Telemachus. Besides all this business is a personal affair, an obsession if you prefer, but I have a feeling that I'm on to something important.'

'Yannis, you know how fond I am of you. If your intuition takes you somewhere, follow it. I'm happy to see you enthusiastic about something at long last. Albeit about a book, a name.'

Arnold Hansen

I spent a rather boring weekend with Anna in Aegina, and on Monday morning I stayed at home re-reading *Bar Flaubert*. In the evening, I waited for Telemachus while listening to the news on TV. The main story concerned a large naval and air exercise called 'Flexible Tongs', being carried out by the Turks in the Aegean. The instigator of the exercise, a Turkish General and repressed author so it seemed, had imagination if nothing else.

The doorbell rang bringing me back to reality. It was Telemachus with a bottle of Barbayannis ouzo under his arm – our host's favourite kind. Before long, the Mini Cooper was on its way along Asclepiou Street, heading towards Bulgaroctonou Street, where Mr Arnold Hansen lived.

We were greeted on the doorstep by an elderly man, around seventy-five years old. He was tall, though his body was bent with age, and on the chubby side, with a face in complete contrast to his body. It was the face of a child, with large blue playful eyes, rounded cheeks, a roguish mouth and unnaturally red lips.

'Come in, come right on in.' He welcomed us in his New York Greek.

Telemachus made the introductions.

'Arnold Hansen, poet and critic – Yannis Loukas, literary scholar.'

Hansen looked me up and down.

'Telemachus tells me that you're Markos Loukas's son. I knew your father, I met him years ago. It must have been '78 or '79. Very good writer. Has he passed on the bug to you?'

'No signs of the illness as of yet. So far, all I've managed are a few short stories…'

'Short stories… It's a start. Though I was never one for them myself. Castrated tales, that's what short stories are… Oh and from the moment you step inside here, I'm Arnold and you're Yannis,' said the effusive Mr Hansen as he led us through to the sitting room.

Arnold Hansen's room was full of books. On the shelves, the table, the desk, the floor, books everywhere, books flung down, books in piles, hundreds of books swamping the place, giving the impression that someone was reading them all at the same time. The walls, on the other hand, were almost entirely covered with paintings by the same artist. Naïve landscapes with elements of ancient Greek civilisation. Arnold read my thoughts.

'The artist? Ah, he's my favourite. Greg. Greg Corso. You'll have heard of him, I imagine. I've been translating one of his poems today. A collection of his work is going to be published in Greek. Do you want me to read you one or two?'

Before I could answer, Arnold picked up a yellow folder lying half-open on the table and began reading with old-style grandiloquence:

Seated on the steps of the shining madhouse
I listen to how the male bell shakes the bell-tower…

When he'd finished, he gathered up the papers and broke out into a cackling laughter, a childlike laughter that shook the whole room.

'Greg. Crazy old Greg. Great poet. Completely crazy…'

I wanted to get straight down to the main business, and I tried to steer the conversation in that direction, with Telemachus playing a largely decorative role. Besides, Arnold seemed to like me, he kept looking me straight in the eye, while every now and then, he broke out into spontaneous laughter, making communication easier.

We began talking about New York; I recounted my impressions from my years there as a student. About the first time I ever set foot in the big city. The feeling of awe when I first set eyes on the Statue of Liberty.

'A tall, young girl expecting a child. The birth of a nation, I suppose,' Arnold commented with a roar of laughter.

I continued, making some observation about the vertical expansion of the city into the skies.

'New York will be one hell of a place when they've finished it,' he added.

The analysis of New York went on in this fashion with Arnold supplementing my pompous account with one-liners, till eventually this old boy who was full of laughter got tired, opened a cupboard and offered us some nuts and sweetmeats, brought by a woman friend of his from Andros.

'There's only Marianna who takes care of me. It's my leg, arthritis, osteo-something or other it's called, I'm unable to get out. Not that I like going out. I prefer to sit at home. I read, write, listen to music. Radio Three. All day. Today they had Richard Strauss. *Zarathustra* and *Don Juan*.'

Classical music wasn't my forte, so I switched the discussion back to its ultimate aim.

'Arnold,' I said, smoothing the ground, 'will you allow me a somewhat trite question? What were Ginsberg and Burroughs like in the flesh? You knew them. What kind of people were they?'

Arnold broke out once again into an unstoppable cascade of laughter.

'Oh! Allen. Allen was a kid, a clever kid… As for Bill, he was the reckless kind. They died more or less at the same time,' he said, and his gaze fixed on the picture hanging above me.

'And Beckett?'

'Beckett was Irish,' he replied abruptly.

Silence fell in the room and it was as if Arnold's great big eyes filled with tears. I sensed that things were delicately balanced, but I had to go on. From across the room, Telemachus gave me a nod to tell me that the time was right.

'Arnold, forgive me for being so persistent, but there's still something I wanted to ask you about that period. There, round about the end of the fifties in America, did you ever meet a young Greek? He must have been about twenty, he was studying biology, but he wrote his own stuff too.'

'What was his name?' asked Arnold.

'Loukas Matthaiou.'

Arnold laughed – through his teeth this time.

He was called Luke all right. But not Matthaiou,' he said, stressing the surname.

'What do you mean?'

He was called Pateras, Luke Pateras. When we spoke again in '76, he'd changed his name to Matthaiou.'

'Look, Arnold... I'm trying to find this Loukas Matthaiou or Luke Pateras.'

'Why?'

'It's a personal thing... I read a novel by him and something happened to me. I was completely captivated. I want to find the man. Wherever he is. I've not been able to find out anything from my own sources. Telemachus told me that you're the only person who may be able to help,' I said with the boldness of someone with nothing to lose.

'Arnold, I have to confess that it's true. I was the one to put the idea into his head,' Telemachus interjected. 'I told him about that day we were here with Jane and Tom, when you talked to us about Matthaiou. When you said that you knew him.'

'But how can I help you now? Yes, I met him in New York in '57. He'd have been about eighteen or nineteen then... The last time I saw him was in Boston in '65. Oh yes, and there was that time in '76 when we spoke on the phone. But then he was another man... He'd changed. Even his surname.'

'Do you know where he lives?' I asked impatiently.

'No, not even if he's still alive. All I know is that when he decided to return permanently to Greece in '67, it wasn't long before the dictatorship came into power and he was forced to leave the country. He went to Spain, to Barcelona.'

'To Barcelona? What on earth was he doing in Barcelona?' My excitement must have seemed excessive as, out of the corner of my eye, I saw Telemachus gesturing to me, as if to say 'gently, calm down, don't press him.' But Arnold didn't have any problem. He was going to tell all.

'Luke was a very strange lad. Perhaps it was what he was studying, I don't know. He was very young, his mind was over his head. I know about Barcelona, because he sent me a card from there to Utah, where I was living then.'

'Do you remember what he wrote?' I asked.

'No, but I can show you,' and he added: 'Mind you, I don't usually do this sort of thing...but I like you Yannis. There's something original about you. I've kept everything. In the bedroom, there are forty-two files containing my correspondence with all the guys from '45 onwards. Greg and I have corresponded every month right up to today. Excuse me for a moment.' Arnold got up with some effort and went into the other room. Telemachus and I were left alone together for about five minutes. My friend was beside himself.

'He likes you. It's rare for Arnold to talk so openly like that about his personal life. He usually needs half a bottle of ouzo.'

When he came back, Arnold was holding an envelope. He opened it and took out a postcard. It depicted the Sagrada Familia, the church designed by the Barcelonian architect, Antoni Gaudí. Arnold began reading:

Barcelona, 5 May 1965

My dear Arnie,

I've been in Gaudí's city for ten days now. I had to get away from Greece. Things are extremely difficult there. My family are all known leftists, I told you that Christos, my father, was with the partisans during the Civil War. I had to keep going into hiding. God knows how I managed to get away. They arrested my father, but fortunately they let him go after a week. He's ill.

I have a friend here, Ramón Esnaider, who's offered me a room in his house. Ramón is an art dealer, in his forties and very rich.

How's the old gang? Bill wrote to me in Athens, no news from Allen. I hear that Jack's not very well. Drink... Tied to his mother, tied to Stella... I read Satori in Paris. *Tired... As if the flame's starting to flicker. Pity. I'm working on something myself. I'll show it to you sometime soon.*

I've found a good crowd here. Some poets, two Spaniards and a Portuguese, good pals. One of them, Fernando, is regarded here as

the biggest new talent. Every evening we go to the London Bar, in
Ramblas, where Hemingway used to go.
I miss Greece, miss the gang, miss you all.
If you want to write to me, send the letter to:
London Bar, Nou de la Rambla 34
(Give this address to the others too)

Joy, boy
Luke

Arnold put the card back into the envelope. My mind was working
nineteen to the dozen, and for every eventuality I'd memorized a
full name, a first name and an address: Ramón Esnaider, Fernando
and London Bar, Nou de la Rambla 34.

'That's the last news I had from Luke,' Arnold said, 'at least in
writing. For, as I told you, in '76, in the first years after the return
of democracy to Greece, we spoke on the phone. Luke was then
called Matthaiou. He seemed very changed. He spoke through his
teeth as if he were afraid. I asked him where he was phoning
from; he didn't answer me. All he told me was that he'd been
through a difficult time, that he'd got married, divorced and that
he'd never write anything again. When I asked him how he got
by, if he had money, I remember his reply as if it were yesterday:
"Money? The only thing I do have is money." Since then, how
long is it, twenty years or more have gone by without so much as
a word.'

'Did he say anything to you about a novel he'd written, anything
about a *Bar Flaubert*?' I asked.

'*Bar Flaubert*? What's that? The title of a book? The one you
read? No. In America, Luke started out with poetry at first, then
later, with Allen's encouragement, he wrote a couple of stories. I
remember them. They were excellent. His style was overwhelming.
He wrestled with it. Style, dear, is a wild thing. Like a wild animal.
At that time, we were all continually fighting with it. We skinned
it, tore it to pieces, but it always managed to leave its scars on us. In
our insides, on our bones. Luke was at the forefront. I recall him
writing more or less where he stood, in restaurants, in bars,

everywhere… And he read, read all the time. He was far more well-read than me, though I was a good fifteen years older than him.'

'I imagine he must have had a girlfriend at the time…' I said hesitantly. Arnold smiled.

'At that time, Yannis, things were different. Sexually, we were all very free, and though we were forever passionately falling in love, there was no exclusivity, nor any clear-cut distinction between being gay or straight, as we say today. Luke was a real good-looker. They called him the Apollo of Athens, in contrast to the Apollo of Denver, which was Neil Cassidy's nickname, you know, Kerouac's hero in *On The Road*. It was only natural that both men and women chased after him. You couldn't classify him. There was no comparison with the other lads around then, he was quite different…'

'So, to recap, the last place that Matthaiou lived before returning to Greece was Barcelona?'

'Yes, for a year at least. I know that from Allen, who told me in a letter some time in the middle of '68 that he'd met him in the so-called London Bar.'

'Do you know anything about the Fernando he mentions in his card?'

'It's not Pessoa for a start!' once again finding his repetitive laughter.

I turned to my friend. 'What about you, Telemachus, how well are you up on Spanish poetry? What was the scene like then in Barcelona?'

It didn't need much thought on his part.

'What I know is that in Barcelona in the sixties, there was a nucleus of poets centered around the critic, Castellet. I recall that the most notable thing was that they all wrote in Castilian rather than in Catalan. I can give you some names: Carlos Barral, Jaime Gil de Biedma, Claudio Rodriguez…'

'No Fernando,' said Arnold, smiling again.

'No Fernando,' I replied. I'd already learned as much as I was going to learn.

The rest of the evening passed without any further reference to Matthaiou. Arnold downed a good few glasses of ouzo, was in a good mood, and sang us some spirituals in his nasal, out-of-tune voice. At around midnight, he announced that it was time for bed, and the evening ended with me a good bit wiser concerning the Matthaiou affair.

On leaving Arnold's house, I felt an overpowering need for a drink. I didn't drink ouzo and I needed a little beneficial alcohol. I suggested to Telemachus that we go to the Bright Lights, but he was too tired. I thanked him and left him outside his house. Then I headed for Exarchia.

Wordgames

The next morning, with the breeze caressing my face on the balcony, I tried to focus my thoughts. The time had come for me to take serious stock of things and see just where I stood. The previous evening, Arnold, the postcard all helped me to sweep away the dust that had settled over everything. For so long, I'd felt as if I were looking from behind misty glasses, through smudged contact lenses. I needed a cleaning agent to get rid of the dirt from my eyes. And it seemed that I'd found it.

On the one hand, I had before me an unknown manuscript, the existence of which only a handful of people knew about. A strange author with an equally strange history. Someone who lived for many years in America, returned to Greece, disappeared during the dictatorship, reappeared like a comet in '75, wrote a novel that was never published, only to disappear again for good. The only reliable information I had was what Arnold had given me. At least it gave me some direction and led me to a city, to Barcelona, to two names, Ramón Esnaider, Fernando, and to a haunt, the London Bar.

Then, on the other hand, there was me. In a state of inertness, without the slightest desire to go hunting after stories for magazines, with the pressure of my father's autobiography weighing on me, my relationship with Anna more of the same.

I found myself at a junction, with two choices. To the left was an asphalt road that seemed endless, full of traffic, with a strict speed limit, with traffic lights and policemen. To the right was a rough dirt road, without signals or limits and with a name hastily etched on a dusty sign, a name at once dental and labial: Loukas Matthaiou.

So, I had to make an important decision; I was standing naked in front of the mirror. There, looking at my reflection, I tried to totally empty myself of thoughts and remain with the two ultimate choices. Yes or no. Right or left. I went into the bathroom and undressed. I didn't need much time. An overpowering instinct turned me to the right, towards the dirt road, towards the defective half, there where the eight missing centimetres stubbornly stared at me from out of the mirror, as if looking for a complement, an addition, *that something extra.*

For many years now, I hadn't allowed them to speak. As if I'd had them in quarantine, as if I'd ritually buried them in some riverbank, and now, like the weapons for a holy war, I was unearthing them, unearthing my eight lost centimetres one by one, and girding them around my breast, as equipment, ready for the great mission.

I returned to the living room and began reading the novel once again. Four chapters, an epilogue, two hundred and fifty-one manuscript pages. Then, I tried to summarise it in one paragraph. I read the one hundred and thirty words I'd written:

> *It's the story of a young man who meets a girl, Leto, in a certain Bar Flaubert in some American town. They fall in love at first sight. But though the girl loves him, she is afraid of living her love. They separate. Years later, he is on the run and finds himself in a town that is not named. He gets involved there in some unspecified criminal act. He escapes in the nick of time. He is forced to flee to another town. There, he meets another woman and has a child with her. A bloody episode once again forces him to seek refuge, together with this woman, in another town – the third one. His memories of Leto constantly hound him. His relationship falls apart. Eventually, the man succeeds in coming into contact with Leto again. Seventeen years have passed. She remembers, but hasn't the strength to respond to his call.*

How simplistic it all seemed to me like that! You'd think it was a cheap romance, a tearjerker… So why had it so stirred my imagination?

I folded the paper and put it in the file, on top of the first page. My gaze once again fell on the incomprehensible caption to the first chapter:

oral mare
even neat

I searched through my dictionaries but got nowhere. It wasn't some well-known quotation, nor could I recall any verse like that from some well-known poem. Besides, if it were taken from a text, the author would have been obliged to mention his source.

What could these seemingly incomprehensible lines possibly mean? They certainly didn't come from the work of any poet I knew. 'Oral mare'… Could he mean the sea of words? Speech as a single unity? Possibly. But 'even neat'? This is where I completely lost him. Did it refer to something that happened in the novel? It had nothing to do with the sea, far less with an even and neat one. All I could suppose was that, with poetic licence, the author was commenting on the speech of his heroes. But here was a total discrepancy, if ever there was one. The heroes – or rather, the hero, who was obviously Matthaiou himself, except that he never once raved throughout the entire length of the novel.

I then tried to decipher the phrase as a whole. Did it refer to the expression of a discourse that flows regularly, obeying some force keeping it under control? Was it perhaps an allusion to the narrative 'plod', the type of prose so fanatically advocated by my father? Or had Matthaiou, who employed anything but a linear, smooth discourse, chosen that caption precisely in order to mock the straight, traditional narration that prevailed in the novels of his fellow authors? Or was it perhaps, after all, no more than a cryptic game, a game with the words themselves, some kind of anagram, a cryptograph? I played for quite some time with the letters, mixing them up and trying to form new words, or an entire phrase with meaning. Nothing came of it. After several failed attempts, now disheartened, I wrote them out in turn, one beneath the other. I stepped back and stared at them as if looking at a painting. Oral, Mare, Even, Neat. Four words, each one of four letters. At that moment, it was as if the Gold Bug had shone within me and revealed the solution to me. The first letters of each word, placed in a row, formed a new word. So reading the letters vertically, I had in my possession four new words, each one again made up of four letters. I wrote the two four-word groups out clearly:

ORAL	OMEN
MARE	RAVE
EVEN	AREA
NEAT	LENT

Omen, Rave, Area, Lent. Another riddle. Even more difficult that the previous one. The omen that raves in the area of Lent? The omen concerning the rave in the area of Lent? The omen concerning the rave area in Lent? No combination made any sense. So this Loukas Matthaiou was either mad or amused himself by devising riddles for his readers, who – it must be said – he never acquired. And he didn't seem mad to me. Or inclined to jesting either.

Wanderlust?

That evening, I wasn't in the mood for going out. I decided to invite Telemachus and Kostas to my place for dinner. I saw it as a kind of farewell meal. It was as if months and years had been condensed into the previous few days. I felt that something had changed in my life – and very quickly too.

I served my friends and the three of us began to eat heartily, joking with each other at the same time. Just before dessert, I broke the news:

'I'm leaving for Barcelona.'

'Oh, so it's that serious, is it!' remarked Kostas, who'd been filled in on everything by Telemachus.

'It's as if you'd fallen in love with that Matthaiou character! It couldn't be, could it, that in your old age you've found your true nature?' said Telemachus, laughing.

'When I've got something on my mind, it stays there. If I've inherited anything from my father, it's his obstinacy. Then again, there's not a lot keeping me here. To tell you the truth, I'm bored,

I need a change of scene. The trip alone will do me good. I've never been to Spain.'

'And the money for all this, old boy? Who's going to pay?' asked Kostas.

'There's a solution. I've three million drachmas in the bank from a small piece of land just outside Volos that I sold recently - an inheritance. I was keeping it to buy myself a new car. I'll keep my old banger for the time being and allow myself some leave. I'll go to Barcelona first and then wherever things lead me. But all this is just between us, okay?'

'That's called late-developing wanderlust,' quipped Telemachus in a highbrow tone.

'Wanderlust… Always wanting to move on. Yes, that's exactly how I feel,' I said sceptically.

'Aren't you a bit old for such things, Yannis?' Kostas asked.

'How d'you mean old… It's nothing to do with age. Do you know how I feel? As if I've been waiting for ages for some sort of sign and now it's come. That's how it is in life. You go out to buy a newspaper, turn the corner and everything changes. All this business with Matthaiou appeared at the right time.'

'The crisis of the approaching big Four-O!', said Kostas, laughing, and explained, 'I mean your forties, Yannis, old boy.'

'You don't seem to remember how you were a couple of years ago. You weren't so cynical and detached then. Myrto had you by the nose…,' I said sarcastically.

'Yes, till I got myself together. If you recall, Yannis, I went off to Melos for two months, shut myself up in a hovel, drinking and reading, till I finally made up my mind. A relationship means war! Those who live by the sword shall die by the sword.'

'I sometimes wonder why we two keep company,' I said with a sly smile.

'Opposites attract, my boy…' came the riposte.

'Let's get serious,' said Telemachus. 'I think Yannis should follow his hunch. He's probably chasing a chimera. Matthaiou could very well be a minor clerk in some library or a miserable teacher in a private school and have relegated his youthful writing aspirations to the dark recesses of his memory.'

'He may even be dead,' said Kostas with a strange grimace.

'How old will he be now? He was at most nineteen in '57, according to Arnold, so he must be around sixty now. Yes, he may no longer be alive...' I murmured.

Female intuition

I devoted the whole of the following morning to preparing for the trip. The first thing was to book a ticket to Barcelona with Iberia on the Sunday flight. I left the return open to allow for every eventuality. Then I booked a single room for ten days at the Hotel Oriente, following Arnold's advice:

'If you want to stay in a real hotel in Barcelona, then stay at the Hotel Oriente. It was opened in 1842 and included part of a Franciscan monastery that had been built two centuries earlier. One of the most illustrious guests at the opening and a regular client was the then American Ambassador to Spain, the author Washington Irving, who in 1819 had published the well-known story of Rip Van Winkle, the tale of a farmer who drank a potion given him by some strange characters and who woke up twenty years later, an old man with a white beard, with his wife dead and with a portrait of George Washington hanging in the place where the portrait of King George III had been. The Hotel Oriente, my dear boy, has entertained famous writers, such as Hans Christian Anderson, statesmen, such as General Grant, movie stars, such as Mary Pickford and Errol Flynn, and countless other celebrities. Oh, and Maria Callas, of course. I remember when Bill and I had stayed there in '63, he'd riddled the wallpaper. He kept aiming at Franco's portrait. He wanted to get him between the eyes. The problem was that Bill Burroughs's aim wasn't always spot on,' Arnold had said before breaking into a torrent of laughter.

It seemed, however, that the Hotel Oriente didn't cash in on its fame, since it charged the relatively cheap room rate of ten thousand pesetas per night – around twenty thousand drachmas at the current exchange rate – though even if it had been more expensive, my mind was made up; the money from the piece of land would be squandered in style, without stinting, for as long as it lasted.

Now, all that was left for me to do was to take care of a few loose ends. First and foremost, to reassure my folks that everything would be all right. I phoned my father and, after cancelling our usual appointment, I told him that I'd accepted an offer with good money from a magazine to do a travel piece on Spain and that I couldn't turn it down. I relied on the fact that my father – who'd never done any work in his life other than lift his pen, if we exclude his courses at the university – respected people who earned their living outside the four walls of their house. Of course, it was to do with writing again, but the trip, the feature, the difficulties with the foreign language made my fabricated assignment seem attractive in his eyes. So much so that he agreed to go on with his autobiography alone for a while. In fact, he took it upon himself to talk to Viliotis and to reassure him with regard to deadlines and practical matters.

The second phone call was to Daniel, who, on hearing the word 'Barcelona', jumped out of his chair. 'I want a piece on the night life and the tapas bars!' he cried. 'Oh yes, and on the Barcelona designers! Remember what we said. Go on, and find your old self again!'

I replied that I'd try to write something and I closed the door, reflecting that the idea of the trip wasn't a bad one after all.

The third contact was also the most difficult one. I would have preferred to announce my decision to Anna over the phone, but, sensing the sadness in her voice, I suggested that we went out that evening.

Women have a strange intuition. Something goes on in their systems, some mysterious elements seem to interact in their cells. Through complex chemical processes, inconceivable to the male organism, they apparently produce certain substances that allow them to communicate with the real 'intentions' of the other person, without being in possession of any clues whatsoever.

Perhaps it was something in the tone of my voice on the phone, a pause that lasted longer than it should, an adjective, a pronoun put in an unusual place. At any rate, when Anna appeared before me, she had the look of a woman betrayed: a slight flush, her hair done up in spikes, her skin swollen and rows of tiny red patches covering her bare back.

'What's up, Yannis? Are you taking off somewhere?' she asked, following a rushed kiss.

'Yes, I'm going. Somewhere,' I said with a half-grin. Then, seriously, 'I'm leaving for Barcelona for a while. How did you know? Have you been talking to Telemachus?'

'There's no need for me to talk to anyone, I can see it in your eyes,' she said sharply.

'I need a change. My mind has come to a standstill, lately. I can't concentrate, can't work…'

'It's obvious that you can't concentrate. You don't have to tell me about it.'

'Don't go imagining anything else. It happens to people.'

'It doesn't happen to people. It happens to you. And as always, the only thing that concerns you is yourself. Of course, I'm not at all surprised. I'm no fool. Right from the beginning I realised you wanted room to breathe in the relationship, that you need your own space, some distance to make you feel safe. You made sure it was all quite clear to me. The type of relationship you wanted became quite clear after the first week, after the first couple of dates. What happened afterwards was simply a cyclical repetition, a variation on that first week, but without the passion, of course.'

This last phrase was uttered with neither aggression nor jealousy. She articulated it under her breath, as if not wanting to believe it even herself.

I tried to explain to her that the trip had nothing to do with what was between us, that I was going through a difficult period, that it was an entirely personal need.

'Your personal need! That could be a perfect motto for our relationship,' said Anna, seizing the occasion.

'You don't waste any opportunity, do you?' I said, irritated, as it was precisely that aspect of her character that irritated me the most.

'Look, Anna, if you're trying to tell me that you've made your decision, then say it now. But come straight out with it and stop all the hinting,' I continued, trying to get the upper hand in the exchange.

'Come on, Yannis, calm down. Let's not make a big thing of it. What do you want me to say to you? To ask you to stay here? Since

you need to get away so much…go. Make sure you have a good time and come back a new person.'
I caressed her cheek and kissed her. Anna closed her eyes. We spent a tender night together, the love-making was what it should be, though above the candelabra I kept seeing a blinding neon light flashing on and off with the two words: Bar Flaubert.

…Exams. So many exams. To have graduated from university and to be still taking high-school exams. How can that be? But I have the certificate. In the room, framed and hanging behind the door. So why are they taking me back? And the Army. The Army again. '*Is ordered to return to his unit no later than 06.00 hours…*' But I have my discharge papers. In the top drawer, under the parental bequest. It explicitly states: '*Discharge and Call-up Papers. Category: Active Service: Intake of '86… Reserve private is discharged…Iin the event of mobilization, to report for duty at the Camp.*' Okay, but we're not at war now, why do I have to report for duty… Yet another document, deferment papers this time: *Certificate Type B: 'is exempted from military service for the duration of his studies.*' Good Lord! How can that be? And that man? Who's that in the painting? A teacher? On the Ministerial Committee? Yes. Summer. In Athens. A heatwave. Me in a blue T-shirt. '*Turn over your papers. You have three hours beginning now. Absolute silence. Your time begins… Now!*'

At that moment, the sound of an alarm shattered the silence. Some car in the neighbourhood had become the target for theft, with the result that I woke up just as I was about to start the unseen ancient Greek passage. The same damn dream for so many years now. Exams that never end. And the Army, always the Army and mobilization, endless military service.
I felt thirsty and got up to get a glass of water. I was so shaken that I didn't notice that next to me the bed was empty and so I got a shock when I saw her in the living room, lying on the green sofa. Anna was wearing her dressing gown, curled up on her side and quietly crying. Trying not to be heard, walking on tiptoe, I turned on the spot and went back to bed, leaving her alone. Her crying was barely audible, yet its volume filled the whole house.

Deep in the Zarzuela

Air pockets

...In the plane full of anxiety. With every hundred feet we ascended a new butterfly burrowed into my stomach, till at the peak of the flight I felt a whole forest of butterflies — bombyx quercus, Lycaena phlaeas, Silvius skipper and about a thousand more types — had set up a demonic dance in my guts. I tried to sit back and enjoy the flight, the view I had from my tiny window, with the gold-tinged clouds and sparkling blue sky. My body succumbed to hyperaemia, I became inexplicably flushed, as though a rash escaping from the clouds had put down roots in my skin and was establishing a colony, till it filled it with a multitude of tiny red spots that gaped, invincibly gaped, and made their home all over my body. It was completely new to me; my body gradually abandoned me and endeavoured to leap outside, to escape through the oval window and dissolve into myriads of dust particles in the sky. And with me resisting and reacting with a deep sigh and with the cabin shaking and me falling ever deeper into the void. And as a murmur rose from the direction of my fellow passengers, with my red skin tightening, I turned to look at them; I looked behind at the people fidgeting and with their eyes bulging and I was gripped by a fear that I had never felt before. And then, indifferently and with a cold hard gaze, the stewardess told me to fasten my seat belt, it was over, we were about to land, we had reached Athens...

I was exactly at that point, where the hero is returning from New York, when by a devilish coincidence, there was a violent jolt that caused the blood to drain from my face. A terrible buffeting accompanied by smaller vibrations gave rise to uncontrollable panic. For between one and one and a half minutes, that seemed like an age to me, I sensed that the plane was continually losing altitude and plunging out of control straight into the waters of the Mediterranean. And then, during that short space of time, I saw my entire life before me as in a video clip. People and places passed like lightning before my eyes. Each image merged with the next. I saw the house of my childhood in Holargos, the summer house in Varkiza, the student room in New York, my present apartment and, together with all these, the faces of my father, mother, grandfather, and of my grandmother who I knew only from photos, of Anna, as she was when I first met her, and finally the vague outline of a man unknown to me. There, on that face, the image froze, the jolting stopped and the plane returned to its normal course. Fortunately, it was just a minor fault caused to one of the engines by a large bird that was sucked in by the turbine. With some skilful flying, the pilot managed to regain control and the flight continued without any further excitement to the capital of Catalonia. The introduction was a warning, I reflected.

I took a taxi from the airport to the hotel. The taxi driver, Pablo, was a young man with shaved head – à la Ronaldo – who spoke English fluently and drove like a madman. After we had discussed at length the gap left by the young Brazilian in the ranks of the Blaugrana, the Barcelona football team, I asked him, before he left me at the hotel, to take me for a tour round the city.

We began by crossing the Eixample, the residential area. At one moment we passed by a building with a tiled roof and mosaics on the facade, and I remembered Matthaiou's card – Gaudí's poetic architecture. We went down towards the port passing through Barrio Gòtico, the hub of the medieval town. A network of backstreets crossing an area full of 14th-century churches, museums, squares and palaces. Before long, Pablo was in the traditional district of Barceloneta. In front of the port, at its entrance, was the towering monument to Christopher Columbus. Then the Olympic village, built on the site of an old, derelict factory. To the right of the port was the large hill, Montjuïc, the centre for the 1992 Olympic Games. At first sight, Barcelona looked like a multifaceted city of an ideal size for exploring on foot.

We turned back, passing through the Plaça de Catalunya and then drove down towards the Ramblas, a wide pedestrian avenue, one and a half kilometres long.

'Here you can smell the heart of the city, you can see clowns, street artists standing motionless for hours like living statues, fortune tellers, musicians, booths belonging to anarchic organizations and flower stalls, the one next to the other. Madness! And whenever Barcelona wins some European Cup or other, you should see what happens,' said the young man, finishing his guided tour, given that it was on Ramblas Avenue, at number 45-47, that the Hotel Oriente was situated.

Despite all the recent additions and the successive restorations, the Hotel Oriente was unable to hide its history. Apart from the structural features of the building that revealed its former function as a monastery, I also noticed on entering my room that the floor was a step higher than the corridor. The bellboy informed me that in olden times that step was intended for kneeling during the evening prayers.

'In the basement there are still the remains of a crypt and also the entrance to an arched tunnel that once led to the Capuchin Monastery, where the Plaça Reial is today. You have to visit it, it has some of the best clubs,' the young man added.

On opening the window, I saw with some satisfaction that it directly overlooked the Ramblas. Exactly opposite was a building under construction; it was the Opera House, the Opera Liceu, which at that time was being rebuilt from the foundations after having been destroyed by a major fire.

My room was large, with a marvellous oval period mirror facing the three-quarter size bed. Three silk prints of the *Maja desnuda* adorned the other walls, while a heavy curtain covered the balcony door entirely protecting the room from the Catalan light. I got a beer out of the minibar and gulped it down.

I took from my bag one of the three manuscripts belonging to
Matthaiou that I had brought with me. I lay down on the bed and
thumbed through the second chapter, when he had now taken
refuge in the first city. I read a paragraph at random:

> ...*Chinks opened in the sky and the light streamed down. And it
> at once spread diffusely over the city. The streets lit up and the glare
> fell upon me like a beam, upon me, a stranger in the street. Yet I was
> neither an emigrant nor a traveller. I had the wanderlust bug and I
> was here, in another unknown place...*

'Wanderlust'? Had Telemachus, I wondered, read the book?

> ...*And the walls here were waves and rippled. The buildings
> flowed, swam in the narrow streets. And I walked over the cobbles,
> vast crowds of people...*

The buildings flowed... Gaudí's buildings with the wave-like
facades... Was this city Barcelona? I put the book down and,
though it was only eleven, decided to get some sleep in order to be
fresh on my first day in the Catalan capital, my first day in the quest
for Loukas Matthaiou.

London Bar

The next morning I went out for a walk in Ramblas Avenue. I
began from one end, from the Plaça de Catalunya. Ramblas is the
street that bisects the old town and leads to the port. Passing by a
fountain, the Font de Canaletes, I halted before a group of elderly
Spaniards who were talking excitedly. They appeared to be talking
about politics, sports, or about both. A number of people had
formed a circle around them out of curiosity. My attention was
caught by a container, rather like a ballot box, in which every so
often the spectators cast a piece of paper. As though an informal
referendum concerning some local issue. If I understood correctly
from my elementary Spanish, they would submit the results of the
vote to the mayor of the city. The old men's faces were bright red,

furrowed; they shone from the sweat. I tore a page out of my notebook, wrote 'No' and tossed it into the ballot box. One old man with a drop of saliva hanging from his lips looked at me askance and spat on the ground.

Passing by a portly fellow holding a puppet that was playing the *Für Elise* on the piano, I found myself among a plethora of outdoor shops selling flowers, magazines and even birds – parrots, doves, canaries and some exotic ones I didn't know. A few metres further on there was a huge food market. A bronze sign read: 'Boqueria: the biggest market in the world.' Pandemonium inside. Hundreds of tourists, pushing and shoving, were crowded between the Lilliputian shops, carefully observing the meats, the salamis and the fish as though walking round a sculpture exhibition. The place emitted a variety of amazing smells. But it wasn't only this. The market was a feast of colours; the counters were so aesthetically laid out, it was as if a designer had undertaken to arrange the foodstuffs like exhibits, while women clad in full-length white overalls made sure all was in order. Before leaving, I stopped at a stand selling eighty-one kinds of Spanish cheese and bought a quarter of a kilo of garocha, a Catalan cheese made from goat's milk.

As I continued on my way, I hadn't managed to swallow even two mouthfuls when I noticed on the right just below my hotel a narrow diagonal street; Nou de la Rambla.

The glass front of the London Bar was filled with posters announcing jazz concerts and literary evenings. Stuck on the wall under the period lamp to the right of the entrance was the week's programme. That evening there was live jazz with Tete Montoliu on piano. The next night there was an American Blues artist while on Wednesday the evening was devoted to poetry. Manuel Ferrer and Fernando Salinas were reading.

Poetry, Fernando? Such luck, I thought to myself and knocked on the door. I had to wait quite some time and knock twice more before a female voice in Spanish asked me who I was.

'Would you open up, please, I'd like some information,' I replied in English.

'Just a moment,' came the voice from inside, this time in English, and presently the door opened.

Before me stood the personification of Spanish elegance. A woman of between thirty and thirty-five, tall, thin, wearing a red mini-skirt, wavy jet-black hair and huge eyes the colour of the sea.

'What do you want?' she asked again.

'May I come in?' I asked politely. 'If you don't mind, I'd like to speak to you for a few moments.'

The woman looked at me searchingly from head to toe.

'Ok, but I don't have a lot of time. I have to close up soon.'

'It won't take long,' I said and followed her inside.

The London Bar was relatively small. A long, narrow place with mirrors covering the oblong walls, a dance floor of sorts in one corner, metal designer tables and dozens of portraits on the walls. Distinguishable among well-known jazz artists – Duke Ellington, Dexter Gordon, Miles Davies – was a photograph of Hemingway, who was posing narcissistically, with a pipe in his mouth and with his arm round a dark-haired Spanish woman. We sat on the bar stools; she lit a cigarette and said with a formal smile:

'My name's Tina, Tina Tobosa, what is it you want?'

'Nice place,' I said to break the ice. 'A combination of traditional and modern.'

'We are one of the oldest bars in the city. The London Bar opened in 1910. But what is it you want?'

'My name is Yannis Loukas. I'm from Greece, from Athens. I work for a literary magazine and I'm here for a specific reason. I'm looking for a Greek writer who has not been seen for twenty-five years. The last place I know he was for sure is Barcelona. He was here in 1967 for at least a year. I know that he was a regular customer of the London Bar. But before I go on and without wanting to be indiscreet, may I ask you what you do here?'

'I'm in charge of all the literary events,' said Tina, 'I contact the writers and poets and I arrange the literary evenings. I was also responsible for the design of the place. It's changed a lot since the time you're talking about,' she added, laughing.

'You can say that again, your parents most likely hadn't even met each other then,' I replied in a similar playful mood. The woman lowered her gaze coquettishly. Nevertheless, I sensed that she was much tougher than she showed. 'The man I'm interested in is called Loukas Matthaiou,' I went on, taking care to pronounce clearly the 't' and the 'th', forgetting that I was speaking to a Spaniard, and one by the name of Tobosa.

Tina showed no signs of recognizing the name.

'I know that while he was living in Barcelona, he stayed in the house of a certain Ramón Esnaider and kept company with a poet called Fernando. Do those names mean anything to you?'

Her sea-blue eyes flickered:

'Señor Esnaider no longer comes here. For years now he's been paralysed, he never leaves his house.'

'Do you know him?'

'Ramón Esnaider was once king of the city. A veritable Croesus. He owns an entire block in the city centre. One of the three richest men in Barcelona. Before his accident, he used to come often to the London Bar. Señor Ramón is a lover of the arts. In the sixties he had three art galleries in the city, his personal collection is priceless. But some years ago, in the early seventies, he got into an argument somewhere abroad and he was shot. Since then he never leaves his house, he has withdrawn to the Pedrera.'

'Pedrera?' I asked.

'The apartment block by Gaudí with the wavy balconies.'

'Where Antonioni's *Professione: reporter* was filmed?'

'Yes.'

'What you've told me is very useful. I'd be especially grateful if you would bring me into contact with Señor Esnaider. It's very important for me,' I said, almost pleading.

'I'll do what I can. My father, who owns the bar, is a personal friend of his. Señor Esnaider helped him to buy it. Ramón Esnaider has done a lot for my family. But as I told you, he hasn't left his house for years, I don't know if he receives visitors. Anyhow, I'll try.'

'Thank you. What about the poet, Fernando, do you know anything about him?'

Tina smiled, almost ironically. 'The only poet I know by the name of Fernando is Fernando Salinas. He happens to be one of my favourites. He'll be reading his poems at the London Bar on Wednesday.'

My intuition proved right. 'The only poet by the name of Fernando...' Two birds with one stone!

'Could you tell me a little more about him? How old is he?'

'Around sixty. He was considered to be one of the main representatives of the poetic generation of contestation at the end of the sixties. Then his writing was in the forefront, he experimented with the shape of the poem on the paper, what we call visual poetry. But for around twenty years he wrote nothing, he completely disappeared. He started publishing again in the nineties, which is when I first read him, in a new, condensed style. His work speaks to me directly here,' said Tina, pointing to her left breast.

'I think there's a good chance that he's my man. Do you perhaps know of any relationship between Salinas and Esnaider?'

Tina seemed to hesitate:

'Listen, back then in the sixties, Esnaider supported all the new artistic currents in Barcelona. He was well known throughout Spain, a personal friend of Franco, they used to go hunting together, you understand. His collection of paintings is one of the most famous in the world, and he hobnobbed with celebrities, Andy Warhol, Maria Callas... In Barcelona, he was something of a sponsor to everyone, he had all the young artists under his patronage. At that time Salinas was one of the major new talents in poetry, so naturally there was a relationship between them.'

The images began taking shape in my mind, the faces began to arrange themselves one beside the other with an arbitrariness that for the time being worked in my favour. As though reading my thoughts, Tina put things in order:

'So, I'll make sure Señor Esnaider is informed that you want to see him. As for Señor Salinas, you'll have the opportunity to see for yourself on Wednesday if he's the one you're looking for. Shall I reserve you a place for the event?'

'I'd be only too pleased. So I'll see you again the day after tomorrow. And if you have any news from Señor Esnaider, I'm staying at Hotel Oriente, room 14.'

'If there's any news, you'll be informed,' said Tina, noting down the address. Then she got up with all the grace of a ballerina.

'Pleased to have met you.'

'Me too, very,' she said and I took my leave of her with an old-fashioned kiss on the hand. This classic gesture must have counted for something because on going out I felt her gaze boring into my back.

I spent the rest of the day walking the streets. Barcelona is a city that lends itself to walking. It is essentially a rhomboid complex of narrow streets which constitute the old town and which are divided in the middle by a large avenue, the Ramblas. At one end of the Ramblas is the central hub, the Plaça de Catalunya, from which begins the rectangular outline of the Eixample, the new district. The hills, Montjuïc and Sierra de Colserola, form the natural borders towards the hinterland.

In the evening I found myself in Barrio Gòtico. After visiting the cathedral, I went into a charming little café. It was called the *Quatre Gats*. Large posters on the walls testified to the fact that it was the centre of bohemian Barcelona at the beginning of the century. Modernist artists had painted the walls and the menu had been illustrated by Picasso. The café served tapas, Catalan appetizers.

Drinking white wine out of a ceramic cup to accompany the crab claws, I indulged myself in the most popular sport in the Mediterranean; the critical observation of everything going on around. Without being particularly good-looking, the people of Barcelona had an innate charm. I remembered Tina's dress, then her eyes, and then I wondered whether I would eventually get anywhere with the London Bar.

Keep cool, I said to myself, in an attempt to exorcise my impatience, my biggest weakness.

It appears that my appeal was heard as, on returning to the hotel, I found a message for me in reception. 'Señor Esnaider is expecting you tomorrow at seven o'clock at his home in the Pedrera, 92 Passeig de Gràcia.'

Immediate interest. The fellow was instantly hooked, I thought, silently thanking Tina. It seemed that Barcelona hadn't forgotten Loukas Matthaiou's stay there. And yes, fortune favours the brave.

Two days in Barcelona, Ramón Esnaider tomorrow, Fernando Salinas the day after, what more could I ask? I decided to celebrate this propitious start at the most in-club in Barcelona.

I drank, danced for half an hour or so with a succulent Spanish girl, who left me when her boyfriend arrived, and at around four, exhausted after a tiring though productive day, I returned to my room, tripping, faithless soul that I am, on the step.

Rip Van Winkle

…And I'm at home, young, aggressive and tempestuous; the only instrument I use well is my tongue, and when even this is insufficient and I get angry, outside my house there's a basketball court above the entrance to which is the symbol of the Junta, the phoenix rising from its ashes and the solitary soldier. And my father gripes and we argue and I can't stand it. I take my ball and go to the court together with my dog, a white one with curly hair, called Nat, and I continually throw the ball at the basket, sometimes it drops in sometimes not, it spins a little round the rim and goes out, and while the ball is turning I pray that it goes in, but it doesn't, and I continue to make shots, alone as I am, I'm always alone when I go to throw the ball because I don't want the others to see me shooting without the eight centimetres, I want them to remember me as before, and after an hour of continual shooting, I collapse exhausted onto the concrete court. And lying there I see, as in the films, the whole of my neighbourhood, the court is on a rise, I can see the black concrete, the narrow balconies and apartment block entrances. Night begins to fall and I reflect that I'll see my father again and I sigh and my fear returns in waves. And at that moment I hear a voice in the distance: 'Yannis Loukas! Yannis Loukas!' Nat, who was curled up beside me, stretches and begins to bark, and I get up and see, ten metres away, a tall, bony old man, with glasses, a gabardine and a hat. He is the image of death and he has in his hands a pile of such thick books that he is unable to hold them and they look ready to fall at any moment. He comes over and asks me to help him. I obey because of some unknown power and take hold of half the books, we leave the court and begin walking through some narrow back streets, and as we are walking I hear a pattering as though it were raining, but there isn't a drop of rain about. After quite some time we have passed through areas that I don't know and we haven't encountered anyone nor have we exchanged a word between us. And we arrive in front of a black building, as though it has been burned, and outside is a red flag with a star. And I go inside with the bony old man and we climb a wooden staircase, an extremely old winding one that creaks. And we reach the first floor and find ourselves before a large room with two men wearing baggy clothes who are smoking something strange and drinking greedily out of a large bottle. They are much younger, one plump, bald and with round glasses, the other handsome, dark and with sorrowful eyes as though he is crying. Though they are supposedly having fun, their faces are grave and they don't speak to each other. The moment we enter, they stare at us with a strange, blank expression and my heart begins to flutter. Then the bony old man, that the fat one called Bill, tells me to put the books down on the floor. They both take a book and begin reading. At one moment, when no one is watching and the three are absorbed, I too take hold of a book, a thin, illustrated one, and I delve into it. It doesn't take me long to become absorbed and I begin to feel that I too am in the story, and my eyes close with a sensation resembling sleep. Before very long I feel them opening again. But now I see that it's daytime, the sun is out and I am back in the court. Lying on the concrete floor. Nat is missing. All around me is dust, thick dust enshrouding me, and I shudder. The baskets are different, of a different material, space-like. An electronic scoreboard is behind them. I've never seen anything like that before, only at the cinema, in *2001: A Space Odyssey*. Terrified, I get to my feet and dust myself down and I tremble at the thought of my father and his rage that once again I imagine coming in waves. As I begin to move, I feel as if my joints aren't obeying me. My body is heavier, as though I have gained not only weight but height too. I leave the court and see with surprise that the emblem with the bird is missing. In its place hangs a colourful, glossy sign. I read: 'Athens 2004'. As I head home, I see the surroundings, how they have changed. Taller buildings, unfamiliar people on the streets, new shining signs over the shops. As though someone had polished them all, given them a new lustre. My house is completely different, but for the worse. The well-tended garden is now a field with weeds, the newly-built single-storey house has the look of a bombed-out shack. At the gate, an old mangy dog growls sadly. Its eyes are the same as Nat's. The gate is open. I enter. 'Dad!' I shout. Silence. I go into the living room. Our furniture has vanished. Just various odd machines with green and red buttons lined up in the place. I go into my parents' bedroom. No one. Through the half-open door of my father's study a dim light appears. I am exhausted and go over with difficulty. On opening the door I see the back of a man wearing my father's dressing gown. He is sitting at the desk and reading. 'Dad!' I shout again impatiently. The man turns his head. It's not my father. It is a pale-looking man with a tin face and hollowed cheeks. A deathly silence fills the place. The man shuts the book and gets up. 'Yannis,' he says. I turn and see my face in the mirror. It's someone else, a grown-up man…

I awoke suddenly, with the man's face glued to mine. Thick beads of sweat dripped onto my cheeks, my bones ached and my head was spinning as though I had smoked some weed with inscrutable qualities. No doubt the five or six vodkas of the previous day together with the wine had done their job well, nevertheless what I felt inside my head was rather like a battlefield, bombs and mines were exploding in my temples, arquebuses and pistols were firing in my ear drums, the clashing of swords and the lamentations of the wounded filled the hypothalamus. As for the dream, Freud for beginners was enough. All I had to do was to remember Arnold's words:

'One of the regular visitors to the Hotel Oriente was the then American Ambassador to Spain, the author, Washington Irving, who wrote the famous tale of *Rip Van Winkle*, the story of a farmer who drank a potion given him by some strange men and woke up twenty years later as an old man with a white beard, with his wife dead and the portrait of George Washington hanging in the spot where previously the portrait of George III had been.'

In my case, there was no wife – the image of Anna had begun fading some time ago – George III was naturally Mark I, but

George Washington, the man with the hollowed cheeks, who might he be?

I left aside the difficult questions and went into the bathroom to take a shower. By the time I had come round it was almost midday.

I strolled down the Ramblas and turned right in the direction of Montjuïc. I walked mechanically, the images of the city passed before me all jumbled up. A strange nausea led me along. Close to the statue of Columbus, I found myself before a sign that woke me from my lethargy: 'Museum of Erotic Art'. I went inside. I had never seen anything like it; Indian engravings from the Kama Sutra, sculptured phalli, designer condoms from the '50s, aphrodisiac philtres and ointments, and the finest exhibit of all, a porno movie from 1926, with an enormous actress who did everything, and I mean everything, with an amazing indifference. After watching it till the very end, till, that is, this porno star from the beginning of the century had worn out a whole gang of men, I continued in the direction of the hill and ended up in a tiny tapas bar. There I savoured a wonderful zarzuela, a gastronomic stew with pieces of lobster, prawns, mussels and various other seafoods cooked with garlic, onions, tomatoes, cloves, laurel, peppers, cinnamon and saffron, all floating in the same sauce in precisely the same way that swimming in my head were a handful of names: Rip Van Winkle, Fernando Salinas, Tina Tobosa, Ramón Esnaider and, of course, Loukas Matthaiou.

Confined in the Pedrera

The Pedrera is a building that looks as if it has been designed by a poet. It resembles a mountain sculptured by human hand. Looking at it from the pavement opposite, you got the impression of a hill full of holes, an object trying to imitate the rhythm of nature itself. There was a constant motion in the facade, like a stone sea rippling on the streets of Barcelona. I again thought of Matthaiou: '...*For the walls had waves here and lapped...*'

The building was constructed entirely on columns and parabolic arches. I couldn't see even one straight line; it was a construction that flowed before my eyes. So it was in this

undulating monument that Ramón Esnaider lived. And for this
reason alone he must have been one of the most privileged citizens
in Barcelona. From what the sign in the entrance said, the building
belonged to the Bank of Catalonia and was full of offices, while the
top floor housed the 'Gaudí Area', a permanent exhibition on the
architect and modernism. Esnaider appeared to be the only person,
apart from the guard, who slept all night in this architectural
mausoleum. I rang the bell, and after waiting a minute or so, I heard
a deep voice ask me in English:

'Are you Mr Loukas?'

'Yes, I have an appointment with Señor Esnaider at seven.'

The door opened and I found myself in a courtyard open up to
the top of the building. A circular staircase facing me led to the inner
areas. Before long I was on the third floor facing an oak door with a
sign on it: 'Ramón Carlos Esnaider, Art Dealer'. I took a deep breath
and discreetly rang the gold doorbell next to the silver handle.

The door was opened by a servant – or was he a butler? –
impeccably dressed; silk shirt, black waistcoat, white gloves and an
enigmatic Anglo-Saxon smile. He was red haired, tall, scrawny and
his face revealed the signs of acne treatment.

'Wait here for just a moment, Sir. Señor Esnaider will see you
shortly,' said the fellow, pointing to the couch in the hallway.

I sat down and my gaze explored the surroundings. I was in a
white room, which, apart from the green couch, contained a glass
table in the shape of a rhombus, an antique chandelier and two
large paintings. A flashy Chagall and a bright pastel. A dancer was
rehearsing her movements in front of a large mirror. I was unable
to hold back my smile on recognizing my favourite impressionist.

Fine, I thought, the hall alone is worth half a billion drachma…
And supposedly the man isn't in his prime…

After twenty minutes or so had passed, a length of time Señor
Esnaider considered sufficient for testing my patience, the butler
appeared again and announced to me with comic officiousness:

'Señor Esnaider is now ready to receive you. If you will be so
kind as to follow me.'

We walked down a long white corridor. On the walls the
Polaroids by Robert Mapplethorpe shrank inside their huge

frames. At the end of the corridor was a large iron door. The butler took from his jacket an object resembling a tele-control and pressed a button.

'Come in! Pedro, leave us alone,' said a husky voice from inside and the iron door slowly opened with a slight creaking noise.

I went into the large room. This time the walls were jet black. At the far end of the room was a huge carved antique desk, while on the left-hand wall a large portrait of Velasquez stared at me threateningly. The right-hand wall was entirely covered by two rows of heavy purple curtains. In the middle of the room was a kind of couch, of amazing elegance, made of steel and marble, and beside it, in a high-tech wheelchair sat Señor Ramón Esnaider.

From Arnold's postcard it was clear that Esnaider must have been around seventy. Yet the person I saw before me in the wheelchair had the face of a man of forty-five, fifty at most. The plastic surgery had been an exceptional success, nowhere was the skin unnaturally tight, the silicone was in complete harmony with the tissues of the lips, and only the nose created something of a false note in what was otherwise a splendid restoration. Perhaps some would regard this overall repair work as being exceedingly refined, given that the delicate face was in sharp contrast to the gruff voice, the old, pocked hands and the aggressive look that pierced you like an arrow.

'Good evening, Señor Esnaider, my name is Yannis Loukas,' I said and paused.

After looking me up and down, Esnaider replied, also in English, 'Yes. You are a Greek, Sir. A true Greek. All the features… I have met a number of your countrymen, sir, major figures: Callas, Tsarouchis, Iolas… I like your race. You are aggressive, and I like aggressive people. Of course, you don't seem so fierce; you have a clean face, though that difference in your arms suggests a certain dynamism.'

Any person with a profound disability immediately senses the least disharmony in others. Practised in detecting even the slightest discord, Esnaider immediately grasped my physical dissonance despite my long-sleeved shirt that supposedly concealed it. Before I could say anything, he skilfully changed the subject.

'Do you like Velasquez, Mr Loukas?'

'Very much,' I replied. 'Though my favourite painter is a French impressionist.'

'I have no doubt that one has to be an impressionist to charm you,' said Esnaider, interrupting me with a smile and, pressing a button on his hi-tech wheelchair, he approached to within a yard of me in the wink of an eye.

'Mr Loukas, I enjoy introductions, but I am not a person who likes to waste time. I was told that you know something about an old acquaintance of mine.'

'I know nothing about Mr Matthaiou. On the contrary, I am trying to find him,' I said.

'Oh, so you're looking for him… But do you know if he's still alive?'

'No, I don't. But if he is I must meet with him. Let me explain.'

I told him the story, omitting only the name of Fernando Salinas. I had decided not to mix my sources. At least not until I was aware of his intentions. Esnaider hung onto every word. At the same time, he made a great effort to appear calm. In fact at one moment he squeezed the arm of the wheelchair so hard that he accidentally pressed one of the buttons, with the result that the purple curtains gradually began to open, revealing part of a miniature painting hidden behind them. Esnaider closed them again immediately, but not so quickly as to prevent me from seeing on the right-hand side of the canvas the characteristic brushstrokes of Picasso in his blue period.

'So you have never actually seen him? Never spoken to him. Pity…' said Esnaider when I had finished my story, seemingly lost in thought. Then he paused for some time. 'Listen, young man,' he said suddenly. 'You story is undoubtedly a moving one. And understandable, I'd say, in terms of its motivation at least. Your father is a writer, you said. And you too want to write. How old are you? Thirty-three, thirty-four?'

'Thirty-nine, I'll be forty in July,' I replied.

'Well, you don't look it… Evidently no excesses, Mr Loukas, *nada*, eh?' And he added sarcastically, 'So you're almost forty and you're still concerning yourself with your father. I ceased to think of my own father from the time I first got laid. And how old would I have been? Thirteen, fourteen…'

'Please, Señor,' I said, cutting him short, 'I'm not interested in your opinions. That's not why I'm here.'

'Really? Perhaps I haven't figured you out properly after all! You are not as mild as you seem. Listen, young man, you can see for yourself that I have been in this life a good few years longer than you have. I have drained it and it has drained me. Believe me then, this is precisely why you are here. Your father, that is. Young man, when I was forty, I had this entire city in my hands!'

'That's your business,' I said, feeling the blood rise to my head. It was clear that the slightest conflict of opinion was enough to irritate him. It seemed that Señor Esnaider was surrounded by people obliged to conform to his wishes, otherwise… Evidently Matthaiou was not one of them. 'If you don't mind, could we get back to the reason for my visit,' I continued, trying to regain my composure. 'I would like you to tell me what you know about Matthaiou.'

'Matthaiou? What Matthaiou? You mean Pateras. Matthaiou is a pseudonym. He used it when he left Barcelona.'

'Anyway. Do you know where he went after here?'

'No, young man, I simply heard that he had changed his surname,' said the old man before sinking once again into silence. Presently, he lifted his head.

'You are in too much of a rush, young man. If you rush like that, you'll never write anything worthwhile. He, too, was in a rush. And much more so than you are. But the man had talent. A rare talent. One of those talents that appear only every fifty years. I have to admit that.'

'But how so, given that he hadn't published anything?'

'I don't mean a talent for writing, young man. A talent for life is what I mean,' said Esnaider, stressing every word. 'To satisfy your curiosity, Lucas Padre, that's how we called him here, lived in this city for about a year, from April 1967 to the summer of 1968. At that time, Mr Loukas, I was not confined to the wheelchair you see now. And I never would have been if… Anyhow, I stood firmly on my own two feet, I was in my prime, I was known throughout

Europe and half of America. Lucas came to Barcelona because he couldn't live in Greece with the Colonels in power. He was a leftist, a young man, you understand... I didn't agree with him at all. In my opinion, the basic foundation of democracy is discipline. Discipline and respect. Politics is not a flexible concept, it's a solid one. It doesn't call for Munch but for Mondrian, do you understand? Were we any the worse for Franco? What we are today we owe to him. Anyhow, Lucas came here recommended by a Greek friend of mine, an art dealer. He was a hounded young man and a handsome one... He had every gift in the world, but inside he was pure venom. Venom...' Esnaider continued with an uncontrolled burst that he immediately tried to constrain. 'He stayed in Barcelona; I offered him hospitality, introduced him to the whole city, and then he left. I don't know where he went, I have no idea. Perhaps he returned to Greece, perhaps not. At any rate, I have had no news of him for at least thirty years. That's all I have to tell you, young man, concerning your business,' he said, and pressing another button he withdrew towards the couch.

I listened to his account with eyes wide open. My gaze was fixed on his in an effort not to miss so much as a flutter of his eyelashes, or the slightest movement of his tongue over his lips. I was certain that he was lying. Ramón Esnaider may have been a good actor, but he certainly wasn't trained in method acting. He didn't identify with the role, he interpreted it from a distance. No, this man wasn't a selfless patron of the arts or of political refugees. He was an old narcissist, arrogant to such a degree that he had made a big mistake. Esnaider had underestimated me, he thought he had before him a two-bit philologist who, in order to overcome his boredom, was looking for the ghosts of Greek writers in Spain. And it was at precisely that moment that I chose to play my next card, hoping that Tina hadn't mentioned what I knew concerning Fernando Salinas.

'Of course, you must know the poet Salinas, Fernando Salinas,' I said, supposedly by chance.

The old man with the face of someone much younger started to crack up, the skin tightened to its very limits:

'Salinas? How do you know about Salinas?'

'I haven't met him, but I intend to see him soon.'

'Fernando Salinas is a no-good alcoholic who thinks that he can write poetry. He knows nothing. Leave him alone!' said Esnaider, raising his voice. Then he immediately pulled himself together and added, 'Well, Mr Loukas, to finish with all this. I'll give you a piece of advice. You seem like an intelligent young man, heed my words. Forget this business. What does it matter now what happened thirty years ago? If you want to write something, write about today, about the new millennium. Things in the world change so fast. Stay in Barcelona, I can recommend two or three places to you where you'll have a most wonderful time – and all on me. I'll get Señorita Tobosa to accompany you. You know, she liked you…besides, you're a likeable fellow and the girl has had her fill of neurotics,' he said, winking at me. 'You'll have a wonderful time and then you can go back home and get on with the book about your father.'

The man was mocking me good and proper. Of course, he didn't know the information I had from Arnold's card concerning the relationship between Fernando and Matthaiou. But what was it that he was afraid of? My prospective meeting with Salinas was becoming even more intriguing. And Tina? What was her role in all this? Was she Esnaider's ward? All I knew was that the old man had helped her father. And the neurotic lovers? I decided not to say anything else about my movements. Besides, I had already got from Esnaider whatever I was going to get.

'Thank you for your offer, Señor. But I prefer to discover the beauties of your city by myself. As for Mr Matthaiou, I realize that he belongs to your memories of the past and, if my intuition is correct, not one of the most pleasant ones. Greek and aggressive, you said. It seems it is in our make-up. In any case, I thank you for seeing me. Oh, and Señor Esnaider, most people would jump for joy if they owned a Picasso. Why do you hide yours?'

The old man flushed. He hadn't expected that. He had reached the end of his tether.

'You are extremely inquisitive and rude! I was completely wrong in my estimation of you! I have nothing else to say to you!' he said indignantly and pressed another button. The butler appeared in the wink of an eye. 'Pedro, show the gentleman to the door. And you heed what I told you. Heed it well! You have no idea who you are dealing with!' he added in a threatening tone, but one which sounded comical considering the height from where it was coming.

'Good day, Señor,' I said and followed Pedro, till the iron door closed behind us.

On leaving the apartment, I went up to the roof of the building. The area was open to the public to see Gaudí's statue. In the middle of the most eccentric setting that the history of architecture had ever seen on a rooftop, in front of the anthropomorphic chimney stacks and monstrous ventilators, I imagined Esnaider in his room with his draped Picasso, alone in his futuristic wheelchair playing with the digital buttons and thinking of his next move. I wondered which scene was the most surreal.

That evening I again did the rounds of the tapas bars and the clubs. Barcelona at night was one big party. The bars on the seafront remained open till daybreak even on weekdays. I noted with some dismay that my average consumption of alcohol had risen dangerously. I normally tried not to go beyond the limit of three hard drinks each evening. Here I had almost doubled that.

Wednesday was another sunny day. It was the day of Salinas's reading. I reflected on how lucky I had been up until now, without having had to wiggle even my little finger, I had come far without even getting my feet wet. And now came the next stage. I considered it virtually certain that the Fernando referred to on Arnold's card was Salinas. How should I behave then towards the poet? Should I reveal to him that I had seen Esnaider? It was clear that the old man didn't like him, he had even tried to dissuade me from seeing him. I decided to proceed intuitively, assessing the situation at first hand. I bought a blue notebook and began recording my movements and my thoughts since setting foot in Barcelona.

At around nine in the evening, I went down towards the London Bar. It was a cloudless night, and the sky was so clear that it gave me a sense of tranquillity, I felt as light as a feather. I realized that this is what had changed since I had arrived in Barcelona. As though a weight had been taken from me, as though the

Newtonian force that had united me with the earth for nigh on forty years was not a weighty vector, but a gossamer thread.

Fernando Salinas

The place was already full. The audience was mixed: young people, but also people of a certain age. All the chairs were taken, as were all the stools. Just as I had resigned myself to two hours of standing up, I saw Tina motioning to me from across the room. She was dressed now in black and had her hair tied back.

Making my way between the throngs of people, I went over to her.

'You see what a crowd poetry draws in our city,' she said smiling.

'Yes, I should have come earlier.'

'Don't worry. I've kept a seat for you. Here in front, you'll sit with us,' she said, pointing to a small table at which two young men were sitting. 'Did you see Señor Esnaider?'

'Yes, and I want to thank you for intervening on my behalf.'

'You know, he was particularly interested in you. He asked me a load of things. I didn't know what to say to him.'

'There's just one thing I'd like to know if you told him. About tonight's event. About Salinas. Did you tell him I intended to come?'

'Oh didn't I tell you the other day, I never imagined that you would talk to him about Fernando. You have to understand that Señor Esnaider and Señor Salinas are not on the best of terms. I take care not to mention anything concerning Señor Salinas to Señor Esnaider. Was your meeting productive?'

'Reasonably, I have no complaints.'

'Come and sit down, the event is about to start.'

I sat next to Frederico who was a musician. The other young man was called Gillermo, and behaved as though he were Tina's escort. Sitting alone at the next table was a fifty year-old woman, in good shape, who, Tina informed me, was Salinas's wife, Victoria. Señora Salinas was constantly playing with her bracelet, as though something was bothering her.

Before ten minutes had passed, Tina went up onto the makeshift stage and announced the evening's event. Two men got up from the front tables and went up onto the stage. My first reaction was to try to hold back my laughter. The scene was comic to say the least. The one looked to be around sixty or sixty-five, very short, around five feet two, fat and bald, and the other, of around the same age, was extremely tall, almost seven feet, lanky, with long white hair and faded blue eyes. He was quite charming with his face deeply furrowed. Frederico whispered his name to me. It was Fernando Salinas.

The short, fat one, Manuel Ferrer, began the event. He was an unusual type of poet, he wrote both in Castilian and in Catalan. First, he read from the collection, *Burning Sea*, which he had published in 1967. Then he proceeded to his most recent work. His poetry, judging from the little Spanish I knew and from the booklet with the English translation, was influenced by Lorca, though somewhere I sensed the shadow of *The Waste Land*.

Then, Salinas took over. With a slight tremor of his hand and, given his appearance, a surprisingly high-pitched voice, he first gave a brief introduction to contemporary Spanish poetry before reading a poem by Pierre Jean Jouve in French.

Then he turned to his own work, which he read alternately in French and Spanish. Verses from his early period, from the sixties, then from his most recent. Just from listening to the poems you could sense the change that the years had brought to Salinas's poetry. From a psychedelic feast, full of exclamations, he had moved to short, sparse compositions. Salinas ended with a love poem, allowing the final four lines to fall like drops of water:

For all that has passed
A half-open door suffices
And a mark on the left of the neck
This too faded.

The reading finished to warm applause and the two poets disappeared behind a curtain only to reappear shortly afterwards holding a drink. I looked across at the other table. Señora Salinas had left. Tina beckoned to Salinas to come over to our table. He raised his glass in a form of toast and made his way over to us with an unsteady step which, given how tall he was, made him look like a clown on stilts.

'Señor Salinas, this is Mr Yannis Loukas, a journalist from Athens. He would like a few words with you.'

'Athens? Ah! Griego! Homer, Solomos, Cavafy!' shouted Salinas in approval.

'Congratulations,' I said, 'I liked your poetry very much. I thought your last poems in particular were exceptional.'

Salinas pulled up a chair and ensconced himself beside me.

'Ah! Young man. Now I've started to write. Till I was fifty I simply played, experimented,' he said in impeccable English.

'From what I know, you belonged to the Castellet group in the sixties, and you wrote in Castilian then, if I'm not mistaken.'

'You are very well informed! Yes, together with Barral and Gil de Biedma,' he said, totally confirming what Telemachus has said in Athens. 'Times were different then, young man…' and he paused.

'Loukas. Yannis Loukas.'

'Juan, that is. I'm Fernando. Let's use our first names, all right?' said Salinas, taking from his coat pocket a black case with cigarillos and a lighter. He went on, 'Loukas, you said? I once had a friend by that name. We called him Lucas here, He was from Greece too.'

'Do you mean Loukas Matthaiou? Oh, sorry, I mean Lucas Padre,' I said, thanking my lucky Barcelona star for this unexpected gift.

'How do you know him?' asked Salinas sharply.

'It's about him that I wanted to speak to you,' I replied.

'About Lucas? Lucas Padre. Is he alive?'

'It's a long story. If you're interested, I'll explain.'

'If I'm interested? Do you know how long it's been since I've heard any news of Lucas? You're a godsend. Whoever knows Lucas is automatically a friend of mine.'

Salinas had already downed the whisky he had brought with him to the table; he immediately ordered another.

'I don't know him yet but I feel that I'm beginning to learn about him,' I said and started to explain.

Halfway through my story, at the point where Arnold was reading to me the card sent to him by Matthaiou, Salinas interrupted me. His face had taken on a strange expression. The furrows in his cheeks had deepened, his thin lips appeared even more pursed:

'Okay, my friend, once upon a time I knocked around with Lucas, then he left, we lost touch. It was a long time ago.'

So, I reflected, here was one more person who wanted to avoid the subject. Yet Salinas wasn't aggressive like Esnaider, it seemed that Matthaiou was for him a dear and intimate friend. Nevertheless, the person I had before me appeared scared, as though the memory of his old friendship had upset him. When I had finished, Salinas's eyes looked like those of a wounded dog. The poet was moved. Yet he was struggling to restrain himself, a difficult undertaking, given that the drink didn't allow him much room for self-control.

The opportunity of a lifetime, I thought to myself, and I ordered him another whisky.

'Lucas must have been very fond of you.'

'We were very close, my friend, like that,' and he brought his two index fingers together. 'But life is unpredictable...'

'His novel is exceptional. You should read it one day.'

'Yannis, this man came to Barcelona one day from nowhere and changed my life. You heard how I write now? Do you know to whom I owe this? To Lucas. He's the one who opened my eyes. We spent whole days and nights talking about poetry, philosophy... Of course, I realized all this years later. Lucas was so ahead of his time, so charismatic and so peculiar...'

'Listen,' I said, putting my cards on the table, 'you are the only person I can rely on. There's a whole pile of information I need. Your friend Lucas disappeared one fine day and was never heard of again. The only concrete piece of evidence I have is a novel that was never published. If you were such a close friend of his, help me to piece things together. I imagine that, if he's alive, you would like to see him again, right?'

'Would I like to see Lucas again? Do you realize what you're saying? My friend, it's not a simple matter. I've been carrying all this around with me for so long. You have no idea what you've got yourself into... Better let it be. Whoever's gone is gone.'

'Who's gone? What are you all so afraid of?' I burst out. 'Just who was this Matthaiou? Listen, Fernando, I'm trying to find a lead. And you have to help me.' The poet said nothing. 'The business is quite simple,' I continued. 'You've forgotten the man. And just as he suddenly came into your life so many years ago, now a countryman of his has come to you and is asking you to help find some trace of him. You have to choose. Either talk to me so I can continue my search or keep silent and Lucas will simply remain a memory, pleasant or unpleasant, for all concerned.'

Salinas looked up from his empty glass and fixed his eyes on me. It was clear that he was wrestling with himself. Nevertheless, the drink proved to be a valuable ally of mine. There was a period of silence. Then Salinas spoke in a low voice:

'You're above board Griego. You talk straight. I'll talk. But not here. We have to be alone. I'll talk to you but on one strict condition. You won't say a word about what I tell you. Not a word. Because then it won't be just me who is in danger. You'll be in danger too.'

I didn't want to hear anything else. I paid for both of us and said goodnight to Tina, who gave me a strange smile. We emerged from the London Bar with Salinas swaying slightly, and we headed towards the Hotel Oriente. Once again I felt Tina's gaze boring into me. Even sharper this time.

Stolen blue

I ordered a bottle of whisky and some nuts from the reception. Salinas seemed somewhat better. He had made his mind up. Before we went upstairs, he took out his cellphone and made a call. 'If I'm late, don't wait up,' I heard him say.

Before long we were in my room, sitting opposite each other in two wicker armchairs. The bottle was in front of us. Salinas took a cigarillo from the black case and lit it with his silver lighter. Before beginning, I showed him Matthaiou's manuscript. He took it from my hands, perused it, smelled it, and put it down with reverence as though he were holding something precious.

I went on with my story from the point where I had left off in the bar, from Arnold's card, but leaving out the meeting with

Esnaider. When I had finished, Salinas took a gulp of his whisky, then a deep drag of his cigarillo and instead of commenting said:

'Well, Yannis, I've listened attentively to your story. Now listen to mine. It was towards the end of the sixties, '67 I think, when the dictatorship came to power in Greece. I was around thirty years old then, I had a good name as a poet, I had published three collections, the literary circles showed particular interest. You heard in the bar that I wrote at that time. Of course, and you ought to see my books, I experimented with the image of the poem itself, I was influenced by Cummings, you know… Well it was then that I met Lucas. We met there, at the London Bar. He had just arrived in Barcelona and was staying at the home of some wealthy fellow by the name of Ramón Esnaider, who was at the height of his fame in the artistic life of the city. Esnaider was a socialite faggot who didn't know what he had. Lucas at the time was a man of rare good looks, extremely handsome. A lot was said about the two of them, but I had it from Lucas that there had never been anything between them. From the moment Lucas realized his interest, he dropped him like a hot potato. Esnaider had worshipped him almost like a god, he was madly in love with him. His house was full of enlarged photographs of Lucas. But he wanted nothing of it. One day, he said to me: "That poofter is not going to get anywhere near my ass!" That's why I believe Esnaider got him to do what he did. Because he couldn't have him.'

'What did he get him to do?' I said, interrupting.

'Wait…first of all I have to tell you about my relationship with him,' said Salinas, who, in spite of the whiskies, was keen to continue his story uninterrupted. 'Lucas and I loved each other, Yannis. As friends I mean. He became my brother, the person closest to me. He was a man with such inner wealth. But at the same time, he was an extreme type, aggressive. At least with those he didn't get on with. Because for Lucas there were two types of people; his enemies, for whom there was no mercy, and those he loved. With the latter he communicated through the deepest part of his being. It was as though he was in direct contact with your soul. And yet this man suffered from an unbearable realism… A realism that was poetic, however, of a sensitive nature… Perhaps this sounds contradictory, but if you had met him, you would understand. He was completely aware of what he was, but he never exploited it. He had a mind that was constantly restless. Every moment had to be glorifying; nothing sufficed him. That's why he was so unfortunate in love. I'll never understand how that man got married…as far as I knew, he had only fallen in love once in his life, in America when he was still a young lad. He never wanted to talk about it.'

'It seems he talked later on paper,' I added.

Salinas lit another cigarillo.

'So then, Lucas and I had lots of ideas. We wanted to start a literary magazine; an English-language one. We had already begun looking for associates when it happened,' he said, suddenly stopping, clearly moved, while his eyes had begun to grow dangerously red.

'When what happened?' I said, pressing him.

'Yannis, I haven't spoken about it for thirty years…what I'm about to tell you is known only to Lucas, Esnaider and myself. And Esnaider doesn't even know that I know. It's dangerous ground you're treading on, my friend. I don't know why I'm telling you all this, there's something about you that makes me trust you. Perhaps I just can't keep it inside any longer. I've been looking for an excuse all these years. Before we came here, I was undecided… But when I saw the manuscript…' Salinas swallowed a good mouthful. 'Well, Yannis, in 1968 Lucas Padre got himself involved in a shady business,' said Salinas hesitantly.

'In a shady business? In what exactly?' I asked.

He spoke in a low voice. 'In a robbery. In the robbery of priceless objects. And it was Esnaider who put him up to it.'

'What did he steal?'

'Four paintings. Four paintings by Picasso. He stole them on behalf of Esnaider. Esnaider was to pay him one million dollars. Dollars! Then, in 1968. You realise what a sum we're talking about!' said Salinas, stressing every word.

'Where did he steal them from?'

'From the Museu Picasso. A few blocks from here. In the end, Esnaider got his hands on just one of them. And that by chance.

Another went elsewhere… Lucas took the other two, with half his fee, half a million, and left.'

And went where?'

'To Florence. He stayed there for four years. Till '72. He got married there and had a daughter. Until Esnaider found him. And so he was forced to leave again.'

'And go where?'

'That's something I don't know, but let me tell you what happened in the order it happened.'

'Yes, I'm sorry, I'm interrupting you.'

'So, as I said, Esnaider regarded Lucas as his personal property, just like all the other young men under his "protection". We're talking about a man without compunction, who was insatiable. He was in his prime then, he had unlimited money and one of the richest private art collections in the world. Esnaider had two passions. Painting and handsome men. His collection was complete, he had at least one work by every great artist, only one was missing: Picasso. Equally complete was his collection of young men. He had whatever toy boy in Barcelona he desired, whenever he desired and for as long as he desired. There was only one man that he was never able to make his; Lucas. And how ironic; the only painter missing from his collection was a fellow countryman, who lived in the very same city, while the one young man that he hadn't managed to conquer was living in his very own house! It would seem, then, that the idea he came up with was by no means a coincidence. Esnaider is a ruthless character. Ruthless and clever at the same time. Only a mind like his could conceive such a plan. He set the one unattainable object of his desire to steal the other. But someone with such arrogance, however clever he may be, runs the risk of underestimating his opponent. And Lucas played him at his own game, beat him hands down and cleaned him out. At first, Esnaider enticed him with money,' said Salinas and went on, 'Lucas pretended to have reservations, the job, naturally, was an extremely difficult one, even more so if you consider that basically it would all be done by one man. In the end, he accepted. The plan was to steal four paintings from Picasso's blue period that were being exhibited for a month, on loan from the Prado, in one of the rooms in the Museu

Picasso. Lucas would deliver the paintings to Esnaider. His fee would be one million dollars. Naturally, the plan put Esnaider at risk too. But he believed in Lucas, believed that he would succeed, which is why he set up the trap, taking for granted the success of the robbery. Lucas imposed his own terms concerning his fee; fifty in advance, four hundred and fifty straight after the heist and the rest when he delivered the paintings to Esnaider.

The job was to go down on Sunday, after the museum had closed. According to the plan, Lucas would go on his own as a visitor, in disguise, wearing a wig and moustache. Just before the museum closed, at three in the afternoon, he would go to the toilet, would force open one of the panels in the WC's false ceiling and would hide there for some twelve hours. Then he would climb down, emerge from the toilets and, with an anaesthetic spray, would knock out the guard in the adjacent room where the paintings were being exhibited. The Museu Picasso is a medieval palace from the 15th century with a courtyard. The toilets are in two of the rooms that open onto Montcada Street. As soon as he had the paintings, which were not particularly large – the largest was roughly eighty by seventy centimetres – he would get the keys from the guard and would leave though the emergency exit directly onto Montcada Street at four in the morning, an hour that in Barrio Gòtico in those years there wouldn't be a soul. There, a motorbike would be waiting for him, driven by José, one of Esnaider's henchmen. He was to give the four hundred and fifty thousand dollars to Lucas, then they would go to Esnaider, they would hand over the paintings and Lucas would get the rest of his money.

I shuddered. Pages from *Bar Flaubert* began to rise up before me and mix with the fleeting image of a Picasso from the blue period behind the purple curtain in the Pedrera.

'But why did Matthaiou agreed to all this? The man was an intellectual, he wasn't a thief,' I said.

'Lucas was everything. He could be whatever he wanted, whenever he wanted. Besides, he had his reasons. Lucas had other plans, and the only one who knew about them was me.'

Salinas downed another mouthful of whisky and breathed a sigh:

'Goethe says somewhere in *Faust*: "*Two souls cohabit in my breast. The one desires to break free from the other.*" In Lucas there weren't only two but innumerable souls. That's why he could never find any balance… In the end one thing was certain. You couldn't ignore him. He had completely captivated me, I have to admit. I recall that Lucas had numerous dreams, Barcelona couldn't suffice him. What he wanted above all was to write in a style that would communicate with language's deepest origins, or so he said. Though he wrote wonderfully in both English and French, he wanted his work to be written in Greek. His exile from Greece had cost him dearly. Perhaps he saw Esnaider's offer as a great opportunity to solve his problem of how to make a living. But, as I told you before, this didn't suffice him. He wanted to humiliate him, to walk away with the whole pot himself.'

'But wasn't Esnaider his benefactor in a manner of speaking?' I asked, puzzled.

'Yes, but he was a person who did nothing without wanting something in return. Lucas wouldn't give in to him so he would sacrifice him. But Lucas had no intention of going back on his principles. His ethics demanded that he break Esnaider, that he crush him. Besides, it was also a matter of self-preservation; he had realised that the whole business was a trap. Esnaider was certain that he had come up with the perfect plan that would bring him four Picassos. But to get back to the night of the robbery, the first part of the plan went like clockwork. Lucas hid himself in the false roof, knocked out the guard, neutralized the alarm in the room, – Esnaider had assigned "professionals" to train him – took the keys, packed up the four paintings, opened the emergency exit and went out into the street, temporarily leaving the four paintings behind. And from then on began the real game. The agreement was for him to meet with José. The henchman was in place with his motorbike. José went over to him and handed him the bag with the four hundred and fifty thousand dollars. Lucas took a look; turned round, opened the door again, and brought out the wrapped-up paintings together with the spray. José had returned to his motorbike. Lucas walked over to him. Naturally the henchman didn't imagine that Lucas would have a gun, how would he get it through the museum's security? And, of course, Lucas didn't have one, because he didn't need one. He went up to the bike and just as José went to take out his gun, he sprayed him in the eyes. But the henchman was a tough nut. Lucas kicked the gun away and they began struggling. In the end, he managed to get the better of him and ran off in the direction of my place. Amid the fracas, one of the paintings, the *Omen* got left behind.'

Bar Flaubert. The text and narration by Salinas. The sculpture and its mould.

'Your place? Were you in on it too?'

'Lucas had confided in me. He knew that I too was no fan of Esnaider. We had been close friends for a year, he considered me the only person in Barcelona he could trust. We were both sure that the whole business was a set-up and we had made a counter-plan. Lucas would remain with me for a couple of hours and at eight he would board a plane for Italy. So that morning, at around 4.10 – I remember it as though it were yesterday – Lucas knocked on my door in Argenteria Street, two blocks away from the Museu Picasso. With him, he had the three paintings and the money. We took care of the final details and, at six in the morning, we set off for the airport. Two hours later he was flying to Florence with a fake passport that I had procured for him earlier. I too had my contacts then... And so Lucas Padre became Loukas Matthaiou.'

'And what happened the next day when the theft was discovered? How did he get the paintings through the airport?'

'The theft was discovered at nine-thirty, when the museum opened for maintenance work; on Mondays it was closed to the public. Lucas was already flying to Florence. He had the paintings in his suitcase. However, what any customs official opening it would see – not that anyone did open it – would not have been Picasso in his blue period. It would have been romantic Tuscan landscapes, works by the supposed painter, Loukas Matthaiou. We had camouflaged the paintings at my place. Of course, concealed beneath the cypresses, the hillsides and the olive trees were the blue brushstrokes of Picasso,' said the poet grandiloquently, and went on, 'You would only have been a child at the time, it caused a huge stir. For several days it was front-page news in the biggest papers in Europe. The case was never solved. No one ever learned what had happened to the paintings. Naturally, Esnaider was furious given that all he had was one painting and he was five hundred thousand dollars out of pocket. But the worst of all was that the Greek had made a fool out of him. He combed every inch of the city looking for Lucas. But in vain. He made it his life's goal to find him and make him curse the moment and hour he'd been born. His sidekicks put pressure on me too, but I said nothing. But I believe that even today Esnaider still suspects me, though he doesn't have any evidence. What I'm telling you is known only to me and you. And to one more person, who is above all this...'

Salinas's face darkened slightly before he continued, 'After four years had passed, Esnaider got onto Lucas's trail in Florence. What happened next, I'll tell you presently. It's a story that Lucas himself related to me over the phone. The crux of it is that Lucas took his wife – he had married an Italian woman – and left Florence. I have no idea where they went. That was in 1972 and it was my last contact with him.'

'So he got married in Florence?'

'Yes, in 1970. He got hitched to a quite well-known Italian actress by the name of Magdalena Gentile, and he lived the life of the blessed, filthy rich, with a new name in a new country.'

'And was he never linked to the theft?'

'Never,' said Salinas, filling his glass again with whisky.

'You're probably wondering why I'm telling you all this. You might very well be an agent from Interpol,' he said, laughing nervously. 'But then again so many years have passed since that time,' he continued, 'crimes are time-barred. Isn't that so? Come on, Yannis! Don't worry... I'm only joking... As soon as I saw his letters, I was convinced. That text was an omen, it was the sign I needed to open my mouth at last. Listen, my friend, fate united me with that Greek, with that man who passed like a comet through my life. Because I owe my very life to Lucas. It was he who once saved me from a knifing. We lived wild then and the city was rough. At nights we roamed the seafront, the night-time wasn't sophisticated like it is today. There were a lot of dangerous types around at the end of the sixties. Pimps, cut-throats and the like. I was drunk one night and got into an argument in the street with a whole gang of them over a woman. Three of them had surrounded me and had taken out their knives and were about to butcher me in cold blood. Then Lucas got among them. Like lightening he took out a pistol, stuck it in the face of one of them and told them to be on their way or he would blow their brains out. The bravos shit themselves at the sight of the gun and disappeared. And the joke was that it was a fake one. And that wasn't all. Lucas showed his appreciation for my help in a practical way too. On the morning he left for Florence, I took him to the airport, and when I got back home, do you know what I found?

'What?' I asked inquisitively.

'The *Rave*, wrapped like gift with a dedication "To Fernando, for everything" – and an envelope.'

'The *Rave*?' I said, puzzled.

'One of the three paintings. Lucas showed his appreciation for my help by making a gift of an authentic Picasso. I hadn't asked him for anything. Now do you understand what kind of a man we're talking about?'

I suddenly felt something like an electric discharge going through me. Oral. Mare, Even, Neat. Then Omen, Rave, Area, Lent... The *Omen* that was dropped in the scuffle with José and is now in Esnaider's house, hidden away behind the purple curtain, and the *Rave* that ended up with Fernando. Two of the words in the motto to the first chapter of *Bar Flaubert* were anagrams of the titles of two stolen Picassos!

'Area, Lent,' I muttered.

'What did you say?' said Fernando alarmed. 'How... How do you know!' Salinas's face lost its colour, as though all the blood had suddenly drained from his veins. 'Damn Greek, are you a cop?' he said, getting to his feet threateningly. His huge body virtually blocked out my entire field of vision.

'Fernando, calm down. Let me explain. I'm not a cop. I'm an unbelievably lucky chap,' I said calmly, and I explained to him the riddle with the names. Fernando was reassured only when I showed him the manuscript with the four encoded words, explaining to him his friend's word game.

'Yes, the other two pictures were *Area* and *Lent*... It seems he wanted to leave a reference, a mark to remind him of the day that his life changed,' Salinas mumbled.

'Fernando,' I said, 'Matthaiou is writing about his life. I'm certain now that the city he mentions in the second chapter is Barcelona. But on the basis of what you've told me, there's a passage in the text that can't be anything else but a direct reference to the theft. I'll give you a rough translation of it,' I said, picking up the manuscript again. It wasn't at all easy, but the passage that Salinas heard was something like this:

...With the heavens lamenting and me listening, hidden up above in the boards, listening to the lightning and thunder, and with the dark hour slipping softly into my mind when I decided and agreed to be here, among the alarms and electric wires, that I try not to touch, otherwise...

Now, after twelve hours, comes a deep sigh and I let myself down with my hands. Ah... I must be careful, I let myself down with my hands and detach myself from above to tumble onto the cold marble. In the bathroom with the square joints and tiles, snakes that flirt in the silence. And I support myself so as not to slip and be met by betrayal, me, alone in the night, virtually daybreak, a wrapped-up canvas, I have to unfold and protect the loot.

With my right hand I touch the door handle, – tiny uneasy movements, my palm becomes greasy on the cold sphere as it grips it, one movement and the door opens like a transparent portal. And with the spray in the other hand I approach on tiptoe, the man in the uniform and I see him before me as he will be when I have anaesthetized him, like the Zen archer I see the after before the act. And the act is done and is successful. And with the coast clear I am alone once again. Alone in the room and I have a human failing. To look everywhere, to dawdle, to blow through the hole so the roar I have been waiting for so long will emerge. But I am in a hurry. I spread the canvas and the images dive head first and now subaqueous to glisten. And the whole package is but a mummy powdered with blue and how the forms overflow. And I return with the mummy. Terrified I pass through the rear exit at once. He is in his place, a fierce man with his mercy consumed. We look each other in the eye. Immediately the intention is revealed and the instruments of pain flash in the night. In the hollow of a skull my self struggles and prevails.

'It appears your friend Lucas has written an autobiographical novel,' I said to Salinas, adding under my breath: And I too seem to be moving back and forth between one biography and the other.

Salinas seemed impressed. The excitement from the way the evening had evolved had even made him forget his drink. The last whisky had been sitting there untouched in front of him for a good half hour.

'So did Esnaider find Lucas in Florence?' I asked.

'Yes, I don't know how, but after four years he managed to find him. It was autumn of '72. He went there himself, together with his henchmen. At that time, Lucas was strangely enough living a quiet, family life. His daughter, Caterina, was only three. His wife was an actress, in fact she'd appeared in a film by Antonioni and I think in one by De Sica. He was involved in anti-dictatorship organizations and such like. With the help of his contacts, Esnaider eventually managed to track him down. He lay in wait for him with his henchmen in a deserted area outside Siena, close to his summer house. His plan was to take him alive, get the paintings, supposing of course that they hadn't been sold, and then make him suffer. But once again Lucas was not taken by surprise. Since arriving in Florence, he had been carrying a gun and could take care of himself. There was a fierce fight. On the one side Esnaider and his three henchmen and on the other Lucas, a friend of his and his wife. The daughter happened to be at her grandmother's in the city. The outcome was that two of the henchmen were killed together with Lucas's friend, and Esnaider was wounded in his spine. Since then he has been paralyzed, in a wheelchair. After this bloody event, Lucas left Italy. Before he left, however, we spoke over the phone. He was in a state of shock. After relating to me all that had happened, in the end he said to me, "Fernando, I can't stay here any longer, I'm afraid for the child, I'm afraid for her. I'm leaving with Magdalena. No one must know where we're going…

I can't even tell you. We'll leave Caterina with her grandmother, she'll be safer there. They'll think we've taken her with us. She'll go with her grandmother to Pisa for a while until the business blows over. As for me, I just don't know, I don't know where my life is going…" I'd never before heard Lucas admit to being scared. That was our last contact. Since then, the only time I've ever heard anything about him again was tonight. From you,' said Fernando, nervously brushing two white tufts of hair from out of his eyes.

I understood that the poet had tired himself out. But there was still something else I wanted to find out:

'What happened to his wife and daughter?'

'I don't know about his wife. They left together as I told you. They left the girl with her grandmother, Magdalena's mother, in Florence. I saw Caterina in 1989 when they invited me to the university for a poetry reading. She was a grown-up girl, twenty years old, a real beauty. She was studying architecture at the city's university. It wasn't difficult for me to find her. She came to the event and we met. She told me that all traces of her parents had disappeared in 1972. Naturally, I told her nothing about the past, about the robbery I mean. Caterina had been raised by her grandmother, Sophia. Her grandfather, Magdalena's father, had died. The only thing linking her with her family was an annual income that went into her bank account. The depositor remained anonymous, the bank knew nothing. Naturally, it must have been Lucas. Now why Lucas and Magdalena never communicated again with their child is something I don't know. I have to tell you that it occurred to me that perhaps they were dead.'

'Do you have Caterina's address in Florence? A telephone number?'

'At that time she was staying at her grandmother's house, somewhere close to Duomo. Where exactly, I can't recall. All I know is that she told me that after her studies were over she would go and live in the city. She wanted to find work there.'

'Did the girl keep her father's surname?'

'The pseudonym, yes. Italianized of course. She introduced herself to me as Caterina Mateo,' said Salinas, breathing a deep sigh, while his eyes revealed someone who has just had a great weight taken off his chest. 'Well, that's all I have to tell you, Yannis,' he added, 'now, don't ask me anything more, I'm tired, I've had a lot to drink and I want to go to bed. But, before I leave, I want you to promise me something.'

'Whatever you want, Fernando, you can't imagine how much you've helped me.'

'If you ever find Lucas, tell him that I still have the painting safe at my place. I didn't sell it, though I was in dire need in the early eighties. I didn't have enough even for a beer and I was living with a hidden Picasso! It was then that I married my wife. Victoria lent me every support. She also put up with a lot from me... You know how it is Yannis, I was always fond of women in my life. Even now, at my age, I've been carrying on for the last five years with a woman much younger than me. But it's over now. I've grown up.' Salinas had tears in his eyes. He lowered his head, 'Now I'm ready to make it up to Victoria for everything she had to put up with...' he said, wiping his eyes. I said nothing. I let him regain his composure. After a short while, Salinas turned to me, 'May God forgive me.'

'God?' I asked. 'It's not easy for me to think of you in terms of the divine.'

'The divine, Yannis, is envious and unpredictable,' he said wearily. 'God doesn't leave us in peace, he has us going up and down, back and forth. And I can't take any more. I want to savour whatever's left to me in peace.'

'But that's how it is Fernando, man is curious and he circles around the unknown like a moth around a flame.'

'But the poet dares to put a stop to the circling. He stands on the circumference and resists the centripetal force pushing him towards the centre. And like that he tries to find himself...'

'And do you think you've found him now?'

'Who? Me? Yes, Yannis, I've found myself. And I've realized that this same self was unknown to me. And I'm happy. Just imagine if I'd been searching for forty years to find something that was known to me.'

At that point, it was my turn to fall silent. I wondered if that was perhaps what I was trying to do. To find someone unknown...

'Anyhow. Let's not go on with all that, it doesn't lead anywhere. If you ever find Lucas, tell him that I still love him and that I want to see him one last time before I die. And give him this. It's his,' said Fernando, and with a trembling hand, he held out his silver lighter. I looked at it. There were a number of bees carved on it. I counted them. Eleven. 'Will you do that for me, Yannis?' he asked as he got to his feet.

'Yes, Fernando, I'll do it, because I'm certain that sooner or later I'm going to find him,' I replied as I showed the poet to the door, forgetting, however, to warn him about the step. Despite all the whisky he had drunk, Fernando managed to avoid falling flat on his face and stepped out into the hallway in one piece. Before he left, he embraced me and kissed me on both cheeks.

'Bye, Yannis, you're all right. I hope I'll see you again,' he said with emotion.

'Me too, Fernando, And thanks.'

I embraced him too and watched his lanky figure disappearing down the narrow hallway of the Hotel Oriente.

Deep in the zarzuela

The next morning I awoke with my head swimming. Without a doubt, operation Barcelona had gone unbelievably well. I had found the people I had wanted to, I had collected a pile of information, a number of obscure points had been cleared up and I already had a pretty good idea concerning the even murkier ones. The question now was what my next move would be. I didn't want to see Esnaider again, besides, with what I now knew it might even be dangerous. I had most likely drained Salinas, and as for Tina, I wouldn't say no to seeing her again, but the presence of Gillermo had a negative effect on my disposition. As for the indisputable protagonist of the trip, Loukas Matthaiou or Luke Pateras or Lucas Padre, he was gradually being revealed to me – first through his writing, then through his personality.

I was looking for a man who lived on the razor's edge, who saw both faces of Janus. Yet what impressed me even more was that in his novel Matthaiou had revealed the suit's inner stitching, had shed light on the secret mechanisms, on the inner forces motivating him to confront life's major issues. Anyhow, it appears that this is what Loukas Matthaiou was seeking; a direct confrontation with life, a duel with fate. Which would end where? In reconciliation? In defeat? I didn't know... But what I had now understood was the genius, the vision of this man, who, while experiencing all these intense states in his inner being, was at the same time able to observe them, condense them and transform them into art. And so the big question arose. Why did Loukas Matthaiou, why did such a man need his work to be approved by someone else? And by an author who was poles apart from him in terms of his temperament and technique? Why had Loukas Matthaiou sent *Bar Flaubert* to my father? The question was now posed, clear and relentless.

My father came to my mind. What a difference... Markos Loukas, a man who in essence had never gone beyond the four walls of his office, who went through life together with his huge library, with his studies and his family, had also fashioned his own world. But he had constructed it piece by piece, in the way you build a house, from the foundations, the columns, the doors, the windows. When his construction was finished, he coated it with plaster, painted it in earthy colours and handed it over clean and shining to the future buyers. On the contrary, what had Matthaiou done? He had jumped into the materials himself, rolled in the mud, scraped himself on the gravel, cut himself on the glass, and when he got to the end, dirty and bleeding, he had nothing else to hand over other than himself. The final product was his own self. That was Loukas Matthaiou's literary output. Fragments and splinters. Dust, rocks and blood.

Yet the strange thing... Putting them side by side, on the left my father's craft and on the right Matthaiou's flesh, my heart once again tilted towards the side that was disadvantaged, I felt the shorter arm reaching out towards the crude material – that protoplasmic mud that I longed to glue to my elbow in order to complete the imperfect limb, to transform what was missing into a circle. A circle, an eternal beginning.

On Friday, at around eleven in the morning, Tina phoned me. We arranged to meet in the afternoon in a tapas bar close to my hotel. I wondered what was behind all this interest. Perhaps Gillermo was simply a smokescreen? I recalled that on that evening she hadn't appeared to return his attention.

Tina looked different to how she had been on the two previous occasions. She seemed to me to be somewhat taciturn, I tried to discover whether she had spoken to Esnaider or Salinas, but she avoided all reference to it, talked to me about literature, about Lorca, Pessoa… She was trying to avoid the burning question, as though she hadn't been the one to point me in the right direction for my contacts in the city. All she asked me was how my talk with Salinas had gone. I spoke in general, without going into detail. But at one moment in the conversation, I came out with the wrong question:

'Have you heard anything about a robbery that happened in 1968 at the Museu Picasso? Salinas…' and I immediately clammed up.

Fortunately, Tina didn't appear to be surprised at the information I had. She blew away the locks of hair falling over her face and said:

'In 1968? How old was I then? Three?'

Her answer allayed my momentary concern. We continued to chatter about everything under the sun as though the reason for our meeting had been Spanish literature or my tourist's curiosity and not my quest for Matthaiou. So much so that after the meal, she offered to take me on a tour to the Sagrada Familia. After having crossed half of Barcelona in her little Fiat, we reached a rather drab district in the middle of which loomed a black skeleton, a half-finished church, this too one of Gaudí's works. It was an otherworldly construction that had no connection at all with the urban landscape surrounding it.

'It's the most famous skeleton construction in the world, it's planned to be ready in 2045,' Tina informed me as we climbed the inner spiral staircase.

When we reached the top of the staircase, I turned and looked at her. Tina was an extremely beautiful woman. Yet there was something behind her sea-blue eyes, a steel base that supported the iris and spread like a barrier around the optical cavity. There, as we were at the highest point of the church looking down at the people below who resembled ants, I suddenly leaned over and kissed her.

At first, she let me; her lips' initial reaction was for them to give way to the slightest pressure from my own. But this lasted only momentarily. She regained control of herself, pulled away, looked me straight in the eye and said:

'Don't do that. You know nothing about me.'

'No,' I said, 'but I want to.'

'You won't like it,' she replied.

'Does it have to do with Gillermo?' I said boldly.

She smiled:

'Gillermo… Gillermo is a child. A child who happens to be fond of me.'

'But you're fond of him too, right?'

'Yes, but not like…'

'Not like what?'

Tina paused for some time:

'You're so elsewhere…' She took hold of my hand. I felt awkward. 'Do you know what it's like to have given your best years to someone and for him not to be able… And how can someone possibly love when he can't even bear his own self… How scared people are of love! When things get tough, they go back to being safe, they seek refuge again where they were before…'

'Who are you talking about?'

Tina moved her gaze away from me. She took a deep breath and looked down at the tourists. Then she turned and gave me a peck on the cheek:

'Forget about us. In our madness we've found our equilibrium. I like you a lot, but there can be nothing between us. Different worlds… If the circumstances were different, the timing… I don't know… Come on, let's go back down.'

We went down the stairs in silence and when we reached the ground, Tina said goodbye to me and walked off hurriedly without even suggesting we return together. As I watched her going off, I hoped that this time it would be her who would feel my gaze boring into her back and would turn to look round. But she continued straight on till her unscathed back disappeared from my view. All that remained was the shadow of the black skeleton. I once again felt myself swimming in the zarzuela, I too an ingredient in a Barcelonan mixture that was becoming ever more strange.

Parc Güell

On Saturday morning I went out for a stroll round the shops. I returned carrying two bags with a pair of striped trousers and two large white shirts with narrow collars. I hadn't even managed to remove the price tags when I heard the piercing sound of the telephone. In response to the instinctive Greek 'yes' that escaped me, the unfamiliar male voice at the other end spoke in English:

'This is a friend. If you want to know where Lucas Padre is, be at Parc Güell at six o'clock this evening, in the arcade with the slanting arches, at the far end.'

Before I could say anything, the man hung up.

So now it was anonymous phone calls… It seems that the Matthaiou business had alarmed a number of people in Barcelona. I now knew that Loukas Matthaiou was a man who had committed an act of hubris, who had removed a piece of contemporary art history from the place that had given birth to it. An act of hubris, for which the one responsible was known only to Esnaider, Esnaider's associates and Salinas. And probably the former had no idea of the involvement of the latter in the business. These were the only two, apart from Tina, to whom I had confided my own interest. So from where had the anonymous phone call come? Was it perhaps Esnaider, who wanted to use me in order to discover Matthaiou's whereabouts? I needed no more evidence to convince myself of the undying hate he felt for the one-time object of his desire. For the man who had humiliated him not twice but three times. He had refused him, tricked him and left him confined to a wheelchair. Esnaider had many reasons for wanting to find Loukas Matthaiou. Yet, on the other hand, was it perhaps Salinas who was playing some kind of strange game? Who could guarantee that his story was true?

At five-thirty, I took a taxi to Parc Güell. The park was on a hill at the edge of the city. At 17.50, the taxi left me at the entrance with its mosaic composition of dragons welcoming me. Gaudí's hand had worked its miracle here too. It was Saturday evening and the park was buzzing with life. There prevailed an atmosphere of elation, as if the whole of Barcelona had gone up to that magic garden with its animal statues in order to enjoy the good weather. At the centre of the park, in the large square with the wavy benches and colourful mosaics, two teams of kids were playing football.

After gazing for a while, I asked where the arcade with the slanting arches was. I walked to the left and before long I was standing in front of a stone-lined shelter.

Strangely enough, there weren't many people in the arcade. It was a concave walk of about three hundred metres. Precisely because of the incline, as I walked, I had no visual contact with the far end of it. Along the way the only people I met were two or three couples going towards the square. It was a hot day, the sun was scorching, and the Mediterranean humidity making me sweat was only slightly offset by a light breeze. Somewhere in the middle of the arcade, I saw a young Spaniard coming from the other direction. Our eyes met and immediately stayed fixed on each other, as though some magnetic force existed between us. We walked towards each other. Each step brought us twice as close. We had become involved in a psychological duel, our eyes were two guns waiting for the right moment to speak. The Spaniard was around twenty-five, tall, dark, with wild good looks and resembling a toreador in his red and black clothes. In such cases, one of the two, the more insecure, is the first to lower his gaze. At three metres' distance, I could bear it no longer. I admitted my defeat, lowering my head. As the Spaniard passed me, he shot me a sideways glance accompanied by a smile of contempt. The informal duel had left me defeated and I still hadn't reached the end of the arcade.

However, the distance that I had covered allowed me to see that there was no one at the end of the dirt path. I walked the last fifty metres to the end. Not a soul. The nearest people to me were two Japanese couples roughly in the middle of the arcade. All I could see was a stone bench, this too slanting. I looked at my watch. 18.03. I was on time.

I sat down on the bench and lit a cigarette. There was a magnolia in front of me. An old dog was watering its root. The atmosphere was suffocating. I unfastened the top two buttons on my shirt. From behind, excited children's voices could be heard. One team had scored a goal. I again looked at my watch. 18.06. The Japanese came closer, waving their automatic cameras like trophies. One of them turned his camera towards me, most likely wanting to photograph the end of the arcade. I had never liked being photographed, particularly not by some unknown Japanese tourists in Barcelona. I made a sudden movement to the right in order to escape the shameless Nikon's sights. At that moment there was a hollow sound and I felt something hot whiz past my ear. A second similar noise was heard and a cloud of dust rose up before my feet. I realized I was being shot at. Instinctively I leapt up and took cover behind the bench. I only just made it as a third bullet came and wedged itself in the edge of the bench, exactly where, just a few seconds before my belly had been. Terrified, the Japanese began running back, towards the exit of the arcade. The only sounds to be heard were the distant cries of the kids. It seems that the people in the park had understood nothing; evidently the gun had a silencer. I calculated that thirty seconds must have gone by since the first shot. I tried to regain even a modicum of self-control. The gun had fallen silent, so it seemed the bench was sufficient protection for me. Through a chink, I could see opposite me. Fifty metres in the distance there was a kiosk with three dark openings. I guessed that the marksman had hidden in there. I wasn't mistaken, as I saw something straight, like a rod, moving in the middle opening. At that moment, the arcade was completely empty. The Japanese had vanished. I couldn't keep hiding forever behind the bench. The only solution was for me to attempt to get out, to escape. I thought of shouting for help, but it was pointless, there wasn't a soul around. Given that the marksman was hiding in the kiosk, I calculated that I would have to cover roughly half the arcade, about a hundred metres, in order to be out of his range. Then I would be protected by the tall trees that would come between us. I took a deep breath, got up suddenly and stooping parallel to the ground, I began running with all my strength, zigzagging along the curved walkway. The combination of my unorthodox running and the slanting course seemed to have disorientated the prospective killer. I ran the distance with the speed of a sprinter, while three more stifled sounds followed me, three bullets that whizzed past me or over me only to be embedded in the far end of the arcade. Reaching the middle of the curve, protected now, I stood up and continued running like a madman till I reached the centre of the park, with everyone staring at me in amazement.

I didn't stop until I reached the park entrance. Someone had tried to get rid of me. It was incredible, but no one, apart from the Japanese who had immediately rushed to get out of the way, had realized anything. My situation was comical. I had just escaped a murder attempt that no one had got wind of. I looked around me. At the cash desk at the entrance, I saw three Spanish policemen looking at me suspiciously. Unconsciously I made a movement to go over to them, but I immediately checked myself. Something inside me prevented me from reporting the event, a strong inner impulse drove me to get away from that place as quickly as possible, to get out of Parc Güell, to get out of Barcelona.

Under the watchful eyes of the three policemen, who were undecided as to whether they should concern themselves with me or not, I hailed the first taxi that I saw and told the driver to take me to the Hotel Oriente.

I rushed up to my room and, still shaking, poured myself a double vodka from the minibar. Then I sank into the armchair and tried to calm myself, to take stock of everything that had happened. A week earlier, I had been in the safety of my flat, in my own city, with my family, my friends and my, albeit routine, work. Now I was alone, in a foreign city, a stranger among strangers, with my only misdemeanour being my search for a Greek who had passed through here like a whirlwind thirty-one years before and I had been the victim of a murder attempt. Who was it that wanted to shut me up?

I tried to look at everything with a sober eye. Logic told me that the business had to have been the work of Esnaider. Given that he hadn't succeeded in using me as bait to lead him to Matthaiou, I was useless to him. Not only useless, but dangerous. Naturally, what had been said between us didn't constitute any special danger for the old man, so he must have learned that I had spoken with Salinas. And here was perhaps the clue to solving the riddle. Who else could have given him that information apart from Tina? Besides, that would explain the change in her behaviour. Tina must have owed Esnaider something – something much stronger than the flirting of an inquisitive Greek. But still, something wasn't right. Even if Esnaider had found out about my conversation with Salinas, how did he know that the poet knew and told me about Esnaider's own involvement in the robbery? Salinas himself had told me that he had never revealed his own part in it to anyone, or at least only to one person who was above suspicion... Consequently someone must have told Esnaider about Salinas's part in the business. Someone whom Salinas considered to be above all suspicion. Yet that information must have been given recently, after my meeting with Esnaider. And once again the only person I could think of was Tina. The circle was closing...

There was still one crucial question; what was Tina's relationship to Salinas? Perhaps the two of them... Despite the shock from the attempt on my life, my mind was working perfectly. I recalled her words from the Sagrada Familia:

'Forget about us. In our madness we've found our equilibrium...'

Tina and Salinas. Salinas and the fifty year-old woman who lent him support. The man who was unable to love. Salinas who had drunk a whole bottle of whisky in front of me. The landscape was gradually starting to become clear. The woman who Salinas had talked about, the one much younger than him, the unusual woman, must have been Tina. And the man who was unable to love, who was scared of love and took refuge in security, in his wife, must have been Fernando Salinas.

So here was a possible scenario. Tina is working for Esnaider; it was he who had helped her father to buy the London Bar. She meets Salinas and falls in love with him, and flattered he leaves his wife for the younger woman. Eventually Salinas confides in Tina concerning his involvement in the robbery. Naturally, at first, being in love with him, Tina doesn't even think of betraying her lover to her benefactor. *Amor omnia*. With the passing of time, from what Salinas himself gave me to understand, the moment comes when the poet, either out of remorse or the burden of his age, considers that the care of a devoted wife suits him more than the demands of a mistress. Besides we're talking about a man who is virtually an alcoholic and who needs help and support. And so the poet leaves the young mistress and returns to the wife he's been cheating on. Tina is hurt and decides to destroy the cowardly lover. Her opportunity for revenge comes through me, the night before, when I let slip the question about the robbery.

Through my irresponsibility, Tina realizes that Salinas has told me about the paintings. And she thinks how she might use this unexpected gift. The path is wide open before her. She now has the perfect alibi for betraying Salinas to Esnaider. By giving the old man the double piece of information that it was Salinas who had harboured Matthaiou and that I knew this, she both repays her debt to her benefactor and also gets revenge on her lover. Naturally, I get swept away in it all, too, yet I don't think that Tina, despite all the fondness she showed towards me, is the kind of woman to allow such sentiment to influence her. I recall when I first met her, she had revealed nothing on hearing Matthaiou's name. Apart from being a doll, the girl was also a tough cookie. She wasn't one of those birds who can put up with playing second fiddle.

The fact was that Esnaider had learned from Tina that Salinas had helped Matthaiou. And what's more, he now knew that I knew everything about the robbery. I had commented on the Picasso painting behind the curtain... Given then that he knew that he couldn't exploit me, since he believed that I still hadn't found any clues as to where Matthaiou was, he decided to get rid of this inquisitive Greek who had in his hands information incriminating him.

In the end, reality far surpasses imagination. Despite all the pressure I was under, I couldn't but smile at the scenario I had come up with. A ready fictional canvas! If only I could concoct stories like that in Athens! Naturally, though my intellectual meanderings had some form of plausible coherence, they were still no more than conjecture. The question was what was I going to do from here on. One thing was sure. If I stayed in Barcelona, my life would be in danger either from Esnaider or from someone else. I had to leave as soon as possible. Besides, everything there was for me to learn about the life and works of Matthaiou in Barcelona was already recorded in my notebook. And finally, even more important, I had found the next person that I had to meet. Caterina Mateo, Loukas Matthaiou's daughter, in Florence.

What took precedence now was for me to get away immediately. I phoned Iberia and booked a seat for Athens on the morning flight. My stay in Barcelona had lasted just one week. I decided to spend the remaining time in the one place offering me the greatest protection, in the hotel, that is. I phoned down for my evening meal and poured myself another vodka. Outwardly, I had almost recovered, inwardly however I felt a trembling, as though some foreign body were vibrating in my belly.

That evening Barcelona beat Real Madrid 3-0 at the Nou Camp, with two goals by Luis Enrique and one by Rivaldo, and the city went wild. Crazy Blaugrana fans kept Barcelona humming until the early hours. From my window in the Hotel Oriente, I stared at the blue and red crowds drinking and dancing, while my mind, despite the unbearable noise, travelled with a rhythmic undulation.

Again on the plane, this time going in the opposite direction. So quickly. So much. A week in Barcelona, three meetings, six gunshots, a new destination. My trip in a nutshell.

I had instinctively gone through all the procedures at the airport with an inner fear, with a vague sense of guilt. Now I was sitting in my favourite place, in the non-smoking section, next to the right-hand window, over the wing. Beside me was a young Spaniard of around twenty. Pale, dark, with something delicate about him. It seems that the events of the previous day had left an indelible mark on my appearance, as my neighbour kept glancing at me out of the corner of his eye, pretending that he was reading his newspaper. Annoyed, I suddenly turned round and stared at him. He immediately went red in the face and lowered his eyes behind the newspaper. And so I came virtually face to face with one of the inside pages of *El País*. And it was then that I saw something that shook me. Exactly in front of me, some nine inches from my nose, I saw in large, bold letters the name of Fernando Salinas, and beside it a photo of him at a young age. Putting aside all reservations, I peremptorily asked the young man to give me the newspaper. I was so astounded that I was unable even to read the headlines. With the same brash tone, I demanded that my thunderstruck fellow passenger translate the passage for me. The young man knew English and, despite still being taken aback, began translating for me in a low voice:

STRANGE DEATH OF RENOWNED POET
Fernando Salinas dies aged sixty

The renowned poet Fernando Salinas, aged sixty, together with a woman who was subsequently identified as Tina-Maria Tobosa, aged thirty-three, were found dead last night in Salinas's house at 17 Argenteria Street. The poet and woman were found naked together in bed. The first reports by the coroner suggest that it is a case of joint suicide, most likely by poison or pills. However, the police rule nothing out. Investigations are being carried out in the poet's immediate environment, though it seems he had no enemies.
Fernando Salinas was born in Barcelona in 1938. He studied literature at university...

'Enough!' I said to the young man, who seemed relieved. He hurriedly handed me the newspaper and turned his gaze in the direction of the aisle.

The article said nothing else after the short biography. I folded it and cheekily put it in my bag. Yes, reality far surpasses imagination.

The eye twinkles again

On arriving in Athens on the Sunday, I began to prepare for my next trip. I decided to stay put for five or six days to see friends, parents, probably Anna too. The events in Barcelona had been so intense that I couldn't, didn't want to think any more. The story was evolving by itself. Like a game of dominos. The one piece caused the next to fall and I was following, running in pursuit. I opened the notebook that I had bought in Spain. It was full of my jottings. I wrote on the cover in thick, black felt-tip: 1. Barcelona. The next notebook would be bought in Italy and would be entitled: 2. Florence. I booked a seat with Alitalia for Florence via Rome; I would leave on Saturday. I once again left the return open.

On the Monday evening I ate with my parents. I said nothing at all to them about what had happened in Barcelona. I simply told them about the city, about Gaudí, about the museums, even about the zarzuela, on a gastronomic level, naturally. My father showed particular interest in my trip and asked me a pile of details. It seems that he approved of the role of travel correspondent for his son. My mother appeared even more sunk in her own world. At one moment, when we went into the living room for coffee, she dropped her cup and it shattered into a thousand pieces. I kept up the fairytale about the travelogues for my parents, I told them that the magazine wanted an article on Florence as soon as possible and that on Saturday I was leaving for Italy.

'My son is going to be the new Bruce Chatwin,' said my father – who had got onto the whisky – full of pride, to my mother, who stared at him in bewilderment. 'What, don't you know anything? Bruce Chatwin was the Egon Shiele or…what's the name of that new painter? The Damien Hirst of travel correspondence!'

'Come on, Dad, slow down,' I said, wondering what I would do if he wanted to read one of the articles. 'All I'm writing are some basic guides, what to see, what to eat, where to stay and a couple of words about the atmosphere of the city.'

My father, however, was inexorable. After four whiskies, he began planning my future trips to Patagonia, Tierra del Fuego, and in the end he began envisioning me as a future explorer, so we had passed from Bruce Chatwin to James Cook and onto Nuñez de Balboa. My old man was in good form that night. Later he played the piano for us and then read us one of his adolescent short stories that he had kept in his drawer, this too a part of the endless paper kingdom of Markos Loukas. I really liked it; it was very moving to hear his juvenile scribblings. Naturally, the firm structure was there, even then. Strong characters, conflicts, social surroundings, beginning, middle and end, an organized world... When I left, he kissed me and, handing me a folded piece of paper, said:

'Yannis, this is the address of a friend of mine in Florence. His name is Theodore Skylakis, he's a professor of art history at the university. I met him at a conference they had invited me to there when the city was the cultural capital of Europe in 1986. Since then, we've kept in contact, he's been to Greece on several occasions... A good chap, aristocratic, he may be able to help you. Give him my regards.'

'I will.'

'Yannis, have a safe trip and watch out for the women in Florence. They have lovely eyes, like almonds... And such grace... I've never seen women move with such grace,' he added as he said goodnight to me.

I saw Anna the next day; we had lunch together in Kolonaki. I told her a few things about Barcelona and that on Saturday I was leaving for Florence. She looked at me with tired eyes. She seemed to be lacking sleep, had lost even more weight, and it didn't suit her. There was a kind of dejection in the whole atmosphere, a difficulty in everything, even in the conversation. I noticed that, while we were speaking, neither of us interrupted the other, neither of us raised our voices, it was all very civil. Anna told me that she had a lot of work that week and suggested that we meet on Friday. We parted with a formal kiss. The next day, she phoned me to postpone our meeting. Some relative of hers had come from abroad and she had to put him up. 'We'll talk when you get back,' she said, and in her effort to sound natural, her voice sounded as if it didn't belong to her.

On Friday, I invited two friends round to my place for dinner. This time I experimented with a Barcelonan speciality. The result was pitiful. Kostas couldn't refrain from commenting:

'I see you're on a high, Loukas. Shame your cooking is at still at a low...'

I told them everything, down to the smallest detail. They listened to my account with great interest, only when it came to the murder attempt did Kostas remember the doubting Thomas hidden inside him:

'Come on Yannis, are you having us on? Are you saying they tried to bump you off among crowds of people, in a park?'

On the contrary, Telemachus was pensive.

'You've got yourself into a pretty mess. Perhaps it would be wiser if you gave up now, before anything worse happens.'

'Telemachus, I'm in so deep that there's no room for backing out. I'm going to see it through to the end whatever happens.'

'Listen, pal, we're talking about blood. Real blood. That Salinas is dead. And the bird too. How come you're so sure that the old man bumped them off?' asked Kostas.

'For me it's all too clear. A translator friend of mine read the recent articles in *El País*. The first accounts talk of a double suicide. But the authorities have ruled nothing out. They are waiting for the results of the post-mortem. There's always the passion scenario, liberation through suicide. But look what we have here. An old man and a woman in her prime, Tina was jealous, but not enough to turn into a female Kleist... And Salinas too, at least as I saw him, wasn't the type to commit suicide. He was a man who had reached the age of sixty, had affairs, played to the extent that he played with life and now had decided to return to his wife and write his masterpiece without any distraction. But the bird wasn't the type that you squeeze dry and then throw away. Of course, she paid for her stupidity. And I'm certain that Esnaider paid to have the job done professionally... Don't take me as an example. I was lucky. If it wasn't for the Japanese, I wouldn't be here now.'

'Damn it, they're always springing up where you don't expect them!' said Kostas, jokingly.

'Fine, laugh all you want,' I said, in no mood to continue the joke, 'anyway, as things have turned out, I'm one of the last obstacles to Esnaider. Me, Matthaiou if he's still alive, and most likely Caterina, his daughter. Though Salinas gave me to understand that the girl didn't know any details. But I'm going to find that out for myself...'

'Great, so now in your old age, you're turning to detective work?' said Kostas sarcastically again.

It was an important evening for me. Despite all their ostensible objections, I sensed that my friends supported me in my quest. Perhaps it was the fact that, as both of them said in their own way, they hadn't seen me so active for years: 'You're looking better, you old rascal, there's a twinkle in your eyes again,' Kostas had said.

Blood from the ceiling

...I don't know what it was that parted me so forcefully from our union, a strange power pulled me out of her, she had long black hair, blue eyes, smooth skin, earrings and bracelets that constantly rattled, and jingled even louder when I pulled away. As she turned on her side, I saw that she had started bleeding, a few drops of pale-coloured blood stained the white sheets. I was lying on my back on the bed, feeling dazed. Everything started swirling around me, till my gaze fixed on the ceiling above. I saw that blood was dripping from the edge of the ceiling, a strange kind of blood, that didn't belong to the woman, no, the woman's blood was pale and there were no more than a few drops, this was different blood, darker, and it was spreading thick and menacing from the floor above. My folks lived on the floor above. The blood licked the ceiling; eventually the drops became heavy and dripped into the room. The flow gradually increased. I got up, she screamed. A crack. In the ceiling. Barely discernible. It grew larger. Through the opening flowed more blood, uncontrollable. I opened the door. The hallway was a pool four inches deep, blood that kept rising. Splashing in it, I reached the front door. I opened it with difficulty and a red torrent gushed into the house knocking me over. The level kept rising, lifting me upwards, the blood rose higher and higher. Before long my head was just eight inches from the ceiling. I only had a small pocket of air left to breathe. There was no sound any more from the woman. I guessed she must have drowned. Suddenly the flow of blood stopped and the level remained constant. I tried to breathe, at the same time frantically kicking with my legs in order not to sink. Then something touched me. I turned round. It was a hand, severed, pale, as though

all the blood had been drained from it. It was floating on the surface.
I heard a cry. Not mine. I woke up…

It was five in the morning; the day was breaking. I felt shaken,
inwardly shaken, my tissue was wavering deep in the darkness. A
firecracker had taken root within me and was about to explode. I
wanted to talk to someone, but to whom? I was suffocating. A pile
of condensed emotions had collected in my lungs and prevented
me from getting my breath. How I wanted to go into my body, to
cross it from end to end, to grab hold of them and clear them up.
But I was there, on the outside, alone, at five in the morning. I
gazed at my reflection in the glass balcony door. Naked, I had lost
some weight. I gazed at the pale shape reflected in the glass. So
short, so long… I'd known it for years. It was mine. I knew that
shape as nothing else. That is, as I knew nothing.

The Mateos' Garden

Theodore Skylakis

'Mr Loukas, when talking of Tuscan cuisine, we are talking of a cuisine that is essentially simple. It is based on the local olive oil, which in my opinion is *sans rival*, unrivalled. Its other basic element is its combination of carbohydrates, so don't be surprised if you are served spaghetti with broad beans or tortellini with lentils. Here, we use carbohydrates in salad too. What we Greeks call salad is the garniture for the Italians, in other words, that which accompanies the meal and which might be beans, boiled greens or lentils. As for the wine, my friend, Tuscany is the home of one of the best red wines in the world. The king of Tuscan wines is to be found in the region of Chianti, between Florence and Siena,' said Theodore Skylakis. The professor, a portly fifty-year-old with a ruddy complexion, flicked the ash from his impressive cigar.

'Tuscano Orizinale, one of Garibaldi's favourite cigars,' he informed me.

'You've been living here for many years, isn't that so?' I asked.

'Since I was appointed Reader in the Department of Art History.'

'And you chose to remain here permanently...'

'My dear boy, I don't know whether we choose in life or whether life chooses us,' said Skylakis interrupting me. 'That's true about the city we live in, about the woman we live with... I had opportunities to live in other places, but I always returned to Florence, it was here that I met Paula in 1980. We were married the following year. Even though I adore Florence, I don't think that you can ever say that you've found the ideal place. We make that mistake in Greece, we have a tendency to create myths. Besides, didn't the English Romantic poets of the 19th century idealize Tuscany too? Florence, Mr Loukas, is an open museum, a place that allows you to come into direct contact with western culture and to become deeply acquainted with medieval and renaissance art.'

Professor Skylakis was by nature talkative. I had only been an hour and a half at his home in Via Faenza and he had already explained to me in detail the entire anthropological map of the region, while his wife, a very likeable Florentine woman of about forty-five, kept serving us with espresso and home-made cakes. The house, full of bookcases and paintings, was spick and span. At the other end of the living room, the daughters of the family, two gorgeous fifteen year-old twins, were painting each other's nails and stealing glances in our direction.

'By the way, Mr Skylakis, I'd like to ask you about two Greeks who you may have heard of given all the years you've lived in Florence. One was called Loukas Matthaiou or Luca Mateo. Of course, he lived in Florence between '68 and '72, but perhaps you've heard of him?'

'Luca Mateo… The name doesn't ring any bells. I first came here in '77. What line of work was he in?'

'I don't know…he was a writer. Of course, he had studied biology and he had money, a lot of money. Anyway, no matter. You came to Florence five years after he had left… But I wonder if you perhaps know his daughter, she's called Mateo, Caterina Mateo.'

'Do you mean the girl who is an assistant in the School of Architecture?'

'Yes, she's studied architecture. Is she around thirty?'

'Somewhere around that age, I think. I known Signorina Mateo from the society. The Greeks in Florence have a society: 'The Greek House'. We engage in various activities, largely cultural but also educational ones. Signorina Mateo is responsible for the Greek school, we have some problems at the moment, we're looking for a new teacher, someone seconded from the Ministry of Education in Athens.'

'I imagine then that you must have the addresses and phone numbers of the Society's members,' I said, interrupting him. 'I would like to speak to Signorina Mateo. I was told that she may be able to help me with the article I'm writing. Part of it is going to be devoted to architecture, on how it's possible to intervene in an environment with such a strong cultural backdrop,' I added so as not to provoke any suspicion.

The professor went into his study and soon returned with a piece of paper on which was written: 'Caterina Mateo, 45 Via Ghibellina, 248 331.'

'Caterina is a very charming girl. Now that I come to think of it, she has never once spoken to us about her father. I think that she was born here. At any rate, she speaks Greek perfectly.'

Theodore Skylakis then took up the thread of the conversation from where he had left it. He spoke to me about the modern Italian language, which had been born in that very city:

'The first person, Mr Loukas, to write in the Italian we know today was a Florentine, Dante. The people here, even the peasants, use the language exceptionally well; if you go to Chianti, you'll see for yourself what wonderful Italian they speak there. Italian, you know, is a very difficult language, particularly when it comes to conjugating verbs…' Undeterred, the professor went on with his lecture on the level of social culture, which, in his opinion, was particularly developed in Florence. 'There is still in Florence that which we call taste, which is a direct reflection of tradition.'

Then he referred to the innate humour of the inhabitants, mentioning the school of Tuscan comics, Roberto Benigni and Leonardo Pieraccioni, and he concluded by talking passionately about the *Fiorentina* football team and Batistuta, the point at which the sober professor suddenly turned into a fanatic follower of the *Viola*. Three hours passed before I was permitted to leave, with my head full of the Renaissance, my stomach full of Florentine cakes and my wallet bulging with the folded piece of paper on which was written the precious address.

That evening, I phoned Caterina Mateo. Her answering machine played Brahm's *Hungarian Dances*. I spoke in Greek.

'Good evening. I am phoning you on Sunday evening, 17th May. My name is Yannis Loukas, I am in Florence and I would like to meet with you about an important matter that concerns us both. I was given your number by Mr Theodore Skylakis. You can reach me at the Hotel Loggiato dei Serviti…'

Duomo

It was Monday afternoon and almost night-time in the Duomo. Inside the church, strangely enough, there weren't many tourists. I walked towards the centre. Having just left behind me a noisy square, I felt benumbed by the sudden silence. I kept on walking. On the right, kneeling in a pew, was a young man dressed in leather from head to toe. His head was shaved and he had an earring in every possible part of his face: his nose, his eyebrows, his ears, his lips. The young man was praying with the utmost piety. Kneeling down there, with a faint beam of light emphasizing his outline, he looked like a black angel. As I was passing by him, he turned and stared at me. His gaze was black too, a dark well. I shuddered. I speeded up my step and headed towards the left wall of the church. About halfway along the wall, I found myself in front of the painting by Domenico de Michelino, with Dante holding the *Divine Comedy*. Absolute silence. I recalled:

Midway along life's path
I found myself in a dark wood
and my life as I had known it was lost.

The motto to the second chapter of *Bar Flaubert*. And then:

…Eight months passed. Hard months, cylindrical with openings like an aqueduct where our love surged like a wave. I was overcome by vertigo scattered in my innards by the weakness. For it was a weakness that this love brought, and I had to defend myself…

I was overcome by vertigo… Dizziness. Rise and fall. The one in love leaves traces on the body of his beloved, and then looks at her from above. Vertigo. The dizziness caused by the vertical distance. Of the mind from the heart. The one in love touches his beloved, makes love to her, destroys her. Rise and fall. Matthaiou in '75, midway through his life, his natural life, his love life, at his peak, suddenly finds himself in his own dark wood. And there, his entire life, the life he had known until then, was lost. He had now seen. He had seen with the eyes of his soul and had understood. He was never again going to experience such beauty. The decay had begun. The love itself had suffered nothing. It was Matthaiou who was dying. This is why for the rest of his life he would feel nostalgia for that dark paradise. The dark wood, which for Matthaiou had begun in a bar. A bar named *Flaubert*.

Next to the Duomo, inlayed with white and pink marble, was a tall campanile, a work by Giotto, with a narrow stairway leading to the top. I began climbing it with some difficulty. The steps were extremely narrow and I thought they would never end. After three or four stops, I managed to reach the top. Below, Florence spread out like a carpet. The height made me feel a kind of vertigo, my legs ached. But it was worth it. Florence was a dream-like city, as though unreal. A place where the only risk you run is to be bored by so much beauty... I instantly thought of Matthaiou and I tried to see him in such a city. It wasn't his style. I somehow couldn't envisage him in this living museum. No, this was a city more suited to my father, I could imagine him in a house overlooking the Arno, with his huge library like a fortress all around him, writing on his carved walnut desk. And at weekends going to his cottage in Tuscany, reading, picking wild mushrooms and playing with his dogs. While my mother, all alone, would lose herself in the endless rooms of the museums with all the Renaissance at her feet...

At the hotel. Monday evening. No word from Caterina. I phone her again. Again the answering machine.

Tuesday morning. The telephone rings. A warm female voice speaks Greek with a slight accent:

'Mr Loukas?'

'Speaking.'

'My name is Caterina Mateo, I got your message. I'm sorry for not contacting you earlier, but I was out of town. Can you tell me what it's about?'

'Ms Mateo, I'm so pleased you contacted me! I've already been here two days and I'm in Florence for no other reason than to speak to you. I'd like to meet as soon as possible, it's about something that particularly concerns you.'

'What exactly?'

'About your father, Ms Mateo, Mr Loukas Matthaiou.'

Silence at the other end of the line. Then after a short while:

'My father? But how do you know... Do you know something about my father?'

'It's a long story. I need to see you in person as soon as possible. We have a lot to talk about. Do you have time this evening?'

'Yes... Of course, we must meet. This evening...' answered Signorina Mateo tensely and added, 'This evening, an architect, Bruno Rotta, is giving a lecture at the university and I have to be there. Could you come so that we can meet afterwards?'

'Yes, of course, but how will I recognize you?' I asked.

'You'll see me on the podium. I'll be welcoming the speaker. But, Mr Loukas, where did you find out about my father?'

'Ms Mateo, it would be better if we spoke in person.'

'All right. This evening then.'

She gave me the address, we made an appointment in the university canteen after the event and she hung up quickly as though she were afraid of continuing.

On putting the phone down, I wondered what Loukas Matthaiou's daughter would look like.

Caterina Mateo

'...And I come to the main point, which I would like you to give thought to. Contemporary architecture has to re-find, to again bring to light the original values encompassed by life. The most important artists in this century always maintained a vital connection, an inner link with the past – Picasso through symbols spoke to us of the vital, erotic force in man; Henry Moore referred us to primitive elements, Paul Klee to the child inside us. We can see that these artists had the ability to interpret the forces of the past, the *valeurs primordiales*, the constant, primordial values, and promote them in contrast to their historical circumstances.

Architecture, in my view, is the formalistic reflection of history. If today we are not content with our cities, it is because we are not content with the societies supporting these cities. The ground on which the contemporary architect has to work is the ground of memory. Without memory we do not exist. I live means *I remember*.

In conclusion, my friends, I would like to stress that architecture is an art, a science that begins before the existence of the architect and continues after his death. And thus it remains a monument for future generations and intrinsically includes the concept of memory, a concept so vital for the evolution of the environment that surrounds us. I thank you for your attention.'

The packed auditorium rang with applause. Bruno Rotta, a likeable fifty-year-old with round glasses and wavy hair, bowed to the audience. Beside him a tall blonde girl stared at him in awe. In presenting the guest speaker, she had introduced herself as Caterina Mateo, Loukas Matthaiou's daughter.

A few minutes later I was in the canteen. Before I had even had time to order an espresso, a coffee as the Italians call it, I saw her coming over towards me.

She held out her hand with a light, elegant movement. White and delicate, her neck stood out against her black dress.

Caterina Mateo had a singular beauty. At first sight, her hands reminded me of the description given by the French author of Emma Bovary's hands; not particularly beautiful, slightly pale, dry at the joints, yet long-fingered and relatively well-shaped, pink nails, shining and sharply rounded. She had fleshy lips, almost violet, and when she smiled, they accentuated her delicate chin. Her hair, blond and shiny, fell to the left and right like doorposts on a particularly expressive face. Her cheeks stood out noticeably, the line of her cheekbones had been worked to perfection. Her eyes, green and tender, resembled those of a deer. She was tall, around five foot ten, her body was trim and firm. Yet it wasn't the individual features that made this girl beautiful.

'Did you like the lecture?' she asked me, after the introductions, in a slightly nasal voice. Its undulation seemed so suited to her features that it was as though the pores of her face were speaking.

'Very much. Rotta is one of my favourite architects, I wrote a short piece on him in a magazine.'

'Are you a journalist?'

'You could say that. But I prefer to say that I write for various periodicals to make a living.'

'Oh, a columnist then.'

'Of a sort,' I said and, after pausing for a moment, added, 'I had a different picture of how you would be.'

'How were you expecting me to be?' asked the girl, surprised.

'I imagined you more Italian…'

'I'm as much Greek as I am Italian. So, shall we go somewhere to talk?'

'With pleasure,' I said and followed her outside.

In a quarter of an hour we were at Giubbe Rosse in Piazza della Republica, a café frequented by the literati in the twenties. The weather was warm, the night pleasant, and we sat outside.

'Mr Loukas, what do you know about my father?' asked Caterina after the espressos had arrived.

'You haven't seen him for years, isn't that so?'

'Yes, it's exactly twenty-six years since I last saw him, he left Florence together with my mother when I was three years old. I don't know where he is, or whether he's alive or dead. But first I'd like you to tell me how you found me. How you know about me…'

I looked at her. Caterina had a face that revealed two different characteristics: spontaneity and caution. Though my diagnosis was instantaneous, I was certain of it. Sometimes you communicate with the other without needing to say a lot. That's how I felt then. Face to face with something recognizable, something familiar.

It was Caterina's turn now to hear my involvement with *Bar Flaubert*. This time without any censorship. I told her everything. The only things I deliberately left out were any hints concerning her father's relationship with the Beat poets and with Esnaider. Caterina listened to me intently, almost with fear. She had hunched her shoulders and entwined her fingers in a stance that made her look as though she were praying. She didn't interrupt me even once.

While I was talking, I noted her every expression. I found myself facing a real transformation. During the course of my narration, the somewhat reserved, polite girl sitting at the table turned into an emotional wreck. Her green eyes gradually misted over and her cheeks flushed, which made her even more beautiful.

When I was done, finishing with the deaths of Salinas and Tina, Caterina could barely hold back her tears:

'It can't be, all this simply can't be true. It's like a novel. And yet it explains why…'

'It is a novel,' I replied. 'I have your father's manuscript with me.'

Caterina stared at me intently and said straight out:

'I'd like to read it myself. Will you lend it to me?'

'I've brought a copy with me just for you.'

Caterina took hold of it devoutly. She opened it, examined the pages and said:

'What lovely handwriting. It's the first time I've ever seen anything written by him.'

'And what he writes is lovely,' I said.

'Yannis,' said Caterina hesitantly, 'not one day passes without my thinking of them. Not one. I don't know whether they are alive or dead. Not even my grandmother knew. I lost my grandmother Sophia two years ago. Right until the end she tried to fill the gap. The only information I have is that in autumn 1972 my father and mother left me with her and vanished without explaining why. When I was six, my grandmother told me that my parents had been in great danger, though she didn't know what, and that they had had no choice but to leave the country. Until then, I believed they had gone on a long trip and that they would return. As I grew up, I began pressuring her, asking persistently. Naturally, my grandmother knew about the gunfight, she had made a statement to the police. But she only revealed this to me later, when I was fourteen. My father had phoned her immediately after the incident. He hadn't told her who had attacked them. Only that some of them had been killed and that he and my mother had to leave as quickly as possible. From then on we never heard anything ever again about my parents. At first, my grandmother believed they would return, but as the years passed she came to accept it. The only link was an amount of money that went into my bank account every year. I enquired at the banks but came up with nothing. The money is transferred from an anonymous Swiss account. That's the only thing that makes me optimistic, that they're living somewhere, that they are alive. Apart from my grandmother, the only other person who ever talked to me about my parents was that Spanish poet, Fernando, who you said is dead. But he too had had no word from my father after 1972.'

'Salinas didn't die, he was killed,' I commented.

'It's all so terrible... Did that Esnaider hate my father so much?'

'Caterina, your father was a very idiosyncratic person. He exercised great influence on those around him. It seems that he also provoked great enmity.'

Caterina played nervously with her necklace.

'I'd like you to tell me about your mother's family,' I continued. 'Did you know your grandfather?'

'My grandfather died in '65 a couple of years before I was born. He was German, he met my grandmother during a trip to Florence before the war and fell in love with her. They lived in Germany for a time; my mother was born there, her second name was Margarete. When the war broke out, they tried to leave the country, but didn't succeed. It was only after the German capitulation that they were able to get away. They came here and, after '45, lived in Florence.'

'So your mother was a little girl in Germany during the war?'

'Yes, my grandmother told me some horrible tales. Of bombings, air raid shelters and carnage. Naturally, they wanted to leave but couldn't.'

'Did your grandfather fight in the war?'

'No, he had some health problem and was exempted.'

'What kind of problem?'

'With his heart, the arteries, I don't know exactly. What I do know about my grandfather is that he was from a good family, the Hardenbergs from Oberwied...the Oberwiederstedt of Prussian Saxony. His name was Friedrich Hardenberg. His ancestors were barons. Grandfather must have been a very well-educated man. We still have his library at home. Five thousand volumes, the whole of German literature.'

'What work did he do?'

'Bank manager. The war ruined him. When he came to Florence, he had to begin from scratch. He had some contact with a bank in the city and in a relatively short time was back on his feet again. They say he was a very able man. Unfortunately, he died quite young; he was only fifty-four, his heart. My grandmother lived for thirty-one years on her own. I was all she had, particularly after my parents had gone.'

'Your grandmother must have been like a mother to you.'

'Mother and father together,' said Caterina. 'That woman was a rock, she was strong, proud... The money that went into my account may have been enough, but it was my grandmother who gave me moral support. It's not easy for me to talk about all that... I went through some very bad times. I found it terribly difficult to reconcile myself with the fact that they had left. If they were forced to leave back then, why later didn't they give some indication that they were alive? One of the last things I have of them is this photo,' Caterina continued, taking out her purse. 'My grandmother found it by chance in a book and hung onto it. Everything else, photos, documents, books, they either threw away or took with them. All that remained were the properties, the house in Via Ghibellina and the summer cottage in Siena.'

I took hold of the photo. It was the first time I ever set eyes on Loukas Matthaiou. It was a colour photo, very poor quality and fuzzy. It depicted a couple arm in arm. The Duomo was just visible in the background. Though it wasn't easy to distinguish his features, the photo absolutely confirmed everything said by Telemachus, Arnold, Esnaider and Salinas. Matthaiou, around thirty, dressed in the kitsch style of the period – colourful shirt, unbuttoned down to the chest, huge collar, bell-bottom trousers – cut a most impressive figure. Tall, brown hair, with the profile of an ancient Greek statue, high forehead, pronounced cheekbones and pale eyes that, though the pose didn't help, looked as though they would pierce the photographic paper, Matthaiou had something aristocratically diabolic about him. Classic good looks together with provocative impertinence. Despite the wayward dress, his expression recalled something of Terence Stamp in Pazolini's *Theorem* – in a more rugged version. A magnetic presence that dominated the place with its appearance and imposed itself on whatever existed around it. As, for example, on Magdalena, who, captivated by that enchanting aura, appeared to be overshadowed by her husband's radiance, even though she took up the biggest part of the photo. Not that Magdalena wasn't a beautiful woman. Tall, blond, delicate, in a short white dress, a red scarf blowing around her neck and a pile of bracelets around her wrists, she was a woman who wouldn't pass unnoticed. What made an impression on me, however, was her gaze. A slant gaze, defensive, that betrayed a certain discomfort, reservation in front of the lens, something strange for an actress.

'Your mother was an actress, wasn't she? What was her professional name?' I asked.

'Gentile, my grandmother's maiden name.'

I looked again at the photo:

'Your parents are both very good-looking. I think you take more after your father.'

'Oh, my grandmother used to tell me that I was the spitting image of my mother. Of course, I've seen my mother on video. But what use is that… I'll never know how she is in real life…'

'Don't say that. You might find out one day. You ought to try at least,' I said earnestly.

'How?'

'Why did you think I wanted to meet you? We'll find him, we'll find them together,' I said, trying to sound as convincing as I possibly could.

'Find my parents… Do you realize what you're saying? I've lived so long without them, it's an infirmity, as though someone had cut off my arm.' At that point, I shuddered. 'Do you know what it's like living so long with a severed arm?' Now I began to perspire, though somewhere deep inside I felt relief, given that she couldn't have noticed anything for her to have come up with that simile so spontaneously. 'And you've turned up today, out of nowhere, and you tell me you'll help me to find my father. Yannis, I'm twenty-nine years old, I've found an equilibrium, I've come to accept certain things. Such as the fact that I'm never going to see my parents. And you say we'll find them. I'll never understand you journalists.'

'I'm not a journalist, Caterina,' I said, almost in a whisper.

'Look,' she said after a short pause, 'I have to go now. I want to spend some time alone to think over everything we've talked about.'

'Caterina, we still haven't begun. There's more, much more…'

'But you don't know me. You know nothing about me. I don't work that way,' she said nervily and two beads of sweat appeared on the sides of her brow, 'all this is too much, much too much at one go. I need time. First I have to read the novel and then I'll think things through. Don't call me. I'll phone you when I'm ready.'

'As you wish. All I want you to know is that I'm not out to gain anything. I'm looking for something too and, to be honest, I don't know exactly what. After Barcelona, an image started to take shape, but it's still unclear. I know I'm entering someone else's house uninvited. A house that's been locked up for years. If you want, I can help you discover what's hidden inside there,' I said with fervour.

'I don't know… I need time. I'll read it and I'll get in touch with you.'

'You know where to find me. I'll stay in Florence for as long as it takes.'

Caterina put the folder into her bag and got to her feet. Her face was wet. She was about to take out her money but I grasped her hand to stop her. Her pink nails dug slightly into my wrist.

'Thank you,' she said and, leaving, gave me a look that, if it had been a flower, would have been one of those that sprout in the crevices in rocks after the rain.

It was a lovely evening and everyone was out in the streets. The Piazza della Republica was full of young couples. In the centre of the square, a mime was giving a performance. The perfectly round moon rose in the sky. I felt as though I had done something bad, half of me was up in arms against the other half. I wasn't an indiscreet person. I knew that approaching Caterina in that way – head-on – involved risks that could destroy the whole venture. Already the girl had retreated after the first shock and her reaction ought not to have surprised me. She had quite rightly demanded time in order to examine the meteorite that had suddenly fallen into her life. And me? How would I handle the situation? At the present time, there was no question of tactics. I had before me a person who was flesh of Matthaiou's flesh, with whom I had, though for different reasons, a common aim; to solve this advanced crossword puzzle.

For there were certain things that I couldn't explain at all. Not even guess at their causes. Why, for instance, had Matthaiou and his wife shown no signs of life since '72? We know that at least three years later he was preparing to enter the world of Greek literature before my father blocked his path. Why did he leave the girl to grow up alone with an old woman? Did he think that the financial support made up for the absence of her parents? Did he never want to find out how his daughter had fared? Even that convict, Pip's invisible benefactor in *Great Expectations* eventually re-entered the life of his grown-up dependent, albeit out of curiosity, to see what kind of fruit his sowing had produced.

I again felt something pressuring me. My faithful Fury, my Impatience was visiting me again.

That same night in my sleep I saw Caterina pregnant in her last month. She had had a terribly difficult pregnancy and four doctors had had her isolated in a lonely house in the country in order to take care of her. The four doctors were Esnaider, Salinas, Tina and me. We guarded her night and day because she had become terribly aggressive, she screamed constantly, swore at us with unrepeatable words and hurled whatever she found before her at us. At times she was beset by awful pains and her cries were like those of a wild animal in captivity. When the time came for her to give birth, Esnaider took a large sword, like a yataghan, and cut open her belly from end to end. Caterina writhed, flailed like a mad woman, the blood ran everywhere. Then Salinas went up to her, put his hands inside her womb and carefully took out a small bloody lump and handed it to me. With the blood dripping from it, I took it over to the sink and washed it. Before me, wet and bloodstained, was a book. The title, with the letters distorted by the water and blood, was only just discernible. Two words: *Bar Flaubert*.

The Garden of the Finzi-Contini

The next day, I saw Skylakis again. We had breakfast in a café in Piazza San Lorenzo and then went to the Uffizi gallery. I halted before Botticelli's *Spring*. Flora, the figure with the flowery dress to the right of Venus, reminded me of Caterina. When I mentioned it to him, the professor chuckled and said:

'Mr Loukas, you evidently haven't understood that the advice I gave you the other day doesn't apply only to the landscape. It holds true for the women too. Don't idealize everything, my dear young man. Don't make a myth of things. Beauty on its own is nothing. It's an empty word. You recognize it, lay siege to it, wrestle with it, and if you're lucky, you conquer it. Then it gives you every right to caress it, bite it, penetrate it… But when all this ends, beauty suffers nothing. You are the one who suffers…'

'I think you are exaggerating somewhat,' I murmured.

'All right, but we were once where you are now, young man,' said Skylakis meaningfully. 'What happened with your article, was Caterina helpful?' he asked after a while as we walked along the corridor in the gallery. 'I hope she told you something about the city's modern architecture. Of the moderns you ought to write something about Michelucci and Italian rationalism, and include some photos from the Santa Maria Novella station and the church in the autostrada.'

'Of course, she gave me a complete picture. I have all the material I need. Mr Skylakis, shall we go and take a look at the Michelangelo? The *Doni Tonto* is one of the main reasons for my trip,' I said, skilfully avoiding the pitfall.

The Teatro della Pergola is the oldest theatre in Italy. Judging from its programme for that year's season, you would classify it as a venue for plays, but which also staged concerts and, naturally, opera. In the high-ceilinged foyer, next to the pay desk was a poster with performances for that quarter. The repertoire was mostly Italian classic playwrights: Goldoni, Pirandello, De Fillipo – *La Locandiera, Henry IV, The Millionaires of Naples.*

Going further inside, an archway spanned the wide staircase. From there you came out into an intermediate area in which, to right and left, towered two lines of columns leading to an even higher level where there hung a board with all the services housed in the building. It didn't take me long to find what I was looking for: 'Theatre Archives of Florence'. In a couple of minutes I was in front of an elegant sign: Claudio Netti – Theatrical Archives Manager'. I was greeted by a well-built sixty-year-old with glasses and a moustache. After introducing myself, I got straight to the point:

'I am a journalist from Athens. I am researching into European cinema and theatre, particularly concerning actors whose careers ended suddenly at an early age. I am interested in a certain Signora Magdalena Mateo, or rather Magdalena Gentile, because I understand that she used her mother's maiden name. She lived in Florence till 1972, I know that she played some minor roles in films by well-known directors: Antonioni, De Sica… I imagine she must have also acted on stage.'

'Gentile, Magdalena-Margarete Gentile! Of course I know her. I even worked as stage manager in a play by Ibsen that she acted in – she played Reggina in *Ghosts.* A very good actress and a beautiful woman. But you're right, for many years now I've heard nothing of her.'

'Could we check what films she played in?'

'There must be something here…'

Signor Netti went to the computer, opened some files and after searching for a short time, exclaimed:

'Eureka! Gentile M. Magdalena, born 1938, here we are… I'll print you out a copy.' He pressed some keys and before long I was reading:

Gentile Magdalena-Margarete

Theatre and screen actress. Born in Potsdam, Germany in 1938. Living in Florence since 1945. Worked with the Teatro della Pergola between 1961-1971. Acted various roles in plays by Goldoni, Pirandello, Tennessee Williams, Jean Genet, et al. Also appeared in the following films:

Michelangelo Antonioni's *Il Deserto Rosso* (1964), Ermano Olmi's *One Fine Day* (1969), Mario Monicelli's *La ragazza con la pistola* (1969), Vittorio de Sica's *The Garden of the Finzi-Contini* (1971).

'Is that all there is?' I asked.

'I'm sorry, but the archives are updated every year. There is nothing about Signora Gentile after 1971.'

'Perhaps you know where I might find some of her films on video?'

Signor Netti gave me the address of a video club specializing in old films.

'Thank you very much,' I said, taking the piece of paper, 'but, as you know, I don't know Magdalena Gentile by sight...'

'Ask for *The Garden of the Finzi-Contini* and come back here with it so we can watch it together, it's a superb film and I haven't seen it for years,' he said, pointing to a TV and video player at the other end of the room. 'Come back at three when I get off work.'

The video club was close to the hotel. At 15.05 I was back at the Teatro della Pergola with *The Garden of the Finzi-Contini* under my arm. It didn't take Signor Netti long to recognize Caterina's mother. In the first scene of the film, among a group of young men and women, dressed in white and on bicycles, who were visiting the home of the Finzi-Contini in Ferrara in 1938, there appeared a beautiful blond woman who looked appreciably younger than thirty-three, the age, that is, that Magdalena Gentile was in 1971.

'That's Magdalena Gentile, the blond,' said Signor Netti.

In fact, it was Magdalena who, on arriving at the front door of the house, says the first lines in the film: 'Is anyone here?' Later, when the group of young people is welcomed into the garden, she is introduced to Dominique Sanda, who plays Nicole, the main character.

Caterina resembled her mother. Except that Magdalena had something reserved about her here, she seemed to me sad somehow, in her lily-white tennis clothes and with her blond hair blowing in the wind. And when Sanda appeared on the screen, Magdalena Gentile's star faded before the blinding radiance of the French actress.

Albertina, the character played by Magdalena in the film, is engaged to one of the young men in the group, but later leaves him because he is a Jew. We learn this from the accounts of the rest of the characters, because from the end of the first scene to the last scene in the film, which Signor Netti insisted that we see to the end, we waited in vain to see Magdalena Gentile again.

'Wonderful film. One of the best films in the seventies. And a lovely woman, shame she stopped so soon,' said Signor Netti.

'Yes, beautiful. But she never played any major roles,' I commented.

'In a film about Jews in Italy in 1940, the Aryan fiancée had very little opportunity to develop the role,' was his reply. Tuscan humour…

The second city

CHAPTER THREE

> *Those anxious go to bed prepared,*
> *go to sleep fully equipped*

For a long time I felt like a frog at the bottom of a well. I stared at the rounded wall, the blue circle up above, I paced round the circumference and said, here, this is my world.

Till eventually, the elements of my character rebelled. As though the baroque revolution had taken place in my soul. Every single thing, from the trunk's furrows to the innermost branches, was driven towards excess, unwound itself in ever more pointless meanderings. I was lost in a delirium, in a wild festivity, in which my self, crowned with laurels, celebrated the end of a long confinement.

But now, in this city, every time I open the window and gaze upon nature, the houses, the streets, my soul becomes detached. It hovers for a while in the atmosphere, rises, then liquefies and drips on the vines and the grass. I drip and am dissolved into countless tiny soul-drops throughout the city and beyond.

No, what I feel is not happiness. Happiness is forbidden to me. Anything precious I touched I touched only once and then was shaken. My soul returned to the sphere of routine and remained there, as redemption. Of instincts.

There is no tragedy more terrible than to have had your hands as a young man on what you will eternally desire. None more terrible. Naturally I went on. I survived. I chose a new love. Yet what love is ever chosen?

I continued for two pages more:

...And why all this anxiety? How I would like for me not to have known, for the lights of my soul never to have opened, for me to have been a disenchanted, frightened, real person!

Yet now, here, how come I feel like this? How I love that creature I fashioned, with light from my darkness! With a love greater than myself even. Eternal love. A prison of tenderness. And this is a sentence. An unbearable one.

I gaze at her. How unworthy I feel! Unworthy even to love her.

And she? Not a day passes without my thinking of her. She too floats in the same love. Where is she? How much time has passed? Why did she go? A birth from another body, a different one, came and stood between us. For the first time, whenever I think of her, that tiny shadow comes to cover her. For the first time I want her to go from before me, to fade, to disappear. How I'd like when my daughter casts her first shadow for it to fall on her!

Second city. 4.6.69. From today I will forget the name Leto...

Yes, Matthaiou wants to forget Leto. Only the child can cast a shadow over the love that was lost. He can't, however, get Leto out of his mind. He sees her constantly, in his second wife, in this second city. Nothing can hold him back; doors and windows are open, squares and churches are deserted. Yes, Florence is no place for Matthaiou. And it won't be long before fate appears in the form of Esnaider to remove him for good. He loves the child, but feels unworthy. He's afraid. *'A prison of tenderness.'* Matthaiou is not

someone who can exist within limits, not even the limits of love.
Here's the first hint, the first explanation for his leaving, for
abandoning... Matthaiou speaks sharply, with one phrase: *'How
unworthy I feel.'* Unworthy. How, I wondered, would Caterina read
this.

Second city. 4.6.69. From today I will forget the name Leto... I
wondered whether Caterina's birthday was the 4th June. If it was,
then on the following Thursday she would be twenty-nine. It was
already Saturday, four days had passed since our first contact, and
still there was no news from her.

Quiet days in Florence

That night I couldn't sleep. I wrestled with the bedcovers all night
long. The next day would be Sunday. We were into the last week
of May. I reflected that it was only a month or so ago that I had
discovered Matthaiou's manuscript. Given that I was unable to get
to sleep, it was five in the morning, I decided to go out and watch
the day dawn over Florence. From the hotel, I took the Via Guelfa,
turned into the Via Cavour and walked down it as far as the
Duomo. I continued along Via Calzaiuoli and kept going straight
as far as the Piazza della Signoria. Day was just breaking and the
city was deserted. The dawn's soft colours bathed the churches,
reddened the white statues, made the water running from the
fontane look so soft that you wanted to caress it. I walked amid
perfect beauty, in a renaissance picture. When I reached the square,
the dawn's first gentle red brushstrokes had begun to colour the
torso on the statue of David. A golden ray crowned his hair and
made his proportions seem even more harmonious; the head no
longer seemed so large, the arms no longer appeared so out of
scale. Everything was tranquil, in the proper proportions. A poem
by Katerina Anghelaki-Rooke came to mind. I remembered it line
by line:

> *The angel becomes perceptible*
> *and at some intermediate stage*
> *in the Piazza della Signoria*

at dawn, with a rose-tinged David
raising his silent
limbs to the sky…

At that moment, as I was standing before the statue, the silence was broken by an unexpected snort and the sound of hooves on the marble. I turned and saw a horse coming towards me. A grey, riderless horse was crossing the Piazza della Signoria, with a grandiose step that caused its scrotum to swing first to the right, then to the left. At its every movement, its adornments, red and blue beads sewn in intricate patterns like arabesques, clinked against the leather saddle, producing a rhythmic accompaniment that sounded like a tambourine in an oriental group of musicians. The stirrups were lined with gold-braided red fabric, the bridle was decorated with silver stars and the leggings were of patent black leather that shone in the dawn light. Its mane, rich and well-kept, shook aristocratically as the horse advanced with its head upright, proud, as though on parade. I recalled… The rhythmic step, the clinking of the adornments, the two fleshy lumps that were swaying…

It was the first time I had ever seen my mother ride. I would have been seven or eight years old, and we were in the countryside, at the home of a family friend, who persuaded her to mount his prize foal. I gazed at her skintight breeches, – it was the first time I'd ever seen my mother in trousers – her white shirt with the top three buttons undone, and her breasts which, together with her necklace, bobbed up and down with the movement of the horse. I had never seen my mother's breasts pounding like that. My perception of the maternal bust was of a soft and gentle surface, of two small mounds that balanced parallel to the ground. I couldn't imagine them moving violently like that; I had never dreamed that they might have a life of their own. Nor had I ever before seen her legs so shamelessly open, forcibly gripping the animal's vibrant, coarse body. Yet even more, I had never before seen her expression, an expression that I felt destroying, in the wink of an eye, everything I considered familiar. Her features were made taut by a strange intensity, as though some secret power had taken hold of her. Her lips were half-open, I felt her losing her breath, her eyes burning. That woman before me bore no resemblance to the ethereal, almost invisible woman who was my mother. This was an excited creature and one that scared me. My father was standing beside me and he too was watching her in amazement.

When the horse passed before us, my mother turned and looked at him. Her wild gaze made my father unconsciously lower his head.

'Markos! Look! That's it!' she shouted in a hoarse, trembling voice.

I looked at my father and, for a brief moment, I sensed that he was frightened; it was the first time in my life I had ever felt my father to be scared.

The horse in the Piazza della Signoria had come up to within a yard of me. It suddenly halted. It whinnied and tossed its head to left and right. I lifted my left hand and stroked its mane. It was soft and smooth. For a moment it was as though I saw my mother in the saddle telling me to climb up. The colours from the dawn in the Piazza della Signoria changed from violet to deep red. The crimson dripped onto the leaves of the trees and fell as a rose sheen on the marble slabs. The reflections of yellow gave an amber hue to the facades of the churches. There was no sound apart from the horse's rasping breath. I took hold of the reins and held them tight in my hands. Again I saw my mother's figure calling me, I took two steps forward and realized that her eyes were not turned to me, but above me, as though she were motioning to someone standing behind me. I turned round. There was no one there. No one at all. Just a deserted square filled with renaissance fountains and white statues.

I spent another four hours wandering the city. I visited the churches, the monasteries, the museums, I even went to an exhibition of – who else? – my favourite impressionist. That same evening in a café I met an English painter, Karen, a tall, gangling woman of around forty-five who looked like Virginia Woolf. We ate together, talking all night about literature and art. During the following days, I met with Skylakis another three times: on the Monday we went to the opera with a doctor friend of his, on

Tuesday we went to one of Fiorentina's friendly matches and on Wednesday we went on a day trip with his family to Certaldo Alto, a village outside Florence, which was the birthplace of Bocaccio. We laughed a lot, Skylakis continued his lecture on Tuscany, his wife was constantly stopping on the way to pick flowers and the young girls competed as to which of them could impress me the most. It was midnight when we got back to Florence, slightly tipsy, with a cassette of songs by the popular Greek singer, Marinella – the professor's secret passion – playing at full volume.

Gibreo

On Thursday morning Caterina phoned me. Nine days had passed since the last time we had spoken. She sounded calm. She told me that she had read the novel carefully, had wanted to be alone for a little time and was now ready to talk. We made an appointment for that same evening at Gibreo, a restaurant in the city centre.

When I arrived, Caterina was waiting for me at the first table to the right of the entrance, facing the small bar. She was wearing a blue dress, white necklace and the slight tan she had as a result of the bright sunshine of the previous few days made her look even more Greek.

Even before the arrival of the first course, a tomato jelly with chilli and basil served by Fabio, the restaurant's proprietor, Caterina had already got on to the subject.

'I read it and re-read it. It was very harsh... Very harsh about my mother too. There were a lot of things I didn't understand. It's not that what I read was incomprehensible. Behind the words, behind the images, his thoughts are crystal clear. It's perhaps that I don't think like that. But there are some passages...' and she stopped as though not wanting to explain.

'Do you think that in the end it's entirely autobiographical?' I asked her.

'A large part of it, but not all... The second woman, in the second city, as he calls Florence, is certainly my mother. He even describes her somewhere: *'A blond shadow caressed my cheek. Shrouded in Italian melancholy, her brown eyes relegated the honey colour*

Alexis Stamatis

to the periphery of the iris'. It was as though I could see her before me. It's not the image I have from her films. It's from my intuition.'

I spoke to Caterina about *The Garden of the Finzi-Contini*.

'Yes, of course, I've seen it. I have more of her films on video; if you're interested, we can see them together...' she said and, after a brief pause, added almost hesitantly as she finished a glass of Montalcino: 'Leto appears to be the person who marked his whole life. I wonder if perhaps she's not a real person, but rather a vision of the ideal woman... Of course, that doesn't change anything...'

As she moved her wrist, I noticed she was wearing a silver bracelet on which were engraved the words: '*Amor nel cor*'.

'The heart's love?' I asked.

'A gift from an old friend,' she replied, almost as an obligation.

'My opinion is that Leto is a real person,' I said, getting back to the subject. 'Besides, Salinas told me that Matthaiou had met the love of his life in America at the end of the fifties. It was also probably his first. Tell me, when was your father actually born?'

'My grandmother told me that he was born in 1938, on the 4th August.'

'The 4th August? What a coincidence! That number four follows me everywhere! And the number eight too!'

'What do you mean?'

'It's incredible! I was born on 4th July 1958, my father on 4th October 1928, my mother on 4th January 1938. This year, we'll all be rounding up our ages. I'll be forty, my father seventy, my mother sixty. And all of us born on the 4th of the month! And your father will be sixty on 4th August!'

'Do you want to know something else of interest? Do you know when I was born? On 4th June, but in 1969! Next Thursday I'll be twenty-nine. I'll be one year short of rounding up my age...'

So there, Caterina had answered my question before I had even asked it.

'*Second city. 4.6.69. From today I will forget the name Leto...*' I mumbled to myself.

Caterina's eyes filled with tears.

'I cried at that part. And that's where all my questions were answered. My father is writing about his life.'

I didn't speak straightaway. I knew it was the hardest part. I let her play for a while with her spoon in the jelly.

'Then he's forced to leave the second city, Florence – after the gunfight with Esnaider. Do you recall the passage, at the end of chapter three?' I asked.

'With the car chase on the autostrada? It must be on the outskirts of Siena. Where he describes the shots as *"dizzy arrows laced with death"*. And then the scene with the death of his friend: *"He the silk crumpled in his handkerchief, and a burning spread the creaking in his limbs... Not you! Not you! Not you!"* Something like that, I don't recall exactly...'

'What do you mean you don't recall, you know it all by heart...' I noted with a smile.

Fabio interrupted us, bringing us the main course, calamari with spinach for me, sausage with beans for Caterina. We were both in a state of excitement, we ate quickly, drank a lot and it wasn't long before we ordered a second bottle of Montalcino.

'When you try to fashion an image of people as close to you as your parents, the one who creates the strongest impression is the one about whom you have the least information. I know almost nothing about my father. All I have is this photograph and now the novel. My grandmother didn't tell me a great deal. Except that he was handsome, very dynamic. "A real Greek," she stressed. She also kept her final promise to him. To have me learn the language perfectly. I had Greek lessons right up until the end of high school, and throughout my life I've had close ties with the Greek community in Florence. Tonia, my best friend, is Greek. And the most important relationship in my life was with a Greek.'

'With a Greek?' I said, interrupting her. 'With a Greek in Florence?'

'Yes, he was a painter, older than me, he had a studio in the centre. He's gone now.'

'Was he the one who gave you the bracelet?'

'Yes,' answered Caterina, taking a large sip of red wine.

The dessert kept us quiet, absorbed in the tasty delight. She was the first to speak.

'While reading the novel, I understood that my father must have been a very lonely person. From what you've told me, everyone who met him talks of his dynamism, of his strong personality. But behind those lines I saw a man who was unhappy. He can't even communicate with the woman he falls in love with. Perhaps it's then that he feels even lonelier. In love... *'I gazed at her as she slept, and it was only then that I felt I was nestling inside her; only then that my love was unlocked and I spoke to her.'* Those words... It's words like those that stuck in my mind while reading the novel. I reflected that in the end I've inherited other things from my father apart from the annual income. Those words constitute his will. And you're the one who revealed them to me. That alone is enough for me to think of you as someone close,' said Caterina full of emotion.

'When I read the novel, I felt something else. A sense of familiarity.'

We stared at each other embarrassedly, Caterina played with her bracelet a little and then we went back to eating.

'Which do you think is the third city?' I asked Caterina after a while.

'After Florence? I don't know. At any rate, there's nothing to be got from the description. At least it's not a city I'm familiar with. It has a dark, suffocating atmosphere. Everything is grey, depressing... The inhabitants are described as being emotionally dry, harsh people. The hero — my father — can't bear that environment and leaves...'

'I'm asking you because, if it's all as I imagine, your mother must be living today in that third city.'

'Don't you think you're going a bit far?' said Caterina, sceptically.

'Not at all! You agreed that it's a kind of autobiography, isn't that so? An adventure that begins in the first chapter; he meets Leto in America. It's his first love, we have that confirmed by Salinas. Second chapter, the separation from Leto and refuge in the first city, Barcelona. Meeting with Esnaider, the robbery, the escape to Italy. Third chapter, here in Florence, in the second city, the second woman, your mother, your birth, the fight with Esnaider and, fourth chapter, the third exodus, this time to the third city. Finally, one more flight and the epilogue; the last refusal. It's a journey that is described exactly as it was in the book... Don't you find this interpretation logical? The problem is precisely the one you said, that your father obscures this city, the third one, he doesn't give us any clue.'

'To be honest, that's just how I see it too,' said Caterina, blowing a tuft of hair out of her eyes.

'And that's how it has to be… We have to find which is the third city. Till now I've been following your father's course from '67 to '72. He left Florence in the autumn of '72, right? He wrote the book in '75. So we're left with the period '72 to '74. If we can discover where he was for those two years, it will help us get to him.'

'Why do you only talk about him? I want us to find my mother just as much as I do my father.'

It was the best thing I could have hoped to hear. For the first time, Caterina had spoken openly about a common search. It was only the second time I had seen her, yet I felt as though we had been together right from the start, from that evening in my father's basement.

'I'm glad you see it that way,' I said softly.

We stayed until late at Gibreo. We had drunk quite a lot and the atmosphere had lost all the earlier tension. By the end of the evening we were talking about other things, about Greece, Italy, painting… We were the last to leave at around one-thirty, when the restaurant closed. We walked to my hotel, which was only ten minutes away. Before I moved close to kiss her goodnight, Caterina shook my hand warmly.

'Yannis, tomorrow, Friday, I'm going for a long weekend to the cottage in Chianti. I'll be back on Monday morning for my lessons. It's not a long trip. Would you like to come?'

'I'd love to,' I replied, kissing her on the cheek as I had planned.

Twenty-six rosebushes

The Lancia Ypsilon with Caterina at the wheel crossed a landscape on which rolling hills stood out like arpeggios on a musical stave. I could see all possible hues of green; light green, almond-green, olive-green, turquoise, emerald-green, not to mention the silver green of the olive trees and the deep green of the cypresses, that like grassy poles created a natural windshield around the isolated villas clinging to the hillsides. The Tuscan sky was wrapped in an aggressive blue and an explosive sun hurled its golden darts in all directions.

I observed this landscape as I did all the beautiful things in my life; from a distance. The gaze, when it sees beauty, acquires an authority all its own, the eye imposes itself on the face, dominates it. You begin by looking at a vine radiating a brilliant green, then you stare at a stone house at the top of a hill and a ray of light slips into the retina gently triggering the muscles, that move slightly, just enough so that the inside of the vehicle carrying you is also included in your visual field. And from there, your peripheral vision grasps a fleeting sense of naked flesh, a white hand as it moves back and forth changing gears, and while you turn your neck in order to include the blond of the blowing hair, the slight breeze obliges you to turn even more, you are now between two temptations, the natural beauty of the countryside on the one hand and on the other her still unformed image, gradually revealed to you by your eye's iris, which longingly races to the left corner of your socket. The vine becomes Caterina's face, the radiant green a red dress outlined by a blond frame. And then it suddenly strikes you what it is that fascinates you so much about that face. It is the extension of the landscape's breath, the reflection of the interminable in its existence. But isn't this what beauty is in a person? When the ineffable secretes tiny explanatory droplets.

Caterina's country cottage was twenty miles outside Siena. On arriving at Poggibonsi and having San Gimignano on our right, we turned left, leaving the main road and following a narrow road leading to a hill, three or four miles away.

'Now we're in the heart of the Chianti region. Can you see that vegetation up on the hill?' said Caterina. 'That's where the house is.'

The road passed through an expanse that was full of vines. All around there was nothing but a few scattered cypresses and a few cows grazing at the foot of the hill. The only sound to be heard was Mahler's *First* coming from the cassette player. I reflected that somewhere along this route was the scene of the gunfight with

Esnaider. The main road was quite busy; no one would have risked an ambush there.

Two cars in chase on the road we were driving along. In front, Matthaiou, Magdalena and their friend, behind Esnaider and his thugs. The acceleration, the braking, the cornering... Then the shots, the blood... Matthaiou returning home, hastily packing, notifying the grandmother to look after the girl and then disappearing with Magdalena. Leaving... But to go where?

'What car did your father have?' I asked suddenly.

'A red Alfa-Romeo convertible. I know from my grandmother. But why?'

'How does a car chase with three people dead on the road you're driving along make you feel?'

'How do you know that it happened here?' Caterina asked.

'Why, is this where it happened?'

'It couldn't have happened anywhere else. You realize it would have been impossible on the autostrada.' Caterina stressed and, turning off the cassette player, continued, 'I've done this journey hundreds of times, knowing that this is where the gunfight happened. It's the first time I'm doing it aware of the reason why it happened.'

'Your parents' friend who was killed in the fight, who was he?'

'I don't know, somebody called Luigi. I never met any of their friends. Apart from Salinas, of course...' said Caterina as we reached the foot of the hill. 'Look, it's up there,' and she pointed to the top.

It was a white two-storey building, surrounded by cypresses. The car began winding its way up the hill. As we got closer, I was able to get a better view of the small cottage. Its architectural design was simple, a row of large openings in the facade, a gable roof and eaves decorated with floral depictions. It had a large double-leafed front door with a carved escutcheon on the lintel. When we pulled up outside, I saw that it was a small elephant.

'My father made it himself. A week before they left, so my grandmother said. It's one of the few images that I have left of him. Here, in front of the house, my father carving a large piece of wood and gradually an elephant appearing. Of course, I may have made it up myself...' said Caterina as she parked the car beside a cypress tree.

No sooner had we parked the car than the door of the house opened revealing an elderly woman wearing a white lace apron. As soon as she saw Caterina, she rushed up to her, hugging and kissing her.

'Yannis, this is Rosa. She's been taking care of the house since the time that my parents bought it,' said Caterina in Italian.

'Pleased to meet you,' I said, holding out my hand to Rosa. She was a restless woman, short and plump, with hair dyed blond that stood up with the help of some strong lacquer. Her face was a map of wrinkles, but her eyes, two blue buttonholes incessantly moving, missed nothing. Rosa seemed to be a woman well-versed in the art of observation...

We crossed the front garden passing beneath the pergola that was covered in climbing plants – ivy, clematis, creepers. Before we went inside, Caterina wanted to show me something. She took me round to the back of the house, where I found myself before an impressive sight. It was a large garden, I estimated about a quarter of an acre, full of plants, some in flower some not; honeysuckle, begonias, oleanders, jasmine, hyacinths, poppies, mimosa and whatever else you could think of.

'The Mateos' garden,' said Caterina with a wry smile.

I looked to the left. In a separate flowerbed, arranged in a line, was a row of rosebushes.

'Twenty-six,' said Caterina, 'one for every year since my parents went away.'

I noticed that the flowerbed was quite large. There was room for at least as many more.

Inside the house, I found myself before an apotheosis of wood. A floor of fir, a ceiling of walnut, an open kitchen with wood panelling, couches, armchairs, chairs and a semicircular interior staircase all made of wood.

In the dining room was a large portrait of a middle-aged man with a bushy moustache and coarse features. He was holding a seal and a scroll of paper on which were written the words: 'Glauben und Leiben', faith and love.

'My grandfather, Friedrich Hardenberg,' said Caterina, 'my mother's father.'

We went upstairs, where there were three bedrooms and a bathroom. Caterina showed me where I would sleep. I arranged my few things; after all we would only be there three nights.

Caterina went into the bathroom and I went downstairs. Rosa was in the kitchen preparing something.

'The signorina tells me that you are Greek too. Like Signor Mateo,' she said in a funny, squeaky voice.

'Yes, I'm from Athens.'

'Athens, he was always talking about Athens, about his house in Filiro.'

'You mean Faliro,' I said, laughing.

'Faliro, yes, that's where he lived, by the sea, he said. Signor Mateo was a very good man.'

The housekeeper appeared talkative by nature. I wasn't going to let the opportunity be wasted.

'Were you with them from the beginning?'

'From the time they bought the house in '69. I'm from San Gimignano. I was hired by Signora Magdalena to take care of it. We had three wonderful years. And then that thing happened, and they left. Since then...'

'What thing?'

'The killings... The blood... I don't even want to remember,' said Rosa with a theatrical gesture, 'but why I am telling you all this, it doesn't concern you.'

'I know all about it, Rosa. I've talked to Caterina. Wasn't it somewhere near here that it all happened?'

Rosa got going.

'Very near. Two miles from the house. That morning, the signor and signora left here with Luigi, a lawyer friend of theirs who was staying with them. The signora was wearing a blue dress with yellow lace, she was beautiful. After half an hour or so, I remember Signor Luca, covered in blood, coming back to telephone. I thought he would call the police. I shouted to him, 'Call the police! Call the police!', but he didn't, he called Signora Sophia and spoke to her for a long time. He said, 'Great danger, we have to leave, take care of the child,' and such like... Then they left and I never saw them again.'

'And the police didn't come?'

'Of course they came! But a long time afterwards. The road is usually deserted. A tourist out walking saw the dead bodies and informed the police. The house was full of *carabinieri*. They took us to the place of the killing, there were three bodies, one was that of poor Luigi, it was horrible, the bullet had hit him in the head, you understand… I didn't recognize the others - swarthy types. I'd never seen anyone killed before and the blood drained from me. I couldn't breathe. Then they took statements from us, from me and Signora Sophia, Signora Magdalena's mother, who came later from the city. There were four in the other car. The swarthy types chased our people for some miles, shooting at them. Our people defended themselves and that's how the killing happened. If Signor Mateo had stayed, he would have been acquitted. Legitimate defence. And he had a licence for his gun. They searched for the other two for days, throughout the whole of Tuscany. But they never found them. It caused a great stir. It was even on the news.'

'Rosa, you're at it again.' Caterina's voice came from the top of the stairs. 'Don't take it the wrong way, Yannis, Rosa has been with us for so many years that now she's like one of the family. In fact, she is family. Come one, let's go for a walk and I'll show you round. It's so beautiful. I suggest we stay here tonight and go to Siena tomorrow.'

We walked for two hours in the surrounding area. Caterina, dressed in jeans and a yellow T-shirt, with her hair in plaits, looked like a little girl. The countryside suited Caterina. As I looked at her, amid the natural surroundings, amid the bright colours, I couldn't but help think how unconnected she seemed to be with all these tragic events.

That evening, Rosa made us *polpette*, something like meatballs in a tomato sauce, we opened a bottle of Chianti Classico, she told us tales of the past – what a handsome man Signor Mateo was, whenever he went to the bank in San Gimignano all the girls would gather to look at him, but Signora Magdalena too was a real lady – then she said goodnight to us and went upstairs to bed.

We went out into the garden with our drinks and sat in the bamboo armchairs. It was a moonlit night; the hills shone. Every so often there was the sound of a cuckoo. In the distance, sparkling like candles on a cake, were the lights of San Gimignano. I felt as though I were sinking in a viscous liquid and slowly melting. The liquefaction was very gradual. As I melted, I turned and saw around me people and places whirling, distorted and misshapen, into a funnel that would swallow them all up. The world became removed from my visual field, as though the people around me were flaking and dissolving. I didn't know what this feeling was. I had no idea, it had never happened to me before. I looked at her and saw a drop of blood collecting in the socket of her eye. She felt it too. She felt that we were falling, dissolving. Together. And we were doing all we could to slow the fall.

'Give me your hand,' she said.

I unconsciously held out my left hand.

'Not that one, that one is for touching the heart, the other,' she said, constantly looking into my eyes.

I gave her the other hand and she held it till the moon was high, the time passed, and we went to bed, each in their own room.

Siena

We arrived in Siena at noon the next day. It was Saturday and the town was packed with tourists. At first sight, Siena was a reddish mass of brick houses. If you added to these the monuments and churches, you'd think you were in a small medieval town discreetly infiltrated by late 20th century civilization. We roamed the narrow streets, halted in the tiny squares, visited the churches and museums. Caterina went into great detail for me about the local architecture, showed me around the renaissance treasures and, finally, initiated me into the custom of the *palio*, a horserace which takes place twice a year in the main square and in which participate all the castes in the town, the seventeen *contrada*. The race only lasts one and a half minutes and the winners celebrate with night-long dancing and singing.

In the evening, we sat down to eat in a trattoria in Piazza del Campo, the square where the horserace takes place. In the entrance was a banner depicting a brick tower on which a red flag was flying. The tower was supported on the back of an elephant. It reminded me somewhat of Matthaiou's carved escutcheon, but this one was the emblem of the *Torre*, the *contrada* that had won the last *palio* in August of the previous year, becoming champions of Siena.

The separation into castes that had an animal as their emblem, the singular appearance of the inhabitants, who bore no resemblance to the Florentines, the mysterious looks from behind half-open shutters lent an air of strangeness to the place. A strange image took shape within me. Of the town becoming transformed at midnight, of the inhabitants coming out in colourful animal costumes, with masks of pigs, wolves, boars and bears and giving themselves up to pagan rites, with the slaughter of cocks, sacrifices and orgiastic dancing.

I was lost in my fantasy when a little girl carrying a balloon passed in front of me. As soon as she saw me, she turned and smiled at me. She had braces on her teeth. For a moment, I thought a little blood was trickling down her face. I went to talk to her and the girl, as though sensing something, touched her forehead, then looked at her hand, saw that it was red, and immediately ran scared towards the centre of the square shouting 'Mama, Mama! Blood…' while the balloon slipped from her hands and began floating upwards till it eventually stopped, a red oval star above the square. A square that had a strange shape, like a shell, with hundreds of tourists lying over its entire length and resembling little molluscs lazily undulating on its brick surface.

'Notice the way that the architect has made use of the perspective. The sections of the square are fashioned so as to lead the eye to the Palazzo Pubblico,' said Caterina, pointing to a Gothic building on our left.

'Angelos staged an entire exhibition with subjects from this square,' she added.

'Angelos?'

'My friend, the one I told you about, the Greek in Florence…'

'Ah yes… How long were you together?'

'Nine years, from the age of eighteen, he was sixteen years older than me.'

'Sixteen years…'

'Yes, I was young and he was so…so…'

'Did it end badly?'

'Yes… I gave a lot to that relationship. In fact, it was my only relationship of any note. I knew from the beginning that it wouldn't be easy. Angelos had problems, many problems. He was a wonderful painter. I'll show you some of his work, I have a lot of it at home. But he was tormented, self-destructive. Later, he got into drugs and that's when we broke up. So talented and so self-destructive…'

'I don't imagine you fell in love with his talent,' I said somewhat provocatively.

'No, of course not. I fell in love with him. But he didn't consider himself capable of being loved. It's terrible for a person to have that feeling.'

'To consider himself incapable of being loved?'

'Yes.'

Pause. The balloon started to come down till it fell, deflated, at the foot of a statue.

'Do you still see each other?'

'No, it's been two years since I've seen or spoken to him. When we broke up, he went back to Greece.'

Caterina looked up, into the Siena sky:

'He's spoken about that too. My father, I mean… "*There are people who are born with anxiety hanging from their eyes. And when they open and close them, the anxiety flies away and they remain alone with its memory.*" Another tiny inheritance.'

The situation was right and so I boldly asked the question:

'And have you been on your own since then?'

'In effect, yes,' said Caterina in a manner as though wanting to put an end to the conversation.

I was slowly starting to understand her manner, her character. Caterina was honest; she would give you the information but then would let you interpret it yourself. She wasn't secretive. But neither was she open. She allowed you a zone of safety in which you could move freely. But when you came any closer, you felt a ring of fire, a burning aura protecting her.

On the way back home we didn't talk very much. We let the landscape pass before us to the strains of Brahm's *Hungarian*

Dances. I suddenly realized that during the entire course of the day we had had no physical contact at all. As though the emotion of the previous evening had evaporated into the Tuscan countryside.

In one hand – yes, the right one – I was trying to carry a tray with a porcelain tea service along the length of a large room. I was somewhere in the middle and the delicate cups, though shaking, were still there, in their place, intact, finely balanced.

The third city

At midday on Sunday, we went to the neighbouring San Gimignano, a beautiful village that you could walk round in half an hour. Most of the coaches that went to Siena also made a stop here, and we encountered a veritable invasion. Every inhabitant in the village seemed to be working to serve the invaders, with a view to profit of course. In the bars, you even paid for the tap water, while the sign 'Sexy Pasta' outside the food stores gave a whole new dimension to the country's national dish. We wandered around, had a snack, and returned, deciding to stay the night at the house and leave early the next morning for Florence.

Rosa prepared yet another specialty, vitello tonnato – thinly-cut pieces of veal with a tuna sauce – and then went home, after bidding me goodbye with a comical 'Byes-byes, Griko' and adding, 'God willing, we'll all be together again next time.'

'Rosa really loved your parents,' I said to Caterina once she had gone.

'Yes, she did... And she's understood about you, she thinks you're onto something. The poor woman still has hope...'

'Why, don't you have hope?'

'I've learned to expect the worst. In that I take after my father it seems,' she said, suggesting that we go and sit by the fire.

'I'd like to read you something concerning what we talked about the other day,' she said, taking hold of her father's manuscript.

She read slowly, stressing the words one by one. A different impression. Completely contrary to the rhythm of the text.

'*My time is barred by an unbreachable portal.*
Absolute silence. Neither bird nor human. The cypresses the sole
witnesses. I don't wish to see his blood stain the grey. I see him lying
with eyes open on the road. I stoop and kiss his white lips. The last
touch he feels. Beside me, scared, covered in blood, she separates the
dark under the eyes. She whispers: "Die Kirche, die Kirche! Mein
Gott, die Kirche!" The red river. The black milk. The dark over the
city. 22nd December... Over there, on the asphalt, the two bums.
We leave. As quickly as we can. Far from here. For all the hues
of green have been swept away by a fire and consumed. And I had
plans here, I had plans.
I abandon the second city. I leave, we leave in the darkness. Up
there, northwards, to a harsher darkness. A new glimmer appears
before me, the third...'

'The third glimmer, the third city,' I muttered.

'Wait, I want to read you a passage from the next chapter. It talks about...'

'The third city. Up there, northwards...' I persisted.

Caterina put the manuscript down on the coffee table in front of her.

'The third city! You're obsessed with it! I think it's all just a game for you Yannis. For me it's not though. You can't find a person through a text. That doesn't happen even in novels. People, when they exist, show some signs of life. Otherwise, they fade and disappear. Forever,' she said getting to her feet. 'Excuse me, I'm a little cold, I'm going upstairs to change. Fix me a drink would you?'

Caterina went upstairs and I remained seated in the armchair in front of the coffee table on which she had placed the manuscript. It was dim in the living room, Caterina had only turned one light on, a spot fixed to the bookcase that emitted a single beam. The light fell directly onto the table, on the photocopy of the manuscript. I couldn't take my eyes off it. I had to smile. It was because of this small dog-eared pile of papers that I was here. These two hundred and fifty pages that I had discovered by chance a month and a half ago in my father's basement were the reason for my having met Caterina, Skylakis, Hansen, Esnaider and the late

Salinas and Tina. It was because of this text with the strange title that my life had been endangered, that five people had died, and that this girl had begun to hope that she would once again see her parents. It was because of this peculiar writing that I had travelled to Barcelona, to Florence, and soon, if everything went well, that I would find myself in the third city, wherever that might be.

Barcelona, Florence. Third city… I looked again at the manuscript. As the beam of light fell on the title, it brought Matthaiou's strange handwriting into sharp focus. The cover was creased roughly in the middle and only the two first syllables of the title were visible.

Suddenly, I felt as if an electric charge had passed through me. As though for a fraction of a second, a bolt of radiation had passed through my body and momentarily turned on all the lights in my mind enabling me to see. I stared at the manuscript's half-hidden title. What I had been looking at all that time was: 'Bar Flau…' The neurons in my brain grasped the message. You can't see the parts for the whole… Yes! Till now, yes! Now I understand. And then? I picked up the creased manuscript, straightened out the paper to reveal the part that was hidden and excitedly read '…bert'. *Bar… Flau…bert.*

The man had explained it all from the beginning! Why hadn't I seen it all this time! *Bar…* Barcelona, *Flau…* Florence, *bert…* bert what? Of course! Berlin!

Barcelona, Florence, Berlin.

Matthaiou had concealed the third city in the most obvious, in the most secure hiding place. In his book's title.

When Caterina came back down, I told her of my discovery. As soon as she heard the word 'Berlin', she was taken aback.

'I don't believe it!' she cried out.

'What?'

'Tell me first and then I'll explain.'

'Well, your father liked word games, hiding messages in places where no one would think to look. Remember the four paintings. I had to rearrange the letters in the motto to find them. And now we have another word game. This time he played with the obvious. He hid the clue in the most conspicuous place; visible to everyone. And what we see before us all the time, we take for granted and don't bother to examine it. Your father has condensed in the title of his novel the three European cities where he lived during the time he was away from Greece, between '67 and '74. From '67 to '68 he was in Barcelona, from '68 to '72, following the robbery, in Florence, where he married your mother, and following the gunfight with Esnaider, he must have gone with her to Berlin, where he lived till '74, when he returned to Greece after the fall of the Junta. He must have written the book between '74 and '75, given that Berlin is included right from the beginning in the whole concept.'

'Hang on a moment! You've made everything seem so simple and clear-cut. And you're going too quickly. Let me play the devil's advocate for a moment. For a start, how do you know that the 'bert' is referring to Berlin. It might refer to some other city.'

'What you say is quite possible. But I don't know of any other major city that would fit. Do you have a dictionary at all?'

Caterina went over to the bookcase and came back with a thick *Longman's Dictionary*. Apart from Berlin, I found only two more cities that 'bert' might refer to: Bergen and Bergamo.

'I don't think either of those cities is of any help to us. Bergen is a seaside town in Norway – no, I don't think so – and Bergamo is highly unlikely given that your father wouldn't have left one Italian town for another.'

'Okay. No more doubting,' said Caterina and, taking a deep breath, went on, 'Yannis, I think you're totally right. Before, when you told me about Berlin, I was taken aback. I'll explain why. There's something that you don't know and that supports, almost verifies, your supposition.'

'What's that?' I asked impatiently.

'Friedrich Hardenberg, my mother's father, lived in Berlin. He had a house there. Before he came to Florence with my grandmother Sophia, they lived with my mother in Berlin… That's why I was taken aback when you mentioned the name of the city.'

'But, of course! How did I overlook it! Your mother was born in Germany! Yes, It's all coming together now. Barcelona, Florence, Berlin: *Bar Flaubert*. On leaving Florence, your parents took refuge in a city where they had some roots, with which they had some relationship. They had money, more than enough, but in Berlin they would also have people to help them. But let's take a leap in time. No later than 1974, your father returned to Greece. And if we accept what he says – and we've no longer any reason for doubting that he's describing events exactly as they happened – he must have returned alone. In the last chapter, he leaves his second woman, your mother, in the third city and *'returns home'*, as he states. If everything is as I think it is Caterina, then your mother must still be in Berlin! There are even German words and expressions in the text... Everything points to it! Despite the confusion, everything seems to be pointing in that direction.'

'You're getting ahead of yourself, Yannis, way ahead of yourself...'

'But can't you see that it's all coming together? Everything's falling into place and we're getting somewhere at last.'

Caterina looked at me sceptically.

'Tell me about your grandfather, about the house in Berlin,' I said excitedly, trying to impart some of my enthusiasm to her.

'From what I know, my grandfather's family came from that region. They were all bankers, from father to son. As for the house, I remember my grandmother saying that the neighbourhood was bombed twice. By the English and Americans in December '43 and by the Russians in April '45, a few days before Hitler committed suicide in his bunker. I have some photos in Florence, I'll show them to you tomorrow. My grandparents never went back to Germany. My grandfather severed all ties with the country. He never saw his family again, nor did he claim the property that he had left behind.'

'Are there any other relatives in Berlin?'

'I don't think so. Following the defeat the family scattered to various cities in Germany. I remember that after my grandfather's death, my grandmother kept up correspondence with her in-laws in Munich. In fact, we were once visited in Florence, in the early eighties, by my grandfather's brother, Frank, his wife, Hilda, and their son, Lothar, who was my mother's cousin. I recall Lothar very well. He was a painter and he showed me slides of his work.'

'And naturally they had no news of your mother.'

'No, they'd heard nothing. We had no information at all that might link my parents with Germany. Before leaving, my father had made no mention of Germany to my grandmother. All he had said was − I remember I had made her repeat it to me over and over − "We're in danger, Sophia. We must get away. And you'll have to take care of Caterina. As soon as I'm able, I'll contact you".'

'Which never happened... But if your parents did go to Germany, didn't they try to come into contact with your mother's family?'

'It's strange, but it seems not.'

'Your mother must have been a little girl of around five at the time of the bombings.'

'Yes. My grandmother told me a terrible story. It's mentioned in the book, the German words and expressions you noted, but I never thought anything about it. You remember, about the little girl, who was called Katrina...'

'You should have told me...'

'Perhaps, but my father includes it in other episodes without linking it to the third city. That's why I didn't mention it to you. I'd never linked the title to the cities. Now things are clearer... So, in 1943, just before Christmas it was, the allies had begun bombing the city. The RAF in the daytime and the Americans at night. My grandparents were constantly in the shelters together with my mother. However, the major bombardment in December found them at home. They only just managed to get away before the bombs hit the neighbourhood. They ran towards the shelters but my mother let go of my grandmother's hand and got lost. My grandmother was afraid that she had been killed. She looked for her in the streets with the bombs falling all around. It's a miracle that she wasn't killed herself. They eventually found my mother hiding under a car, next to a large church, the Gedachtnis Kirche, that was later destroyed. She wasn't on her own for longer than about half an hour, but during that time she must have experienced some terrible things. My grandmother said that from that day she never cried till she reached her adolescence.'

The photo with Magdalena beside Matthaiou. Her hesitancy. Her eyes. The eyes of someone who had seen... And had never forgotten.

'*Die Kirche, die Kirche! Mein Gott, die Kirche!*' 22nd December... *Bar Flaubert*, everything, absolutely everything was in it.

'Do you know where the house was? Do you have an address?'

'I have photos, I don't know, perhaps I have an address somewhere. I'll look tomorrow when we get back to the city.'

I picked up the manuscript again and straightened out the folds in it.

'Three cities,' I said. 'And four villages too. There's another passage, incomprehensible to me, that talks of four villages.'

'Four villages? Somewhere at the end, right?' said Caterina.

I searched for a moment. It was at the end of the book.

I'm coming to the end. Origin's root has stretched back, to the depth of existence. New fruits have sprouted. Earth... Air... Water... Fire... The four elements. The four paintings. And one more with the plaque. That's where I'll go. Back to where I come from. To the four villages. Where the towns tumble down the precipitous slopes. The mountain. Four villages. L.D.S.K. I choose one. The destination. For ever.

'What does he mean? He mentions the four paintings and then talks about a mountain. He says that he'll go there. Where? '*The destination. For ever*'. And those four letters L.D.S.K... I don't understand'

'The three cities and the four villages...' said Caterina.

'*Bar Flaubert*. It's like a hiding place...a hiding place for three cities.'

'Do you think there might be a bar with that name somewhere in the world?' Caterina asked me.

'Perhaps in New York, where your father met Leto. But that's of no concern to us now. We're following the flow of the story. The flow of *Bar Flaubert*. What interests us now is Berlin. Where your mother must still be. Where he left her. It seems he couldn't endure Berlin. Whereas your mother sank into the city, as though blending in with it.'

I put the manuscript down and went over to her. Caterina was crying softly. I put my arms round her and gently caressed her hair.

'We have to go to Berlin as soon as possible,' I said.

Caterina burst into sobs on my shoulder. I needed no answer. It was as though every sob said 'yes'.

I was now well and truly in. Not in the novel. In reality.

Via Ghibellina

The next day, Monday, was the 1st June. Caterina went to the university to arrange her leave. The faculty closed on the twelfth of the month. We decided to leave for Berlin on the Saturday. On Thursday, the fourth of the month, she had her birthday and she wanted to celebrate it with a few friends at her place.

I booked open tickets for Berlin. I found a hotel in the centre of what was formerly West Berlin. It was called the Hotel Funk and was in Fasanenstrasse in the Charlottenburg district. From what the girl at the travel agency had told me, the building had once been the home of Asta Nielsen, the Danish star of the silent movies.

That evening, Caterina invited me for the first time to the house in Via Ghibellina. I arrived at around eight with a bottle of Montalcino. However at number 45 there was no one by the name of Mateo. I noticed that one of the names on the door was that of an architect, Marco Forcelli. I rang his doorbell and, presently, a man of around forty with a goatee appeared in the entrance. He knew Caterina and told me that there were two different systems of numbering in the street. The number 45 I wanted was one of the blue numbers, one block further down. I walked a little and found myself in front of a three-storey house with green doors and windows and with an escutcheon on the facade – not an elephant this time, but a giant tortoise with a snake coiled round it. I looked at the doorbells: Abramo D'Ingillo, F. Leonini, U. Gramosa. C. Mateo, Architect. The flat was on the second floor. I climbed the wide spiral staircase and waiting for me in the doorway to the flat was Caterina, dressed in a blue silk knee-length dress; her hair tied back. We kissed. On the cheek.

The flat in Via Ghibellina bore the mark of its architect tenant. Simple, minimal furnishing, straight lines that ended in sharp curves, few objects, and only three, albeit huge, pictures on the walls.

'Where's *Lent*? Are you hiding it?' I said, laughing.

Caterina smiled and took me to see the rest of the house. There was one room completely taken up by her grandfather's library. I had a quick glance: Goethe, Schiller, Hölderlin, Novalis, Tieck, Heine, Rilke, Trakl, Mann, Musil, everything... Grandfather Hardenberg would have got on great with my father, I reflected. Then we went back into the living room.

'No problem with the faculty. They gave me leave,' she said.

'Great. Saturday morning, we're flying to Berlin.'

'This afternoon I looked at the photos of the house in Germany. I want you to have a look at them too,' she said, handing me a folder.

I opened it. There were five or six photos inside together with some papers, letters and cards. The Hardenberg family house was impressive. Four floors with an attic, a red-brick construction, with large windows and a tile roof, looking more like a summer house than a residence in a large city like Berlin.

'Look at the back of it,' said Caterina smiling. 'Oh! Except that it's in German.'

'Don't worry. I know the language well,' I reassured her. I turned the photo over. A date and an address were written in distinct rounded letters:

'*Our house in the gorgeous summer of 1934, Motzstrasse 45, Berlin, Schöneberg.*'

Caterina had a book with maps of European cities and we located the street. It was at the heart of former West Berlin, to the south of the Tiergarten, the huge park.

'The only clue we have in Berlin. The address of a ruined house...' I said.

'For the time being,' added Caterina with unexpected optimism. 'Do you remember me telling you about Lothar, my mother's cousin? I found his address in Munich, at least the one he left me in 1980, when he came to Florence with his parents. There was a telephone number too. I called, but no one answered. I'll try again. I looked through the rest of my grandmother's papers but I found nothing other than a few letters and cards in German. One card, however, is of some interest.' The letters in the folder were mostly from Munich and sent by Sophia's in-laws with various bits of news but nothing of any importance. Among them, however, was one card with a photo of Brecht. It was addressed to her mother. It had been sent here, to Florence, to the Via Ghibellina. 'That's the one. Let me read it for you,' said Caterina.

Berlin, 14 January 1972

My dear Magdalena,

Greetings from Berlin, I hope you're all okay. Roger and I are up and down, you know how couples are… He's made a series of silver bracelets, superb they are!

Here, a light is starting to appear at the end of the tunnel. Thanks to Willy Brandt and his ostpolitik. And that new president in the East, Honecker, seems more flexible. Did you know that his family lives in Saarland, in south-west Germany? We're hoping for some progress!

Next week Arturo Ui *is being staged with me in the leading role. A lot of stress, a lot of work. I've lost some weight, in the first scene I have to crawl on all fours, like a dog… I played in a film by a young director called Fassbinder, he's only twenty-seven, an enormous talent and quite mad. I've no doubt you'll hear a lot about him in the future. Regards to Loukas, tell him to keep wearing black, like in Venice, it suits him.*

Kiss your little girl for me!

Martin Speer

'Martin Speer. Do you know him?' Caterina asked me.

'No, but it's a name that might be useful to us. He's an actor and I imagine it would be easy to find him.'

'Don't forget that things have changed a lot there since 1970. There was the wall then, the two cities, the cold war… If my parents went to Berlin, no doubt they would have settled in West Berlin.'

'I imagine that your mother must have worked.'

'Perhaps she acted in the theatre, she had something of a name, perhaps she even worked with this Speer... I wonder what she did after my father returned to Greece.'

'Logically, she would have stayed there. If we suppose that they separated in '74, and given that your mother didn't return to Florence to find you, she must have stayed there. Of course, the question still remains, why did she never attempt to communicate...'

'Perhaps she died. The dead don't communicate with the living,' said Caterina in a low voice.

'I think she's alive. And that we'll find her.'

The following afternoon we walked by the side of the Arno. Caterina seemed in good spirits. We passed by the Ponte Vecchio and the Palazzo Pitti and, crossing the Boboli gardens, we arrived at the Forte del Belvedere. From the castle courtyard, the view was enchanting. The day was fading and, above the renaissance finesse of the churches, I saw the Gothic arches of the north taking shape, the dark aesthetics of the third city.

I was getting closer and closer. To that charismatic and dynamic being. I slid between his codes, his paintings and his cities, his streets and his houses. I may have been gazing at the panorama, but I was low down, very low. So low that I could smell the rubbish on the edge of the pavements, feel the damp in the sewers. Crawling with my elbows muddied, I felt I was slowly dragging myself towards Matthaiou. Because I knew that I would find him low down. I saw him leading me through a labyrinthine tunnel that began from the medieval museum and the undulations of Gaudí, passed through the frescoes of the Renaissance and the cypresses of Tuscany and through Flora's flowery gaze, to Berlin, to Europe's palimpsest.

At around seven, we walked down towards the Piazza Santo Spirito. Though it was already the beginning of June, it had begun to drizzle. Caterina felt cold and I gave her my jacket to put on.

When we arrived in the square, the rain was coming down stronger. We went into a café called Cabiria, and we ordered a drink. We sat in the window and looked outside at the facade of a yellow church dominating the square. My shirt was soaking from the rain.

'You look funny being wet like that,' said Caterina smiling. 'That's what's good about you. Sometimes you're like a serious, dynamic man and, at others, you're sweet and funny like a little boy. I don't know you well, but you must be a person who has been different things at different times.'

'Yes, perhaps... But now I want to settle down.'

'Your actions don't suggest it. I don't know many people who because of a handful of paper would set out to wander halfway round Europe. Those aren't choices made by someone who wants to settle down.'

'Perhaps those are precisely the choices made by such a person.' Caterina looked me in the eye. She became serious.

'Yannis, I want you to know how grateful I am for everything you've done. It may be just a wager for you but for me it's my life. You're helping me re-find a part of my life that I'd buried. Thank you,' she said, taking hold of my hand.

A wager? Not any more. A need.

I felt like taking her in my arms and kissing her. But I didn't do it. And more importantly, I didn't regret it.

The story repeats itself

On Thursday night, Caterina invited a few friends round for her birthday. Some colleagues of hers from the faculty, Monica, her best friend from school, who was a primary-school teacher, and Paolo, who was tall, dark and handsome and who looked a lot like Paolo Maldini, the central defender who played for Milan. Paolo was a dentist and from what I could gather was a recent addition to the circle of Caterina's acquaintances. He flirted with her throughout the evening. She didn't pay any special attention to him, though one or two gestures, the tossing of her hair to right and left, a slight coyness in her voice showed that she was flattered by the handsome dentist's attentions. When, at one point, we found ourselves alone in the kitchen, I asked her:

'Where did you meet that tall guy?'

'Paolo? I met him at a Christmas party. He's really nice. So polite.'

'Too much so, if you ask me.'

Caterina said nothing. She stared at me for a moment seriously, and then a grin gradually spread over her face till, not being able to contain herself any longer, she burst out laughing:

'You miss nothing, do you?' And coming up to me, she kissed me on the cheek. 'Come on, let's go and blow out the candles. Wish me happy birthday.'

As I was standing there, with my left foot I lightly pushed the kitchen door to close it. Caterina was exactly in front of me, with her face at the same height as mine. A tuft of hair had fallen over one side her face covering it down to her lips. With my right hand, I brushed it aside, caressed her head and, looking her straight in the eye, slowly moved in till I brought my lips up close to hers and then I kissed her softly. Caterina didn't pull away. There was no passion in our kiss. Her lips accepted mine, her eyes fluttered.

'Happy Birthday,' I said when, almost immediately, I pulled away, and I opened the door only to bump into Paolo, who looked daggers at me. I responded with a smile.

All Caterina's friends gathered round and we all sang the customary song, which sounded even more ridiculous in Italian. Caterina took a deep breath and blew out all twenty-nine candles in one go, as though wanting to put them behind her as soon as possible.

The next day, after writing a little in the second, the Florentine, notebook, I went into the centre to do some shopping. I wandered round various shops and in the end I bought a grey shirt with white stripes and narrow collar and two T-shirts. Quality fabric, exceptional cut, Italian fashion always on the highest rung. While drinking a coffee at Giubbe Rosse, I realized that it was time I had a look at my finances. Of the three million drachmas, there were one million eight hundred thousand left. Barcelona and Florence had cost me one million two hundred thousand. Six hundred thousand for each city I thought. Thankfully, there were only three cities. For the present, at least…

Then my mind turned to Caterina, to the momentary kiss with our bodies almost touching, her half-open eyes, with the double significance of both surrender and surveillance. The assent of a person who is cautious, of a person who has been frightened and who requires time. I mustn't be in a hurry, I thought, I have to let her dictate the rhythm, choose the moments, choose me.

I paid and mixed in with the crowds that had packed the Piazza della Republica that Friday morning. Tourists, dressed in every colour under the sun, with faces dripping sweat and red from the Tuscan sun, hurriedly came and went. They all seemed anxious, as if trying to take in as much Renaissance as possible in as short a time as possible.

In Via de Pecori, the street that led to the Duomo, one fellow dressed as Charlie Chaplin had gathered a crowd around him. He chose kids from the crowd and acted out an improvised scene with them, like a silent one-act play, with the youngsters stealing the show.

Walking towards the church, I suddenly felt a tiredness come over me. I had only slept three hours the previous night and I had been out in the streets since the morning. I decided to go back to the hotel. I was roughly in the middle of the square when I made a sudden about-face to change direction. On turning, I found myself fact-to-face with a man. His hair was red like the roof tiles in Florence. He was wearing a white silk shirt and grey trousers, he was a good bit taller than me and his face was dotted with the characteristic marks left on adults by acne treatment. As soon as he saw me staring, the man immediately looked away and, with a few dexterous movements, mixed in with the crowd to my right, pushed through the tourists and disappeared into the church. For a moment my brain stopped. I knew that man, I had seen him somewhere before... Of course! The image returned vividly. Then, too, he had been wearing a silk shirt, but it was accompanied by a black waistcoat, white gloves and an Anglo-Saxon smile. The red-haired man was Pedro, Ramón Esnaider's butler.

I rushed immediately to the nearest card phone and called Caterina on her cellphone. She was at Monica's. I asked for the address and made it clear that she wasn't to move from there till I arrived. Monica didn't live far away, I was there within fifteen minutes. Caterina was drinking coffee in the living room.

'The story is repeating itself. Esnaider is looking for your father for a second time, in the same place. Of course, indirectly now.

We're the bait and he thinks we'll lead him to him,' I said to her in Greek and told her of my unexpected encounter with Pedro. 'We mustn't go out at all today,' I continued, 'we mustn't risk it. Esnaider won't only have sent Pedro. He most probably also knows about you. Perhaps he's found out that we know each other. Of course, he can't know anything about Berlin. We'll be safe there. If Monica has no objection, I think we should stay here tonight. The flight is at eight tomorrow morning. Ask her to stop by my hotel and your place and pick up our things for us. Whatever jobs you still have to do, do them by phone.'

Though Monica was taken by surprise, she had no problem putting us up for one night. Before she left, I gave her money to pay the hotel.

When we were alone, I noticed that Caterina was alarmed. Her eyes were flickering. It was clear that she was frightened.

'Are you sure that it was him?' she asked me.

'More than sure. You don't forget such faces easily. The man was definitely following me. Who knows for how long. It was a stroke of luck that I found you here.'

Caterina came over and sat beside me.

'We're in this together,' I said, 'together.'

That night, I slept on the couch and Caterina slept in the bedroom with Monica. At six-thirty in the morning, with Florence bathed in the colours of dawn, we were in a taxi heading for the airport.

'This must be how my mother felt. Being chased out of her hometown and leaving for Berlin,' said Caterina sorrowfully as she gazed out of the window at the Arno flowing peacefully.

'Except that there's one difference,' I observed. 'When your mother left Florence, she also left you. You're leaving too, but you're going to her…'

She made no reply.

The Church of Memory

The sky over Berlin

The flight from Florence to Berlin was via Milan. During the first part of the trip, Caterina spoke constantly, she was overcome by an uncontrollable garrulity concerning any issue other than the burning one. Eventually, in order to bring her back to this, I told her how scared I had been when I realized I had one of Esnaider's thugs standing before me:

'The man is ruthless; rich and ruthless. The most dangerous combination.'

'But how did my father get involved with him?' she said, puzzled.

I couldn't hold myself back this time.

'Caterina, your father exercised a strong attraction over people,' I said, 'a strong attraction over both sexes. And Esnaider was used to getting whatever he wanted. Esnaider wanted something from your father. Regardless of the fact that he never got what he wanted…'

'You're extremely discreet. Do you think I haven't understood? What I still can't grasp, however, is that because of all this business I was able to grow up and study without any financial worries. I'll always have Esnaider on my heels, wherever I go.'

'It will come to an end eventually. The two paintings are perhaps still in your father's hands. The third is definitely in Esnaider's possession and I read that *Rave* was found hidden in Salinas's house. It seems that the police searched more thoroughly than the old man's stooges. The Spanish police have opened up the file on the robbery again. Of course, it was so many years ago, but I don't think it will take them long to get to Esnaider. And I hope a certain telephone call from me at the right time might help. But let's forget him for the moment. No one is going to find us in Berlin.'

Caterina stretched her head back. Her veins swelled forming two harmonious lines. I sensed that it was the right moment to ask her something that had been bothering me from the very beginning.

'There's something that I've been wanting to ask you since Florence.'

'What?'

'Did you ever try to find your parents?'

Caterina turned her head suddenly, the veins disappeared and her expression became unexpectedly aggressive:

'Why do you ask that? Do you find it strange that I never tried?'

'I'm not judging you, I simply would imagine that a child who grows up missing his parents would try to find them at some stage.'

'And if the child thinks they are dead?'

'Then he tries to find their grave, he moves heaven and earth to find the two missing pieces. Because to miss something means that you had it and lost it.'

Caterina looked ready to break down. I wondered why. It seemed that, without wanting to, I had touched a nerve.

'If you don't want to talk about it, it doesn't matter,' I said.

Caterina lowered her head and stared in front of her.

'In my life I've always tried to find what I knew to exist, what I could have, not what I didn't know. You're evidently not like that.'

'No, I do the opposite. And in the end I discover that what I thought I knew I didn't really know after all.'

'I didn't really know my parents, Yannis. All I remember are two beautiful figures coming into my room for a while, saying goodnight to me and then leaving. While growing up, I elaborated on those two figures a great deal. And I was frightened how they might look.'

'Frightened?'

'Very. And now that we're getting close – if we're getting close – to them, I'm even more frightened.'

After we'd changed planes, Caterina's mood altered. She adjusted her seat and sat back, covering her ears with the earphones of her walkman. I read an article on the techno scene in Berlin and on the Love Parade, the annual music festival. Then I rested my head against the window and fell asleep. When I opened my eyes, what I saw resembled a painting. We were flying over a stretch of countryside, over a patchwork landscape with red and green squares. The sky had a metallic sheen; you could feel the cold condensed in the atmosphere. Fragments of cloud, plucked remnants from a recent cloudburst were journeying here and there. In the distance, I could make out a grey mass. As the plane got closer, the mass appeared to consist of an array of rusty pipes; nearer still, however, I realized that they were tenement blocks. My field of vision gradually began to fill with tiny clusters of buildings, lower this time, punctuated by ellipses and circles. Soon, the grey gave way to a pale green-brown, as if, as we went further west, the town were acquiring colour, waking up from its concrete stupor and freeing itself from the cement bareness. I saw a sports ground, a railway track, a railway station, a copper-coloured river, a majestic archway, a tall telecommunications tower with a sphere on top and a large expanse of green. Tiergarten, the main park, I reflected. At the same moment, thousands of tiny parallelograms filled the streets. They were moving so slowly that they appeared stationary.

What was most impressive of all, however, amidst this austere arrangement of buildings were the openings, countless openings, gaps between the buildings, as if groups of little boxes had been uprooted from the earth. The empty spaces were surrounded by hundreds of orange cranes, like flamingos snatching their prey from the river. At one point just before the park, there was a large expanse filled with these metallic water fowl, so close to each other that it was as if they were performing a dance routine.

I sat up in my seat and gazed directly below. Stretching out a few hundred feet below me was a huge construction, an endless building site; Berlin, the third city, the European capital of the 21st century.

It was the first time I'd ever set eyes on the birthplace of Caterina's mother. I wondered whether we'd find her. All we had to go on were two names and an address, but a strong intuition told me that the woman was there, in one of those tiny boxes. But in what state?

When Matthaiou left her, her world must have ended. Could she have followed him to Greece? I ruled that out. No, from what I'd gathered, Magdalena wasn't a woman to go to any great lengths to win back her husband. She'd seen the workings of fate when she was still a child.

The very idea of meeting her made me nervous. Unconsciously, I turned and stared at Caterina. She was lost in her earphones. Her cheeks had taken on a ruddy colour. I remembered the rosebushes. Would the twenty-seventh ever be planted?

We were about to land. The ground below seemed to be glistening. A few minutes later, while the plane was approaching the docking bay, I gazed at the ground controller directing the plane with two round signs. Blond, with distinct features. He was looking straight ahead, towards the plane, absorbed in his work. Nothing could distract him, nothing could alarm him. That man would never break into a sweat, I thought, and at that moment, I don't know why, I felt a pang of homesickness. I felt that I had lost my sense of direction, that I was a long way from home, alone in a foreign country. Strange, since this whole business had begun, since setting foot in Barcelona, it was the first time I had thought of Greece. For a moment, I imagined Loukas Matthaiou in my place, twenty-six years earlier, landing at the same airport, with his German-Italian wife at his side, in a strange city, far from his homeland, far from his child, holding an icy breath that for years he'd carried with him.

In half an hour the taxi had taken us from Tegel airport to our hotel in what was formerly West Berlin. The sky was overcast. Light rain was falling. On the way, I gazed at the cranes, from ground level this time. They really did look like huge, gawky birds that had landed in the city and were building their nests out of glass and steel. I didn't see much colour, apart from the red and yellow piping on the roads, especially around Potsdamer Platz, the city's main square, which was being rebuilt from scratch. I remembered the scene from a Wim Wenders film in which an old man is wandering around on the west side of the wall and mumbling: 'Where's Potsdamer Platz? It should be round here somewhere...' The old square was buried exactly beneath his feet.

When we reached the hotel, I helped Caterina with her suitcase. Then I paid the taxi driver, and while Caterina was already on her way to the reception desk, I looked upwards. The sky was overcast, menacing. Yet it wasn't a question of the atmosphere. The threat was clear, plain, as if someone were saying to you outright: 'That's how I am.'

The Sky over Berlin, the actual title of Wenders's film was plain, doric, a name that only a German could have given to a film about angels and cities. The melodramatic nature of the Greek translator had led him to render it differently: *The Wings of Love*. I again looked at the grey section of the universe embracing the section of earth on which I was standing. Wenders must have known something, I reflected.

The bellboy took our cases up to the two single rooms that we had reserved. The atmosphere in the hotel was very congenial, old-worldly, the people here had tried to maintain the place as a pre-war Berlin apartment block would have been.

In my room there was a huge photograph of Asta Nielsen in the film *Vanina*, with a date inscribed on the right: 1922. She was a very lovely woman with striking features, elegant, with the typical dress and make-up of the times, curls, hat, heart-shaped lips the colour of a cherry, a longing look. I went up and at the bottom saw a calligraphic inscription: 'Asta Nielsen: The drunk's vision and the hermit's dream.' Signature: Guillaume Apollinaire. The bellboy informed me that on channel 16 of the TV, I could watch all the major films of the Danish star: *Engelein, Hamlet, Dirnentragoedie, Das Haus am Meer, Freudlosse Gasse...*

'You must see her. She's a goddess!' he urged me.

Presently, Caterina knocked on my door.

'Do you have a photograph of Nielsen too? Verses by Apollinaire, eh? Mine has words by Pabst: "To the greatest actress of the modern age."'

'She's beautiful... Do you know that she played with Garbo in *Freudlosse Gasse*?'

'No, I had no idea that she was so famous,' said Caterina unfolding a map of Berlin and spreading it on the bed.

'Come on, let's get organized. Let's see where we are.'

Our street, Fasanenstrasse, cut across Kurfürstendamm, the central avenue in West Berlin. I looked to see where Motzstrasse was, the street where the Hardenbergs's house was located. It was only a few blocks to the south-east, in the Schöneberg district.

'We're very close,' I said to Caterina, 'we could even go now if you want. It looks about fifteen minutes on foot.'

'All right, but first let me try phoning Lothar again in Munich.'

'Okay. I'll go down and wait for you in reception.'

The receptionist gave me some basic information about the city, where to buy tickets for the metro, the opening times of the shops, of the museums and such like. Soon, Caterina came down with a big smile on her face.

'I found him!' she said. 'He remembered me straightaway. We talked about old times. At present he's staging an exhibition in Munich. But he promised me that he would come to Berlin as soon as possible.'

'I like your enthusiasm "as soon as possible". It seems to me that he's most likely written off your mother. Did you tell him why we're here?'

'Yes. He'd had no news of her at all. But four or five years ago, in a photo from a show in Berlin, an adaptation of a Greek tragedy, he saw a woman who looked like her.'

'Caterina, it all comes down to what the two of us manage to come up with. First we'll exhaust the evidence we have and then we'll see. And something else. This evening, I want us to read a passage from *Bar Flaubert* together, from the beginning of the last chapter.'

'All right. But we're not exactly on our own, don't forget Martin Speer,' said Caterina, meaningfully.

'Of course, there's Martin Speer, too.'

Motzstrasse was a street that was between an avenue and a square. Quiet, green, with plane trees to left and right. The neighbourhood had two playgrounds and was full of life. Boys and girls came and went on their roller skates, older boys on bikes held makeshift races. In front of a yellow phone booth, a group of Asians was waiting stoically in line. A couple of skinheads crossed the street. Behind them was a comical dog with a similar haircut.

Number 45 was a four-storey block with an attic roof and a heavy wooden door. 'Restored,' said Caterina with the air of a specialist. In the basement there was a Greek restaurant with a yellow neon sign: 'Kalamboka'. As we got closer, I saw three people talking in the entrance. In the middle was a pretty little blond-haired girl with blue eyes, a blue dress with white flowers, green sandals and a yellow ribbon in her hair. To her left was a woman with hair the same colour as the girl's – I assumed it was her mother – and to her right was a beautiful slender dark-haired girl, dressed in yellow. The little girl was singing a children's song to the older girl in Greek. Before we reached the entrance, the song ended and the girl said to the little girl, again in Greek, 'That was very nice! Bye Elodi, I'll see you at school,' and then she turned to the mother and said goodbye to her in German. Then she opened the front door and disappeared inside the building before we managed to enter ourselves.

The German woman gave us a strange look, took hold of the little girl's hand and walked off. We looked at the names on the doorbells. Schuller, Kutruff, Zimmermann, Grinberg, no luck… We decided to ring one at random. No answer. The second time, we were greeted with some incomprehensible abuse. The third time, however, a soft female voice answered and when Caterina explained that we were looking for a Frau Mateo or Hardenberg, the door opened.

'Fourth floor,' said the voice.

We climbed the winding staircase to the top, where behind a half-open door, a nice-looking old woman with long hair, dyed blond, was waiting for us. She was wearing a flowery dressing gown and metal-rimmed spectacles.

'Did I hear correctly? Who did you say you were looking for?' she asked us.

'Frau Magdalena Mateo or Magdalena Hardenberg,' Caterina answered.

'I don't know any Frau Mateo, but Hardenberg was the name of the owners of the block. It suffered a lot of damage during the war and they repaired it in the fifties. My husband and I bought this flat in 1955. It's been ten years now since he died. His heart. He didn't suffer at all…'

'Do you remember who it was you signed the contract with?' said Caterina, interrupting her.

'Oh dear, no.'

'It's been such a long time. Did you perhaps ever meet a woman by the name of Magdalena?'

'I remember a young woman, many years ago, she had come here with her husband and she told me she was one of the Hardenberg family. I remember her well, her eyes were so expressive yet frightened at the same time, they seemed so… She wanted to know what had happened to the building. I told her that the Hardenbergs had sold it and left.'

'Was that some time at the beginning of the '70s?' I asked.

'Yes, around then. I remember him too. A handsome…very handsome man. Like Hans in his youth…'

'Did you ever see them again after that?' I persisted.

'No, never. I don't go out very much. It was different when Hans was alive, Berlin was different. The sky was even different then, with Hans. We had a life then, do you understand?'

The sound of meowing came from inside the flat.

'Now, please excuse me, I have to leave you, I have things to do. I live alone.'

'Thank you and sorry if we disturbed you,' Caterina said, and we went back down the stairs.

When we reached the third floor, the door of the first flat on the right half opened and the slender girl I had seen in the entrance poked her head out. Caterina was already on her way down to the second floor. For an instant, we looked each other in the eye. She had an intense, electrifying gaze. I was about to say something to her in Greek, when from inside the flat came the sound of a man's voice. He was speaking German.

'Maria, is alles in Ordnung? Is everything all right?'

'Ja, alles in Ordnung,' said the girl, giving me another look before closing the door.

A Greek girl married to a German. Evidently not 'alles in

Ordnung…' Unconsciously, I reflected what 'Ordnung' there could have been between Matthaiou and Magdalena…

Waters of the black forest

Waters of the black forest, how silent you are. How awesome your silence.

I have come to a new city for a third time. Each time for a different reason. The first time, in order to escape from an afflicted homeland, the second, to save myself, the third time, with a member less, like Franz B. When I leave, I'll be minus two members. Because I'll leave alone. Because she is like them. She grew up with the same dark milk, she lives in the same black houses. But not me. Not me. My soul is liquid, my life flows in transformation.

The people here are unable to dream, they are unable to dream even of their own death. And if they were to dream of a death, it would be a death on earth, a death made of earth. Irreparable, necrosis, an end. I dream of a death in water. I die aqueously, constantly, at every moment. Cut the droplet – blood will run out. Death on earth, death in this place is one-dimensional. Death in water, in my own place, is a death without limit…

'Who's Franz B.?' asked Caterina once I had finished reading.

'When I first read it, I didn't understand either,' I said, 'but from the moment we discovered that the third city is Berlin, I remembered. It must be Franz Biberkopf, the hero of *Berlin Alexanderplatz* by Alfred Döblin. It seems that your father was actually giving us a lot of information. The description of the German mentality, Biberkopf… I should have realized sooner…'

'And this Biberkopf, who is he?'

'He's a bum who, on being released from Tegel prison, wanders around Alexanderplatz doing odd jobs. Then he gets involved with a gang and eventually loses his arm under the wheels of a car.'

'Which arm?'

'The right one,' I said in a low voice.

Silence. Silence filled the room. Caterina was sitting in the armchair, I was reclining on the bed. We stared at each other. I wanted her. I wanted her like mad, from the first moment I had seen her. It wasn't just the circumstances, that she was Matthaiou's daughter, that we had got involved together in this business. It had nothing at all to do with coincidence. It was what I had felt the first time I had set eyes on her in Florence. Some kind of common origin, as though I had known her long ago and we hadn't seen each other for years. Just like with the girl that you were in love with at school, and that you see again years later, only to discover that the old flame not only hasn't gone out, but is stronger than ever. Because that's how I felt about Caterina. I was in love with her. How I wanted, at that very moment, in that foreign city, in that old-worldly hotel, to take her in my arms, to kiss her and tell her how much I loved her, how much I wanted her...

Caterina was in front of me, six feet away, staring into my eyes. She was wholly here, body and soul, and I was staring at her, staring into her eyes and reflecting on all this, reflecting on what her eyes said, and that's how we were, facing each other in silence, and I wanted my love to leave my eyes of its own accord and go and meet her, to travel, to cross those six feet and enfold her, to be turned to liquid by her breath and to pour from end to end over the landscape of her body.

I tried to say something. I was unable. Caterina made an imperceptible movement in my direction and at that same moment I heard myself saying:

'You don't have that mentality. The German mentality, I mean.'

'And how would you describe my mentality?' she asked with some coquettishness.

'Like your father's. A liquid mentality. A liquid that flows and babbles.'

'And murmurs now and again,' said Caterina laughing.

'Yes, and is never stagnant,' I said, continuing the joke.

The atmosphere had changed. We were more at ease now. More at ease and more amorous...

'We have to find Martin Speer,' said Caterina, becoming serious.

Beside the telephone was the directory for Berlin. It was new and had been issued only three months previously. There were two

Martin Speers.The second one must have been the one we wanted.
Speer Martin, Pestalozzistrasse 7, Director-Actor.

It was late, around two in the morning. We postponed the
phone call for the next day and went to bed.

Martin Speer

'Herr Martin Speer? My name is Caterina Mateo, I'm the
daughter of Magdalena and Loukas Mateo, you must know them.'

'Yes, exactly, Magdalena Gentile. I'm in Berlin looking for my
mother. I have reason to believe that, if she's still alive, she may be here.
I didn't grow up with her. I haven't seen her for twenty-six years.'

'Do you know me? Oh, so long… I found your name on a card
that you sent her in Florence, a long time ago.'

'You mentioned something about Fassbinder, Ostpolitik,
someone called Roger…'

It was some time before Caterina spoke again. For the next five
minutes, all she said was the odd 'yes' and 'no'.

'Yes, when the dictatorship fell.'

'Do you know where she is today? It's very im…'

'Yes, I understand.When would you be able?'

'And if not…'

'A Greek, in the bar, okay… And the address?'

'B-Flat. Rosenthalerstrasse 13. In Mitte… Yes, in the East part.
We'll be there at nine.'

'A friend of mine. He started the search in Greece.'

'Me too. Goodbye.'

Caterina put the receiver down. Her eyes were shining; I
understood that the phone call hadn't been in vain.

'So, yes… *Bar Flaubert* – Barcelona, Florence, Berlin.You were
right, my parents came to Berlin from Florence in '72. Speer told
me that they became friends in '70.They had met in Florence; he
was on tour with a German theatre company.When they came
here, they saw each other for a while. My mother worked in
Germany as an actress. Then various things happened that he
couldn't tell me about over the phone. Only in person, he said.'

'And when you asked him if your mother is still here?'

'He told me that she probably does still live here, but that they had lost touch in recent years, that there's some problem and that he must see me as soon as possible.'

'Is the appointment for today?'

'Yes. As you heard, I told him about you too. At nine o'clock this evening at a bar in Mitte, a district in former East Berlin.'

'And how will we recognize him?'

'He'll be sitting in the middle of the bar, he described himself as very fat, with an intelligent face. He'll be wearing braces.'

'The description doesn't seem all that helpful to me.'

'He told me that if by any chance there's a lookalike of him, we should ask the manager of the bar, he's a Greek by the name of Thrasybulus.'

That evening, we took the underground from Unlandstrasse and got out at Hackescher Markt. It was quite warm, I was wearing a white shirt and Caterina an open-back dress. We passed by the area of the same name with the cinemas and bars and before long we found ourselves before a large glass entrance that overlooked Rosenthalerstrasse, a street that was full of clubs and art galleries. The name was printed on the glass front: B-Flat. I smiled at the initials: B-F. It was eight-fifty. There weren't many people in the bar. A trio was playing soft jazz music on the stage. The barstools were occupied by a young couple and two girls wearing tracksuits and a lot of make-up. We went up to the counter. A slim, swarthy-looking man, around forty, was serving. He was Greek: Thrasybulus.

'Greeks, eh? You have an appointment with Martin? He's a regular here... No, he's not been in yet, but he's bound to come. Have a seat and let me offer you a drink.'

Thrasybulus was a photographer, quite well known in the city from what he led us to believe, and with exhibitions abroad too. He only worked as a barman occasionally. 'So I can breathe at night,' he confessed. We struck up a conversation, initially about Athens, then about Berlin, and finally about the Greeks living there.

'The Greek community is a composite one; there are two types of Greeks in Berlin. Those who came in the seventies, immediately following the events of May '68, when the city really was leftist and it attracted politically-active Greeks. But they don't constitute the majority. Most are immigrant workers who came in the sixties and seventies. There are a great many Greeks here. Quite a few are painters and sculptors... There's even a school, called the "European School". It's also open to German kids, who are learning Greek as their main foreign language. Would you believe that?'

I remembered the slender girl in Motzstrasse who had been speaking Greek to the little German girl.

'Oh, Berlin is a very special city,' Thrasybulus went on. 'It's like no other city in Germany. And the inhabitants are not your typical Germans. Those who lived here, when the Wall still existed, constituted a special caste of people. Those who weren't happy with life living in the West German economic miracle. Artists and students came in droves, living here was cheap then. Before the Wall fell, Berlin was a place where no one could stay for very long. It was a platform, an island.'

'So did the fall of the Wall completely change things?' I asked.

'Not exactly... The unification may have been signed on paper, but the reality is quite different. Take, for example, this area, Mitte. It's an area inhabited by former West-Germans and former East-Germans. They still have a lot of problems with each other, a lot of differences. Don't forget that the *Ossies*, as the West-Germans disparagingly call the East-Germans, have grown up in that wretched system known as state socialism – God help them.'

Thrasybulus suddenly stopped, turned his eyes to the door and said:

'There's Martin, he's arrived.'

The adjective that came to mind when I first set eyes on Martin Speer was 'enormous'. He was around sixty, over six foot five, and with a huge belly that stuck out ostentatiously. He was wearing a white shirt and corduroy trousers held up by a pair of colourful braces and he had a shoulder bag. His face was swollen, with the characteristic puffiness of the chronic beer-drinker. It was a face in which two things stood out: a sensuous mouth and two bright blue eyes, huge and alert, that swept the area with tremendous self-assurance. Two eyes that were childlike and demonic at the same time, as they blinked beneath thin, curved eyebrows, carefully plucked with tweezers. He had realized who we were and he came up to us with a smile. He reminded me of someone.

'Hallo!' he said in a deep, singing voice. 'Thrasy, beer.'

Martin accommodated his enormous bulk on a bar stool with an incredible agility given his weight. Then he took a large pipe from his bag, a cigarette and a small black slab resembling a bar of soap. He opened the cigarette and took out the tobacco. Then he put it in the pipe. Next he took the slab and, using a penknife, began to shave it. And he did all this in silence, without addressing a word to us. He collected together the shavings and put them in his pipe together with the tobacco from the cigarette. He lit the mixture, drew on it deeply, and when he considered that the ritual had ended, he tossed his head back with a theatrical gesture and turned his gaze to Caterina.

'So you're Magdalena's daughter?' he asked.

'Yes, you must be Martin.'

'Martin Speer. Speer, as in Hitler's architect, Martin, as in Luther King,' he said, letting out a shrieking laugh that was in complete contrast with his voice. Then he brought his face close up to Caterina's. Their noses were almost touching.

'My dear girl, you may or may not believe it, but I've held you dancing in my lap!'

Thrasybulus brought a huge glass brimming with beer. Martin didn't react immediately as I had expected. On the contrary, he barely wet his lips, letting out a sigh of satisfaction.

'Beer, beer, lovely. So, my dear, I won't beat around the bush. Your mother and I were very close friends. We were colleagues in every sense of the word. I also knew your father well. Loukas, what a fine-looking chap! Adonis… When we went to bars, the whole of Berlin would stare at him. Men and women. What a temperament! Your father was an aggressive type and I liked that. He was like me… But your mother didn't like it at all,' he said, lowering his voice.

'Could you please tell us how you first met Caterina's parents?' I said, interrupting him.

Martin turned and stared at me. He looked me up and down for a moment as though I were some kind of exotic bird and then after an embarrassing silence – embarrassing from my point of view, that is – his words crushed me:

'And you, dear, who might you be? Her lover boy?' And turning to Caterina: 'He's not for you, darling, Loukas's daughter deserves better than an impatient little boy. She deserves a man who's balanced. In all respects...'

Martin missed nothing, it seemed. I was about to say something, but I held back. Martin Speer was the most precious contact we had in the city and, whether I liked it or not, I reconciled myself to the fact that communicating with him wasn't going to be easy.

'I'm not her lover boy, I'm a friend,' I said in a firm voice.

'Well, you don't seem gay to me. So you simply haven't had the guts to make a play for her yet. Anyhow, whoever you are, listen to what I have to say: In the early seventies I was with the company on tour in Italy. What were we playing then? Oh, yes, *Macbeth*. I was Macduff. In Florence, Magdalena came to my dressing room after the performance. Alone. We liked each other immediately. She was a charming woman then, but very insecure, highly-strung. She had that insecurity of women who have chosen a man with a stronger character. They know right from the start that they're not going to have an easy time with him, but there's some kind of force, something preventing them from walking away. In your mother's case, and I know this for a fact, what she saw as a little girl in the war played a part. She wanted a strong man beside her. And she chose the one who seemed to her to be the strongest. But Loukas wasn't only strong, he was also a magnet. He attracted people almost against their will, and when they opened themselves to him, he brought them face to face with their innermost feelings, with their most secret fears. Even me. He's the only person who has ever made me cry in front of him like a little child. Loukas as a man, as a person, was inexorable, do you understand?'

Martin stopped for breath and this time took a large swig of beer.

'So, in Florence, after meeting Magdalena, I also met Loukas and they invited me to stay in their house in Chianti, in the country. I remember you too, you were just a baby then, a very sweet little baby, with protruding teeth and freckles. We had a good time. We even went on trips together. I remember one time in Venice, I had won a good bit of money in the casino playing odds and evens. We went through it all in a few days. Good years, I was in love... Roger has been dead for five years now, twenty-four years together, we were just starting out together then... I have everything at home, whatever he left, rings, bracelets, diamonds; he was a jewellery designer. I remember how jealous he was, he thought I liked Loukas. Roger was black, twenty years older than me. Loukas was white and the same age. One evening, out of jealousy, he emptied a bottle of beer over me! We got on well then all of us. And I got on particularly well with Loukas. We shared the same views on lots of issues. Especially when it came to politics. And he was a wonderful soul! Even Fassbinder liked him! When he met him in Venice, he wanted him to play in one of his films. But Loukas would hear nothing of it. About two years later, I was back here in Berlin. One evening the phone rang. It was Magdalena, who said, "We've come to Berlin and we're going to stay here."

"Why, what's happened?" I asked her.

"We had trouble in Florence, just the two of us are here, we left the child at my mother's and we'll see what we're going to do." At first, she told me that Loukas had had problems with his residence permit, later, after he had left, she told me the truth. You know the truth, Caterina, don't you? Because for you to be here, you must know it.'

'The truth? I know enough. What truth are you referring to?'

Martin looked behind the bar and when he was certain that Thrasybulus was occupied with another customer, he said in a low voice:

'I know, Caterina, I know everything. Everything, about the robbery, about the paintings, and about that Spaniard – what was his name? – Snaider?'

'Esnaider,' I said.

'Esnaider, dear,' said Martin and, turning to Caterina, added, 'I know everything, but don't worry, I haven't said anything to anyone. I want you to know that your parents were my friends. And

I love my friends. Besides, I haven't had many in my life. And now it's your turn. I'm all ears,' and he sat back, causing his huge belly to hang over the stool.

Caterina briefly recounted her own story together with what she had learned from me. Martin took it all in greedily. Every so often he came out with thunderous exclamations or broke into shrieks of laughter. Laughter that for a moment reminded me of Arnold. Yes, he was the one who Martin reminded me of; Arnold Hansen, except that Martin had something rough and dangerous about him. If Arnold still had something in his old age, something of the carefreeness of the American Beats, Martin was a living remnant of the German revolutionary avant-garde of the seventies, a tough cookie of the kind that knows nothing of compromise. Martin's revolutionariness, though expressed through art, had no romanticism in it. In his case, there was not the heroism of the outsider, but the absoluteness of the rebel. Just him and the enemy. A fight that was without mercy. Of the two, only one would reach the end. And Martin gave the impression of a person who had looked the end in the eye. And was still alive.

Caterina got to the point where we had visited Motzstrasse:

'That's more or less what I know. The question is what to do now. Whether you can help us. On the phone you told me that my mother is living in Berlin. Do you know where?'

'Hold on, darling,' said Martin in an unexpectedly tender tone of voice. 'You've just told me a tale of wonders. Dear little thing… So in the end they left you entirely alone. I wouldn't have thought that. As regards Magdalena, I'll explain to you. But him… And he wrote it all in that novel? Even about his first love. Magdalena had told me, the poor thing had understood everything. It's not easy to be married to a man who hasn't got over his first big love. Yes, I remember, Loukas was always writing, but he would never show what he wrote to anyone.'

'So where is she?' Caterina asked again impatiently.

'Now? I don't know exactly. I've been here for six months, working on a Berliner Ensemble production of Brecht's *Arturo Ui*, arranged by my late friend Heiner Müller. It's been five years since I last saw your mother. But don't worry. She must still be here, we'll find her. But let's get back to the point where we left off,' said Martin. He downed another swig of beer and continued, 'Loukas and Magdalena lived for about two years in Berlin. From the autumn of '72 to the summer of '74. They rented a marvellous penthouse in Knesebeckstrasse, near Savignyplatz, in West Berlin. When Loukas left, your mother suffered a nervous breakdown. She began drinking, drinking even more than me. For a while we lived together, your mother, Roger and I. She was still able to work then. We even played together in some productions. Your mother was a fine actress. And, strangely enough, when she had the breakdown she became an even better one. But she had begun to lose her mind. Together with her looks. She drank from the morning, hard liquor, her face swelled, she grew fat… And in her private life she did things, dearest, that not even Uncle Martin, who's not the most ethical creature in the world, would want you to know. Naturally, she could no longer play the ingénue. So she played character roles, supporting roles, a whore in one of Fassbinder's films. And she did all this using a stage name. Ursula Link. I still remember it. What an idiotic name!

As for you, at first, when Loukas left, she wanted to bring you to Berlin. But then she had a change of heart: 'I'm ashamed, afraid… How can I let my child see me like this?' she said. 'I'm not even able to take care of myself, how can I raise a child?' And as for Loukas, not a word. He may have sent you money every year, but he left his wife a hundred thousand marks and that was all. Not that it was a small amount, but she had gone through it all inside two years. And not on her own.

When the friendship the three of us had came to an end, in desperation, she even went to Greece to find her husband. She combed the whole of Athens, but found nothing. By the end of the seventies, she was in a bad way. I was always having to take her in and out of hospital. That went on for several years, detoxification, relapse, naturally she had no steady work. The woman gradually fell apart.

Meanwhile, in '88, I had an offer to direct a play in Greece. I was invited by a Greek actress who had just opened a theatre. I was six months in Athens. I had a fantastic time. I went to various gay bars in Kolonaki, to Alexandros, I think that was the name of it.

While I was in Athens, I tried to find Loukas. I searched everywhere, but without any success. And when I say that I searched everywhere, I mean that I left no stone unturned in night-time Athens. Omonia, Syngrou, Kolonaki... I remember it all as though it were yesterday. I wasn't so fat then.

Within a year of my returning, the Wall fell. At that time Magdalena was working as an usherette in a two-bit cinema. She had changed her name to Hardenberg some time before and was living in a tiny hovel. I managed to find her a small flat in an old block in Kreuzberg. Though it was small, at least she was able to live there with some dignity. Later, I was told that she left that place too.

Two months after Roger died, at the beginning of '93, I had a problem with my blood. I became ill. I was in hospital for a whole year and when I came out, I looked for your mother. I was unable to find any trace of her for a long time. Eventually, however, I found out that she was playing in a TV production. It was an adaptation of an ancient Greek tragedy, *Hippolytus*, I think. I got her phone number from the production company, and I called her. At the other end of the line I heard a voice that sounded as if it was coming from the depths of a cave. At first she didn't recognize me. Then she started to cry, she told me she lived in Prenzlauer Berg, in former East Berlin. Then she told me something I didn't expect to hear: "Luca phoned me."

'How did he find you?' I asked her.

'Nothing's impossible for Luca,' she replied.

Amid cries and sobbing, I understood that Loukas had in fact phoned her after twenty years. But all he wanted to know was whether she had news of their child, of you. From what I gathered, Magdalena must have spoken very badly and put the phone down on him. "I'm afraid of him," she told me, "he's a black bat with green eyes, I see him every night, he's trying to get into the house," she said crying all the time.

At one point I asked her exactly where she lived, saying that I wanted to see her as soon as possible. Then she began to get angry and started swearing: "Leave me alone," she cried. "Leave me alone, I want to be alone," and she hung up. I wanted to look for her but my health still wasn't good. When I was completely recovered, I had to leave Berlin for professional reasons. I lived in Dusseldorf for about three and a half years. Since then I've had no contact with her.

When I returned here six months ago for the Berliner Ensemble production, I phoned her. The man who answered the phone told me that Frau Hardenberg no longer lived there. And I didn't try to find her again after that.'

'Did you find out the address, Herr Speer?' I asked.

'No,' Martin answered, in a serious tone this time. 'We can find the address, the question is whether the new tenants will know where she went. And, my dear friend,' he went on, addressing himself to me, 'don't take everything to heart. You don't have to be so formal with me. Call me Uncle Martin,' and he shrieked with laughter.

'Do we have any other sources? Do you know if she had any friends? Perhaps from work?' asked Caterina.

'Friends no, Magdalena didn't have any. Various people came in and out of her life, but it was of no consequence. After a certain point, she was no longer able to have a normal relationship with people. But there's no point in our looking here, there and everywhere. We have to act methodically,' said Martin, who seemed to have begun to get excited at the prospect of joining in the search for his old friend.

'First, and I'll do it right now, I'll phone the house in Prenzlauer Berg, I have the number in my address book. I'll ask whether they know anything, where she moved to and so on. Then we'll go there. The three of us. I can't tomorrow morning, I have filming for the TV. We'll go the next day, Tuesday. A little patience and we'll get somewhere.'

Martin jumped down from the stool like an overweight cat and made a beeline for the phone booth. I shouted to Thrasybulus and ordered another round of drinks.

'A proper steamroller, isn't he?' said Thrasybulus, winking at me.

When he returned, Martin was holding a piece of paper.

'This time a woman answered, who told me that she didn't know where the previous tenant had moved to. But living in the block is a friend of Magdalena's, a certain Max Elsner, who helped her to move her things. We'll ask him. The address is Pasteurstrasse 35 in Prenzlauer Berg.'

We stayed at the bar all evening, Martin downed another five or six beers, smoked almost the whole of the black slab, told us a pile of blue jokes and, towards the end of the evening, invited us to go and see him playing Göring the following evening in the Berliner Ensemble production of *Arturo Ui*.

'Tomorrow is a special performance. I'll have seats for you in the front box. VIPs!' he said with grandiloquence.

In the hotel hallway, Caterina said to me with tears in her eyes:

'I'm scared. I'm scared of what I might find. I want so much to meet her, but I'm scared.'

'I put my arms around her. 'Caterina, I understand…'

And immediately, the opposite reaction:

'Why wait till Tuesday? Let's go tomorrow, today!'

'Better if we go with Martin. You don't know what we might run into…'

'And that Martin scares me too.'

'I think he's nicer than he seems. Patience. We're getting close.'

I looked into her eyes. We were in each other's arms outside her door and staring at one other. Her mouth half-opened. The next moment flashed through my mind. My lips deep in hers. From the next room came the sound of grunting from the television. Obviously some people were not taking advantage of the silent masterpiece with Asta Nielsen. As though wanting to bring the evening to an end, Caterina stretched her neck and gave me a gentle kiss, barely touching my lips. At the same time she whispered:

'Yannis, there's a lot going on …'

And turning round, she opened the door of her room.

'Goodnight.'

'Goodnight,' I said in a low voice and went towards my room. I went to bed with her words tearing into my sleep like a knife, 'Yannis, there's a lot going on …'

Arturo Ui

The Berliner Ensemble canteen is in the basement of the building; the entrance is from the theatre yard. We had an appointment half an hour before the performance so that Martin could get us into the box. The interior was like any other German beer house, except that in this case the majority of the customers were the actors who were having a beer before they went on stage. A number of them were dressed in their costumes. Across from us, a slender forty-year-old with a rugged, angular face, dressed in an army uniform, was sipping his beer and staring in front of him with a vacant gaze.

'He must be playing Goebbels,' I said to Caterina.

At the table to the left of the entrance, a tall, blond thirty-year-old with sunglasses, quite clearly the worse for drink, and surrounded by a group of red-faced Germans, was improvising on the saxophone. Every so often he would stop, put the saxophone down on the table, and greedily drink his beer out of a large mug.

'I know him from somewhere,' said Caterina at precisely the moment that the door opened and Martin's portly figure appeared, dressed more or less as he had been in the bar: white shirt and corduroy trousers with braces.

Martin came over to our table and said good evening. As soon as he saw him, the saxophone player got up and, almost falling over, came up to us and fell into his arms.

Martin sat him in a chair and turned to us.

'This is Axel Hausen. His father may be a great musician, but he's a rare talent too. We'll be working together on the Berliner's next production in the autumn, Axel has orchestrated German lieder. I'll be singing. Just look at him! Pretty as a baby, isn't he?'

'Hello, boys and girls!' said Axel in a drunken drawl.

'Axel, get yourself a cup of black coffee and we'll talk after the performance, you'll come with us to eat, okay? Now the two of you follow me and I'll take you to the boxes,' said Martin, turning to Caterina and me.

As Caterina was getting up, Axel grabbed hold of her arm:

'You, darling, you sit with me, I'll play for you.'

'Cut the crap, Axel,' Martin shouted out loud and the whole canteen turned and stared at us.

'Stay here with me, darling, you'll have a much better time. Why go and waste your time with those faggots,' Axel said again, taking off his glasses. Two lovely eyes, blue and intoxicated, stubbornly fixed on Caterina, who was obviously embarrassed. Axel put his arms round her and tried to kiss her.

And then something happened that I hadn't expected. Instead of intervening, Martin turned and looked at me. His gaze was hard. I understood in a fraction of a second. I stepped forward, grabbed Axel by the collar and slapped him across the face. More out of surprise than from the force of the blow, he collapsed onto his chair.

'That's what I mean by balance, my lad,' Martin said to me as the three of us headed towards the door.

Arturo Ui on all fours, like a dog, with his tongue dyed bright red, grunting, barking, talking as a dog with a human voice would talk. And then, on the enormous stage: Eva Braun, a tall blond, with a narrow face and wide hips; Goebbels or Roma, as he was baptized by Brecht, the forty-year-old with the rugged features, and finally, Göring – Giri in the play – played by Martin, with a look of the devil in his eyes. It was a magnificent production. And the actors… The leading actor, a true theatrical creature, also called Martin, constructed his character with absolute mastery. And our Martin looked at the audience with the same icy gaze that he had fixed on me in the canteen just a while earlier.

The performance ended to a shower of applause. I counted eight curtain calls before the actors finally withdrew.

Later, in the canteen, Speer organized the evening. We would go out to eat with virtually the whole of Hitler's General Staff: With Arturo Ui, played by Martin Rutke; Eva Braun, real name Carlotta Bach; and Goebbels, Heinrich Bayer. As for Axel, he was sleeping on two chairs in a drunken stupor still clutching his saxophone. Martin and the two of us went in Carlotta's car, a Chevrolet that she had just bought. We headed for the heart of former West Berlin. The restaurant was in Savignyplatz, one of the most chic parts of Berlin

It was a scintillating evening. The German actors were incredibly relaxed and unassuming. Throughout the meal, they hardly spoke about the theatre at all. Only Carlotta recalled some moments with Heiner Müller; the writer had died in her arms. Carlotta and Müller had been together during his last years. The evening continued pleasantly. Heinrich spoke enthusiastically to me about ancient Greece. Martin Rutke told Caterina jokes, and our Martin surveyed everyone at a safe distance from behind his curved pipe – which was full of tobacco and black shavings. The reading glasses made him look like a distant critic, like an observer who missed nothing.

Prenzlauer Berg

Prenzlauer Berg is a working-class district with drab buildings. People were walking on the streets with seemingly dejected expressions, quite different from the people in the centre. Speer had warned us: 'Prenzlauer Berg is a district in former East Germany.'

Martin was waiting for us at the underground station. We walked together as far as Pasteurstrasse, passing in front of identical grey boxes, till we reached our destination. Number 35 was a grey multi-storey block of flats, built so as to be free on all sides. Twelve floors. As we entered the building, we were obliged to stoop under a construction of planks that someone, who knows why, had fixed as a form of escutcheon over the door. In the hallway, which was full of torn sports pages and cast-off beer cartons, was a crumpled poster of Oliver Bierhoff, the centre-forward of the German national team. On our right were the letterboxes. We looked for the name Max Elsner. It was the third in the top row. 'Max Elsner, 6th floor.' We began climbing the stairs. A strange smell, a mixture of sourness and alcohol, pervaded the place. Huffing and puffing, Martin stopped on every landing to catch his breath and to curse at the same time. On reaching the 6th floor, we found ourselves before a door with the sign: 'Max Elsner – Sociologist'. Above it was a piece of paper on which, written in elegant handwriting, were the words: 'When everything is going well, do not forget that nothing obliges it to be that way – Gottfried Keller'.

Martin rang the bell. No answer. He rang again two or three times. Just as we were about to leave, the door half opened, as far as the chain allowed. One third of an unshaven face appeared in the gap.

'Who is it?' asked the unshaven face.

'We're friends of Magdalena Mateo or Hardenberg,' said Martin and, pointing to Caterina, added, 'this is her daughter.'

The unshaven face peered in order to include Caterina in its field of view.

'Wait a moment,' the man said. Five minutes passed till we heard the door opening with a creaking sound. Standing in the doorway was a thin man, around fifty, with a hollow face and long hair that appeared not to know the meaning of shampoo. He was wearing spectacles and was dressed in a white vest and threadbare army trousers.

'Come in, I'm Max,' he said, showing us inside. The flat was just one room with a kitchenette in one corner. There was no bathroom to be seen; I supposed that the toilet in the hallway must have been a shared one. The walls were covered with bookshelves reaching to the very top of the high-ceilinged room. Where there were no books, the space was covered with political posters, ranging from Che to Greenpeace. A photo of Petra Kelly was hanging over the washbasin.

'Can I offer you something to drink?' asked Max.

'What do you stock?' said Martin ironically.

'What would you like?' Max asked again.

'Mojito! Do you know how to make it?'

'Mojito… Of course. Take a seat,' said Max and quickly went over to a cupboard and took out a bottle of rum and half a dozen lemons that he cut first into halves and then into quarters. Then he took a handful of mint and chopped it up. He put the rum, lemons and mint in a shaker and mixed them. Then he served the drinks in four tall glasses, adding crushed ice.

Martin tasted it first.

'How do you find it?' asked Max.

'Too little rum, too much lemon,' said Martin, pointing to the lemon peel and adding, 'And now, Herr Elsner, down to business. We are trying to find Frau Hardenberg. The tenant in the flat where she used to live told us that you helped her move. Were you friends?'

'Friends? No, I wouldn't say that. I liked her. Frau Hardenberg was a very troubled woman. I imagine you know that…' and turning to Caterina, he said, 'Did you say that the girl is her daughter?'

'Yes,' said Caterina. 'I'm her daughter.'

'Magdalena never spoke to me about you.'

Caterina was about to say something but checked herself.

'We know that you helped her move. Do you have her present address?' I asked.

'Yes, of course. Knackstrasse 33. It's not far from here, in Prenzlauer Berg. She went to live with a friend of hers.'

'With a friend of hers?' said Martin in astonishment.

'Yes, three months before she left, Magdalena met a man; his name was Volker Eimer. He worked in the Berlin National Library. Strange sort. He didn't say very much. But it seems they got on together and Magdalena decided to go and live with him. Besides, she didn't have much money and in her situation she needed someone to take care of her.'

'What do you mean? What situation?' asked Caterina.

'Frau Hardenberg had many problems, many problems and chronic ones...' said Max faltering. 'But didn't you know? You said you were her daughter.'

'I said I was her daughter, but I haven't seen her since I was three.'

'Fraulein, what can I say. Better for you to go and see her for yourself. But be prepared, Frau Hardenberg, your mother, is a very troubled woman.'

We didn't stay long in Max's flat. The sociologist didn't appear to have any more information concerning Magdalena. Martin downed one more mojito – with a double measure of rum this time – and we left, with Caterina holding a bit of paper with her mother's address, which was in the same neighbourhood, only fifteen minutes away on foot.

Magdalena

Tuesday, 9th June. Knackstrasse 33. A similarly grey apartment block, in slightly better condition. The street was quiet. Caterina examined the doorbells. The second one down in the second row said 'Volker Eimer'. Martin and I stood a little further back. I felt like a stranger, an intruder. There was a humming in my ears. Like a volume of water stirring. I looked at her. Caterina appeared calm. She rang the bell. Absolute silence. Uncomfortable, Martin was gazing into the sky. Caterina rang again. Silence. A boy crossed the empty street on a bike. He turned and looked at us. My legs felt like jelly. The deep voice of a man broke the silence:

'Who's there?'

'I'd like to see Frau Hardenberg, please?'

'Who are you?' asked the voice.

'My name is Caterina Hardenberg, I'm her daughter.'

Silence. There was no sound from the intercom. I looked up. The dull Berlin sky made no reply. In the distance the sound of a police car could be heard. Then, presently, the man's voice again:

'Is it Frau Hardenberg you want? Magdalena Hardenberg?'

'Yes.'

From the intercom came a screeching sound, an out-of-tune wind instrument splitting the silence. Martin and I stood motionless, glued to the spot. Caterina pushed the door open. Without speaking, we climbed the two floors. The block appeared empty. On the first-floor landing a scrawny cat suddenly jumped out in front of us. None of us was startled. At least no one showed it.

The corridor was dim. The walls had the characteristic signs of damp. A man was standing in the doorway of the second door on the left. Caterina went first, with me behind and Martin bringing up the rear.

The man was of average height, thin, with a crooked nose and sparse, uncombed grey hair. He was wearing a threadbare pair of jeans and a loose white T-shirt. I noticed his hands. They were dirty as though he had just left off doing some repair work. A red scar, like a burn, was visible on his left cheek.

Caterina went up to him.

'Herr Eimer?'

The man nodded.

'Caterina Mateo. This is Mr Loukas and Herr Speer.'

'Mateo? You gave me another name over the intercom,' said Eimer and a cautious expression spread over his face.

'Yes, I said Hardenberg, my grandfather's surname. My name is Mateo, the surname of my father. Frau Hardenberg is my mother.'

'Magdalena's daughter… She never said anything to me about a daughter. What do you want exactly?' said Eimer somewhat aggressively.

Martin stepped in front of me and stood beside Caterina, beneath the dim lamp in the corridor, so that the man could more easily see him.

'My name is Martin Speer. I am an old friend and colleague of Frau Hardenberg. I knew her long before you did. Don't be alarmed. All we want is to see Magdalena for a little while. To have a little chat with her.'

The expression on Eimer's face changed again. This time, becoming more friendly.

'Martin Speer! But, of course, I know you! I've seen you at the cinema, in some Fassbinder films! *The Year of the Thirteen Moons*…and just recently, only a week ago, I saw you with the Berliner Ensemble, in *Arturo Ui*! Wonderful performance! I'm very fond of the theatre. But Magdalena doesn't come with me, she doesn't have the strength. She's ill, you know, poor thing. She's ill and she has no one…' And turning to Caterina, he added, 'Wait here a moment. I'll go and see.'

The door closed, again leaving just the three of us in silence in the dark corridor. Across the way, the door of the neighbouring flat half opened. An old woman glanced at us from behind the chain before again shutting the door.

About five minutes passed. From inside the flat came the sound of creaking furniture and a strange noise, as if someone was spraying.

The door opened wide and Eimer again appeared in the doorway. He had hastily combed his hair and was evidently in a better mood.

'Step inside,' he said, addressing himself primarily to Martin. We passed through a white hallway and entered a large room.

The living room was painted pomegranate-red. The place smelled strange. A combination of mint and alcohol, as if someone had sprayed a basement bar with cheap air freshener. A chandelier, with only one bulb in it, dimly lit the place, creating a variety of red hues. To the left was an iron cabinet with glass shelves containing carefully arranged miniatures of animals. A tiny elephant caught my eye. Porcelain. To the right was an oval-shaped wooden cage, but without any bird inside. Beside it was a black and white television, switched on, with a fuzzy picture. At the far end was a yellow couch. Seated on this was a stocky woman. You could see her back and long blonde hair. In front of her was a coffee table with a half-empty bottle of vodka, a half-eaten cake and, beside this, six blown-out black candles.

Eimer went over, treading softly.

'Magdalena, Herr Speer... He's here to see you...'

The woman turned slowly round. We were standing in the middle of the living room. Martin walked towards the couch. Red streaks like gashes fell across Magdalena Hardenberg's face. It was a face on which two opposing forces had fought. There were indelible traces of the struggle on the battlefield. The skin crumpled, the red marks of the wet steamroller round the eyes, the nostrils dilated. The only thing left of the sweet little girl from *The Garden of the Finzi-Contini* was the now artificial colour of her hair. Her facial features had disappeared beneath her swollen cheeks, the eyes had shrunk to a gaze that didn't focus, the mouth, now contorted, left a row of sparse teeth showing behind the marble lips that were caked in red lipstick. With obvious effort, the woman raised herself up on her elbows.

'Martin, is that you?' asked Magdalena Hardenberg in a weak, croaking voice.

'Yes, Magdalena. It's me.'

'Come closer, Martin, I can't see you very well. I'm growing old. I'm sixty today, Martin, sixty.'

Martin knelt down next to Magdalena and took her hand in his.

'I know,' he said, 'I know, and I've brought you a present, Magdalena, a present for your birthday.'

'Present, Martin, what present?'

Martin motioned to Caterina to go over.

'I've brought you one of your own family, Magdalena. Happy birthday,' he said, getting up and taking a few steps back.

Now facing each other, the two women looked into each other's eyes. I felt my body drifting, out of control.

Magdalena gave her daughter a scrutinizing look, at least as best she could from behind her drooping eyelids:

'Who are you?'

Caterina spoke softly, steadily:

'I'm your daughter, Caterina.'

I felt as if the room had flooded with water and Martin, Eimer and I were holding onto the chandelier and trying to stay afloat. Underneath, on the floor, mother and daughter, creatures of the deep, were arm in arm. I remembered. Before leaving for Florence. It wasn't water then. It was blood; up to the ceiling. I was drowning. We were all drowning.

The old woman's eyes opened wider. The veins in her neck tightened.

The text, soaking wet, was floating.

...Shadows, shadows that come and go. Others, other places, other times. They go from one city to the next. Seeking. People. Fashioning. People. An endless line, people succeed one another, wide-open. The one shadow stoops over the other and begets it. And me? I'm a light without a shadow that always falls on the same spot, ever silent...

Magdalena made a sudden movement with her hand over the table. The cake fell on the floor:

'Daughter... What daughter! I never had any children!'

I remembered how Caterina had spoken to me in Florence about the terrible half-hour bombardment.

Then the text. The testimony. The words like water through the fingers.

...She woke in a sweat. 'What's wrong?' I asked her.
She covered her face with her hands. Her voice came out stifled. It was the first time I'd heard about it:
'Black smoke everywhere. Noise. Huge balloons bursting. I'm running. It's winter. Invisible stones whistle above my head. 22nd

December. Christmas in three days' time... I must hide. A huge black balloon falls on the church. 'Die Kirche, mein Gott, die Kirche!...' A car. Black; burnt. I have to hide. Underneath. My mother, where's my mother? I get down. Hide myself. A voice beside me. Liquid. A liquid spreads over my dress. Stains it. Red liquid on a white dress. I reach out my hand. A face. A faint voice. I turn round. She's like me. Her face dirty, a yellow ribbon in her hair. Brown eyes, like mine. She has no legs. No, no legs... She says... says something...

'What's your name? What's your name?'

'Me... My name's Katrina. Ka...tri...na...' in a voice dying away... away... away... .

It was the first time it had happened to her in my presence. There'd be dozens more.

She fell silent. Now she stared straight ahead, without speaking. I imagined the scene.

Evening. Winter. 20th century. On the cobbles the shame, the tiny broken limbs, the thing-man.

'I never had any children!'

Magdalena tossed her head back and remained still. She seemed to be asleep. Her arms remained in front of her stomach, unnaturally extended, as if they had turned to marble. Caterina knelt down and rested her head on her mother's breast.

I looked around me. Martin, yes Martin, was quietly crying. Eimer stared at me in astonishment. Two or three minutes of agonizing silence went by. Water everywhere. No oxygen. We were drowning.

Caterina slowly got up. She came up to me, looked me in the eye. There wasn't a sound in the room. Only drops falling. Tiny cold drops. Inside me.

'What right did you have to do that to me?' she said quite icily. I couldn't speak. I was drained.

Light without a shadow that always falls on the same spot, ever silent...

Eimer took a blanket and covered Magdalena. Martin wiped his eyes. Caterina came closer to me and, with a sudden movement, hugged me tightly:

'Sorry, Yannis, sorry...'

She went over again to her mother. Magdalena seemed to be asleep. Her breathing was heavy. It appeared as though she were cut off from her surroundings. Caterina picked up the cake from the floor, took the bottle of vodka, went into the kitchen and threw them into the waste bin.

Then she turned to Eimer:

'Make sure she gets some rest today. Let her sleep as long as she wants. I'll come back tomorrow morning. At ten. Alone. I'll stay as long as necessary. She's my mother.'

Then she picked up the six candles that had fallen on the floor, folded them up in a paper napkin, put them into her bag, and continued:

'If you want anything, I'll be at the Hotel Funk. My name is Mateo. Caterina Mateo,' and, turning to us, she said, 'Come on, let's go.'

I opened the door mechanically. Once outside in the corridor, I felt a hand pulling me out of the water. It was a soft and familiar hand. Like my mother's.

We walked in silence through the streets of Berlin. Strangely enough, it was Martin who was in the worst state. Perhaps I'd made a mistake. There were some cracks after all in this hard German. We put him into a taxi and continued walking till the tenement blocks gave way to well-preserved old buildings and the empty lots to tree-lined squares. It was Caterina who broke the silence:

'I can't stand Berlin, it stifles me.'

I could hold back no longer:

'I want to say I'm sorry. It's true I didn't have any right...'

'No need to say anything. Today, I feel as if I've been reborn... and you're the one who brought me here. When we spent my birthday together, I never imagined that in five days' time I'd be with my mother on her birthday. Thank you for that. But from now on, I'm taking charge. And that might not be easy for you...'

'I don't know what to say... She's your mother. I think that eventually you'll come to find whatever it is you have in common. There's just one thing I'd like to ask of you. When you can talk again like mother and daughter, no matter how she reacts, try to find out. Find out where he is, and I'll do everything I can to bring you into contact with him too.'

'I promise,' said Caterina. The surroundings had become more familiar. We were now close to the hotel. We had walked through half the city. From East to West Berlin. The third city was actually two cities.

The Death Fugue

The next day, Caterina went to visit her mother. Alone. We made an appointment to meet in the afternoon at a café close to the hotel. I went out for a stroll round the town. I wanted to distance myself, to change my environment. I took the underground to Potsdamer Platz. I wandered round the vast building sites, saw the yellow flamingos in action and visited the Info Box, an installation where you could see the course of the construction works and a view of the square in the next century, when Berlin would be the most important capital in Europe.

Then I went by the National Art Gallery – I stopped to admire Otto Dix's *The Skat Players*, and two rare pastels by my impressionist. Then I walked eastwards, through a half-ruined district that seemed not to have recovered from the bombing during the war. I stopped at a bookshop. Leafing through some books at random, I came across my mother's favourite poet, Paul Celan. My mother wasn't really interested in literature but she adored Celan. I looked for the poem that she liked the most: *Todesfuge*, Death Fugue. Reading it in German, without thinking, I read Magdalena wherever I saw Margarete. In any case, it was her second name:

Black milk of daybreak we drink you at night
we drink you at noon death is a master from Germany
we drink you at sundown and in the morning we drink and we drink you
death is a master from Germany his eyes are blue
he strikes you with leaden bullets his aim is true
a man lives in the house your golden hair Margarete
he sets his pack onto us he grants us a grave in the air
plays with the serpents and daydreams death is a master from Germany

your golden hair Margarete
your ashen hair Shulamith

I continued walking eastwards. Passing by a large vacant lot, my gaze fell on a sign that looked onto the street: 'Topographie des Terrors'. On the right-hand side of the lot, there was an open-air exhibition of photographs and documents from the activities of the SS and the Gestapo. Half a century earlier, the security services of the Third Reich had been located there. I looked across the street. A small park and a row of houses from the beginning of the century. The view from the window enjoyed by the SS officers while they drank their coffee in the breaks between interrogations.

I went round the exhibition. Coming to the end, I halted before one particular photograph of two men. The one on the left was in uniform, – high-ranking, I could make out three medals – narrow moustache, wearing small round spectacles. The other on the right was well-built with a round face, and was dressed in the kind of civvies fashionable in the forties – gabardine, leather gloves and hat. At the moment that the light-sensitive surface captured his expression, he was smiling. I had never seen such a smile. Two fleshy lips formed a bright red curve. The shape of pleasure that springs from absolute darkness. The harmonics of terror. Suddenly, a thought came to me. I had seen that expression somewhere before, the image wasn't unfamiliar to me. It didn't take me long to recall. It was depicted on Martin's face in *Arturo Ui*... I stooped and read the caption underneath it. Nothing happens by chance... The high-ranking officer on the left was Heinrich Himmler, chief of the SS, and on the right, the well-dressed man with the smile was Herman Göring, the head of the Gestapo. Fifty-five years before, they had been coming out of the building situated exactly on the spot where I was standing.

I came to the end of the exhibition and headed for the street. At that moment, a plane crossed the sky, leaving a blue trail behind it. A trail, a blue thread that joined the red curve of Herman Göring's lips with the yellow flamingos of Potsdamer Platz.

Heart laid bare

I had a snack close to the hotel and at around four o'clock I was in
the Litteratur Café in Fasanenstrasse. Caterina was waiting for me
at a corner table. There was a pleasant weariness in her face.

'What happened?' I asked.

Caterina lit a cigarette. It was the first time she had ever smoked
in my presence.

'Eimer welcomed me very warmly. He told me that Magdalena
had slept until daybreak. In the morning she asked what had
happened, she remembered that Martin had come with a friend of
his and with a beautiful girl. We went into the living room. There
was the same dim lighting. The place didn't smell so badly. She was
reclining on the couch again. She had had a bath, fixed her hair –
it was pulled back – powdered her face and pencilled a black line
above her eyes. She had done it for me. I understood from the way
she looked at me. She wanted to please me. Eimer had told her that
the girl would come back. I examined her, a little more calmly this
time. I had never imagined my mother like that. For so many years
I'd had the image of my grandmother before me, my sweet and
beautiful grandmother, and in my mind I fashioned her daughter,
my mother. A creature full of charm. I had the photo and the video.
And yet, Yannis, this morning, the second time, I wasn't shocked. I
was upset but not shocked. I took her a bunch of roses. I went into
the kitchen, cut the stems and put them in a vase. I left them in
front of her. "For your birthday," I said, "even if I'm a day late.
"Thank you, dear." she said.

Eimer offered me a coffee. She drank from a deep cup. Without
my asking, she told me it was orange juice. I didn't believe her. It
smelled of alcohol again when I went up to her. When she asked
me again who I was, I told her my name was Caterina, nothing
else. However, she persisted, "Didn't you come yesterday, weren't
you with Martin? I remember you. I was upset. It was my birthday
and I was ill. That's why I went to sleep. I was in a bad way. All my
body was aching. I was glad that you came. I'm so alone… There's
only Volker. You… I remember you. You speak German well, but
you're not German. And what you said, what was it you said to me,

dear?" "The truth," I replied. "I'm your daughter, Caterina. My surname is Mateo. My father is Luca Mateo. We lived in Florence, you remember... I'm not German, I'm Italian, I was born in Italy. Half Italian, half Greek, on my father's side..." Then her face took on a sad expression and she said calmly, "My dear, I never married, I have no children, I loved a man but he left, he left and I never saw him again." I asked her who that man was and she replied sorrowfully, "My man was a Greek too. A handsome Greek. He left, disappeared, went far away..."

I remembered what Martin had told us and I asked her if she had ever heard anything of him again. "Years ago," she said, "not too many, I can't remember numbers and such like. He phoned me. He didn't want me. He wanted another woman. A young woman." "What was the young woman's name?" I asked. She told me she couldn't remember. "Was it Caterina?" I asked again. She took a big drink and began to cry. "I have no children... I have nothing..." I let her calm down a little and then I took out of my bag the photograph with her and my father in Florence when they were young, the one I showed you. She held it to the light. Her face hardened. "Leave me," she said, "go away, I don't know you! I don't know any of you," and she covered her face with her hands.

Eimer intervened. He took her in his arms and comforted her as best he could. Then I went with him into the bedroom. I explained the whole story in brief. He told me that he had first seen Magdalena at the theatre and he had been very taken with her. One evening, he had bumped into her in a bar. She had been so drunk that she hadn't been able to return home on her own, nor was she even able to remember where she lived. An affair had started between them. "It's not exactly passion, it's more like love between two troubled souls," he added. Eimer was from East Berlin, he had lost his wife through cancer. My mother had spoken to him about a major love of hers in the past, about a Greek who she had lived with in Italy. But not a word about any child... He also told me that Magdalena was now virtually an alcoholic; that she had a problem with her leg caused by uric acid. She had hardly been out of the house for months. With him beside her, she had managed to cut down on her drinking. He waters down her drinks, hides the bottles from her, but she always finds a way to drink. He claims to love her, to feel for her, for him she's a "good person albeit a distressed one". I asked him if he believed that I was her daughter. He replied, "To be honest, not at first. But when I saw the photo, I began to be convinced. Besides, why would you lie? It's not as though Magdalena was wealthy… All she has is a trunk, full of clothes, odds and ends and papers. At least, that's what she told me. And there's also the similarity. Magdalena has shown me old photos of herself. It had always struck me as strange that she never had anyone around her. Apart from those photos from the theatre or from filming, when she was surrounded by other actresses."

I told him that I'd like to see the contents of the trunk. He reacted, saying that he'd have to ask Magdalena first. "But I should tell you, she won't let you. She hasn't shown its contents even to me. She keeps it locked. And she keeps the key in her purse that she has strapped to her waist. You see how she reacts. Absolute denial. The past is sealed, all there is is some handsome anonymous Greek…" he added. "In that case, Herr Eimer, please look yourself without saying anything to her," I said. "More than likely it will contain some evidence concerning her past, something to confirm my relationship with her. If you love her as you say, help her to re-discover who she is." Eimer hesitated, thought it over for a while and finally agreed. He's going to look and let me know. "What you ask me to do is not at all in keeping with my character, you know. I'm only doing it for her in case we're able to help her," he said.

We went back into the living room. My mother had got up. She was sitting in a chair at the table; her arms were folded over her breast. I didn't go on with the previous conversation. I began to talk about other things, meaningless things. I asked her about her health, she said that she was fine, but that she had a problem with her leg and that she got tired easily, then we talked about Berlin, how it had changed following the collapse of the Wall. She found it difficult to express herself, though she was coherent nevertheless. At times, however, she lost the thread completely, sinking into a world of her own. Then she would recover again and look me in the eye. As for me, Yannis, behind that vacant look of hers, I felt… believe me, I felt recognition. Eventually, I turned the conversation, as gently as I could, to Italy. "I lived there, too, dear. A long time ago, I don't remember now," she said. I started to talk to her about Florence, I told her that it was my city and, speaking about the various districts, I said, "The loveliest street in the city is the via Ghibellina…" I'll never forget how she looked at me. Momentarily, I felt her face coming closer to mine. I thought she was going to kiss me. She suddenly stopped and said, "Volker, I want to be alone now." She didn't want me to press her any more. I left, telling her that I would stop by again tomorrow. She gave me a tired look and said, "I'll expect you, dear".

On the way back I thought: my mother abandoned me. Perhaps at first she wanted to protect me, yet she had never once wanted to see me in so many years. It's not something that you can easily forget. Nevertheless, today I'm a healthy woman, with all my faculties, whereas she is a broken creature who has erased half her life from her memory. I'm going to stand by her. She is my mother after all. I'll be beside her from now on.

Then I phoned Martin and stopped by his place. He was extremely sweet, not at all aggressive as he had been in the bar. He said that in his opinion I ought to stay a while in Berlin and see my mother as often as possible. He even offered to let me stay with him. And, you know Yannis, I think that's the best thing to do.'

'I think you're right,' I said, 'you should stay with her for a while.'

'What will you do?'

'I'll stay for a few days too. I think that there's a good chance of finding information in Knackstrasse that could lead us to your father. And, of course, if your mother is able and willing to tell you anything about him, that would help us enormously, but…'

'But what?'

'But I have to be honest. You have to be ready for the possibility that your mother may simply remain the way she is. Maybe for ever…'

'I'm aware of it. It doesn't change my feelings in the slightest.'

'And something else. I know it's personal… If Eimer shows you the things in the trunk then please let me take a look too. We're still only halfway there, you realize that…'

'Of course I do. Whatever I find out, I'll tell you. Besides it all began with you.'

'It all began with *Bar Flaubert*…'

'*Bar Flaubert*. I thought of it while I was looking at my mother today. I swore to myself that, even if she makes a complete recovery, I'll never let her read as much as one page of it. Not even one page! Ever!'

On the question of the trunk, Eimer made a strange stipulation. He would let us see the contents, but the following Wednesday, after midnight, when Magdalena would be asleep and he could get the key from her purse that she kept with her night and day. I supposed that Caterina's insistence had made him suspicious and he wanted time to carry out a little research of his own.

Almost a week passed. Caterina continued to visit her mother every day. She would go in the morning, we would meet at midday for lunch, then she would go back in the afternoon and stay until night-time, when she and Eimer would put Magdalena to bed. Magdalena had come to accept her as a kind of nurse, a private nurse who had appeared out of nowhere. As for me, I roamed the city, wrote in the third notebook that I had bought – the Berlin notebook – and did a lot of thinking. I thought about the time when I would eventually meet Loukas Matthaiou.

Most mornings Martin would come with me and show me around Berlin. He took me to the remains of the Wall, to Checkpoint Charlie, to the Pergamonmuseum and the Bauhaus Museum, walked me round Nikolaiviertel – an amazing district – and took me to restaurants and cafés. After Knackstrasse, our relationship had unexpectedly blossomed. His irony had been replaced by a singular tenderness, his sarcasm had turned into humour, the man had taken the whole business to heart and was deeply concerned. He was concerned not only about his old actress friend, but also about her daughter and, consequently, about me.

Martin even went so far, being a specialist in the field, to give me advice in matters of the heart: 'Don't deny it. I've been watching you. It's written all over you. You're in love, poor boy, head over heels in love. I don't blame you of course, the girl is a jewel, and the way things between you have developed, it's as though you were both living a fairytale.'

'But not yet,' he said to me in another conversation. 'Don't make any move for a few days. Right now her mind and heart are there, with Magdalena. But all this is precisely in your favour. Wait, but not too long. The girl is going through a sensitive phase, her heart has been laid bare. She gives the impression of a girl who has been hurt by love, as though someone has torn her feelings to shreds. It requires care, Yannis, tact... But for God's sake! I mean care, not pussyfooting. The girl needs a man beside her not just someone to lean on.'

In the flat in Knackstrasse, Magdalena gradually became more relaxed and accepted Caterina's presence in her home, but she was still unable to recognize her as her daughter. Caterina for her part did not press her. All she did was to mention names and places from time to time. On a couple of occasions she again showed her the photo with her father in Florence. Sometimes Magdalena clammed up, sometimes she changed the topic or became angry. Nevertheless, one afternoon, Caterina found her looking at the photo that she had deliberately left on the coffee table. She had raised it to the light and stared at it for some time, her eyes had filled with tears. Another day, she spoke to her of her grandmother, Sophia Gentile. 'My grandmother,' she told her, 'had a very beautiful daughter. She was so beautiful that she acted in films, just like you.' 'I never acted in films, only in the theatre,' Magdalena said angrily. Eimer had told Caterina that Magdalena refused to watch her films on video. 'She doesn't want to see herself as she was in her youth, she can't bear it, you see...' On another occasion, Caterina spoke to her about her grandfather, the German, how she had never met him, that he had died prematurely because of his heart. Her mother showed no reaction. It was only when Caterina turned the conversation to the destruction in Berlin caused by the war and to the bombed houses that had since been rebuilt that Magdalena burst out angrily, 'You young people have no right to even talk about those things! You saw nothing! You have no right!' And that day she sealed her lips and said nothing more. On the following day, Caterina cleverly turned the conversation to the subject of the stolen paintings, 'I live in Florence,' she told her, 'in the Renaissance paradise. I'm very fond of art. But my favourite painter is a contemporary one: Picasso. My father liked him too. In fact, he possessed two genuine Picassos. He brought them from Spain, where he'd bought them from a collector friend of his, Ramón Esnaider.' Second outburst. Magdalena was beside herself, her eyes were red and her lips pursed, 'People continually amass objects, collecting and collecting, and eventually they're suffocated by them. Objects and money ruin people. They're a curse! Curse, do you hear? They turn people into egoists, traitors, thieves... I have nothing. I have no money. I was never interested in either money or objects. All I have is a trunk with my memories.' When Caterina again mentioned Florence, Magdalena became adamant, 'I've lived in Italy. There the men are handsome, but they are liars and hypocrites. They're like angels, they tell you they're in love with you and then they betray you. Be careful, dear, don't ever fall in love in Italy...'

One of the first things that Caterina did in Knackstrasse was to get rid of all the bottles in the house. It was up to her to take the initiative. We had discussed it and had concluded that Eimer may have been a dear and devoted fellow and have unselfishly loved her mother, however he had a weak character, completely unsuited to caring for someone on the verge of alcoholism. When Magdalena lost her bottles, she was like a fish out of water. She cried, searched through her secret stores, suffered a few minor crises though nothing to cause too much worry. Martin even sent his own doctor, a gastroenterologist specializing in alcoholism, supposedly to look at her leg. The doctor gave her some tablets and vitamins, and, given that it was impossible for us to put her in a detox clinic – Eimer had made it clear to us that she would never agree to that again – he recommended rest for at least a month and, naturally, total abstinence from alcohol. 'Don't let her even so much as smell it ever again,' he told us. As for her mental state, he didn't have anything original to recommend. 'I'm not an expert, but what this woman needs is on the one hand to close the chapter on drink once and for all and, on the other, to be loved, to be loved and cared for by the people around her. Personally,' said the doctor, 'I see someone who is emotionally transfixed, who refuses to communicate. The woman has given up, for years now she's been letting herself slide towards death. The only way for her to turn back is for her to feel that there's something ahead, some motivation for going on living. And for her to have faith in herself and in those around her. In my opinion, it's going to be a long and slow process. But it's something that is possible. People have enormous strength that is not always apparent. But she has to want it and you have to want it, too, and to have patience.'

Caterina left the flat when her mother was asleep and returned before she woke up. Late at night we would get together and talk over all the events. The possibility that Eimer might give in to her pleas for drink made her want to have total control. Gradually, Magdalena began to feel a little better. She had become gentler, more talkative, and also more susceptible to the tactics adopted by Caterina, who, without pressing her, tried to help her mother remember, something not at all easy. The shield, the liquid protector, had gone, but the wound was deep and the habit had created powerful antibodies.

As for me and my feelings towards Caterina, I felt like the East Germans did towards the West Germans during the period of the cold war. Our rooms were adjacent, our beds were no more than four metres apart, but between us was a wall, a low brick wall that was waiting for the right time to come crashing down. And such things, as history teaches, happen when you least expect them.

Arcadia

On Wednesday the seventeenth, Caterina and I left the hotel shortly before midnight. I had a premonition and took a copy of Matthaiou's novel with me. Half an hour later we were knocking on Eimer's door. He welcomed us with a conspiratorial look. He tiptoed though, as he said, Magdalena was sleeping soundly. She had gone to bed an hour earlier and had even asked him for an extra sleeping tablet.

'She'll be sound asleep for a good few hours,' he told us. He had easily got the key from her without her understanding anything. We sat on the couch and Eimer went into the bedroom. He came out holding three large blue folders and a red album: 'I've brought you everything that may be of interest. The rest is simply old clothes and objects. The clothes are old-fashioned, from the seventies, bell-bottoms and pointed collars. There's some jewellery too, of no great value, an old typewriter, a tiny statue – an award for some performance or other – miniatures of animals like the ones we have in the showcase, and five or six small paintings, nothing special, silk prints and such like. The folders are full of papers, lots of handwritten pages in a foreign language, I imagine it must be Greek. The album has photos in it. Some of them I've seen before. She kept the others, where she's with various people, from me.'

'Thank you, Herr Eimer, I won't forget your help,' said Caterina.

'I have to tell you that I feel extremely embarrassed. I've never before intervened like this in someone else's personal things, never in my life. Yet, Caterina, for so many days now I've felt just how close you are to her, flesh of her flesh. So it's as though I were handing over Magdalena's memories to her natural successor. If these papers can help her to find who she really is, then it will have been worth it.'

Eimer closed the living-room door behind him and left us on our own. We began with the album. It contained around a hundred photos with quite a few scraps of papers. All in chronological order. We carefully examined the photos one by one. In the first, Caterina recognized her grandmother. Twenty years old, she was posing in the Piazza Duomo. Then grandfather Hardenberg, also in his youth. The next one was a photo of their wedding. Below was a date: *Berlin, 13.6.1937*. Afterwards, Magdalena as a baby. Blonde locks, coquettish look. The facade of a house. I recognized the building in Motzstrasse. Different windows, an iron door, but more or less the same. Then the landscape changed again. Florence. Magdalena as a little girl, on the Ponte Vecchio, then the statue of David. Tuscan landscapes. Family photos; mother, father, daughter. Magdalena in her classroom, in school performances. Magdalena growing up, becoming a young woman, extremely beautiful; blonde, slender, sparkling eyes. The school-leaving certificate. The diploma from drama school. The programme from her first performance: Hilda in the *Lady from the Sea*, 1961. A death announcement. Friedrich Hardenberg 1911-1965. Stuck in the album was a sheet of paper with notes. The last words written by the German grandfather. Photos from films: *The Red Desert* by Antonioni, in the background behind Monica Vitti. *One Fine Day*, a photo with the whole cast. A young man with curly hair and a beard. Photos with him on islands. Embracing. Then a large photo of Loukas Matthaiou. A black and white portrait. Caterina wanted to see if there was anything written on the back. I carefully tore it out. The note in Italian: *19.7.1968. Thirty years old. Like me. Different from me.* And Matthaiou again, this time with Magdalena. A series of photos in Siena. The photo of the wedding: *2.9.1968...* A handsome couple. Bridal gown in yellow hues and dress suit with bow tie. Few people. Out of the corner of my eye, I saw Caterina welling up with tears. There followed photos of Magdalena with friends, Martin was in one of them, an appreciably thinner Martin, arm in arm with a tall black guy, older than him – Roger I assumed. Then photos of Matthaiou, as an adolescent, as a young man, with various unfamiliar people in Athens.

On the next page there was a surprise waiting for Caterina. A photo with a baby who was virtually dangling in the air, a baby being held by two arms, just two arms, carefully cut from the rest of the body. The baby was beautiful, with the sweetest eyes. Caterina spent a long time looking at herself as she was twenty-nine years earlier. And once again snapshots from films: *The Garden of the Finzi-Contini*, a photo with De Sica during one of the breaks in filming. Magdalena, slender, dressed all in white, beautiful. Towards the end Matthaiou, with his daughter sitting on his shoulders, her little legs crossed on his chest, her arms reaching up high together with his. Note: *4.6.1972. C. three years old.* A series of other photos of Matthaiou, at a younger age, with other, unfamiliar people. And on the last page another large colour photo of him. Dark green eyes fixed on the lens, a high forehead, long hair brushed back, mouth half-open, sardonic smile. On the back a few words written by him: *In mir habt ihr einen, auf den könnt ihr nicht bauen,* I am one in whom

you cannot invest – Bertolt Brecht. On the back cover a few more
stray photos held with a paper clip. Berlin. The inside of a flat.
Matthaiou and Magdalena in front of the Wall. Magdalena putting on
her make-up in her dressing room. And finally, a photo of Matthaiou
from the back walking down an empty street in Berlin. Caterina's
eyes were moist. Emotional, but composed.

'The poor woman… An entire life in an album. From her
parents' wedding up to 1972. And there it stops. From then on she
doesn't want any evidence. Her life ends in '72. She doesn't want
to remember after that. But you saw for yourself, in the photo
where she's holding me, she cut herself out not me…'

We turned to the folders. The first contained a bundle of letters
and a diary. They didn't appear to be in any particular order. Three
love letters, to Magdalena, signed Fabio. 'The curly-haired chap
with the beard,' said Caterina after reading them, 'very much in
love…' Then letters and cards from various friends, of no particular
interest. Towards the end, there was also a letter in English addressed
to Luke, to Matthaiou. I read it out.

3 April 1965
Hotel Nueva Regis, Bogota

Dear Luke,

 *I read your piece. Allen gave it to me. He told me it was
published in a magazine edited by Nanos. Congratulations!*

 *You know of course that talent is like nobility; it brings with it
obligations. But it also slips away easily, it can lead to its own
independence from the real game being played out there, in the great
Machine. You, dear boy, for the present, you've managed to preserve
your nobility. But be careful…*

 *As for the piece itself, I like your characters' lasciviousness. It's both
poetical and cynical. Exactly to my taste. The bodies in your text are
in revolt, they are conscience's rebels travelling in a universal Arcadia.*
 Don't ever lose that.

As ever
Bill

'It must be from Burroughs,' I said. 'About the short story published in *Pali*, the magazine edited by Nanos Valaoritis, a Greek writer.'

Then a handwritten letter from Matthaiou to Magdalena. Caterina read it out. Like an electrical discharge…

For you,

   When you read this, I'll be far away. Nothing will ever make this moment any less. Nothing will ever bring me closer to what I truly am. The moment is a viper, Magdalena. A bite in time.

   I never understood who I was with you. 'Where are you? What are you thinking?' you'd ask me. Fate, Magdalena. My fate.

   Don't look for me. I'm going to find my own earth and bury myself. There's a lot of chance in what we experience, it hurls us to right and left. And now that I'm standing in the middle of the magnet, on the dividing line, I'm beginning to feel the upper pole attracting me more and more strongly. What is there I don't know. Only that I'm down below and beside me, like an equation, is my present life. And the way I'm living it is not enough for me. It's not the Germans, it's not the city, it's not the girl. It's not you either. It's me who never understood.

   Don't look for me, I don't deserve it. I'll go on helping her. Every year just like now. Sophia, dear Sophia will take care of it. Once she's eighteen, she'll be able to manage things herself. Unless you…

   Go back, Magda, go back to her. There's no future in this city. There's no future in divided cities, in dividing lines, in divided people.

   I no longer want my writings. If you find them, burn them. Please burn them. There's only one thing I want to write and I have that inside me.

   The envelope is for you. I think it's enough.

   Magdalena…

   What else is there for me to say? From now on, more than ever, I don't exist.

   L.

The last nine words, read out by her daughter, echoed like bullets in Magdalena's living room. Silence. My gaze fell on the porcelain elephant. Its trunk raised. Its tusks pointing to the skies. To the upper pole.

Then Caterina continued with a letter from Magdalena to Matthaiou. Undelivered of course. Eight pages... She asks him to come back. *'I don't know where you are. I can't find you. Where shall I send this letter? All I want is for the doorbell to ring and for it to be you...'*

The diary began in 1968; it too continued till 1972. It was written virtually in code. Short, sharp phrases. Caterina went to her birthday: 4th June 1969. *'Everything adorned by my belly. A beautiful little doll. I gave her to him'.* On their wedding day, 2nd September 1968: *'The breeze blew refreshingly between us. My skin against his skin. For ever...'* I looked for the day of the incident. It was 23rd September 1972: *'Blood everywhere. C. three years old. Like the other C. '43-'72. Berlin-Siena. Blood, blood everywhere. Keep her protected. I'm leaving with him.'*

That was the last but one entry in the diary. The last was the following day, 24th September: *'My city split in two. Do something Luca. My belly is split in two as well...'*

The second folder was filled with newspaper and magazine cuttings referring to Magdalena. There were reviews of performances, reports of opening nights, theatre programmes. I looked for the last reference to her artistic career. There was nothing concerning Berlin. The last dated evidence was the programme from a performance in Spring '72 at the Teatro della Pergola in Florence. Pirandello's *Clothe the Naked.*

The third folder contained just one brown envelope. On the outside in thick black felt-tip pen were the words: *'L.M. – Berlin Texts'.*

Inside it were a series of texts, written in Greek, in the characteristic handwriting of Loukas Matthaiou. Literary reviews, monographs, essays on painting. The titles were indicative: *Burroughs and the cut-up technique, Contemporary Spanish poetry, Image in the poetry of Fernando Salinas, Dante:* The Inferno – *notes, Picasso: the blue period, Nicolas Poussin: the classicism of baroque and mythology, Jacopo Sannazzaro and the pastoral romance, Heroic romance: the case of Philip Sidney, Paolo*

Rolli – Pietro Metastasio: Lyricism, libretto and canzone, André Gide: mirror and myth, Abandoning Authority: the literary circle of Queen Christina of Sweden in Rome, The trend against Gongorism in Portuguese poetry, Goethe and ancient Greece, Goethe in Italy – Roman elegies, Goethe: Bucolic poetry and *Die Laune des Verliebten.*

Thumbing through the essay on Poussin, I found a colour photo of one of the artist's paintings attached to it with a paperclip. The title: *Shepherds in Arcadia.* It depicted an idyllic landscape in ancient Greece. Two shepherds dressed in tunics, one red, the other white, each holding a staff, seemingly showing a couple the inscription carved on a stone mound. One of the shepherds has his foot resting on a tree stump. On the left, dressed in a dark tunic, the man is bending down before the tomb trying to read the inscription, while the woman is standing on the right, dressed in yellow and dark blue with a white kerchief over her head. Though the shadow of the man was covering it, I managed to read the carved inscription. It was the familiar Latin saying: 'Et in Arcadia ego'. I recalled the interpretation. 'I too come from Arcadia'. I read the text to Caterina. Matthaiou undertook a detailed analysis of the work of the French artist: the influence of Roman sculpture, his contact with the Italian painter and architect Domenichino, the origin of the mythological scenes...

'We'll read them all, Caterina...all the texts. I've thought of something,' I said to her.

I began to read them all, one by one. Apart from being a gifted author, Matthaiou was also a fascinating essayist. The way he tackled his subjects was in the form of a spiral. He began by surrounding the topic from all sides and then, going deeper and deeper, though without abandoning the circular motion, he made constant inroads into it until he had exhausted it. He was clever enough, however, not to draw any final conclusions. Having floored his topic in the ring, with a gesture of magnanimity – in actual fact of concealed arrogance – Matthaiou stopped the clock instead of basking in his victory. He gave it the opportunity to recover and, after helping it to his feet again, he asked: 'What other sport do you want us to compete in?' And he finished it off.

His topics were varied. Naturally, he had concerned himself with his master, Burroughs, with his friend, Salinas, with Dante – evidently because of Florence – but also with Gide concerning the reciprocal shaping of both the author and the book, a topic that appears to have been of particular interest to him. Reading about Picasso, I couldn't help smiling; it seemed to me a gesture of supreme irony for an art thief to write a study of the painter of the stolen art.

The other essays dealt with more specialized topics. While reading, however, the text on Jacopo Sannazzaro and the pastoral romance and then the one on the historic romance and Philip Sidney, it wasn't difficult for me to detect a common element. An element that in its turn linked these two essays with the one on Poussin. For Matthaiou informed us that it was Sannazzaro who wrote the first pastoral romance entitled *Arcadia* in 1501, while Philip Sidney was the author of the most important English work of the 16th century. Its title identical to that of the Italian romance: *Arcadia*.

I went on with the rest of the texts. The common point of reference didn't end there. Again in Italy, Paolo Rolli and Pietro Metastasio were members of a literary academy founded in Rome in 1690 with the aim of opposing Marinism, the dominant school in Italian poetry in the 17th century. Its name was by no means fortuitous: *Academy of Arcadia.* As for the origin of the Academy, this was to be found in the literary circle of Queen Christina of Sweden, who, after abdicating the throne, took refuge in Rome. And Gongorism? This was actually a baroque poetry movement with Spanish influences, countered by a number of Portuguese poets who in 1756 joined forces against it and formed a literary group under the name *Arcádia Lusitana.*

It appeared that the word, the concept 'Arcadia' was something of an obsession for Loukas Matthaiou. In his article on the Italian academy, he even attempted a definition:

Arcadia: An idealistic landscape, an imaginary, idyllic land, where the shepherds preserved their unsullied customs and the bliss of a peaceful life prevailed. It refers to a scene of enjoyment or delight in provincial innocence and uninterrupted harmony. The name came from a pastoral region in ancient Greece that was presented as a country paradise in Greek and Roman bucolic poetry.

I was still unable to draw any conclusion. Until, that is, I began to read his pieces on Goethe.

In *Goethe and ancient Greece*, Matthaiou investigates the Greek roots of the poet's work, while in *Goethe in Italy – Roman Elegies*, the poet's journey to Italy and to Rome in particular is presented as a gesture of liberation, an artistic and at the same time human turnabout. Matthaiou begins his article with two lines from *Faust*:

> *Zur Laube wandeln sich die Thronen.*
> *Arkadische frei sei under Glück!*

Our thrones are transformed into vines / Let our fortune be free, Arcadian! I went on reading the article and stopped only at the penultimate paragraph:

Goethe published two books from his journey to Italy in 1816 entitled Italienische Reise (Italian Journeys). *In their first edition, on the first page, there was a motto in Latin, anonymous, to which I will return after making a necessary leap in time. Goethe made a second journey to Italy in 1824. On his return, he burned a number of his letters and in 1829 republished his* Italian Journeys, *this time removing the motto. I would ask his readers to note the phrase initially chosen by the greatest German poet of all time for the frontispiece of his work: 'Et in Arcadia ego' (And I too come from Arcadia). The greatest mind in Germany travels to Italy and returns to Weimar only to end up notionally in Greek Arcadia.*

I didn't go on with my reading. I didn't go on because Matthaiou, next to the Latin motto, had put an asterisk, a reference. In the margin of the same page he had written, in Greek, in large letters and in red ink, the following note:

*And I too am going to end up in Arcadia. In the mountain. In the
four villages. L.D.S.K. I'll choose one.*

'Caterina, *Bar Flaubert*! In my bag. In the last pages...' I recalled
the passage. I had read it to her in Florence. It was there, on page
243:

> *I'm coming to the end. Origin's root has stretched back, to the depth
> of existence. New fruits have sprouted. Earth... Air... Water...
> Fire... The four elements. The four paintings. And one more with
> the plaque. That's where I'll go. Back to where I come from. To the
> four villages. Where the towns tumble down the precipitous slopes.
> The mountain. Four villages. L.D.S.K. I choose one. The
> destination. Forever.*

'Arcadia... L.D.S.K....The four villages, the plaque, the inscription,
Poussin, there's no doubt! Your father returned to Greece, to
Arcadia, to the mountain, to the four villages whose initial letters
are L.D.S.K... To the mountainous region of Arcadia. Everything!
Everything is in the book! Matthaiou ends his journey and just like
Goethe asks Magdalena to burn his writings! Barcelona, Florence,
Berlin. The slight curve that ends in the North. And then the
vertical drop, the re-baptism in the South. In Arcadia.'
    I was almost ecstatic.
    'And have you any idea which villages they are?' Caterina asked,
interrupting my effusion.
    'Oh, I don't know. The mountains of Arcadia... The only village
that comes to mind is Vytina. Oh, and Zatouna from the record of
Theodorakis. B.Z., no it can't be them. Though there is a solution.
Let's go back to the hotel, I've a map of Greece in my Filofax.'
It was already four in the morning. I called Eimer, woke him up
and told him that I needed to keep the contents of the three folders
in order to photocopy them. I also secretly took with me a large
photo of Matthaiou and another dozen or so of those where he was
with others. In actual fact, it was a kind of theft, but at that moment
I saw it as a necessary form of confiscation due to the exceptional
circumstances. I told Eimer I would return the folders in the

morning before Magdalena woke up. 'Be here before nine. Without fail!' he said anxiously.

Back at the hotel, we immediately went up to my room. I got my Filofax and took out the small pages. I spread the parts of the Peloponnese on the bed and joined them together. I went straight to the centre, in Arcadia. Oliyyrtos, Mainalo, Lykaio… River Loussios. I looked for an L. Yes. There was a village beginning with L. Langadia. I went south. Dimitsana. The D! Further south, the S! Stemnitsa. A little further down, Karytaina. The K! Another slight curve linked the four villages, which were all within a distance of around forty-five kilometres.

'Langadia-Dimitsana-Stemnitsa-Karytaina. Till now it had been a relay race. Each new piece of information had let to the next. Autobiography-*Bar Flaubert*-Hansen-Barcelona-Tina-Esnaider-Salinas-Florence-you-Berlin-Martin-Magdalena-trunk-Arcadia-the four villages. If we don't drop the baton in the final straight, then we should find your father living somewhere in that forty-five kilometre radius!' I said to Caterina.

Her face had taken on a bright glow. It was as though her eyes had been lit by some secret ray of light, her cheeks had reddened and her features appeared so distinct that it was as though they had become independent of each other. We were sitting on my bed, more or less side by side, with the small pieces of the map of the Peloponnese laid out before us. Asta Nielsen above our heads. The final straight. The baton tightly gripped. With my left hand I swept the pages off the bed and with my right I pulled Caterina towards me with some force. Holding her in my arms, I looked at her momentarily and then I kissed her on the lips with all the awkwardness and expectation of the previous days.

The Church of Memory

There is a certain finality in love. It sets a seal on the moment and at the same time is a synopsis of all that has gone before. The wetland of a constantly present memory. This is how it usually is. However, in some people there is something else too. For those whose soul was never certain, who were obliged from an early age to question the obvious, for those whose world was the part of the iceberg beneath the sea, love was not always a matter of just two people. There was an additional presence, someone else in the space between the loved one and whatever most real the lover brings to the relationship: his own self.

Just as always, the observer of my life arrived at his appointed time. He put his bag down to one side, took off his jacket and sat comfortably in the place that most suited him. He watched me making love to Caterina, noticed that a protective layer had begun to vanish from my skin, heard me unexpectedly uttering words that I had never uttered before, saw my longing welling up, – no longer the controlled flow, the regulated supply, now the liquid flowed incessantly making the bodies gleam – was surprised at the sight of my right hand that for the first time played a leading role, saw in my eyes a transformation identical to those that take place when a person gets a second chance and then, with a lightning movement, with a movement befitting the magic justice of dramatic shadows, he faded and vanished leaving my soul lightened and oscillating to the rhythm of Caterina's pulse.

Thursday morning. By a happy coincidence the hotel had a photocopier and it seems that the receptionist found the sight of a tourist making copies at eight in the morning amusing enough to allow me to have sole use of it for a full twenty minutes. Then, with heart in mouth, we took a taxi and were at Eimer's place at five minutes to nine. He was waiting for us anxiously.

'Quickly! The folders!' he said, panting. 'Any time now, she'll wake up. She's been tossing and turning for some time now.'

I was with Caterina in her mother's living room. From my room, from the undulations of love, straight on to the streets of Berlin and then there. So quickly… I recalled her words: 'Yannis, there's a lot going on…' Yes, there was a lot going on. A lot going on that was inevitable.

'I'll go now,' I said to her. 'I'll leave you two together.'

'No, stay,' she said, tenderly taking hold of my hand. 'This time I want you to be here too. Today is not like all the other days…' she said meaningfully.

I remained in Knackstrasse the whole morning. Half an hour later, Magdalena got up and we had coffee together. Seeing them, mother and daughter, after a week together, I sensed some change in the atmosphere. Caterina had done good work. Clearly more composed and somewhat thinner, Magdalena looked at her daughter with tenderness, on occasion I saw her staring at her, her gaze fixed on her. We were all more relaxed. We joked, made small talk, about the weather, about clothes, about Magdalena's leg that was getting better. At around twelve, Caterina turned to her mother and made a bold suggestion:

'Do you feel like going out to eat? It's so lovely. The weather's good. I'll phone Martin. We won't go far.'

To my great surprise, Magdalena nodded affirmatively.

Caterina helped her mother to get ready. Together they chose a blue dress with a white collar; she fixed her hair – brushing it back – and took care of her make-up. When they had finished, Magdalena looked very different from the abandoned creature we had first encountered on the couch. The abstinence from alcohol, in combination with the tablets, had already brought some results, though there was still a long way to go. Already, however, behind the extra weight and the puffed cheeks, I could discern the charm that this woman must have had in her youth. A charm, nevertheless, that had not been sufficient to keep a man like Matthaiou. How must Leto have been, I wondered. I imagined an oval apparition, an ethereal creature…

Caterina phoned Martin, and Eimer called for a taxi. Before we got into the taxi, Caterina went up to the driver and said something to him in a low voice. In answer to my question as to where we were going, she said meaningfully, 'When we get there, you'll understand.'

Half an hour later, after an exasperating drive through the jammed roads of Berlin, I realized the meaning behind the outing. The taxi pulled up outside a Greek restaurant. I knew it, I had seen it before. It was Kalambokas's. We were in Motzstrasse, outside number 45, Magdalena's family home.

We got out of the taxi. Caterina helped her mother out, taking her by the arm.

'Do you like this neighbourhood?' she asked her.

Magdalena nodded 'yes' and her eyes, hidden behind the black horn-rimmed glasses, turned to the four-storey apartment block. She stood back a little in order to be able to include it all in her field of vision. Her face was calm and serene. Without showing any alarm, she turned to Caterina.

'It's changed. It's changed a lot since then,' she said quietly.

'You mean the house? Since when?' asked Caterina.

'Since I remember it. It's been many years since I was last here. Before the fall of the Wall.'

'Do you want us to go up? I know a lady who lives on the fourth floor. She remembers you from the old days.'

'No…no, I don't want to! Haven't we come here to eat?' Magdalena replied abruptly, and the four of us went into the restaurant, where Martin, impeccably dressed and cheerful, was waiting for us at one of the central tables.

We ate in a pleasant atmosphere, Martin recounted anecdotes from the theatre, Caterina served her mother, who seemed to be enjoying it, Eimer was in seventh heaven, and I watched the woman with whom I had spent the previous night spreading inside me like invisible ink.

However Caterina's plans for the day did not end with Motzstrasse. After the meal, she proposed that we go for a walk towards Kurfürsterdamm, the nearby central thoroughfare in former West Berlin.

We walked slowly, Caterina led the way, arm in arm with Magdalena. It was a summer afternoon and Berlin was teeming with life. A colourful crowd of people was coming and going on the wide pavements. We passed by two or three building sites, some pretty cafés, the large department stores, Wertheim and KDW, till at one moment the two in front suddenly halted. It wasn't the daughter who interrupted the leisurely stroll, it was the mother. Magdalena had stopped dead, her gaze was turned to the left, to the opposite pavement. Looming there was a slender black shape, resembling a sculpture by Giacometti, a tall church with traces of the bombing in the war still visible on it. The Sagrada Familia came to mind and the last time I had seen Tina. Next to the church, almost touching it, was a modern building of glass and steel. A speechless steel object. Like a bomb.

'H Gedächtnis Kirche, the Church of Memory. It was built in memory of Kaiser Wilhelm and was bombed during the war,' Martin whispered to me.

'Die Kirche, mein Gott, die Kirche…' I said unconsciously under my breath.

As though she had heard me, Magdalena turned to her daughter.

'What's your name? What's your name?' she asked her with a trembling voice.

'Caterina.'

'Ca…tri…na…' said Magdalena, stressing the syllables.

'Not Catrina. C a t e r i n a.'

'Ca…te…ri…na…, yes' and, opening her arms, she wrapped them around her daughter. The two of them remained silent, in each other's embrace across from the blackened ruin, while the rest of us stood back like a silent chorus.

Three minutes must have passed with the two women hugging each other tightly in the street. It seemed an age to me. Eventually, Caterina turned her head. 'We're going home. I want us to be alone.' Not one of us said a word. Caterina hailed the first taxi to pass and they disappeared in it. Everything had happened so quickly. We went for a coffee, which we drank in an atmosphere of general dejection, and then we went our separate ways. Martin had a rehearsal with Axel to do with the lieder and Eimer would go to one of his friends in order to leave the two women alone. I went back to the hotel. Having gone thirty-three hours without sleep, I collapsed onto the bed. At around ten in the evening the phone rang. It was Caterina. She had decided to sleep at her mother's. She didn't elaborate. Just, 'My mother…she's been through a great deal'. 'I'm thinking of you,' I told her. 'I'm thinking of you too, Yannis…' she answered tenderly. I went back to sleep with our union of the night before still fresh on the sheets.

The next day I tried to put my thoughts into some order. The previous hours had produced an avalanche of developments. As long as I looked in front, as long as I rushed forward out of control, I noticed the following paradox: events were getting ahead of me. I had to slow down, to look to right and left, to check where I was. Yes, a lot was going on. On every front.

First of all, Caterina's tactics had borne fruit, and pretty quickly too. Magdalena had taken the first step in order to accept her daughter. It was a critical period; for the time being Caterina must stay in Berlin no matter what. At the same time, from the previous evening, the path to Loukas Matthaiou had opened wide. The journey was coming to an end. *Bar Flaubert*, the book that had sent me off wandering in the three cities it incorporated, was now calling me back to base. Arcadia, Langadia, Dimitsana, Stemnitsa, Karytaina. I had to return to Greece, to the Peloponnese, to search those forty-five kilometres inch by inch. To find what? The man who had become an obsession to me, after simply having read his book that had fallen into my hands by chance.

And amid this vortex, the recent developments would on their own have been extremely favourable, if there had not been something else: Caterina. Caterina, the woman with whom, to paraphrase Matthaiou, I felt myself existing as never before. And her father had paid a high price for that 'never before'.

It was Friday, 19th June. I called the travel agency. There were flights to Athens on Monday and Wednesday. I decided to leave on Wednesday, to stay another five days in Berlin, with her.

The wings of love

The days passed with the familiar routine. Caterina would go to her mother's in the morning, then we would meet for lunch and in the afternoon she would return to Knackstrasse. I spent the rest of the time either with Martin or with Thrasybulus, with whom I shared a passion for the Tiergarten. But the evenings belonged exclusively to Caterina. What I felt for her was not simple infatuation, an activation of the flesh, but something more, different, that I was unable to define. Our love was incredibly tender, as though we were both afraid of hurting the other. There were times when I felt I was caressing her as though I were handling a fragile vase that I was afraid of breaking. I touched her with my fingertips and felt a current running through my whole body. And afterwards I gazed at her... Oh, afterwards I lay and watched her, looked into her eyes for hours, trying to understand where they were focused.

Berlin had changed Caterina. It was as though she had acquired more resolve. I saw her need to communicate with her mother, to find a way to explain it all. On the other hand, I sensed aggressiveness and resentment towards her father. When I talked to her about my trip to Arcadia, she showed no interest, as though she were indifferent. The focus of her interest was there, in Berlin, with her mother. I realized that the case of Loukas Matthaiou had now come to rest exclusively on my shoulders. And up to a point I was pleased about that.

On Tuesday lunchtime, my last day in the city, Caterina eventually told me what I had been expecting for some time to hear:

'This morning when I went to Knackstrasse, my mother called me over to her, she kissed me on both cheeks and said to me, "My dearest girl... Will you forgive me... Will you ever forgive me?" I stroked her hair and answered, "From the moment I saw you Mother, everything faded and everything became clear at the same time. From now on, the two of us are going to begin again." My mother didn't cry, she said simply, "For years I was afraid, for years I was all alone and afraid".'

I asked her if they had said anything about Matthaiou.

'She doesn't even want to hear his name. Once, all she said was, "He, he ruined everything, he was only interested in himself, himself and that woman." I took hold of her hand and asked her straight out, "What woman? Leto? " She didn't know any Leto. We said nothing more.'

'What will you do? Will you go straight to the Peloponnese?' she asked me.

'No, I'll stay a few days in Athens first, to see my parents. Then I'll go down to Arcadia. I'll go through the villages one by one. As soon as I have any news, I'll contact you straightaway. How long are you going to stay in Berlin?'

'I don't know, as long as it takes. Besides, I have plenty of time. I don't have to be back in Florence till the end of August.'

'And when will we get together again?'

'I don't know, Yannis, we're bound up with all this, it's we who follow the events, they don't follow us.'

I stared at her without saying anything.

That evening we all went out for a meal. We ate at Diner's, a restaurant close to Martin's house. Magdalena was extremely friendly towards me. To her I was 'Caterina's boyfriend'. Her instincts were fully functioning. Naturally, Martin was informed concerning the developments, while Eimer seemed still in a state of shock caused by the recent events. We had a quiet dinner and then I said my goodbyes first to Eimer and then to Martin.

'And next time, see that you bring Loukas back with you. I'll see you again soon, you rascal,' Martin whispered to me, hugging me in his huge arms.

With Magdalena the goodbyes were slightly less cordial, but equally moving. 'Bon voyage, dear boy. Do come back and see us.'

On the way back to the hotel, Caterina and I agreed that we would be in constant contact. As soon as I arrived in Arcadia, I would keep her informed of my every move.

'And what if he's no longer there? My father doesn't seem to be the type of person to put down roots in one place. He may have stayed there for a while and then moved on somewhere else,' she said as we got into bed.

'But do you recall his last letter? It was a concluding letter, from a person who had ceased searching. In 1972 your father was thirty-four years old.'

'And now he's sixty... Or rather he will be on the 4th August.'

'I'll have found him before then. Before my birthday...' I said, taking her in my arms.

...I was in a semi-open area, something like a churchyard, that was full of women, women I knew well, old loves of mine, and I was passing between them, shoving, pushing through, while, indifferent, they stood around and chatted. Eventually, I managed to reach the entrance to the church. I opened the door and entered a darkened area. I saw two women, two women clad in dark robes with hoods, kneeling and praying before a cross. The cross was neither of wood nor steel. It was of an indeterminable material with successive layers. A hefty priest was standing to the left and chanting. It was Martin. I asked him what the cross was made of. 'From fingernails,' he replied, 'from the fingernails of the dead...' Then the women got to their feet. Their faces were barely visible in the semi-darkness. I recognized one of them. It was Caterina. The other took a step back as though she were hiding. I went over. She had pulled her hood low over her face. With a sudden movement, I threw it back. The first thing I saw was the slanting scar on her forehead. My mother...

The alarm rang shrilly. I woke in a sweat. Daybreak on Wednesday, 24th June. In half an hour I had to be in the hotel lobby. I washed, threw my things together, my notes from Berlin, the photos, the photocopies of Matthaiou's writings, and I got dressed. Caterina was fast asleep. I didn't want to wake her. Before closing the door, I stole a glance at her face. It was serene.

On the plane I sat by the window over the left wing. I was leaving, to meet the father of the woman with whom I had slept the night before. As the Boeing rent the Berlin sky before levelling out above the clouds, I looked out of the window and truly felt like an angel, an angel on a special mission, who was flying over a grey cloud towards a dark forest, searching for the fleeting nature of love as it comes and goes between the wind and the leeward silence.

The Secrets of the Gods

Amor fati

My answering machine was full of messages. So many that even the special thirty-minute cassette had finished. Anna, two messages – 'I'm worried about you'; my father, concerned about the autobiography; my mother, more placid; Kostas – 'so what's going on, have you fallen in love with some signorina?'; Telemachus – 'Arnold has been asking about you'; Daniel, still waiting for the piece on Barcelona, and various acquaintances and oddballs.

It was Wednesday. I would leave for Arcadia on Monday, 29th June. I looked at the villages on the map. In order starting from above: Langadia, Dimitsana, Stemnitsa, Karytaina. I calculated the distances; I would base myself in Stemnitsa. From there, my first stop would be Karytaina. If I came up with nothing there, I would move on to Dimitsana, and again if I found no leads there, I would go to Langadia.

I phoned Hotel Trikolonio in Stemnitsa and booked a single room. Nine thousand drachmas with breakfast, said a woman's soft voice. 'Have you ever been out this way before?'

'No, it's the first time.'

And so it was. I looked through my bookshelves. The only thing I found to do with Arcadia was a textbook by a certain Euripides Yeorgakopoulos, doctor of Philosophy from the University of Hamburg, entitled: *Ancient Arcadia*. I had bought it years before from the Dodoni bookstore. What could a Greek teaching in

Germany in 1938 possibly write? On page eleven, the professor noted:

> 'History, as the politics of the past, provides us with a technique for the future preservation of a people. According to Adolf Hitler, in Mein Kampf, the study of history means investigating and locating the forces, which, as causes, bring about those effects that we regard as historic events.'

However, as it proceeded, the analysis moved away from any wretched propaganda. Further on, Dr Yeorgakopoulos claimed that:

> 'Fate is for the Arcadians a heteronymous meta-logical knowledge. For them freedom meant the expression of a spiritual necessity, in other words, an autonomous and genuine life. The obligation in life was for them to serve their fate. Their reconciliation with fate (amor fati) was the supreme virtue of the hero, the highest experience of the Greek. This was an expression of the deepest awareness of his existence. In this awareness lies the possibility of return by the spirit to itself, of the recollection and discovery of the human character.'

I wondered whether this *amor fati* is what drove Loukas Matthaiou from one city to the next and I remembered my feeling in Florence that I was crawling towards him. Now I had passed the barbed-wire fence, I had wrapped the dirty combat gear in the sack and was walking steadily in a shiny uniform towards the final outpost, to meet that legendary officer, who was either mad or the only rational person in this entire tale. It was no longer about the book. It was about him. Him and me.

As I hadn't shown any signs of life for days, I phoned my father. After he had given me a dressing-down – 'Where have you been all this time? Never mind about me, didn't you think of your mother?' – we arranged to have lunch together the next day. Then I called my friends, Kostas and Telemachus. Bright Lights, on Sunday. Next was Anna. She was restrained. I sensed that she had begun to accept the impending separation. We agreed to meet on Friday evening at my place. The last phone call was to Berlin. Caterina had just got back to the hotel. Her mother was better. She had begun to talk more about Florence and Magdalena no longer reacted, but listened, albeit without commenting. And she now accepted her. 'My dear child, my little girl,' she would say to her all the time.

'I already miss you,' I said to her before hanging up.

'I feel that there's something uniting us,' Caterina replied. 'I don't know what it is exactly. But it's something deep and total.'

I slept again in my own bed after a gap of thirty-nine days, with that word 'total' caressing my eardrum.

It's not all footslogging

'When was it you left? Mid-May?'

'Sixteenth to be exact.'

'Do you know what date it is today? The 25th. And it's June. So what were you doing all that time in Florence?'

'I didn't only go to Florence, Dad. I went to Berlin too.'

'Berlin?'

'Yes, and I'm leaving again on Monday. I'm off to the mountains of Arcadia.'

'Have you gone completely mad? Are you turning into a travel writer? I'd drunk a bit too much that day and I was joking. It must be your birthday that's to blame. Time races, dear boy, it waits for no one. You'll be forty on the 4th July and I'll be seventy exactly three months later. But to get this far, I wasn't continually with a suitcase in my hands. I don't want to start on all that again... So tell me then, what were you doing in Berlin?' my father asked rather aggressively.

'I went with a girl.'

'Don't say I hadn't told you. An Italian girl, eh? Met her in Florence I suppose. Almond eyes, elegant walk... I told your mother it was probably some girl or other. And now you're bringing her to show her the old homeland...'

Since first meeting her, I had decided that I would never reveal to my parents who Caterina was:

'She's half Greek on her father's side. Her mother is Italian.'

'Greek? Do we know him?'

'No, you don't know him, besides it's as though he were dead.'

'I don't follow… What are all these secrets? Didn't you go there to write an article?'

'No. And the trip to Barcelona too wasn't to do with work. Maybe I'll never tell you. It's a personal matter that still hasn't been closed.'

'And doesn't your father have a right to know what it's about?'

'I'm not ready yet. I don't know if I ever will be. Don't press me, please.'

'Yannis, I don't like what's going on.'

'Listen Dad, we're both older, that's a fact. And each of us has his own problems. Don't worry. Nothing's changed. I just need a little time.'

'And why are you going to Arcadia?'

'I don't want any more questions. We'll talk when I get back.'

'Yannis, what's this mania all of a sudden? What's got into you and at your age too? You've got more serious things to do here than go chasing up and down mountains. The book, your career, Viliotis is starting to put pressure… Just when you were starting to find some direction. The way I see it, this editing will help you. It will lead to other jobs. Maybe you didn't do what you actually wanted to do with literature, but I honestly believe that soon you'll find a position in some publishing company, perhaps as a reader or a series editor, I don't know. But these things don't just happen without work. All this business is making you lose valuable time.'

I was unable to contain myself.

'Dad, we have very different views on certain issues. For me neither life nor literature is simply footslogging. Now and again you have to break the routine, take a leap, dive…'

My father stared at me. His eyes had grown even smaller, disappearing into their sockets:

'Symbolisms, poeticisms… You're acting like a child again.'

At that moment, my mother, who had been sitting at the table all the time without saying a word, said, stressing each word:

'Markos, Yannis is looking for something. He's following his instincts, have a little faith in him.' And then, turning to me: 'I want you to know that I, that we, are right behind you… I don't know what it is exactly that's going on or what you're looking for. You always did have a vitality and energy; perhaps in recent years it's lessened somewhat… I don't know what's got you worked up exactly… There may be things you haven't told us. Or you haven't told me. Maybe I too have become withdrawn, have gone into my shell somewhat in recent years and not come out. I understand. I love you and perhaps I'm concerned all the more. Please forgive me.'

I got up and put my arms around her. My father watched in silence, playing with his pipe cleaner in his hands. When my mother raised her head, he stared at her with a look I had seen before. But then it was in the Piazza della Signoria, and it was in a dream.

When the doorbell rang at nine the next evening, I didn't look at the screen of the closed-circuit TV to see her. It was the first time since I had met her that I hadn't done so. Always, before opening the door for her, I would make her wait for a few seconds while I stared at her. What she was wearing, how she had fixed her hair, her expression. This time, I saw it all a little later, live, without the electronic intervention. Anna's hair was longer; she looked more mature, more womanly.

I didn't go into all the details. I simply told her that my life had taken a different turn, that I had met a woman, that I was in love, that our relationship in recent years had begun to wane and that I would always regard her as a close friend and be there for her if ever she needed anything. Anna didn't show any surprise. She told me that she had understood, even before I had left for Barcelona, that it was just a question of time. She had thought it over, she saw the dead-end, the different goals, the different rhythms, but she had never lost hope that something would change. She too had had an affair: 'It was nothing special. I felt alone and insecure and someone came along to give me support.' Two weeks earlier she had completed her thesis. 'At last,' she said, 'I'd got fed up of searching through old books for sculptures of Gothic monsters and heraldic symbols. I need to concern myself with something other than Bosch.' From September, she would be teaching History of Art at a College of Further Education.

It was a tender and uncomfortable evening. We didn't make love. We parted after a long embrace, in which each of us left a part of ourselves. Anna's was the larger part.

On Sunday evening, I went out with my friends. I gave them a summary account of my trips, keeping quiet about the turn in my relationship with Caterina. I sensed Kostas was envious – 'You rascal, you remind me of those old reporters…' – while Telemachus, more pensive, reflected on the crux of the matter: 'How could a fellow like that have withdrawn to a mountain?'

As for Daniel, before leaving, I left him a message on his answering machine: 'I'm working on the piece about Barcelona. I also have material for Florence and Berlin. I'm leaving tomorrow for Arcadia. We'll talk when I get back.'

Stemnitsa

It was Monday morning and my Mini Cooper was burning up the miles on the Athens–Corinth motorway. At the Mandra toll post, while I was gazing at the blue metal roofing over the cubicles, a scruffy little Albanian selling paper tissues came up to me. 'So you'll be clean, Mister,' he said, brandishing a packet of the things under my nose. I gave him five hundred without taking the tissues. The nipper held it up before his nose in both hands, looking at it in the light as though he were a bank official checking hundred dollar bills. I chortled.

About an hour later I was at the toll post for the new Athens–Tripoli motorway. This time the metal roofing was red; it gleamed in the sun. There were no little Albanians here. Just some girls all dressed the same, who were distributing leaflets for a mobile phone company. On the cassette player I was listening to my favourite songs from the eighties. The Clash, The Stranglers, Talking Heads, Julian Cope. The landscape began to change. I was now in the prefecture of Arcadia, in the distance I could see Mainalo. That scene brought something to mind. At first sight it seemed strange, but the surroundings reminded me of Tuscany. Olive trees, vines, shades of green, cypresses… The journey to Caterina's summer house. The shoot-out… Was it Matthaiou, I wondered, or his friend who had killed Esnaider's two henchmen? My prediction gave no chance to his friend. Passing through the Artemisiou Tunnel, I made the dark journey to the accompaniment of The Specials: 'This town...ghost town...' I was now on the outskirts of Tripoli, when on my left I noticed a Gypsy camp – about thirty tents. The Tuscan dream ended somewhere there. Entering the town by Nafpliou Street, I passed by a cemetery. I had never seen such a densely-populated one in my entire life. Hundreds of graves squashed one beside the other in a small space. On the other side of the street was a funeral director's office. It had an incredible name: 'Narcissus'. The city, definitely overbuilt, was a typical Greek provincial town, concrete, dust, cars everywhere. I pulled up in the square for a coffee. Next to the bus terminus; the traffic was unbearable. There was a statue in the centre of the square. Its marble had turned black from the exhaust fumes. The honoured person was Kostas Karyotakis. The poet had been born there; 28 Erythrou Stavrou Street. He was born in Tripoli and committed suicide in Preveza. The major events in his life had unfolded in two of the most depressing cities in Greece.

On driving out of Tripoli, I felt relief. Leaving behind me the last of the houses, the landscape changed once again. The charm returned. Climbing Mainalo, the vegetation became thicker and thicker. A little further and I was driving through a dense forest of firs, interspersed with expanses filled with bushes, hollies and maples. And, again, scattered among the firs and the bushes were cypresses. Some of the hillsides were stepped and planted with olive trees. It didn't take me long to reach the first village. Tselepakos. Virtually no one in the streets. A quarter of an hour later, I was in the second village: Chryssovitsi. Pretty, with large stone houses. From Chryssovitsi, the road suddenly became steep. I was driving up into the mountains of Arcadia at the end of June, the 29th to be exact, through lush vegetation, getting closer to... Getting closer to where? First stop: Stemnitsa.

The village was situated on the western slopes of Mainalo, on the foothills of Klinitsa. On first setting eyes on it, I sensed a strange smell in the air. It wasn't the sweetness of the cherry trees or the walnut trees or even the smell of the soil as it was washed by the stream. It was something else, not any less poetic. The smell of old paper lying for years in a folder in an Athenian basement. The handwritten pages swelled, snapped the thin string and burst out into the atmosphere. And their author? I could smell him, I could sense him in the air.

The majority of the houses in Stemnitsa were stone-built and two-storeyed, huddled together in the centre of the village, more spread out as they climbed the mountainside. The Hotel Trikolonio was more or less in the centre, on the main road. It was a three-storey tower with a two-storey extension, next to a church of impressive dimensions.

The polite woman's voice that I had heard over the phone in Athens belonged to a plump young woman who, with a smile, showed me to my single room: a spotlessly clean room on the second floor with a view of half the village. Before she had even handed me the key, I asked her:

'Do you know if there's anyone by the name of Loukas Matthaiou living in the village?'

'Loukas Matthaiou? No, I've never heard that name before.' She stopped for a moment and added, 'As you walk up the village, ask for old Yorgos Konaris. He knows what's under every stone in Stemnitsa.'

It was two-thirty in the afternoon. I decided to lie down for an hour or so and then I would begin looking.

Before I began, I passed by the village square, which was dominated by a tall belfry with a clock. It struck me as being odd that it wasn't built beside the church, but opposite it and at some distance. Behind the belfry was a row of cafés with characteristic arches. I sat at the middle café, beneath a wonderful acacia. From the hotel, I had got hold of a map of Stemnitsa showing the two basic tourist routes. Finishing my coffee, I decided to take the second route that went higher up the mountain. Leaving behind the village bakery, I began walking up a cobbled path. After passing a stone fount with a large arch, I came to an area with two-storey houses and with an archway running along the ground floor. I supposed that they must have once been shops. All of them abandoned. There was no one outside. The path continued upwards. I halted to catch my breath. As I looked up, I saw an elderly man coming down the cobblestone path. He was walking erect and was dressed to the nines. White starched shirt, waistcoat, braces, well-polished shoes, wooden cane with a silver handle. He looked as though he were from another world, an old bourgeois dandy from the inter-war years who had been beamed into the mountains of the Peloponnese. Just before he walked past me, the mountain gentleman took off his hat and greeted me. I returned the greeting and he halted.

'You're not from Stemnitsa, I presume…' he said with a comic formality.

'No,' I replied. 'I'm from Athens.'

'Yorgos Konaris,' he said, introducing himself. 'Pleased to make your acquaintance.'

'Likewise. My name is Yannis Loukas. I've heard of you. I was just talking to the lady at the Hotel Trikolonio. In fact, I was looking for you, I wanted to ask you something.'

I explained my problem in detail to Mr Konaris and I showed him the photo of Matthaiou that I had 'borrowed' from Berlin. After listening to me most attentively, he suggested that we sit on a nearby bench, from which there was an exceptional view of the village. He began to talk. Yet he avoided answering what was basically a simple question as to whether anyone by the name of Loukas Matthaiou was living in Stemnitsa; rather he deemed it fitting to give me a lecture on the legends and traditions of the area. And so, before I was able to repeat my question, I was obliged to listen to the tale of Auge and Telephus, of the nymph Syrinx and Pan, about the Lamia – the evil spirit of the Black Lake – about the murder of robber Zacharias and about how the locals gather turtle weed on the slopes of the mountain.

Loukas Matthaiou? No. I know a Mathios who lives higher up, next to the house of Kolokotronis the Brave,' concluded Mr Konaris taking his leave of me somewhat hurriedly, 'I have to leave you now. They're waiting for me in the square for an aperitif,' and he disappeared in a flash like a hero out of Lewis Carroll.

I looked at the map. It was true that in Stemnitsa was the house of Ioannis Kolokotronis, the so-called Brave, the son of Theodoros.

After a complicated trek up and down cobbled paths, amid almond and cypress trees, I eventually reached a house with tiny windows that, as the marble plaque said, was once the house of the Brave. An old woman staring out of one of the windows pointed me in the direction of Mathios's house. It was the next one up. Sweating and tired, I found myself before a wooden door with the sign: 'Mathios Katsoulis – Silversmith and Goldsmith'. The door was opened by a most likeable old man who may not have been Loukas Matthaiou, but he was an old 'golder' as they are called in those parts, who considered it essential that he initiate me into the secrets of that old Stemnitsan art in a room filled with anvils, pliers, chisels and moulds. Without the slightest information concerning Matthaiou, but with abundant information on local folklore, I returned exhausted to the hotel.

The following day, I explored the rest of the village inch by inch. No one recalled any author having passed by there twenty-three years before. Not even the director of the cultural centre, a more co-operative version of the omniscient Konaris type.

That evening I phoned Caterina and told her the news. They had gone out for dinner with Eimer and Martin. 'I'm thinking of you,' she told me. 'In what way?' 'In a way I can't specify...' After trying in vain to decode this new message – from 'total' to 'a way I can't specify' – I got between the clean sheets, having erased the first of the four villages from the map.

I was unable to get to sleep. I felt that I was attached to Matthaiou by the same thread. One step nearer to him... One step further away from Caterina... It seemed that I couldn't get closer to the father without moving away from the daughter.

Karytaina

'If you're heading towards Karytaina, be careful of the bends,' they told me the next morning at the hotel. 'They're very sharp. In 1962, when they held the Rally Acropolis in these parts, one driver left the road and fell over the cliff. Poor lad was killed. He was Greek, only thirty years old.'

As I was soon to find out for myself, the trip was indeed a test of driving skill and, as the attractive scenery drew my gaze to the right, I had to have all my wits about me so as not to suffer the same fate as the young Greek... After a certain point, the road began to wind downhill; I descended from an altitude of one thousand and eighty metres in Stemnitsa to six hundred and eighty in Karytaina. On the right, below the now bare Lykaio – a victim of the previous year's forest fires – could be seen the smoke coming from the chimneys of the electricity plant in Megalopolis. I drove through a lovely little village called Elliniko and, after a while, I reached a large steel bridge at the junction for Megalopolis. I left the car and walked down the path until the old five-arched bridge came into sight. Down below flowed the waters of the River Alphaeus, into which, further to the west, flowed the Loussios, then the Ladonas and finally the Erymanthus, before heading all together towards Pyrgos. Looking up, I saw Karytaina, with its Frankish castle on a hilltop, an image that, slightly retouched, can be admired before parting with it, by anyone who owns a five-thousand drachma note.

I parked in the village square and followed the instructions that I had been given in Stemnitsa. I went to the Vrenthi café. Seated at the central table was a small group of elderly men with their sticks – all of them almost identical – stretched out beside them in the sun like the horses of cowboys outside the saloon door. The group was in lively discussion, sipping the first ouzos of the day. I sat down at a nearby table and it wasn't long before I became part of what was going on. Their interest in me proved particularly keen with the result that I had recounted half my life to them before I was able to get to the main point. And it was then, for the first time in my Arcadian wanderings, that a little light appeared at the end of the tunnel.

The oldest among them, old Ilias, who had once served as head of the local community, cried out on seeing the photo of Matthaiou:

'Eh, isn't he the one who wanted to buy Matzouroyannis's tower?'

'What tower? When?' I asked intensely.

'Around the time you're talking about, young man, seventy-something, a stranger came round here, looked a lot like the man in the photo. He must have had plenty of money because he came to me at the time wanting to buy that two-storey ruin, that one exactly below the castle. You'll see it if you go up the road a ways. It's called Matzouroyannis's tower because a homeless family by the name of Matzouranis had once taken refuge there. Squatting, you might say... Naturally, it wasn't for sale, it belongs to the Inspectorate of Antiquities. Don't be fooled by the fact that it's in ruins, it has historical significance. It dates from the middle of the fifteenth century; it's a remnant from the Byzantine village of Karytaina. I explained all that to him but the man insisted, "I have to have that place... I'll renovate it, I'll make it the pride of the village, it'll become as it was five hundred years ago." He went on and on about it. He offered us an enormous sum of money for those times, I can't remember how much exactly. But as you understand, of course, I took the wind out of his sails from the very first, but he insisted. He stayed a week or so in the village and pestered me from morning to night. He was a very smart and handsome fellow, but there was something strange about him, something frightening about the way he looked at you...'

'Did you ever see him again?'

'No, but as he was going, he said we were throwing away a golden opportunity and that he'd find another village more hospitable. You didn't know what to make of him...'

I didn't need to hear any more. I thanked the chorus of elders and a few minutes later I was at the foot of the castle. The building was in a prominent spot, exactly below the stone fortifications. It was a two-storey stone construction, with three windows in its facade, and in ruins. I climbed the hill a little way, turned right from the cobbled path leading to the castle and found myself directly in front of it. Around the windows were traces of the original ceramic decorative surround. Through the central doorway, I entered a small space with a vaulted ceiling. This must have been the cellar that in the past was used as a storeroom or as a stable.

I went back outside and climbed up around the rear of the building. The way it was constructed on the slope of the hill, I was able to get straight onto the second floor through a small opening. I was taken aback on going inside. The vaulted ceiling, the stone carving, the patina left by the years. I was in an enchanting place. The north side, the front wall, that is, as I saw it from the interior, had two large windows, one above the other. The higher one was square, the lower one was arched. A line of stones, barely balanced by their own weight, formed the lower arch. From where I looked, the view was breathtaking – the whole village, the main church, the road, the houses, the Gortynia mountains in the distance and even further mount Taygetus. I realized why Matthaiou had insisted on buying the place. Apart from its architectural value – he had evidently underestimated the locals, believing that they didn't know what a treasure they possessed – the building was constructed in an ideal location. It dominated the entire village and at the same time was isolated, independent. The only building more impressive in the village was the castle, but even Matthaiou would have realized that that wasn't for sale.

On the west side were two arched recesses, or rather one, the right one, because on the left the wall had collapsed, so that through the natural window that had been created, you could see a tall, slender tree standing out amid the greenery. On the east side were two more recesses and various tiny square niches. One of these, between the two recesses, was blocked by a pointed stone. I went over and pulled it out, with not a little difficulty, as it was virtually wedged inside, as though someone had put it there deliberately. At the back of the niche was something that looked like a box. I reached inside and managed to pull it out. It was a black cigarette case with a gilded border, and with all the marks of age and damp. I broke it open as its mechanism had jammed. There was nothing inside it. I took it and put it in my bag.

I didn't waste any more time in Karytaina. On the way to Stemnitsa, my mind was whirling, but none of its frequencies was tuned in to the driving. On reaching Stemnitsa safe and sound, I recalled the accident with the rally driver. He had been a professional, I thought, before getting down to reading about Dimitsana, my next destination. I was so absorbed in what I was doing that it was two in the morning when I remembered to phone Caterina. The phone rang at least a dozen times. No one answered.

Dimitsana

Thursday morning, en route to Dimitsana, I felt the landscape opening like a stage set, as though a curtain had gone up, revealing in all their splendour the mountain ridges with the depressions and plains between them like natural squares. The village itself soon came into view, built as it was amphitheatrically between two peaks that overlooked the River Loussios. A little further down was Zatouna, the village where the composer Mikis Theodorakis had been exiled during the time of the military junta.

The first thing I did was to visit the village library, which was located in a small square dominated by the statue of Patriarch Gregory V, one of Dimitsana's famous offspring. I had been told in Stemnitsa that a visit to the library might be useful. On entering, I was welcomed by an extremely polite woman of around forty, with curly hair. She was wearing horn-rimmed spectacles and was dressed in black, with white lace around the collar and sleeves. She introduced herself to me: Evrydiki Dimitriou, librarian. I explained to her who I was looking for and showed her the photos. She didn't recognize Matthaiou, nor had she ever heard the name, but she would check in the detailed list of inhabitants of the village, which had been published in a recent issue of the municipal gazette. She came back before long. She had found nothing.

'The man you're looking for, what's his line of work?' asked Mrs Dimitriou.

'He was an author.'

'Has he done any work on local topics? Anything about Arcadia?'

'Yes, in his essays. He had written on the influence that the concept of Arcadia had in Europe, particularly in the 16th and 17th centuries. The pastoral life, the place of innocence and bliss… You know, the famous "Et in Arcadia ego".'

'From the painting by Poussin.'

' "And I, too, come from Arcadia," ' I translated.

'Yes, but you're aware, I imagine, that there are conflicting views on the meaning of the particular phrase?'

I shook my head. However, it seemed that the topic I had touched upon was one of her pet subjects, as the librarian adjusted her spectacles and went on:

'Concerning the meaning of the phrase, there are two main, opposing views. Their basic difference is in the determination of the subject and, consequently, in the interpretation of the phrase itself. The confusion, of course, arises from the absence of any verb. According to the first interpretation, the verb "sum", meaning "I am" has been deliberately omitted, while the subject of the verb is death.'

'Death?' I said in surprise.

'Yes. According to that interpretation, the phrase "Et in Arcadia ego" suggests the omnipotence and eternal dominance of death. The emphatic positioning of the conjunction "et" at the beginning of the phrase stresses that there is no place in the world free from the dominant shadow of omnipresent death, not even Arcadia, the earthly paradise, the place of peace, of sublime love and beauty…'

'So, "I am even in Arcadia", is said by death,' I concluded.

'Precisely. Whereas the second interpretation, a more arbitrary one, does not correspond exactly to the syntax of the words. According to this view, the verb that has been omitted is the past simple or past continuous tense of the verb "to be", and thus the interpretation of the phrase, with a minor rearrangement of the word order is: "And I too was, or lived, in Arcadia".'

'Personally, I, together with the man I'm looking for, interpret it as: "And I, too, come from Arcadia",' I said, having in mind Matthaiou's essay.

'You are both closer to the second interpretation, where the subject is not death but some unfortunate mortal who is now in the netherworld, and who is recalling with nostalgia the days of happiness and peace that he experienced in the earthly paradise of Arcadia. In this case, the phrase signals the retrospective vision of a sublime happiness that someone enjoyed in the past. But this second interpretation cannot satisfactorily explain the existence of the conjunction "et", meaning "and", at the beginning of the phrase, of a conjunction, that is, that gives emphasis to "in Arcadia" and not to "ego", as it ought to in order to support the second interpretation.'

I was impressed:

'What you say is extremely interesting. If we accept those two interpretations, I believe that Poussin used the words in the first sense, given that the saying is carved on a gravestone, a symbol of the omnipotence and acceptance of death, whereas Goethe, and Schiller too, who also refers to it, use it in the second sense, indicating the symbolism of Arcadia as the ideal place of origin for a person.'

'You're right. But there's also a third interpretation,' said the librarian quite emphatically.

'A third interpretation? I don't see how the subject lends itself to any further analysis...'

'But it does! According to this third view, the absence of any verb is a deliberate act in order to achieve the exact number of necessary letters. Because this particular interpretation considers that the saying "Et in Arcadia ego" is simply an anagram, a "key", an easily remembered functional tool for decoding some secret message known only to the initiated. There are many scholars who believe that Poussin was an initiate of the occult. Some claim that his painting *Shepherds of Arcadia* conceals a secret. It is well known that the Sun King, Louis XIV, discovered the painting in 1685, twenty years after the artist's death, and for years kept it hidden in his private chambers. Did he believe that it would bring him luck? Was he trying to unravel the secret? We simply don't know.'

My conversation with Mrs Dimitriou continued for quite some time. She was a person who had a passion for her work; I wouldn't have been surprised at all to learn that she had read the greater part of the five thousand volumes contained in the library where she worked. From the saying, we moved on to the Arcadian legends, to Pan, to Callisto, to the theory mentioned in Virgil's *Aeneid* that Rome was built by Arcadians, only to end on more mundane matters such as the state funding for libraries that was three years late in coming and the need for cataloguing all the volumes in electronic form.

On leaving, I had learned nothing about Caterina's father, yet what I had found out about the saying, and particularly about the third interpretation, went hand in hand with the codes and anagrams that appeared to follow Loukas Matthaiou in all his doings.

I took a long walk round the village, went to the castle, to the cyclopean walls, even as far as the house where the Patriarch Gregory V was born and where I admired a rare 16th-century Cretan icon of Luke the Evangelist. In the afternoon, I got talking, over an ouzo and a snack, to the locals in the square. They knew nothing of Matthaiou; they had no recollection of any odd stranger during the last thirty years. As for the photo, all I received were comments of the type: 'You don't forget a face like that; we'd remember such a handsome fellow.'

So I had reached a dead end with D, S and K. Dimitsana wasn't the place where the handsome fellow had settled. Only one letter remained: L.

The ouzo and snack turned into a full meal with local wine and at around ten in the evening, feeling groggy and rather than go on to Langadia, I accepted the hospitality of the local taxi man who insisted I stay with him. 'Don't even think of driving off now in the night, you've been drinking too... You can come and sleep in my son's room, he's away, doing his national service in Alexandroupoli. In the morning, you can get up early, have a coffee and be on your way like a civilized person.'

I slept in a room full of photos of Iron Maiden, of the Greek pop singer Anna Vissy and of Megas Alexandros, the Tripoli football team. At seven in the morning, after a large coffee made for me by the taxi man's wife, I thanked them, got into my car and headed north, towards Langadia, the final destination, the final place where Loukas Matthaiou might have settled.

Langadia

Langadia wasn't far, about twelve miles from Dimitsana. On the way, I stopped at a small village, Karkalou it was called – I recalled the film by Stavros Tornes with the actress Eleni Maniati in a wooden cage pulled by a cart – and I filled up with petrol at an AVIN station. At the junction, I took the main Pyrgos-Tripolis road that led to Langadia. After passing the source of the River Loussios, it wasn't long before I had in front of me a panorama of the fourth village. At first sight, this village appeared much larger than the three previous ones. It was constructed almost vertically on the mountain slope, which it almost entirely covered, while each house seemed to be supported by the roof of the one below. The anonymous town-planner had made full use of the natural incline of the landscape, with the result that the village had the shape of an ancient amphitheatre with the orchestra at the foot of the slope, which was divided by a river valley.

I had no trouble in finding the Motel Loussios; it was situated on the main road. The woman who welcomed me was inversely analogous in weight and cordiality to the one in Stemnitsa. In answer to my list of questions, she replied negatively, almost curtly. She advised me, however, to ask at the town hall. The interior of the motel reminded me of a state hospital. White walls, long, narrow corridors, depressing lighting. My room, despite all the accompanying miserable impression, had an unquestionable advantage that somewhat redressed the balance: a large balcony that protruded like a natural cantilever on the mountainside and from which you could see way down into the river valley.

My visit to the town hall proved fruitless. As I had expected, there was no one by the name of Loukas Matthaiou in the municipal registers and the employees assured me that they had never heard of anyone living in the village, even temporarily, with that name. 'But you never know,' said one elderly employee, 'the best thing is for you to go off yourself and search. It's a big village and you might get somewhere by asking around.'

I had to agree. I returned to the motel. This was situated on the main road that cut the village more or less in half. I decided to begin my search with the upper, slightly larger, half, reckoning that if Matthaiou had chosen Langadia as his place of residence, he would have taken into account the advantages offered him by a house that would have a view of the entire village.

I began walking up, asking whoever I met on the street and whoever I saw sitting outside. I had got quite high up, passing by the village cemetery, which because of the inclination of the ground was built on five levels, when I found myself face to face with a craftsman, who had just come round the corner with a sack on his back.

'Salesman are you, pal?' he asked me staring at my briefcase.

I laughed and explained to him what I was looking for.

'Me, pal, I've been building houses for over fifteen years. I've never heard that name.'

'But I'm talking about twenty-three years ago, about 1975.'

'Ask further up, above the Deliyannayiko, the people there have been here longer.'

I climbed the merciless slope mechanically, in the sweltering heat, among the pines, the oaks and the cypresses, walking towards the top of the village. On the one hand, I felt my breath quickening and on the other I felt a sense of intoxication.

I was here, in Langadia, in the last place where I might possibly find the man on whose account my life had turned upside down. I had enough evidence to convince myself that I was on the right path. Yet what if I didn't find him? What if Loukas Matthaiou had indeed tried to find an earthly paradise in Arcadia but had been disappointed or had even died? But no, there was the phone call to Magdalena. Though he may, in a bout of nostalgia for his daughter, have been phoning from Acapulco or Keylan. He may be living with some pretty little thing, squandering Esnaider's dollars in places far more exotic than Langadia. So what if I didn't find him? What would have remained from all this business? Would I simply go back to Athens, go on with the same life, the same old tune? After all, why had I done all this? What was I trying to prove?

There was Caterina, my heart reminded me. But Caterina had, I sensed, been changed by Berlin. For a moment I reflected how much better it would be if she weren't his daughter. If she weren't the daughter of someone who may be only a few metres away from me, albeit uphill.

I had now reached the highest point of the village. From the front yard of one of the houses, a blue-eyed old man with a likeable face stared at me. 'I wonder if you know...' More of the same... The next house was the last one in the village. From there on, there was nothing but the forest, as I was informed by the little old woman who had the privilege of living in the highest house in Langadia. In front of her house was a small cobbled square with a plane tree and a bench. I sat down for a while to rest. At my feet was the loveliest view of the village. The blue sky, the rooftops, the verdant mountains and, finally, the river valley. My gaze wandered over the landscape and came to rest on the lowest point of the valley that the eye could see. Amid the green, I could make out five or six white dots. I went back to the old woman and asked her whether anyone lived there. 'In the past, the village was large, nine thousand souls. There were houses as far down as there. Now most of them have been abandoned, only a few shepherds live there and some who come just for the summer.'

A new idea shot through my mind. Had I perhaps figured him out wrongly? Perhaps Matthaiou had chosen the other extreme, perhaps, instead of the summit, he had chosen the foot? I had to investigate.

Having walked for almost two hours uphill in the scorching heat, I decided to head down to the square to eat. Then, I would rest and late in the afternoon I would set off in the opposite direction and go down towards the river valley.

The secrets of the gods

At around seven-thirty, I went down to the square. I phoned Caterina. She wasn't at the hotel. The receptionist told me that she had paid her bill that morning and left. She must have gone to stay with Martin, I thought. I had taken the bag with me but not the diary; I'd call her again later from the motel. On hanging up, I felt a stabbing in my chest. I hadn't managed to sleep at all at midday. Something was bothering me, thousands of tiny pins were floating in my arteries. I walked past the kiosk in the square and took the steps leading down. The houses in the lower part of the village were further apart, some abandoned, others in ruins. As I walked down the slope, I encountered three or four spry old men, who must have been craftsmen, given that each of them was fixing something, one a door, the other a window. The area had a reputation for its craftsmanship. In former times, Langadia was the home of the master-builders who had constructed virtually the entire

Peloponnese. I wondered whether perhaps some of their descendents might have built Matthaiou's house. To my now standard question the answer in Lower Langadia was: 'Ask further down, perhaps the shepherds know.' After about a quarter of an hour's descent I had arrived at the last houses, which were barely part of the village. On my left I could hear the river gurgling. In the distance, sheep bells and bleating. The vegetation had thickened. I stood in a clearing and looked even further down, where the ground levelled out. There were only four houses in my field of vision. Two built close together, almost side by side, the third, a large grey building with a tiled roof, lower down, beside the river, while the fourth, a yellowed, two-storey building, was on the opposite side of the river.

I went up to the first house. It was locked up. The double door was barred by two huge bolts. Not a trace of anyone. I went to the house beside it and discreetly knocked on the door. Another old man appeared in the doorway. 'Matthaiou. No, Mister, never heard of him,' he said sharply and shut the door in my face. In order to reach the grey house, I went down to the river. I was now well outside the village, on a stretch of land with less of an incline, with the mountain slopes to right and left embracing it protectively, and with the water flowing like silk with a sound so harmonious that it went a long way to soothing my frayed nerves. The grey house appeared to have been recently renovated, but there were no signs of life. Next to the front door I read the name on the bell: 'Nikolakopoulos's. I rang. Nothing.

All that was left now was the two-storey house about two hundred metres further on, half hidden by the vegetation, on the other side of the river. I crossed it by walking with care over a line of flat stones that served as a makeshift bridge. I had hardly set foot on the opposite side when I heard a prolonged growl. Suddenly, out of the bushes jumped a small grey dog with an aggressive disposition inversely proportional to its size. Two bounds and it had reached me and began circling me and growling threateningly with its sharp teeth in full view.

'Rock! Rock! Down boy!' The voice came from the house and from behind the trees appeared a youngish man. He had long hair and a sparse black beard, was wearing dirty, threadbare jeans and was naked from the waist up. Rock turned round and altering his expression – to the extent that a dog can alter its expression – he lowered his head and began licking his master's bare feet.

'Who are you? What are you doing here?' the fellow asked me in a somewhat aggressive tone.

'I'm looking for the house of a certain Mr Matthaiou.'

'You're looking for a house... Way down here? This is where the village ends. There's nothing else. Only in the forest...' he said and, as though realizing that he had revealed something he shouldn't, he became even more aggressive. 'Be off with you, if you know what's good for you!'

'In the forest? Is there a house there? Where? Is it far?' I asked.

'Look, friend, I told you, this is where the village ends, do you understand Greek or not?' said the man even more angrily, and he put his hand to his pocket, intimating that there were other ways to persuade me to go.

'Okay, keep calm, it's no big deal, I'll go back,' I said and turning round I began climbing up towards the village.

I went a little way up the slope and when I saw the fellow was no longer watching me, I again crossed the river and continued going down. I passed by the two-storey house, taking care not to be seen and I began to make my way through the heart of the forest along a level footpath. The more I advanced, the lovelier the surroundings became. Nature's path led me along of its own accord. The vegetation was sublime: pines, holly oak, redbuds, oaks, acacias and rush all participated in a symphony of green, the water in the river babbled beside the hornbeams and the plane trees. Standing out in the distance were two mountain peaks, while overhead an orchestra of birds was performing a heavenly symphony. Yes, that was without doubt a hike... For a moment I had a sense of déjà vu, as if I'd been there before... In any case, it was the loveliest journey I had made since arriving in Arcadia. I went on, the landscape itself carried me along, time had stood still.

Since leaving the last house in the village, I had walked at least half an hour. I suddenly realized that all along the way I hadn't seen a single sign of any organized life. The daylight had begun to fade.

It would be dangerous for me to be caught out in the wilds at night. And all this was based solely on what Rock's master had said, on the off-chance that I would find a hut in the middle of nowhere. Reflecting with not a little apprehension on the terrible uphill climb awaiting me, I had just decided to turn back when I saw a clearing in the distance. At one edge of it I saw a reflection as though someone were sending signals. As I got nearer, I realized it was the rays of the setting sun falling on a white surface. From afar it looked like a kind of plaque set up before the root of a tree, while behind this, at the far end of the clearing were several taller trees arrayed in a line. On approaching, I saw that it was indeed a marble plaque that resembled a gravestone. There was a grey strip across its upper part. Suddenly, as befits the nature of such an experience, the sense of déjà vu returned. The fragments of the stored image began one by one to be replaced by the actual ones till the landscape turned on its head and I remembered. The two mountain peaks in the distance, the idyllic landscape, Arcadia, the stone plaque in front, the tomb! Even the severed tree trunk on the left. But of course! If you excluded the whiteness and the line of trees that looked as if they were hiding something, the scene was the same, identical to the landscape in the painting by Poussin!

I almost ran up to the plaque. The grey outline that I saw from the distance took on substance. Yes, there was an inscription carved on it! And not only that, but it was in Latin too! Slightly faded, but still readable. Bending my left knee, I adopted a position like the figure on the left in the painting, and in the fading Arcadian light, I read the following:

I TEGO ARCANA DEI

I had never imagined that the Latin that my schoolteachers tried so hard to cram into my head would one day prove useful to me.

'I TEGO ARCANA DEI.' In other words 'Be gone, I guard the secrets of the Gods.'

I remained with my knee bent, in the same position. My mind was working overtime. I felt the sky splitting into huge plaques like the one in front of me. The light spread between them, leaving only one ray focusing on the strange saying. 'Arcana Dei'. The words united, the letters merged… They struck me like lightning. 'Arcana Dei, 'Arcadei', 'Arcadia'. A word game, a play on the letters. An anagram. Dimitsana. In the library. Mrs Dimitriou: '…the absence of any verb is a deliberate act in order to achieve the exact number of necessary letters…an anagram…an easily remembered functional tool…'

I opened my bag, took out my notebook and a pen and copied the saying.

I TEGO ARCANA DEI. Fourteen letters.

I erased the seven composing the noun ARCADIA. There remained another seven: I,T,E,G,O,N,E.

I erased the two letters of the conjunction ET. Five remained: I,G,O,N,E.

I next erased the two letters of the preposition IN. That left three: G,O,E, or E,G,O, EGO!

The phrase 'I TEGO ARCANA DEI' was an exact anagram of 'ET IN ARCADIA EGO'! The half-faded phrase in the painting 'And I too come from Arcadia' became an anagram for 'Be gone, I guard the secrets of the Gods'. Here, in Langadia, in Arcadia, on a gravestone in the midst of a landscape identical to the one in Poussin's painting.

I got up and, having brushed the earth from my clothes, went over towards the tall trees. There were two rows of pines, planted so close together that they formed a natural barricade. It was with some difficulty and not without a few scratches that I managed to pass between them.

Behind them I at last gazed upon what I had so long been waiting for. There was a large stone house with small windows and a huge glass front on the upper floor.

The house was built in the middle of a yard that was barricaded all around with more trees, the one so close to the other that a human body could barely pass through. Two white horses tied to one of the trees were drinking water from a barrel, while a large cc bike was propped up against the outer wall. On the roof of the house, fixed on the tiles, was an enormous concave object that appeared in complete contrast to the natural landscape. A metal disk that looked like a satellite dish.

Before I had managed to take even a few steps towards the house, I heard a woman's voice behind me saying in a commanding tone: 'Don't move!'

I turned round as slowly as I could and saw a thin woman of around forty, tall, with dark skin and long wavy hair. She had a wild look about her. Her face was tanned from the sun. She was wearing a loose dress of black cloth and brown sandals, and she looked to be in particularly good shape. Round her neck she had a string of shiny blue beads and dozens of bracelets on her arms. None of this would have caused me any great concern if she hadn't also being holding a short-barrel shotgun, which she was aiming straight at me.

'Who are you? What are you doing here?' she said, with a strange drawl in her voice.

'Don't be alarmed. I'm a friend. From Athens, my name is Yannis.'

'What do you want?'

'I want to see Mr Loukas Matthaiou.'

The woman hesitated. The shotgun was still pointed threateningly towards me:

'This is private property! You're trespassing! There's no one here for you to see! Be off with you and don't come back!'

'Please, I'm not looking for trouble. I know that Mr Matthaiou lives here. I've not come to do any harm. I just want to talk to him. I have a message for him.'

'What message? Who from?' said the woman lowering her voice.

'A message from the past. From Barcelona, Florence and Berlin.'

'That's not a message!'

I seized the opportunity immediately.

'Then give him a note. If he reads it, he'll agree to see me,' I said and, taking out my notepad, I hastily wrote two words: BAR FLAUBERT.

The woman lowered the shotgun, came over to me and snatched the paper from my hands. '*Bar Flobet…*' she said.

'No, *Bar Flaubert*. Listen to me. I'll wait outside, behind the trees, where the plaque is. That's not private property, is it? If he doesn't want to see me, I'll go away and I'll never bother you again. Please, do as I ask. It's very important for me, and for him too. Believe me.'

'All right. *Bar Flaubert*. Listen, I'll go inside to give him the paper,' said the woman. 'Now you go there and wait. I'll be back soon, and if he doesn't want to see you, make sure I don't see you again. It's the wilds here, no one will come looking for you.'

'Okay, I'll wait. Thank you,' I said and treading carefully distanced myself from the dangerous zone. The woman didn't let me out of her sight till I was on the other side of the trees.

I waited beside the plaque. After about fifteen minutes, I saw her head appear between two tree trunks. To my relief, I noticed that she was somewhat less aggressive.

'He can't see you now. He says for you to be here tomorrow at six-thirty. I'll wait for you beside the plaque. Come alone. Because if there's anyone with you… I've warned you…' she said, rather more politely this time. I thanked her and made my way back.

My head was spinning. No end of thoughts were going round and round inside. Images from the trips, pages from the novel… and three verses.

In the midst of life's path
I found myself in a black forest,
and my life as I knew it was lost

And though night had now well and truly fallen, I continued to climb up, hoping that on the next day, my birthday, I would finally learn some of the secrets, if not of the gods, at least of the man I had been looking for over the past two and a half months.

Forty years old

On the Saturday morning I woke up in a sweat. Perhaps to blame was the fact that on that day I was entering the fifth decade of my life, or perhaps it was the dreams I had had – dark ones, with cemeteries, tombs, mysterious women dressed in robes and lonely houses bolted and barred – or, again, the fact that I was all alone in the middle of summer in a shiny white motel room with my first image of the morning being a handful of papers on the pillow next to me.

I phoned Berlin, this time Martin's house, and at last I found her.
'Many happy returns! Now you've turned forty, you'll have to
start acting your age!'

Caterina was in good spirits, but when she heard the news, her
enthusiasm was less than I would have expected.

'So you were right after all. About that too…'

'Get the first flight and come on out,' I urged her.

'It's not possible, Yannis. My mother needs me. She's getting
better but it's going to take a long time. For the present, my place
is here, with her. I'm not ready for him. He's strong, he doesn't need
me. I'm thinking of taking her to Florence with me. So she can live
in her own house, like a civilized human being. That's what I want
you to tell him, that for the present my place is with my mother. I
want you to stress that to him.'

We hung up somewhat at a loss. Caterina had made her mind
up. Most likely not only concerning her family. I felt her outline
thinning at the same time that the image of her father was
condensing like a piece of clear, geometrical ice.

EPILOGUE

The numerator

When together with the forest, death too with all its trees will climb up.
Crawling, creeping, from night to day, to the edge of time.
Yesterday; everything is yesterday. The jostling yesterdays of the
dead. Tiny pasts that crawl; as far as the forest's last leaf.
Disappear; vanish, sun ray. You don't exist; vanish. Nothing
exists save the language that fashioned you in order to swallow you.

Saturday, the 4th July. Five o'clock in the afternoon. Once more the
epilogue, before meeting him. I put the manuscript into my bag
together with the photocopies from Berlin and a photo of Caterina.

6.25 p.m. and I was once again beside the plaque. I hadn't been
there more than two minutes when the woman appeared. More
presentable this time; two loose cloth garments, one blue in the

form of a skirt that reached down to her ankles, and a yellow one that was crossed over her breast. Her hair was tied with a mauve scarf with a gold border.

'Follow me,' she said curtly. While crossing the yard, I got a better look at the house. The walls were very old, the stonework betrayed its age. At certain points it seemed that later additions had been made – the building had been reinforced with horizontal concrete bands. I wondered how the work had been carried out. The doors and windows on the ground and first floors were simple, traditional. But the second floor, at the front and sides, was constructed entirely of smoked glass, right up to the tiled roof. The glass must have been of the type that only allows you to see from the inside.

We reached the front door. The woman unlocked a series of bolts, which surprised me, given that she must have come out only shortly before to meet me. Before entering, I caught a glimpse of an escutcheon in the doorway. It was a small, carved elephant, identical to the one in Caterina's summer house in Tuscany. To its left, my practised eye noticed a tiny video camera hidden in one of the joints between the stonework.

We descended three or four steps and found ourselves in a space that must have served as the living room. The interior was dark. The small windows were half-closed and so it was with some difficulty that I distinguished the couch made of expensive wood and invested with a heavy material, and the bookcases that covered over half the surface of the walls. The rest of the surface was covered with paintings. I didn't have time to see very much as the woman, pointing to a semi-circular interior staircase, said:

'This way, please, follow me.'

We climbed the iron stairs to the first floor. An open-plan high-tech kitchen and beside it an oblong monastery dining table with benches on the longer sides. The area was lit by an antique chandelier hanging from the carved ceiling. Beyond the dining room was a corridor, on either side of which were two doors. The bedrooms, I imagined.

It seemed, however, that the meeting was going to take place on the upper level, since, before I even had time to ask, the woman once again pointed to the stairs. On the second floor, we emerged into a small area that had but two armchairs, a small bookcase and an old cabinet. On it was a vase of flowers and three silver picture frames. Exactly opposite me was a heavy oak door, this too covered with bolts. The woman turned to me:

'Sit here. I'll call you.' And after knocking discreetly on the door, she disappeared inside.

I waited, looking at the photos. In the one on the left, there was a baby in a pram – Caterina? The middle one was a black and white family shot, showing only the faces: a child of around five with a crafty look on his face – Matthaiou? – and a couple. On looking at the photo, I realized that I knew virtually nothing about his family. Whether he had any brothers or sisters, his family origins... The third frame contained a letter, yellowed by time. From where I was sitting, I was unable to read it clearly but I didn't want to get up and go over in case the door suddenly opened.

Opposite me was a small oval mirror, with a gilded frame. I stared at my image in it. It seemed strange to me in those surroundings. I reflected on my situation. I was waiting outside a door that would open to reveal standing there, before me for the first time, the man I had been searching for: Loukas Matthaiou. A part of me was afraid, I was scared at what I would confront. But the emotion that prevailed inside me was one of longing, the pressing need for me to set eyes on him. Despite the heat, I felt a numbness in my limbs. My brain was working overtime; it was drawing all the blood from my heart.

Loukas Matthaiou

For each of us there is something secret, indescribable perhaps, yet real, that waits in the dark nest of our inner self. It waits for the right moment in order to fly up and cast its shadow over our hearth, over the white eggs that await, warm from the expectation, to crack open in the sunlight. And when they finally break, it is not the sun or the light that they first see. It is this shadow, the black veil of the creator.

At that moment from inside I heard a man's voice: 'All right, Atalanti.'

Presently, the wooden door creaked, a cloud of flies fluttered momentarily and the woman once again appeared before me.

'He'll see you now, please go in.'

I entered a large, open space. Two or three metres behind Atalanti stood a tall, pale man who looked younger than his sixty years. All my senses were on the alert. It was my sight that was the first to be sensitized and it recorded an image I'll never forget. Loukas Matthaiou was even more impressive than in his photos. He had a classic face, of the kind that the Chinese call 'a king's face'; very fine, angular, with a high forehead, pronounced cheekbones and a square chin. His gaze was amazingly direct, with a composure that was at once cold and bright, his eyes focused on you like rays. His neck was long, his eyebrows, arched shields, grey domes above the green weapons. His hair was grey, quite long, brushed back, somewhat dishevelled. He had a thin mouth, with two deep wrinkles that began on either side of his nose and reached down to his lips. In the colour of his eyes, lip-shaped – the corners with a slight upward inclination, the notional line joining them absolutely straight – I saw the likeness with Caterina. A small scar, rather like a circumflex, over the left eyebrow, gave an additional charm to this man who, dressed in black from head to toe, greeted me politely in a husky voice:

'Good evening. With whom do I have the pleasure of speaking?'

'My name is Yannis, Yannis Markou,' I said and I had my reasons for giving that surname.

'Loukas Matthaiou, but of course you know that… Come in, Mr Markou. Atalanti, leave us alone please.'

Atalanti immediately disappeared and Matthaiou led me to some seats in the centre of the room. I noticed his step. It was so light that you had the impression that he barely touched the floor. Then there were his hands. The second point of likeness with Caterina. We sat down, I in a green armchair and he on a couch with marks like a tiger's footprints. I looked around me. We were in a rectangular room about ten by fifteen metres in size. One entire side of the room overlooking the yard was made of glass. Langadia could be seen high up, nestling on the slope like an eagle's eerie. The room was something between a medieval library and a space centre. On the wall next to the door was an oblong construction resembling a console with digital numbers that kept flashing. It was set in a metal bench at least four metres long, while three large computer screens were linked to the central system. On the left wall, on a metal tripod, was an enormous telescope, turned to a part of the ceiling that had been transformed into a glass dome construction, through which could be seen the Arcadian sky. On the right-hand wall was a huge screen. Heavy wooden bookcases, bursting at the seams with books, covered the rest of the area. All around were carved candelabras and extinguished torches. In one corner I noticed the stuffed head of a bear. Next to the telescope a vaulted opening led to a short corridor, with small, illumined showcases on either side. From where I was sitting, I was unable to see their contents. Matthaiou noticed me looking:

'My collection, miniatures and rocks, nothing special.'

I put the bag down next to me. Opposite me, Matthaiou folded his arms.

'It's not exactly the castle in Karytaina, but it serves my purpose,' he said, with his eyes fixed on my every movement.

'Yes, it's very comfortable,' I replied, ignoring the challenge. 'And the style of the place is very original. Technology and tradition.'

'I am totally wired, Mr Markou. Totally wired in the total wilds.'

'From reading your novel, I didn't expect you to have such a relationship with machines. Such poetry doesn't easily combine with so much technology.'

'Then you read only the surface. Do you remember what Heraclitus said? *"Everything is interrelated, what is whole and not whole, what is brought together and brought apart, what is in tune and out of tune; out of all things there comes a unity, and out of a unity all things."* '

I began to understand the rules of the game and I adapted myself as befitted:

'Yes, you're right. Everything is interrelated, even three cities so different from each other.'

'Do you mean *Bar Flaubert*? So how did you come across the book, Mr Markou?'

'Before I answer you, I should tell you that this is precisely the reason why I'm here today. The book. From the moment I read it,

I felt the need to meet the man who put me back in the world. Mr Matthaiou, all this time I've been searching in the setting for your book and I've found pieces of me virtually everywhere...'

'Really?' said Matthaiou coldly. 'And where did you find the manuscript?'

'That's not important. By chance, in a friend's bookcase,' I said, and, taking a folder from my bag, I took out a copy of the novel and handed it to him.

Matthaiou took hold of it, examined it for a moment or two without even opening it and gave it back to me:

'I have no need of it any more. It belongs to your friend, as you said. It's a little strange, though, as it was never published.'

'My friend is a collector. He paid a lot to acquire it.'

Matthaiou sighed deeply.

'Naturally, you don't expect me to believe you. Listen, Mr Markou, I don't play around with people. I very quickly become bored. You sent me a message through the title of the manuscript. And for that reason I agreed to see you. For your information, it's something I've not done for the past twenty-three years. I am sixty years old; I no longer have any time for chit-chat. So to put it plainly, there is something beyond any doubt. For you to be here in my house at this moment means that you have been to Berlin. Only there is there any evidence to connect me with this place. Though I thought that all the evidence had been destroyed. I imagine you understand what I'm talking about... And that means that you must know a great deal about my life. I'm interested in what you know, what your motives are and what demands you have. Then we can deal with the details.'

'There are no details, Mr Matthaiou,' I said, feeling insulted by his insinuation. 'As for Berlin, yes, I went there,' and taking the essays out of my bag, I handed them to him. 'And not only there. I also went to Florence and Barcelona. And as you might expect, in reverse order. Bar, Flau, Bert...'

I was skating on very thin ice. And my only ally was speed.

Matthaiou took hold of the papers and flicked through them. He remained totally composed:

'I had said that these should be burned…'

The trace of the steel on the ice. Sharp.

'Magdalena was very unwell. For years she was like that. She was in no position even to strike a match,' I said.

He put the essays down beside him on the couch.

'Mr Markou, I think you'd better start at the beginning.'

The same story once again. One version of it. I began with how I had found the manuscript in a friend's bookcase, how I had been intrigued and had begun to investigate, how I found Hansen, I told him about Barcelona, about my conversations with Salinas and Esnaider, how I had found out about the theft, how I had decoded the motto, I told him about the attack on me and about Salinas's death, – Matthaiou's green eyes glistened, but he didn't make as much as a sound – about Florence, Caterina – naturally without saying a word about my feelings for her – about Via Ghibellina, the summer house and the gunfight, about how I had discovered that the third city was Berlin, about my decision to go there with Caterina to look for Magdalena, about Martin, the meeting with Magdalena, the trunk, the essays, the 'Et in Arcadia ego', about the note in the margin – L.D.S.K. – about the return to Greece, the four villages, my wanderings in Arcadia and, finally, the plaque and the secrets of the gods.

'That is my *Bar Flaubert*, Mr Matthaiou. It may have lasted only two and a half months but, believe me, it has changed the way I think about life. So that then is my motive. To find the man who wrote that book. It may seem naïve to you, but I haven't regretted it even for a moment. I have no demands. All I wanted was to find you and I did.'

Matthaiou remained silent. He said nothing for a good two minutes. It was a silence that was not, however, a pause. It was an inner conversation, a period where we looked each other in the eye, not as we usually do to test the other's endurance, but in the way that happens when two people are trying to fathom each other out.

He spoke to me in a more familiar tone:

'Either you're mad or you're still trying to find yourself. And you don't seem mad to me…'

Now it was my turn to fall silent. Matthaiou never took his eyes off me once. Looking inquiringly. The water from Knackstrasse had returned. Icy cold. I spoke slowly:

'From the time I first began to become aware of myself, I started to withdraw from the world, others seemed more and more foreign to me, I was unable to accept that I had the same limbs and the same functions. At first it cost me. But now I know that I have no need of anyone.'

Matthaiou gazed up above:

'Do you know what a book is? The story of a conflict of characters?' Before I could answer, he shook his head. 'No… The only true conflict in literature is between the author and the world. And now you expect me to explain to you in detail my own involvement… And unfortunately we have to speak, and that is not only very tiresome but also unimaginably unproductive. Because, whatever I tell you, you'll never be able to understand why I live here in isolation, why I went through with the theft, why I married Magdalena, why I left Berlin, why I never saw my daughter again. And of course why I wrote that novel.'

'I could at least try,' I said.

'Yannis – isn't that what you said your name was? – how old are you?'

'I'm forty years old today.'

'Really, today? The 4th July, eh? Are you married? Do you have any children?'

'Neither wife nor children.'

'Then not even life can help you. Much less the novel.'

'Mr Matthaiou, the novel has helped me a great deal. I have read it and re-read it. I don't know who I identified with. Perhaps I should tell you about my life. But I never lived such intense situations, not even in my imagination. Don't underestimate the book. I've seen you before me… I've also met your daughter, your wife, your friends, I've visited some of the houses where you lived. And I think I've understood why you left all that behind: "How can so much fit into a numerator. You divide love, divide the unknown… Inappropriate. It's so much."'

Matthaiou stared at me in astonishment:

'You remember whole passages!'

'Pages, more like.'

I sensed him hesitating. I felt that he would have been glad to kick me out, yet at the same time I saw that something had stimulated him; he didn't want it to end so easily with me.

'Novels are gas chambers. They suffocate their contents. Whatever part of my soul I put in here atrophied. It died in this fake world's asphyxiation. Don't believe what you read. Books aren't people.' He paused for a moment and looked aside. '"*So much in a numerator…*". Do you know what fraction's numerator I'm talking about?'

'About life's fraction, I imagine.'

'Right. And what's the denominator?'

'Man.'

'Precisely,' he said and his eyes sparkled. 'You really did read the book. So in a fraction that equates with life and has man as its denominator, what is the numerator?'

'That's completely subjective, some will say love, others death, others…'

'Others God, right? Or what each one takes to be God.'

'Yes, the numerator can be many things. It may never become known. There's only one thing I can think of. The one we know, the one with which we have dealings on an everyday basis without being able to describe it, is the Greatest Common Factor of all the fractions that make up the lives of each one of us.'

Matthaiou seemed excited:

'The Greatest Common Factor… I'm happy, I'm very happy to be talking to you! Tell me what it is you're referring to.'

'Time, of course. Time. Time divides all lives, all fractions.'

'The great adversary,' said Matthaiou ritualistically.

'That divides all fractions…'

'Yes, it's true. But every fraction is also a logos, in both senses, a ratio and a word. And as you well know: "*In the beginning was the word.*" '

' "*In the beginning was the Word and the Word was with God,*" ' I added.

' "*And the Word was God. The same was in the beginning with God.*

All things were made by him; and without him was not any thing made that was made. In him was life; and the life was the light of men. And the light shineth in darkness; and the darkness comprehended it not." '

Matthaiou was silent for a while and then said:

'You have two Evangelists in your name, Yannis. That was the first paragraph of the Gospel of the one whose name you bear. The Gospel according to John. Mark begins differently: *"The beginning of the Gospel of Jesus Christ, the Son of God..."* A different order. Linear.'

He was right. In terms of the number of Evangelists, not in terms of the particular names.

He went on undaunted:

'Matthew begins by listing names, ancestors and descendants: *"Abraham begat Isaac; and Isaac begat Jacob; and Jacob..."* Luke, somewhat more modern, uses a narrative device to relate the story in the second person, to a listener, Theophilus: *"For as much as many have taken in hand to set forth in order a declaration of those things which are most surely believed among us...it seemed good to me also, having had perfect understanding of all things from the very first, to write unto thee in order, most excellent Theophilus, that thou mightest know the certainty of those things, wherein thou hast been instructed."* That's how things are. The same story written from four different viewpoints, in four different ways. And the greatest character in literature. Jesus Christ.'

'It's an amazing coincidence,' I said. 'My name includes two Evangelists. Yours the other two.'

'Your arithmetic is flawed, Yannis. Pateras never wrote a gospel.'

'Oh yes... Loukas Pateras...' I remembered.

Matthaiou smiled. His face took on an incredibly charming expression. But his eyes, his eyes focused on me with the attention of an entomologist, they looked right through me. He was the one to speak first:

'You said you had studied literature. Have you written anything?'

'I've tried...'

'Don't do it again, don't ever attempt it. Literature is unbearable. I've never written anything again since then. Nothing more in written language. There's no need. Life itself is a language. There's a grammar behind everything. Even in this 20th century of ours, this truncated century…' he said with emphasis.

'Why truncated?'

'It begins at the end of the First World War, in 1918, and ends in Berlin, in November 1989, with the fall of the Wall. You were there recently, weren't you?'

'Yes.'

'Then you must have felt what it means to be on the fringes of history, in the dead zone. I never went back again after '74.'

'But Magdalena remained there,' I said suggestively.

Matthaiou shot me another deadly look. He took a deep breath:

'Do you know how many times Berlin was bombarded during the course of the war? Three hundred and sixty-three. Seventy-five thousand tons of bombs and explosives fell out of the grey sky you saw. Magdalena was in Berlin on the 22nd December 1943. She was only five years old and she was there. The previous days had seen the destruction of the Opera and the old library in Unter den Linden. The Church of Kaiser Wilhelm, the Church of Memory, was destroyed on that same day. Since then it has been a blackened ruin. And Magdalena was there. From that day, Magdalena was always there. Always. And every week the same dream. The same crisis. There was no Florence, no cinema, no career. Not even Caterina. There was nothing but a little girl mutilated and slowly dying beneath a car. And her obligation was to give birth to her again. That's where her maternal mission ended.'

Molecules of water tightly knotted. They congeal. Afternoon in Kurfürstendamm. Magdalena and Caterina before the Church of Memory. *The sky over Berlin.* Black angels in the black forest.

'Yet, that woman loved you. She loved you very much,' I said.

Matthaiou made no reply. He paused, tossed his head back and stared at me:

'My mother died when I was thirteen, Yannis. All the tenderness I felt for her disappeared in the space of one evening. After she had died, for two years, during the time just before going to sleep, I felt a hand touching me on the face, on my body, all over. It was neither a maternal caress nor an erotic one. It was an appeal, a call. As though the dead body were calling me downwards, towards an unknown nature.'

His eyes fixed themselves on the chandelier hanging from the ceiling.

'I was made of stuff intended for things more peaceful than those I experienced. For a more harmonious relationship with my fellow man. I once came near to what would bring me back to such a state. There was a possibility of happiness then. It disappeared. And I returned. To my fate. I haven't regretted it.'

He leaned over towards me:

'People are fashioned of the same stuff as events, they are equal to what happens. There's no rehearsal in life. Everything is once and for all. I have never regretted it.'

'Even at a cost to other people?' I asked.

Matthaiou put his hand to his mouth as though wiping it:

'You have to know who you are at every moment. To smell your own air, however polluted it may be...'

It had started to get dark. Matthaiou got up and lit three candles in the candelabra on the table between us. The light highlighted the lines in his face even more.

'Do you smoke?' he asked me, holding out a black cigarette case. I smiled.

'Thank you, not just at the moment.'

He sat down again on the couch. He was now much more at ease.

'I come from a family of scholars,' he said. 'My father was a doctor, just like my grandfather, but his real passion was literature. He had a huge library with all the classic authors. By the time I left for America, I had more or less read everything in it.'

'You must have come into contact with some great minds...'

'Depends how you see it,' he said sarcastically, 'I set out to do biology and ended up going around with the Beat generation.'

'They seem to have believed in your talent,' and I referred to the letter from Burroughs.

'In my talent... For a young man there were plenty of temptations. My life then could have taken a completely different turn. But at that time I was somewhere else. I don't mean drugs and the like. I mean other things... Not everyone is bound by their appearance. And that's something certain people couldn't accept.'

'Salinas told me about a girl.'

His expression changed. He ignored the hint:

'Fernando... I was very fond of him...'

A suitable opportunity. I again opened my bag and took out the silver lighter that Salinas had given me in Barcelona.

'I think this belongs to you,' I said, handing it to him.

Matthaiou recognized it immediately.

'Fernando...' was all he said.

'As I was saying, he told me about a girl...' I said, returning to the topic and, on seeing no reaction from him, I continued, 'Before coming here, I re-read the end of *Bar Flaubert*, the last pages. The phone call after seventeen years. Leto answers, remembers, but hasn't the strength...'

Matthaiou fidgeted with the lighter for a while. For a moment I thought I had annoyed him, but he replied:

'There are things that we'd like to happen but won't take the risk and things that don't happen because they're not possible.'

'Like the phone call?' I asked.

'That particular phone call never happened. Besides, I never found out...'

He stopped. I wasn't going to leave it like that. I persisted.

'Who was Leto, Mr Matthaiou?'

He ran his fingers through his hair.

'Who was Leto? You want answers? Answers to everything? Well, sometimes they're aren't any.'

'There are answers and you know it,' I said, amazed at my own boldness.

Matthaiou cast a venomous glance at me. It was now clear that he regarded me as an equal in the conversation. And he replied:

'My fragments. Leto is my fragments. Discarded, scattered fragments. That constituted the harmony I was looking for. That whole "being". But as with whatever anyone longs for, this too is scattered to the four winds, fragmented, almost invisible. If you're lucky, you find it once in your life in one piece. And it immediately begins to fall apart. And for the rest of your life you run after its fragments. Or you find some support to face together the one certainty: death. But death, Yannis, is always visible, apparent. Whereas happiness prefers to conceal itself.'

'Did that woman exist?'

'Of course, we were together for almost a year, in America. It was Christmas when I met her and October when she left. 29th October, 1957'

'Why did she leave?'

'She dried up. When souls become moist, they get scared. And they dry up.'

Silence. And more silence. He was the first to break it.

'Does Caterina know that you found me?' he asked suddenly.

'Yes. But she thinks that her place just now is with her mother. She asked me to make sure I told you.'

'I understand. I was never a father, just a name, a… I'm a private person. She'll never be able to understand. Does she know where I live?'

'Now she does.'

'So, whenever she wants she can find me.'

Matthaiou stopped. Without saying anything, I took the photo of Caterina out of my bag and handed it to him.

He got up from the couch, went over to the bench with the computer screens and put on his reading glasses. I once again observed his movements. He was extremely lithe, a person continually on the alert. I wondered at how such energy could remain fixed in a wilderness like that.

'She's grown up to look like her mother, perhaps she has my eyes…' he said under his breath and added, somewhat hesitantly, 'May I keep it?'

'Yes, and there's her phone number in Berlin on the back. She's staying at Martin's.'

'Martin, Salinas, Esnaider. You're bombarding me with names. Names of the living, the dead and the crippled.' And he immediately asked, 'Did the police find the painting at Fernando's place?'

'Yes. How did you know that he had hung onto it?' I asked instinctively.

'Even if he'd been starving, Fernando would have hung onto it,' Matthaiou replied softly.

'You're right. He'd even made me promise to tell you just that.' And I added, 'The case concerning the theft has re-opened.'

'Esnaider is well connected. He's got away with it more than once, I can't see them catching him. Till now it was more than enough for me that he was left crippled. But now that Fernando...' Matthaiou stopped short and put the lighter down on the table.

'Fernando was like a brother...'

'On leaving here, I'm going to make a phone call to Spain,' I said. 'I'm going to name names.'

'If they get to Esnaider, then...'

'Then they'll get to you too? No way. To find you, they'd have to read *Bar Flaubert*. Even Esnaider got no further than Florence,' I said, smiling.

'Yes, you're right,' said Matthaiou, smiling too. 'The Spanish police don't have your learning. Nor your motivation.'

'I explained to you my motivation, Mr Matthaiou, I have it at this very moment before me.'

He again stared at me enquiringly. The ice broke:

'But what is it that you want? Every story is an answer to that very question. What does the hero want?'

'If that's the case, then what did you want when you went through with the robbery?'

Matthaiou leaned over towards me:

'Do you think it was the money? No. It was Esnaider. He underestimated me. And that was his big mistake. Naturally, I would never have undertaken anything like that on my own... But I was challenged. I had a peculiar idea about honour then. And the fact that he was left with the *Omen* was just luck.' He turned his gaze to the showcases at the far end of the room. 'The *Omen*, the *Rave*... I would never have imagined that someone might decode all that.'

'Oral, mare, even, neat. It wasn't easy. Do you still have the two paintings Mr Matthaiou?'

'On account of those paintings and a little pride, three people died and one remained crippled.'

'Not three, five. You lived a comfortable life and your daughter never lacked anything,' I added.

Silence. I let the minutes roll by. The light had now all but faded. Through the glass front I saw the Arcadian mountains like grey caresses. The lights on the console were flashing on and off. The digits on the clock showed 20.26. The time had come for me to probe deeper.

'You seem to be very fond of anagrams, isn't that so?' I asked him.

No reply.

' "Et in Arcadia ego", "I tego Arcana Dei". More difficult than the paintings,' I went on.

He said nothing for a while.

''The thing with the paintings is a game,' he said eventually.

'And the other thing, with Arcadia?'

'The other thing is a matter of life and death.'

'Life and death?'

'You're smart. But perhaps not enough to know why I carved that inscription in front of the house. The motto to a book is a game; the motto to a life is something unbelievably more complicated. I thought you'd understood the book. But you're still only looking straight, linearly…'

'Concerning "Et in arcadia…" I know that there are three interpretations. In the Renaissance…'

'The phrase is older than the Renaissance.'

'Older?'

'Get up and let me show you something.'

He led me to the corridor with the small showcases. We went to the last one. By contrast with the others, this one wasn't lit. I took a quick glance at the others. They shone. Not from the artificial light. From the light of the precious stones.

Matthaiou pressed a red button. The last showcase was flooded with light. He motioned to me to go closer. Inside there were neither precious stones nor miniatures. Just an old family emblem. Visible at the bottom was the inscription with the family name: 'Plantard de Saint-Clair'. To the right and left of the coat of arms were two bears. Each bore an inscription: 'Arcas' and 'Callisto', while in the centre of the coat of arms, axially placed, was an identical one, which gave the impression of doubling it.

'Callisto,' said Matthaiou, 'was the daughter of Lycaon. She lay with Zeus and gave birth to Arcas, the primogenitor of the Arcadians. In order to punish her, Artemis transformed her into a bear.'

Yet that wasn't it. Matthaiou had a more important reason for showing me the showcase. On the upper part, on both coats of arms, on the small one but also on the larger one containing it, in an arched arrangement, were eleven bees, while on the escutcheon, in calligraphic characters easily discernible, was the well-known phrase: 'Et in Arcadia ego'.

'France, 1210,' said Matthaiou abruptly. 'As you can see, the phrase dates back a long way. Some say that the Plantard family has its origins in Arcadia, others in the tribe of Benjamin, others in the Merovingian kings.'

'The Merovingians?'

'It was the Merovingian kings who introduced Christianity into the pagan West. On the tomb of the last king they found three hundred tiny bees. The sacred symbol of the Franks. Do you know where they are also to be found?'

'No.'

'At the coronation ceremony of the Emperor Napoleon in 1804. He had them pinned to his cloak to show that the Merovingian dynasty continued through him.'

'Why is the coat of arms reduplicated internally?' I asked.

'The second one is positioned inside the first, "en abyme", the smaller is inserted in the larger, copying it and reflecting it. It's a technique that also is to be found in literature. Have you read Gide's *Paludes*? If not, then you'll at least recall *Hamlet*. The smaller drama is incorporated into the larger, mirroring it. The Greek word for "paludes", written backwards, gives us Hamlet.'

Matthaiou switched off the light in the showcase. The show was over. It seems that the phrase was an open mystery. Just as he was.

'It was in Dimitsana that I learned about the interpretation with the anagram,' I said when we had sat down again. 'Till I arrived by chance at the plaque outside. From Arcadia to the secrets of the gods...'

'Yes, that's precisely what I wanted to say to you. From death to life,' said Matthaiou and his eyes lit up. 'How from death, which is said to exist even in a place like Arcadia, are we led to where the secrets of the gods, the secrets of life, are kept? How from the grave do we reach the cradle? How does that turn come about?'

'Turn?'

'Yes, it has to do with a turn.'

Matthaiou was talking now with excitement in his voice.

'The material is the same. Fourteen letters, fourteen lifeless symbols. We are still on the symbolic level, in the realm of signs, there's no problem here. But we have to pass on to the level of life, into the realm of the body. And that's where it starts to get difficult.'

'And in what way do those word games help?' I asked.

'In no way. In no way and in every way. Fourteen letters that form four words, an unfinished phrase that alludes to the existence of death as being omnipresent even in an earthly paradise. A pretty phrase that leads nowhere.'

'I agree.'

'Let's return to the fraction we were talking about before. The fraction of life. The denominator is man, me, you. What is it that we divide in order to participate in life? Of what overall total are we subtotals? How from the certainty of death can we return to the beginning, to the secret of the numerator? What is this numerator? All we have are those fourteen letters that hold us bound to the unshakeable presence of death. How can we intervene?'

'We can break the series…' I said mechanically.

'Yes, that's it! People are bound by the series, the sequence. When the series begins, the alienation begins too. Each new thing leaves its odour on the previous one and so on, till the original, the kernel, has accumulated so much waste that it is no longer recognizable. And then whoever is not satisfied with the obvious destroys the series. He throws the letters to the wind, breaks the sequence, creates chaos. And this is the truly wondrous thing. In order to change, in order to anagrammatize, in order to create a new meaning, you have first to break, to destroy, to pass from order to chaos. And then from the scattered parts to create a new meaning. Only in this way, from the certainty of the existence of death even in this idyllic place, or out of a simple nostalgia for this paradise, can we get to the deeper essence, to its secrets. You'll tell me it's just a game, right?'

'An exceptionally intellectual exercise…' I answered sharply.

'Yes, but now you're called upon to go through all this on the level of life, in your body and your passions. Just as with the scattered letters, you have to reconstruct your scattered fragments. To create a new meaning. That's what I meant before about Leto… But that's a titanic struggle. We're born whole, break into fragments as we go along, and right to the very end try to weld ourselves back together again. I wonder who it was who made me such a wretched denominator so that I've been striving all my life to understand what is hanging over me,' said Matthaiou, stressing the word 'who'.

'Perhaps you've succeeded in opening up a chink.'

'A chink, so that I can breathe a little of the air of the numerator. That's how I passed from the one phrase to the other. Through language. Because no matter how much I hate it, it's language that opens up that chink.'

'A slit from the grave to the cradle… Yet you chose a combination. You inscribed the key to the equation on a tomb.'

'Yes. Just imagine; you might have read *Bar Flaubert* from a wrong perspective. There is another way to see…'

I no longer followed him. 'For me, the numerator is not in the grave…' I stressed.

'Perhaps. But when I explained to Atalanti what the inscription means, she found my choice very apt,' Matthaiou said smiling.

I didn't want him to go any further. I seized the opportunity:

'Are you two married?

'Married? To Atalanti?' said Matthaiou, roaring with laughter. 'No, no, you don't understand. I found Atalanti here in 1975. She was just a girl of sixteen then. I took her under my protection. Now she's the one who protects me…'

'Have you lived here all the time since 1975?'

'Basically, yes. After Karytaina, I went to Dimitsana to find a house. My last opportunity was here in Langadia. I tried to find a house high up…'

'That's what I imagined,' I said, interrupting him.

'But once again I found nothing that I liked. Then I came down to the river and began walking till I was completely lost and had no idea of how to get back. Eventually I found myself in a clearing, there where you saw the plaque. I sat down and admired the surroundings, it reminded me of the painting by Poussin. I noticed a ruin, the trees hiding it today weren't there then. It was an old stone building of which only the four walls had remained. Inside I found a girl. She was in a semi-savage state, barefoot, dirty, dressed in rags. They'd told me in the village about some orphan living in the forest like a wildling. At first, she attacked me. She was very savage, she bit me, clawed me with her nails. I gradually managed to win her trust, I used to come every afternoon and bring her food. I thought she didn't know how to speak, but after the first week she found the courage to start coming out with the odd few words. She was a gypsy, her parents had been killed in an accident in Corinth when she was only six. Since then she had lived alone roaming through the villages of the Peloponnese. I took her in with me. I liked the place, it was precisely the kind of place I had been looking for. I got hold of three builders from Tripoli, paid them double the normal price, and made them promise not to divulge anything about the house. We all lived here in tents and began work on the construction. I had a large jeep and I brought the materials and tools along a dirt road on the other side of the mountain. It took us three years. A lot of the work I did myself. Atalanti helped enormously. Of course, it's a village and word got round, now and again some of the more inquisitive would come and we had one or two incidents, but eventually they left us alone. For a long time now, no one has set foot in this place.'

'You said that Atalanti found the inscription apt. But how…'

'How did she learn to read?' Matthaiou cut in. 'And Latin too? In all the years we've been here, we've exchanged our knowledge. I gave her her name – Atalanti – taught her to read and write, and she taught me other things, more useful.'

'What do you mean?' I asked.

'She taught me how to survive,' he replied.

'And will you go on surviving here?'

'This is now my place, my earth.'

' *"I'm going to find my own earth and bury myself."* ' The words escaped me. The book…

Matthaiou's gaze momentarily turned inwards.

'Magdalena... She kept it. That too...' he said in a low voice.

'But the letter also had a postscript,' I reminded him.

' *"From now on, more than ever I don't exist."* '

Matthaiou uttered the last words with some difficulty. He seemed tired.

'A harsh farewell,' I commented.

He made no reply.

'Would you like to see her? I could bring you into contact...'

This time Matthaiou replied immediately:

'Magdalena? No. Not now.'

'And Caterina?'

'I told you, now she knows where I am...'

'Is that what you want me to tell her?' I asked.

'Yes.'

He uttered the last word abruptly, as a kind of conclusion. I sensed that he wanted to put an end to our conversation. But almost immediately he turned once again towards me:

'But you haven't told me the truth about the novel. How did you find it? There aren't many people who have read it. And most of them live abroad. In Greece, apart from sending it to Hestia, I only sent it to one other person. To Markos Loukas, the author. But it seems that I struck a wrong chord. He was full of animosity. The man considered himself the guardian of Greek letters. He thought his duty was to protect them from infiltrators like me.' Matthaiou suddenly stopped, as if not wanting to go on. I said nothing. 'The publishing company rejected it. It was no doubt acting on advice. But never mind. That novel never existed. It began from nothing, ran its course, and ended in nothing.'

He himself had brought the topic to the point that was of burning concern to me.

'Yes, you're right,' I told him. 'With regard to Markos Loukas, I mean. I kept something from you. The truth is that I discovered the book in his basement. I am editing his autobiography and I found it in his archives together with other manuscripts that he had rejected.' And I went on, 'But I want to confess something else to you too. During all this time that I've been looking for you, reading your book, following your life, meeting the people close to you, a great many questions have arisen within me. You told me before that there are some things I'll never be able to understand. About the robbery, the fleeing, the abandoning. But there's something else. I can't not ask you. Why did a man like you feel the need to send his work to another author? Particularly to someone at the other end of the spectrum. Why did you send *Bar Flaubert* to Markos Loukas?'

The green rays focused on me mercilessly:

'Perhaps I had my reasons.'

'But why him,' I persisted.

'You never know who people really are,' came the reply.

'But Markos Loukas is an open book.'

'Do you know him well?' asked Matthaiou, evading the stumbling block but without lowering his gaze for an instant.

'Yes, very well,' I answered calmly.

'Then you must have met his wife...'

'Of course, often.'

Matthaiou stroked his chin.

'They have a child. He must be a grown man now.'

'Yes, he's my age. We see each other.'

'So you must have been born in 1958.'

'I told you. Today is my fortieth birthday.'

Loukas Matthaiou got up from the couch. He went over to the oblong table with the console and switched on one of the computers. In just a few seconds an image appeared on the huge screen. It was totally black with a faint circle of light in the centre.

'Take a good look at it,' he told me, leaving it on the screen for a minute or so. 'Now I'm going to show you another one.'

On the screen there appeared another almost identical image. Black background and a faint circle in the centre.

'What's the difference between them, can you tell me?' he asked.

'No, at first sight, I can't see any difference,' I answered.

'The first,' he said, going back to the first image, 'is from the far reaches of the universe. It is the image of a carbon atom as it appears from a distance of one light year, 9.4607×10^{12} or one trillion kilometres, from its centre. The second,' and he turned to the twin image, 'is inside the particle, a distance of one pico or 10^{-12}

from the centre of the same atom. The macrocosm and the microcosm.'

'Why are you showing me this?' I asked.

'Because the numerator may perhaps be this very image.'

'But they are virtually identical. Which one?'

'Both. The inner and the outer, one and the same.'

Matthaiou remained with his eyes fixed on the huge screen. He leaned over and moved the mouse. I imagined him over twenty years before with a hammer and chisel leaning over and engraving the inscription on the stone plaque. From the grave to the cradle, from the plaque to the screen.

But before leaving, there was one more question I wanted to ask: 'Mr Matthaiou, why do you have all these machines?'

'I've just shown you. For the outside,' he replied.

'The outside?'

'The image, the outer one that we said…it's my link to it. Technology allows me to be everywhere. It's the common blood of the future.'

'Electronic heredity,' I said.

'Heredity is an inactive virus that develops only when you remember that you are its carrier. It's like the mark of God. It obliges people to live and constantly remember the cause of their existence.'

Matthaiou switched off the screen and suddenly turned round towards me:

'Do you recognize within you the cause of your existence, Yannis?'

I didn't have to think.

'No,' I replied.

Night had now fallen. Together with the darkness, I also felt a black veil falling over Matthaiou and covering him. The only part of him still uncovered were his eyes, which, though tired, sparkled. I had heard all I wanted to hear. I was ready to leave.

As though sensing it, Matthaiou asked:

'And now what will you do with all that you've learned?'

'I'll keep what's mine. What's become mine during these last two and a half months. I know what I'll do with all that.'

'And the rest?'

'I'll leave the rest to those who lived it,' I replied and I meant it.
Matthaiou said nothing. The time had come for me to leave.

'And now I'll take my leave of you,' I said, 'night has fallen and
I have a long trek back to the village.'

'If you'd like Atalanti to go with you as far as the first house…'
he suggested.

'No, thank you. I want to walk on my own a while. I have a
torch.'

I got to my feet. Matthaiou came over to me. With his right
hand he patted me on the shoulder.

'Thank you, Yannis. It was a pleasure to meet you. You're a smart
and sensitive fellow.'

'It's I who should thank you for seeing me,' I said and made for
the door.

I was wearing a long-sleeved blue shirt over a white T-shirt. It
was hot in the room but I had been so riveted by the conversation
that it had never occurred to me to take it off. But now on leaving,
before I was out of his sight, I instinctively took it off.

Matthaiou, who was standing only a few feet behind me, shouted,
'Yannis!' I turned and stared at him. His expression had changed. 'Stand
there a little, in the light. I want to look at you before you leave.'

I stood for a moment beneath the chandelier in the hallway.

He looked at me intently. I was uncomfortable. I felt myself
turning numb. Especially on my right side. I didn't understand.

After a while, he lowered his eyes. I understood that the
examination was over. Before I had begun even to go down the
stairs, he stopped me again:

'I'd like…'

He tried to say something, but it wasn't easy. The sentence
eventually came out with some hesitation.

'I'd like to see you again. Could you come tomorrow?'

'I'm afraid not, Mr Matthaiou. I'm leaving in the morning. I'm
going home, to Athens.'

'You're going home…'

'Yes, back to find my own earth. Goodbye, Mr Matthaiou,' I said
and descended the stairs without looking back.

Atalanti was waiting for me on the first floor. Her look was different from the last time. I sensed a mixture of envy and admiration. Which was only natural if you consider that, from the time she had first met him, I was perhaps the sole person to have kept her companion-master busy for such a long time. We went down together to the front door. 'Did you know him from before? You must have for him to have agreed to see you. He is a very special person! No one has ever understood him. Except me... Only to me has he spoken about everything!'

'Yes, he told me.'

'Oh yes! He told you! He's a very special person!'

'Indeed he is. Quite remarkable. But now I have to leave.'

'Shall I go with you to the first houses?'

'No, thank you. I'll walk on my own. I know the way,' I answered politely.

I was about to step outside when I suddenly thought of something. I turned to Atalanti:

'I want to ask you a favour. Please tell Mr Matthaiou something I forgot. The numerator, tell him, is fate.' And I said goodnight to her. As I stepped out into the yard, one of the horses whinnied.

'Fate? Yes, I'll tell him. The numerator is fate,' Atalanti repeated behind me like an echo.

On emerging from the clump of trees, I continued for about two hundred metres and then turned to look back. It was a beautiful night. The moon was full and its light was bathing the plaque. The inscription appeared even more deeply engraved in the Arcadian stone: 'I TEGO ARCANA DEI'

I began the climb. I was walking on clear ice. I looked below, at the denominator. On the bottom was an arm. Severed. At the root.

I went back to the motel and before going to sleep I read once again the last page:

I'm getting close. A sharp sound and deep darkness. The constellations are changing direction. Suddenly a flash. The enigma appears over a cart of freshly-cut wood that tosses in the middle of the ether. On it is an oak chest with the initials 'L.P.': 'L for lonely,

P for psyche'. The cart enters the fear. In the edge of the vegetation, where nature ends. It is then that the entire sky rises from the diamond seat with a great cry:

'No, it's too much. Too much.'

And I am seized by the ellipse, which is a violated circle, just like life.

There is no end to this story. There is no end to any story. Only beginnings exist, millions of beginnings that jostle in the stone entrance in order to disappear, alone, in the black forest that no one guards.

End

Athens 1975

Amor omnia – Amor fati

The next morning I drove to Athens with my eyes on the road, hardly casting even a glance at the landscape. I speeded along as though wanting to get away from Arcadia as quickly as possible. I called Caterina from a payphone. Martin told me that she and her mother had gone to the Tiergarten.

'Magdalena is a new woman. She's lost weight and her features have softened. She's started to remind me again of that sweet creature that I knew in Italy,' he added.

'How is she getting on with Caterina?'

'Better, much better. She remembers, she keeps calling her "my dear little girl". So what happened, did you find Loukas?'

I gave him a brief account of everything.

A cry of approval echoed at the other end of the line.

'Yes! Well done. What's the darling up to? Is he all right?'

'He seems to have found what he wanted.'

'How is he? Has he grown old and ugly?'

'No, he's fine.'

'What about Caterina, what did you say about her?'

'The father is waiting for the daughter and the daughter the father. It's their business now. What about you?'

He told me that the following month he was going on tour with the Berliner Ensemble to Latin America. We continued chatting for a while and agreed to meet the following February in Athens when they would come to Athens to stage *Arturo Ui* at the Athens Concert Hall.

On arriving home, I listened to my phone messages. My father, Viliotis – he wanted to see me as soon as possible – and Caterina. It was early in the evening in Berlin. I found her and told her of my meeting with her father.

'Is he waiting for me to come?' she asked me.

'He didn't put it as plainly as that. He's waiting for you to make contact with him. I told him about your priorities.'

'You did right. I'm still not ready. I don't know if I'll ever be. I've been doing a lot of thinking. At the end of the month I'm leaving for Florence with my mother. We've talked everything over. We're going to live together.'

'And Eimer?'

'Eimer is going to stay in Berlin. He doesn't feel up to such a big change. I'm going to get hold of Rosa and the three of us will live together in Via Ghibellina.'

'Is that what you want?'

'Yes. I hope you'll understand why. If you see him again, tell him that we'll be there. In Florence.'

'I'm not going to see your father again, Caterina.'

'Anyway. Let him know where he can find us if he wants.'

'I suppose the same is true for me too, right?'

'Yannis, please... I owe you so much... so very much. If you care for me, try to understand. I can't fit everything into one package.'

I understood her. I understood her perfectly. The course was pre-planned: Bar, Flau, Bert. And it ended in Berlin. After all, I was the one who had planned it, or rather the one who had followed it. Faithfully. Step by step. Till the final syllable.

I didn't have any problem. I was learning. At last.

Amor omnia – Amor fati.

On Monday morning, I made the phone call to Barcelona. I tipped them off – anonymously. A name, known to everyone in the city, the title of a painting – *Omen* – and a famous address, on the third floor of the Pedrera, in the large room on the left behind the purple curtains. From then on it was a matter for the Spanish authorities.

Then I called by the offices of *Nomos 2000*. The smoked-glass mirror behind Daniel Triandafyllides had been replaced by a giant split screen that displayed numerous channels at the same time. I told him straight out that I hadn't written anything and that I was stopping work for the magazine. I handed him a folder with an unfinished article on Barcelona. 'Give it to Dimitris to finish, I don't want a cent for it,' I said. Daniel was taken aback, he had recourse to flattery – 'but to let such talent go to waste' – he tried to make me change my mind, he eventually switched off the channels and began talking to me about our years together at school, but I left him in no doubt.

'I'm worried about you. It's as though something has happened to you,' he said as I was leaving.

'Something *has* happened to me,' I replied, shutting the door behind me.

That night I went with my friends to the Bright Lights. Before leaving home, I had already begun to make the most of a bottle of vodka. At the bar, I continued with whisky and by the time I'd related everything to them I was completely sozzled. In the end, Telemachus was obliged to carry me outside and take me home in his car. I was awoken around noon on Tuesday by the sound of the phone. I was in bed, still wearing my clothes. At the other end of the line was Kostas, who related to me all the happenings of the night before:

'I've never seen you like that before, Yannis, I think it's time you put an end to all that business. Stay here in Athens, rest up, and get yourself sorted out.'

'For you to say that, I must really have scared the lot of you, eh?'

'Take it easy for a while. You've turned forty now. Round figures… You've got yourself into a rut. Remember where you were in spring and where you are now.'

'Naturally I remember. That's exactly what I remember. Where I was then and where I am now,' and I got up to make a coffee, with my head still pounding.

That afternoon I had an appointment with my father. Before

setting off, I called a writer-friend of mine who was looking for work and made him an offer. To my great relief, he accepted.

My father was on his own. He greeted me coolly as though he knew what I was going to say to him. He didn't start grumbling or preaching. I spoke in a way that brooked no objection.

'Dad, I'm not going on with the editing.'

The wrinkles on his brow changed their curvature slightly:

'And now you're telling me? With all these loose ends? So was that your problem? The editing of your father's autobiography?'

'Don't take it the wrong way. But it's high time I started to do my own thing. I've already found a friend to replace me. He's someone who is totally trustworthy.'

'I can't pretend that I'm not disappointed. These last months…'

'You don't understand me.'

'No, I don't understand you at all.'

I didn't stay very long. We had a drink together without saying very much, then he made the excuse that he was tired and wanted to lie down. Before leaving, I kissed him. His cheek was burning, he was bright red.

As I went down the stairs to the basement, I recalled my feeling in Barcelona, that I was constantly coming and going between one autobiography and another. Now, as I went down the stairs, I felt that the toing and froing had stopped, I was moving back, into my own life.

I made straight for the blue bookcase. I took the mauve folder out of my bag, tied the string, climbed up the stepladder and put it back in its place. Exactly where I had found it on the evening of the 22nd of April. On the top shelf, at the end on the right.

I had hardly managed to open my front door when the phone rang. It was my mother.

'I'm coming over,' she told me, without waiting for me to reply. In less than half an hour the doorbell rang:

'No, he told me very little. You know your father doesn't say very much. When something touches him deeply, he doesn't discuss it, not even with me. Since you left home, you haven't been there to see, you don't know… And if you had been there, you wouldn't have attributed the blame to him. Your father's been through a lot, Yannis.'

'Didn't he tell you anything? Not even about the autobiography?'

'No, he said virtually nothing. Other than, "Yannis is backing out." I didn't understand and I came so you can tell me what you're backing out of and why.'

'I'm not backing out of anything, Mum. Just the opposite. I'm going back to where I was. To where I ought to have always been.'

My mother sighed deeply:

'Your father, Yannis, is a very special person. Only I know him. I had to face a lot of difficulties in my life and he always stood by me. Only someone with such a broad mind could have accepted everything he did. Never forget that.'

'Accepted what?'

'Me, Yannis, me the way I was.'

'Yes, but you accepted him too.'

'I was the one who was wayward. Perhaps it's something you can't understand. He was the one who had to surpass himself. When your father first met me I was only nineteen.'

'And he was twenty-nine.'

'Yes, with the mind of a forty-year-old. Yet he didn't follow his logic. Perhaps it was the first time that in real life he did the things he wrote about in his books.'

'I don't follow you.'

'Never mind. What I'm going to tell you I want you to keep to yourself. Your father is not just what you see. He has made some brave choices. He has taken risks in his life. And very serious risks too.'

'And now it's my turn,' I said in absolute earnest.

My mother came over to me, took my head in her hands and put it gently to her breast, caressing my hair. It was something she had never done before in her life. At least insofar as I could remember. We remained like that for a long time. A very, very long time.

The numerator

…The body stretches. Slender, exercised. An arm, a woman's arm. It touches me. The feeling is one of total softness. Fluff with fluff. I turn towards her. Her features espouse an innocence that makes her face seem wide open with abundant light shining brightly from within. I go inside. A stone door bars the entrance. I utter the password. 'Et in...' A crack opens in the stone. I proceed. Light rain. I proceed. Now everything is black, pitch-black, and in the distance, far off and dim, a light. I approach. Nearer and nearer. The light splits. The upper light and the lower light. Like a fraction. A straight line between them. The lower light begins moving, is transformed. An oval shape, a vertical line, a horizontal one, two holes. A face. My face. The upper light begins to coil, like a snake attempting to bite its tail. The rain increases, thunder, lightning rends the darkness and the upper light continues to whirl, till it races off and fades into the black background, covering a space that cannot be measured in length – only in moments, in duration – and becoming fixed once again in the distance; a silver glimmer, a dim light...

'The numerator', I cried, while my eyes were still blinking from the first light of day as it passed through the thin curtains. 'The numerator is inside her. In her belly, high up. In the sky... Caterina!' I cried.

Yet this wasn't the woman I was calling.

Epilogue

Yannis Loukas got up slowly, at around seven, from a long afternoon siesta. Through the window he saw the rain falling. He looked at his face in the bathroom mirror. People are simply images, reflections. They acquire life only when we touch them. They exist only when we exist – and at that moment he existed as never before.

Then he phoned Caterina in Florence. He informed her of Esnaider's arrest. 'That's a weight off our shoulders,' he heard her say with a sigh of relief.

Martin was touring in Italy with the Berliner Ensemble and they were going to spend Christmas together. The previous day she had gone with her mother to the Teatro della Pergola – Pirandello. Magdalena had been extremely moved. She had cried.

And they were doing fine together, mother and daughter. At the weekend they would go to Chianti; she wouldn't be planting another rosebush that year. Her father, no, they had still not been in contact.

'Perhaps I'll write to him in the new year,' she told him. She thinks of him, she'll come to Greece at the beginning of April and meet with him.

He quickly made a coffee, got dressed – he liked to be dressed when writing so as to be ready to go out at any moment – went into his study and turned on the computer. The date appeared: 24th December. Christmas Eve. Gracefully curtseying to him from the poster on the

285

facing wall was a dancing girl painted in pastel, a characteristic impressionist work. By his favourite painter. Edgar Degas.

He created a file, named it wip.doc – work in progress document – he had his reasons, all writing is a work in progress, and put his notes down beside him. The three notebooks he had kept, one from each city, took up a hundred or so pages, not counting the notes he had from Arcadia.

He already had before him the manuscript he had been writing over the previous few months, it was going to be a big book, over three hundred and fifty pages. The first draft had come easily.

By Easter, he would have the final draft ready on computer. He imagined Viliotis's face when he would read it. If there was one thing he was sure of, it was that he wouldn't reject it...

He had collected together in a file all the photos that Caterina had given him together with whatever other material he had gathered during his trips. He picked up the large photo of Matthaiou, the one he had taken with him to Arcadia, and he propped it up against the thick autobiography of his father that had come out just the previous week. It had coincided, in fact, with his unanimous election to the Athens Academy. Naturally, his name was nowhere mentioned in the book. He himself had requested that. The way he positioned Matthaiou's photo, it covered part of the cover of the autobiography, leaving half his father's figure appearing in a complacent pose, slightly bent forward as he noted something in a book.

He looked first at his father's photo and then at Matthaiou's. He recalled the first time that he had seen his face in Florence, with Caterina in the café.

As he was straightening up his things, a photo fell out of the files and dropped to the floor. Stooping to pick it up, he saw something strange on the floor.

A second photo, stuck to the back of the first, had come unstuck. He brought it to the light. It was Loukas Matthaiou with an elderly man.

If he had looked at it more carefully, something he would do years later, he would have noticed that it showed Loukas Matthaiou or

Luca Pateras, in the garden of his house, around seventeen years old, standing upright with a dog curled at his feet. Matthaiou's father was standing beside him. He resembled his father, except for one slight difference. Given the way Christos Pateras was standing, erect, almost at attention, with his hands at his sides, it was clearly visible that his right arm was a good hand's breadth shorter than the left one.

He might very well have noticed it then.

But he didn't.

Instead, he struck the first key on the keyboard.

It was a capital B.

He took a sip of coffee and continued:

Bar Flaubert by Yannis Loukas

Novel

omen rave

area lent

I was down below, exploring her. My tongue teased the opposing skin, twisted it, smeared it with its warm lubrication. My mind wasn't in it though. My thoughts raced off, elsewhere. At one moment, my gaze fixed on the facing wall. It was my wall, marking the confines of my room. Three candles were burning in the silver candelabra. Their candescent light flooded the room. I drifted in their warm glow. I gazed again before me; only darkness now and a dim light in the distance. I proceeded. A stone door barred the entrance. I uttered the password. A crack opened in the middle of the stone. Light rain. I proceeded still further. Vegetation, mountain peaks, a stream babbling. Yet it was as if nature had faded away. Everything was black, draped in darkness, with only a dim light in the distance, a silver glimmer in the pitch black forest.

Acknowledgements

My thanks to Andreas Yiakoumakatos for Florence, to Eleftheria Sapountzis and Volker Spengler for their help in Berlin, to the lady at the Dimitsana Library, to my translator David Connolly, to Maria, to Gary and to my family for their support. The stranger who first talked to me about Langadia verified the meaning of 'The mechanics of Life', as Paul Auster puts it.